THE FARMER AND THE FALD

J R Leach

Illustrated by Hilary James

For Limelight.
For the lessons and the laughter.
And for reminding me why stories are important.

CONTENTS

The Farmer and the Fald	
Dedication	
The Calendar	1
Foreword	3
Bundon I	15
Bundon II	33
Bundon III	37
Tyr'Dalka I	40
Tyr'Dalka II	59
Tyr'Dalka III	74
Tyr'Dalka IV	87
Tyr'Dalka V	93
Bundon IV	103
Bundon V	123
Bundon VI	144
Will I	158
Will II	169
Will III	181
Tyr'Dalka VI	202
Tyr'Dalka VII	210

Tyr'Dalka VIII	262
About The Author	273

VII

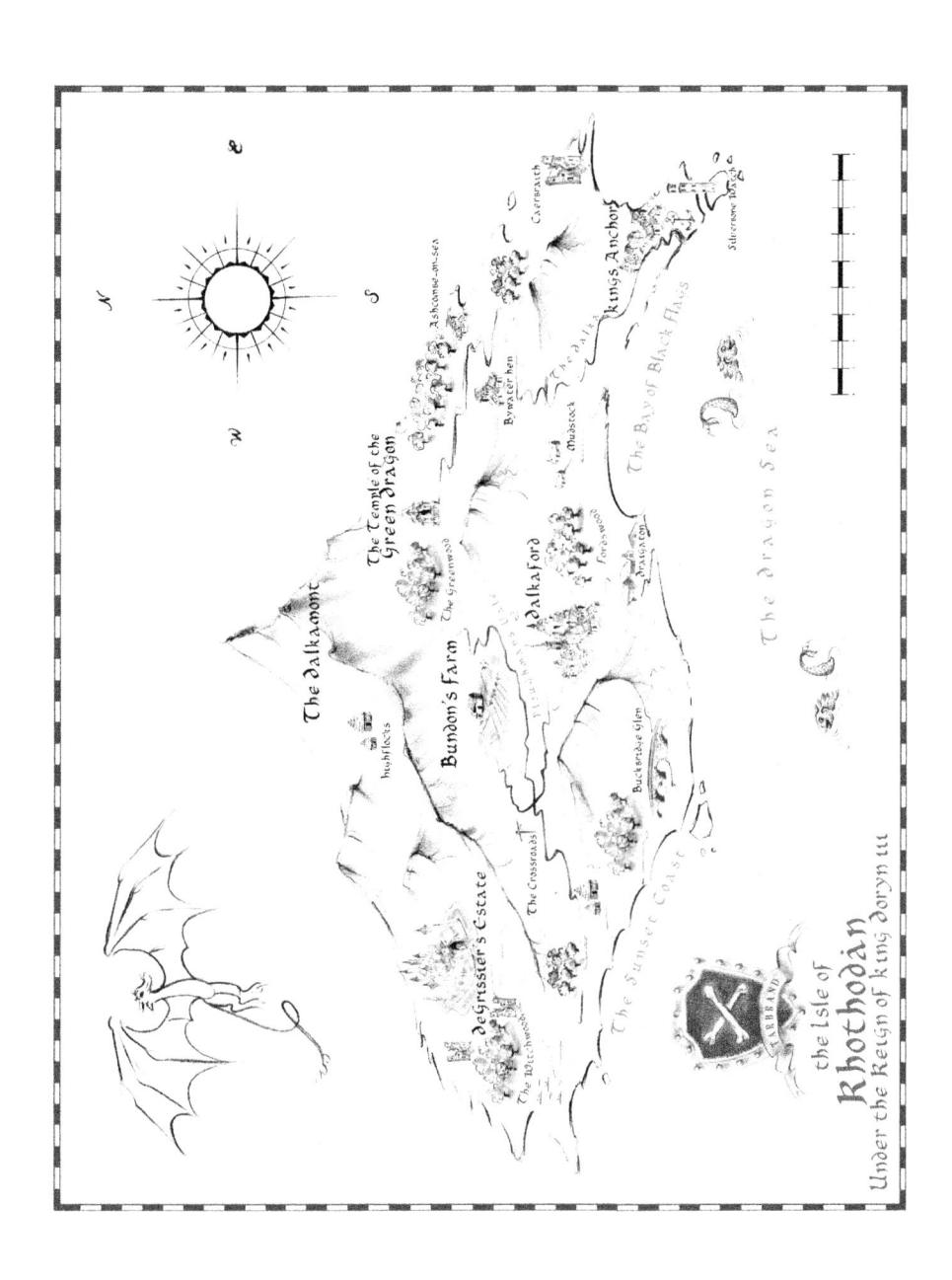

THE CALENDAR
Of Sathillian Agriculture

H are doth leap, and lambkin prance,
All within the Month of Dance.

Lovers sow through fresh spring showers,
All within the Month of Flowers.

Foals are born, on grass they lay,
All within the Month of Hay.

Crops doth yield with horse and harness,
All within the Month of Harvest.

Bright skies shine as spring is done,
All within the Month of Sun.

Queen's yield gold; so sweet and runny,
All within the Month of Honey.

Berries sought through moorland rambles,
All within the Month of Brambles.

Thread wheels spin as linseed blooms,
All within the Month of Looms.

Blood is spilt as journeys halt,
All within the Month of Salt.

Weave and hearth, while prayer proceeds,
All within the Month of Reeds.

Thresh and winnow, stripping weeds,
All with the Month of Seeds.

Tilling earth through years end toil,
All within the Month of Soil.

Through sun and joy or rain and hurt,
The year storms on; from Dance to Dirt.

- Common Nursery Rhyme

FOREWORD

By Greenjack Jorkin

I first heard the tale of The Farmer and the Fald in an alehouse in Kriscany, our most beloved and beautiful capitol of Kraigwyn, on the southern isle of our Eastern Kingdom where, on Harper's Street, wandering elves had made their humble mark upon the white city.

The singer in question had told the tale a hundred times by his own reckoning. It had the ring of an ancient story, altered through many a retelling. You can imagine my surprise when the singer informed me that it was not so ancient as that—happening in fact, in my own lifetime. And not that long ago.

He had first heard the tale from a band of goblins, those nomadic elves from the Farhogian Plains, the flat, steppe on the eastern side of the continent. The singer gave much useful information and told me that this band of elves gave him an account of such adventures, with the claim being that they had seen them firsthand.

As someone who grew up on the Isle of Rhothodân, you can understand my delight upon hearing such a local tale. With all these place names and landmarks, I knew so well. The Dalkamont, King's Anchor, the Bay of Black Flags, the Temple of the Green Dragon. These were names I grew up on, now given new life and fresh magic. A magic I had never known was there while I habited the isle in my youth. I wasted no time as this fresh endeavour blossomed in my mind.

Histories and lore have been written for the eyes of the wise and the wealthy only—all in old Brentiri runes or the Sathillian script of the Thrice Drowned Empire. But none in our humble Trade Speak. The language the merchant-folk had created through the natural courses of common use and time.

And so I resolved to write a tale that all could read, with another promise to ensure that many more Brothers from the Temple would make it their mission to teach the reading and writing of words to as many souls as wished to learn. For, in the time of writing this, even in the courts of King's (as well as the courts of highborn lords and prideful jaerls of both the southern and northern islands), just shy of half have mastered the art of the written word, by my reckoning. And that needs to change. For in written words are the key to understanding, and with understanding... it is my humble belief, and I dare say the belief of our Noble Dragon, that war and conquest shall hold little to no relevance.

But first, I think, a little about me.

My name is Brother Jorkin. Known to many as Greenjack for the Brotherly robes of green linen I wear, coupled with the princely sigil of my noble family, a black raven on blue. These robes set me apart from my other Brothers-in-Prayer, as they wear black robes with red sashes, and carry tall staves of solid blackwood. While I, decorated as I am in accordance with my heritage and some few... 'good deeds' (shall we say?) was adorned in green. For I number one of that elite order of knights non-combative: The Order of the Quill. Brothers of the Temple who are set apart; the most promising to rise to Krillian. So I was not anointed, not yet, but still in my apprenticeship, with the vague promise of a title, a 'sir' before my name if I wished it.

Which I did not. The title of 'brother' suits me well enough.

I returned from King Doryn's Third Crusade, along with his crown, his ravens and his fair body. Now still. Now broken.

The crusades, both the second and third, and the foul mockery of governance upon our return, took twelve years of my life all told, from the age of four-and-ten to the age of six-and-twenty. And now I sit in the years of my thirties; and I look back most fondly, not at those times of conquest and death, (which others name as valour and glory)... but at those quiet times; those lazy days in the Temple at Rhothodân, playing tricks on my cousins, brother and Brothers-in-Prayer. Of those warm summers by the banks of the Dalka. Favouring the skimming of stones and courting of maids over wearisome study and long, monotonous oration. For the old Krillian valued little else more than tired, weary wisdom. Passive in its execution, but prickly as brambles if interrupted out of turn. Or worse yet; ignored entirely. (As I favoured in my youth).

But I had royal blood, diluted and part forgotten by most, but there in my veins it lay. Carving out a fair future for me. For things were made easy for me, and they could have remained such if I had chosen it. But that ceaseless call to adventure compelled me to answer the summons of my cousin, the Good King Doryn, and bid all those warm summers and quiet meditations farewell.

But it is only when these everyday comforts and joys are gone that one truly starts to see their merit. For when I returned from the abhorrent sandy shores of Arencia, that inhospitable and unconquerable southern continent, I found none of the comforts had stayed in my absence. Either that, or perhaps I had grown blind to it through weary riding and numbing battle and could no longer see what was clearly there for some.

For the banks of the Dalka felt grey even by the light of the sun. The stones would not skim so beautifully as before. And all the fair maids in the realm could not bolster any amorous intention in me. For their faces reminded me of the many that lay dead upon the sandy roadsides down south; many was the number that we had a hand in killing. Innumerable, I'd say. Though only through fear of the number, I think.

But after the Good King had died, and his son, the Young King Eiric, had been crowned, I thought my future to lie in the capitol, guiding, counselling and penning the Young King's letters. But no. Destiny, it seemed, had other plans for me.

I was dismissed from courtly duty. Through an altercation with our late King's son, King Eiric. The reasons were countless, and the effort to remove me, I'd say with total certainty, was not solely down to our Young King... the little cousin I had been so close with in my youth. However, *that* story may bleed into this one... the two are separate. And I shall speak more on it in time.

On the matter of my dismissal, I was free to continue my studies, with a generous annuity of one-thousand golden monarchs from the crown to see me sheltered, fed and served suitably for a man of my standing.

So you see... my removal was not so hefty a punishment. But the Young King had made it plain that he wanted nothing more to do with me, nor my counsel, not then. Not yet. But his grace did not know what a boon this would be for me, and, one hopes, the rest of the known world; in time.

For I vowed on the shores of Brentir when I first returned; on the thirteenth day of Apys, (the Month of Honey in the common Trade Speak), that I would partake in no further acts of death and war. Nor would I put my hands to the signing of any papers, nor lay my voice to any order or command that would result in such. This solemn promise alienated me from my dear family, my cousins and brother, who were walking roads far different to mine own. On courses I could neither understand, nor condone.

Understand that for a Brentiri, especially one of royal blood, to waft away conflict as though it were a petty nuisance was not done. And I received no blessings on my journey, not even from those I held most dear to me.

I held the blood of kings in my heart; warriors, liberators and crusaders all. Who did not gain their crowns by fair heart and wise words. Only by the strength of their sword arms.

However, I have found there to be great strength in the former. Even though the latter makes for better songs. But I have a fair few songs of my own. Tales; grand and old... and powerful, I'd say.

And so it was on the ninth day in the Month of Brambles that I, with a meagre retinue of scribes, servants and a few companions I had gathered on my adventures, travelled back to my old home of Rhothodân. In my company was the elven singer who had first told me of the Farmer and his Fald, who named himself as 'Cân-o-Carreg'. He, on our travels, coined the phrase I often use in my writings: 'The world hates me for naught but the point of my ears.'

A wise soul and a fair companion, he became my scholar in all things elven within the story. Providing me with such wonderful words as: 'Hiraethi', 'Kin'Slaen' and, of course, 'Tyr'Dalka'.

For did you know that the elves also practised the Green Dragon's Prayer? Kri, our most Noble Dragon, was but one lesser god amongst their pantheon. They scattered ashes across their babes' heads, as we do now. We call it an 'ashening'; the ritual we Brother's oversee when a newborn's fire is first kindled. Elves named it 'Heninyath', or 'a birth from the ashes'. This means that our ancient customs are more ancient than even the wisest of our brother's ever knew. And it leads to the ofttimes controversial question of... 'how much else do we not know?' as well as 'How much else have we forgotten?' These are unpopular questions at the Temple and are even held as contemptible by many of the Order of Natural Philosophers in the high courts of both

Brentir, Kraigwyn and beyond. These philosophers, who seem to value certainty above truth, would have us think that nothing is 'unknown' and that we have merely not yet asked the right questions. An odd belief, to be sure, when held hand in hand with their secondary belief that the asking of such questions is akin to heresy. But I digress. This is not an essay on the paradox of the modern intellectual but an exercise in how the pursuit of knowledge can, in fact, be of great service.

It was little over two days later, on the eleventh day of Brambles, that we arrived at Rhothodân's self-styled capitol. King's Anchor. Though, to be sure. it was a sorry size for a city. And a sorrier state. The buildings half crumbling, the roads two-thirds mud to one-third cobbles, and the people... I try and save judgement for those who come seeking it, but by my fire. There are some sorry people in the world. And most of them seem to dwell in King's Anchor.

The lord cutthroat of the isle, the Lord Killian Tarbrand; now old, sea burnt, and as unkindly as ever, gave his blessings for our project with an indifferent waft of his gnarled hand. I dare say he did not understand it, but at least he did not refuse it, as I had half-expected he might. He bore no memory of the events, save for some glimmer of recognition when the name 'Lady DeGrissier' was mentioned. But no more than a glimmer. And some half-remembered rumour that she had returned to Autreville on the continent after some letters of altercation shared with her noble father; some half-forgotten duke of some whole-forgotten duchy.

We made the quick decision not to lodge in the capitol, favouring instead a ride onwards to a small village by the name of Bywater Hen, a humble fisherman's rest nestled on the banks of the Dalka, just before she splits off into her many hatchling streams. The village doubled as a waypoint for travellers on their way to the Temple, or further, and had in its humble streets a stable, an inn and an alehouse; all run out of the same ancient, half-reconstructed building. It seemed to stoop over itself like a crooked old man, its third-floor windows inspecting the ground before it. The Hen and Hook was its name, with its weather-beaten sign hanging over its old oaken doors, showing us the reason for it.

We found that only a few had heard the tale we were hunting after as we drank strong ale and chatted with the locals. But none shared any useful insights. The common instruction was to head to Dalkaford if we wished to learn more.

"They have many queer folks and fanciful tales down the ford's way," I recall a fisherman saying as he cracked his clay pipe over the old, smoke-stained hearth.

And so it was on the thirteenth day in the Month of Brambles after our horses were watered, our wineskins refilled, and our provisions bolstered by fresh river fish that we journeyed north-westwards, further afield to the town-stead of Dalkaford.

We did not reach the town until after dark, where we made fresh lodgings in the 'Good King's Cups', named for our late crusader king. It was clear from the outset that elves were not well trusted on the isle. Cân-o-Carreg received many unwelcome glances. Despite that, the singer gave a song or two that evening, and some coins were granted him by the locals, though warily and with little warmth.

It was not until the morning that I saw the town in all its splendour. For it was in Dalkaford that I discovered the true shining capitol the isle deserved. Where the streets were cobbled, and the buildings well-raised with wattle and daub and good solid timber. A watchtower stood in its centre, of quarried stone and slate— four, maybe five stories high, while the streets were busy with trade and chatter around this central citadel. Dalkaford was half the size of King's Anchor, perhaps, but with twice the beauty, and thrice the gentility.

In our search for answers, there were some who knew the names of Bundon and his daughter. But they were old and half-remembered. Many fellow farmers regaled the name of 'Bundon', claiming that he was the picture of honesty and humble generosity.

"Old Master Bundon," one large-bellied old baker gave,

with long grey muttonchops growing determinedly down both cheeks. "A fine fellow. With a tragic old story. Haven't seen him these last seven years. But then many moved away after news of our Good King's death."

Another gave (a fellow Brother from the Temple by the name of Kindur):

"A fickle chap was Farmer Bundon; trouble seemed to follow him likes flies follow horses. And his daughter was no better. That beast of hers was no suitable pet for a farm girl. Our Young King's Decree was much needed if you ask me. I haven't seen them since that law was forged."

The law he spoke of was, of course, the law of 'In Fortys'Bestias', or 'The Ban of Magical Beasts', in common parlance. Which saw that none but the King could hold, breed or rear elder species or any ancient beasts that the crown deemed 'magical'. Wyverns, manticores and griffons were all on the decree. As were falds.

This was the first mention of the fald that I had heard from any save the elven singer himself. And it spurred us ever forwards to discover more.

In truth, I had not even stopped to think how this decree might have effected the common folk, for it was mighty rare that any even dared to wrangle such dangerous creatures, save for highborn lords with their fanciful menageries.

We stopped by the smith's shop to replace our horses' shoes, as the cobbled streets had battered them mercilessly. Some brutish female blacksmith answered our call, as did her brother, a dyer, who lived above the smithy. She shod our horses well enough and even gave us a brief, albeit refreshing, affirmation to our task.

But they seemed to regard our honest questions as threats and unwelcome prying, and the blacksmith resolved to not spill the secrets she had made oathless promise to keep. A scribe wrote down the brief conversation, and it went so:

The blacksmith, a woman with a man's bearing, thicker wrists and broader shoulders than half the men in our company, told us that she knew the farmer in question. And that they knew the tale. But she was adamant that this was solely her business, and the business of the farmer, and his fald. And their late mother, who they both, judging by their downcast expressions, sorely missed.

The leader of our company, our own Brother Greenjack assured the blacksmith and her brother that we meant no harm with our questions and promised that it was a purely academic endeavour, of some own personal interest, nothing more.

The blacksmith seemed to mistrust this phrasing. Stating that she'd 'been fooled before by fair words and false promises.' At that point, to punctuate her words, she threw her hammer down upon the anvil, shaping a horseshoe, red and glowing from the forge. She then, by my own study, eyed the golden dragon that was embroidered onto our Brother Greenjack's robes, and this instilled firmer defiance in her.

She spoke no more until her brother asked what payment they might expect for the story. He was a small man, of unfortunate feature, and half his sister's size. With his arms stained blue to the elbow.

Once informed by our treasurer that we had some small amount of silver to grant those who helped in our effort, the brutish blacksmith slammed her hammer back down onto the anvil, silencing her brother before he had a chance to reply.

The sister then said something most odd. She stated that "even gold can tarnish, I've found", which we all regarded as a most peculiar thing to say, as it is safe knowledge that gold is completely inert. Both that and we were offering silver. Not gold.

She reiterated that it was not our business to be asking such questions, but gave us a sliver of information, claiming the story was a true one. Perhaps not as true as our resident elf had described it, but true enough. And after that was said, she left little room for negotiation. Refusing even the small amount of silver offered her. However, her brother took it happily, though he had certainly been the less helpful of the two.

Scribes account, on the fourteenth day in the Month of Bram-

bles, year 987 by Sathillian Reckoning.

And that was that. Though the dyer, once a safe distance from his sister's wrath, did give us some small advice:

"Go follow the northern road from Dalkaford, deep into the Ploughman's Vale. There to look for a farmhouse raised in the valley of two hills."

We gave the fellow another silver, which he grabbed before scurrying away without farewell.

And so we had our next destination.

We lingered in Dalkaford for a further few days. In part because none in my retinue wished to leave so soon. The autumn days were warm and splendid that year, and there was no finer place, in my mind, to enjoy the falling leaves of the riverbank's golden willows and rich, auburn light of the setting sun. It was in those pleasant days that I first penned a rough map of Rhothodân, with naught but spare parchment paper and sticks of charcoal. Making plain to all that Dalkaford stood as proudly (if not prouder) amid the hills and mountains as King's Anchor.

But soon, though solemnly, we left the town-stead. And we arrived in the Ploughman's Vale on the nineteenth day of Brambles and visited many farmhouses (and many wary farmers) before we found, what we assumed to be the farmstead the dyer had described to us.

But when we arrived, our hearts were sunk, for there was nobody there. A big green door lay off its hinges, now half rotten. The farmhouse sat covered in a layer of dust and cobwebs, with a well-used hearth in its centre… now cold. Though not as long abandoned as we dreaded. The elven singer, with his kind's aptitude for nature and tracking, informed me that this place was only recently abandoned- as little as a year or less.

As we explored the hills, we found some old graves; two sat in a long overgrown field. Humble wooden planks atop cairns of moss-covered stones. One, the more weathered of the two, read; Meat, while the other, fresher than the first, read: Veg. But further afield, atop the farmland's highest hill lay two other cairns, piled either side of a large oak tree, where wild cattle still grazed. One seemed old and overgrown, and the writing on the grave had worn to nothing. But a fresher grave lay too, with a beautiful old calendar acting as its headstone. An old cartwheel, with the months of the years painted around its outside, with the days, one to thirty, etched onto the interior. A straw cap lay atop the cairn. And so did an inscription, in trade speak, so all could understand it.

"Here lies Bundon, my papa, whose proud fire dwindled to nought but humble ash in his winter years. He who had touched destiny, diced with dragons and tilled earth with honest effort, till the end of his days. A farmer. A father. And a hero none shall sing for. Save us. And ye few who read this."

So overcome was I by such a message that I found myself weeping. That a girl, a farm girl, no less. Common born and near-forgotten. That she could write this was more inspiration than I could ever have wished for. But stranger still. When I leant over the gravestone to lay a copper piece and the dragon's prayer atop the cairn, I was struck suddenly by a thought, or perhaps a memory. It was as though some great recollection had planted itself within those deep grains of old weathered wood, which awoke in me when first I touched the calendar.

Now perhaps, as a Brother of the Temple, I had simply inhaled too many of those sickly, sweet smokes we favour. For they do make one see things if one smokes enough of them. Or perhaps through long years of prayer and blessing, the Dragon himself had bestowed to me a small boon. I could not say for certain.

But I knew things. And saw things. As though glimpsing through another's eyes, just glimpses, nothing more. But I feel it now, as I felt it then. That there was a touch of... destiny to all of this. And in my heart, I knew the story already. Every part of it, every player within it, every tragedy, every bit of luck and every joy.

I began work at once, taking lodging back in Dalkaford in humble rooms above the Good King's Cup. A long year of studious work followed, obsessing endlessly over each account and infinitesimal detail. Through my small effort of seeking such a story out, I felt compelled and duty-bound to see it told well. It was as though, in my mind, the story had already been written, and all I need do (through a tireless process of elimination) was decipher it from the mists of memory and time. In this process, I encountered many other players and tellers within the tale, but I shall leave these delayed accounts for a spell lest I spoil some of the twists and turns that gave peril to our humble farmer.

My own sacred flame is intermingled with every word of this fair story, in the vague hope that it might spark the fiery imaginations of others. So I present to you, the reader, the tale of The Farmer and the Fald.

>Greenjack Jorkin
>Dated: The first day in the Month of Brambles - Year 990 by Sathillian Reckoning.

BUNDON I

The Twenty-Fourth Day in the Month of Harvest

Farmer Bundon had never dreamed of fancy. His father was a farmer. And his father was a farmer, and his, and his. And so on, and so on, as the usual story goes. Fancy was not to his liking; he mistrusted it. Why wear silk or samite when linen and wool were as warm as any? Why stuff a peacock with cinnamon and cloves when bacon and bread filled a belly just as well, if not better? Why bow and curtsey away your hours of leisure when a cup of ale and a jolly tune could be enjoyed? It made no sense to him.

If my herd were to make me a rich man, I would buy more cows, not a cow made of gold. Why hoard what you can spend? Sow a thousand fields instead of one if you've the coin to front it.

The thought of such fancy confused him, as things often did.

Words, and the writing of them, had both escaped Bundon. His mam had tried to teach him on many occasions, he remembered. She used to love the old poems, the tales of dragons and monsters and the clashes of good and evil. He had tried to learn for her sake; she missed her father reading to her, she used to say. But the words never looked right to him; the marks would change and shift and never stay in his head. He had made his peace with that, as he had with her passing, and his father's not long after that.

If you feel naught but grief in times as such, grief is all you'll know.

That's what his mam used to say. He had hated it while she lived; for she said it to any and all daily strife to stop his complaints, its meaning dwindling over the years to mean: *shut yer gob and get on with it.* He had found the wisdom in both since his parents died.

He had had four brothers too; two had died to King Doryn's crusades, another to the rot, and another they lost to a passing merchant's ship' one in need of a cabin boy. So the small farm on the hill was just his. With its crooked barn and its big green door, its herd, two and twenty heads strong, its barley and wheat corn, and its two dutiful horses; big brave Meat, the old and swaybacked plough horse, with his long white whiskers, gloomy eyes and hooves the size of dinner plates. And Veg, the young and fearless palfrey, with his coat of dappled sand and blue eyes as bright as his spirit (and, the farmer knew all too well, the most expensive animal in his care).

I would never have spent such coin on a horse if not for her, he thought fondly. *She insisted. Saying that if I were travelling the roads every week, I should have a quick, stout horse for the job. Her dowry to me. My beautiful Veg.* The farmer felt a swell of pride and lovingly scratched the palfrey below his left ear; the twitchy, floppy one.

Be happy to work, and work to be happy, and happiness is all you'll know.

More of Mam's words echoed in his head. Yes. He was happy. With his barn, his cattle, his crop and his horses.

And her, of course. The farmer thought, smiling. *I have her. And him, soon.*

Veg carried him now, on the long and familiar road to the town-stead of Dalkaford, the same journey he had shared with Veg a hundred times before and a hundred times on Meat before that. But Farmer Bundon did not bring his cart this time, nor any of his cattle. No. This time he came to market just for him, and her, and him.

The dirt and dust roads turned to cobbled streets as he crossed over a high stone bridge. From the small rise, he could see near the entirety of his island home. The Isle of Rhothodân, where dragon's sleep. He could see over the green hills, right down to the coast, where the mighty Dalka crashed into The Bay of Black Flags and further to the jade coloured waters of the Dragon's Sea.

The port town of King's Anchor lies there; they'll have linens, white ones, shining and new. And bread, that black bread she likes with the pumpkin seeds on top, he thought a moment, caught up in the daydream. *But that's another two days' travel and another two to get back. Your son might not wait another four days, Bundon. Best be safe.*

He spurred the palfrey forward to Dalkaford, putting a hand to his belt to check his purse was still there. Bundon had had his purse taken near a dozen times on this road, and each time he had sworn it would be the last. The purse was there. Thank the fire. He hadn't thought of what he'd do, had it not been.

Bundon stepped down from Veg, leading him by the reins into the village square. His was a warm smile in Dalkaford, all men knew him to be an honest trader, and all women knew him to be the picture of courtesy. He nodded to faces he recognised, matched greetings with greetings of his own and swelled with pride at any chance he got to tell the townsfolk his news. He spotted the local baker, a young man with a coarse blond beard and silver-blue eyes. Owyn was his name. He had a large red nose and blemishes that washed over both cheeks. The young apprentice had worked hard over the years, and he had risen to become master of the local baker shop last summer, when the old baker grew too old. All were happy for the boy, the farmer remembered. And his bread was just as good as any.

"Good Master Bundon," the young baker bellowed, a basket of fresh loaves under one arm. "I did not think to see you again so soon. The Harvestman's festival has only just been and gone." Bundon had practised his response on his journey over.

"No, good master, I am not trading today. I have come to market to buy milk, bread and linens for my wife; she is great with child and like to burst any day."

"Has it been that long already? By my fire, how the days go by. Many congratulations, Master Bundon. Truly. And here, this batch was made with your own wheat, so I'll not take any coin from you. We'll drink to your boy tonight, or you could join us in the drowning of our sorrows?"

Sorrows? That would not do. Bundon had news, very good news, and the talk had turned so suddenly to sorrows? He took the bread, wrapped it in a square of washed cloth and placed it in his satchel. He fumbled with his purse, pouring the contents onto the cobbled streets.

"What sorrows? There are sorrows?" He asked, stumbling to pick up his coins.

"Aye, sorrows aplenty," the baker shook his head. "See the man there? You know him, yes? Krillian up at the Temple, him and his Brothers. Even Lord Tarbrand is here. Oi, I said no coin!"

The baker pushed the copper coins away. Bundon thanked him heartily and turned his eyes back to the crowd. Bundon could see the men, and he knew them well. They were holy men. Men of the Temple. The Krillian stood stooped and frail in his resplendent green robes, a golden mantle round his shoulders. His two Brothers wore simple black robes, with sashes of red wool and staves of hard blackwood. He knew one of them, Brother Kindur the younger of the two. He collected the temple's tithes and was always gracious in his duty.

"The harvest goes well; the weather holds," Bundon insisted. "What have we done to anger our godly Dragon so?"

"Not *our* Dragon, Bundon," the baker whispered. "You see that one, that one they're with? The comely one".

Bundon looked toward Lord Tarbrand, the liege lord of the Isle of Rhothodân. An old cutthroat by all accounts, weathered and foul-faced, dressed in a black chiffon surcoat, trimmed with silver thread and adorned with the silver crossed-bones of his lordly sigil. Complete with the strong bearing and thick wrists of a man who had answered all life's hardships with steel. He was escorting a young lady to a carriage - a striking beauty of gentle birth, he was sure. She was pale as the farmer's thigh, with high cheekbones, sharp as anything and a nose that was sharper still. Her eyes were flecks of gold, glowing beneath an ever-present scowl. She wore her deep red hair in an impossibly long braid that swung at her hips. And decorating her was the richest gown the farmer had ever seen. A shimmer of crimson samite with long dagged sleeves cut to reveal golden damask beneath. A golden sash hugged the curve of her hips, wrought with jewels, rubies and zircons, all finished with golden threads, embroidered to the shapes of writhing flames and battling dragons. She wore a thick shining cloak of beautiful copper fox pelts, clasped with a golden dragon, a ruby set in its maws.

"She has the bearing of a queen," Bundon said quietly, awed by the red lady.

"Aye, and a purse to match," Owyn chided. "She's just bought the town-stead, and sworn fealty to our lord of bones there." Bundon could not have heard that right. Bought the town-stead? You can't just buy a town, can you? Did she buy the land the town was on? The houses that made up its streets and roads? Or the people? Farmer Bundon did not think the good people of Dalkaford would like to be bought and sold like so many calves from the Month of Dance.

"She's moving into one of the old slaver estates over the hill, the one the children play at."

"The slaver estates?" Bundon asked, puzzled. "But they're half a ruin. There's a great tree growing through one of their roofs. Every inch is alive with mould, or moss or fouler things. Swear I saw a family of young wolves in one once."

"Whatever the state of it, that's where she's going," he sniffed. "Both tithe and tax will rise for this; they always do when nobles move in." Bundon watched the lady board her grand carriage, a four-wheeled monster of red canvas, gilded steel and golden dragons. Her many servants busied around her, plumping pillows, opening doors, and, if nothing else, just bowing low to the ground. She had guards, too, square-jawed mainlanders. Each had a new set of chainmail, oiled to a black shine with a heavy red sash that hung from shoulder to hip. Half her guard held tall oaken spears with shiny steel points, while others held expensive crossbows, the sort the dwarves made on Copperlee. Bronzed steel and solid blackwood, with quivers of bolts on the bowman's hips. Around their shoulders were red capes; crimson, the same as their lady's gown, each clasped with an iron dragon.

"Those mainlanders are to be our new prison guards, it seems to me," Owyn added in a whisper. "To watch the banks of the Dalka, to cease reckless use of her waters. I heard our Lord Tarbrand name them such. The Riverguard."

"Our mighty Dalka needs no guards, nor any of her hatchling streams," Bundon wrinkled up his face in confusion. "She can plenty protect herself."

"Well, that's not how our nobility sees it," Owyn spat. "Look at them. Our Good King sunders the chains of slavery, only for this sorry lot to forge us new ones." He shook his head and let out a string of tuts, walking off with a heavy sigh. Bundon stayed a moment, watching in dour fascination.

I bet her servants' servants eat better than I do, the farmer wondered, more thoughtful than bitter. He noticed a fat little boy join the lady, dressed in a crimson doublet, peppered with golden studs. A mop of rust coloured curls on his head. He heaved himself up the carriage steps, even as her servants struggled to help. The boy was no more than four or five, but he was beastly plump and red in the face. Once up, he sat himself down, cheeks flushed and sweaty from the effort. His lady mother patted him gently on the top of his head, wincing at the wetness of his now slick hair. The farmer found himself staring, and he had never been much of a starer.

There's always something happening in the world, stop and gawp at every one and stopping and gawping will be all you ever know.

Another of his mam's. There was a certain pattern to her advice; the farmer could not deny it.

Bundon watched as the lady's retinue, along with Lord Tarbrand's knights, packed her up and sent her off to the old Slaver Estates. The old raider-cum-lordling stepped forward to the carriage steps, presenting the lady with an odd gift. A large stone, it seemed to Bundon. Patterned with obsidian scales, so sharp, their edges glinted like shards of black glass. Lord Tarbrand whispered some coy words in the lady's ears, and she wrinkled up her nose with a look of frosty gratitude. She lay a hand against the black stone, and her cold smile became a warmer thing. And as Bundon looked on, intrigued by the strange gift, he suddenly felt the lady's eyes on him; he could swear it. Through the bustling crowds of the market square… she was looking at him. Straight at him. And she was smiling. The farmer averted his eyes, not wanting to seem presumptuous, and turned his mind to the task ahead.

A copper of milk, a copper of bread and three coppers for fresh linens. The farmer tried to recall, but there was something else. *Squared. The linen must be cut into squares. Remember, foolish farmer.*

"Master Bundon!"

He knew the voice; it was Myko, the stable master. An older man, of some five-and-forty years. Coarse grey hair grew thick on both cheeks, while his head hair had retreated halfway up his head, wiry grey curls sat like a garland on his crown. He had a large hooked nose but kind eyes and an easy smile.

"And Veg! You beautiful beast. Look at that gut; he's been feeding you too many apples, hasn't he?"

Myko laughed and slapped Veg's soft underbelly, who whickered and huffed his response.

"No one thought to see you today, with the Harvestman's Festival only just been and gone," the stable master started, already eyeing up the wear on Veg's shoes. "And those I put on only last week."

Bundon took a breath.

"No, good master, I am not trading today, nor am I looking to shoe my horse. I have come to market to buy milk, bread and linens for my wife; she is great with child and like to burst any day."

"Young Alaria is having a baby," the stable master shook his head. "You found a true gem in that one, young master, and I hope she gives you many strong sons and daughters. The wife's in the shop; she'll see to milk for ye if you have a pail for her."

Myko's wife was a stick of a woman who wore her years harder than her husband. Calloused hands and tired eyes, with many haphazard teeth all growing over one another. Daisy was all Bundon had ever called her, though she always attested that Daisy was not her true name. She never gave a different name in its place, though. So Daisy, it was.

She ran a general shop of odds and ends, selling lengths of rope, farming tools, pots and pans and wooden spoons. Spoons above all else, as she had taken to whittling them in her spare time. Spoons hung from the rafters in bizarre bouquets, all of varying sizes and quality. One would usually string up herbs or garlic,or onions. For Daisy and Myko, spoons served just as well. But they also kept two great shaggy dairy cows, horns as long as a man's reach. And the husband and wife were open-handed with their milk.

"You've a pail for me?" The woman asked warmly. "Didn't

think to see you at market so soon."

"I am not trading today. I have come to market to buy milk, bread and linens for my wife; she is great with child and like to burst any day," the farmer said proudly. He handed the pail over, and she returned with it a few moments later, filled with frothy, warm milk.

She did not even take a copper for it. Just smiled and said, "When next you come with your crop, just give us the milk's worth in barleycorn and we'll call it even."

She whispered it as though it were a great secret. When asked, she also handed him four-and-twenty neat squares of freshly woven linen, still smelling of the loom. "And a little something for the little 'un." She secreted a toy in the farmer's hand. A small wooden horse that bore the most uncanny resemblance to a wooden spoon, with little string legs and a painted face.

"You have my thanks and my fire, lady Daisy," the farmer bowed, and the woman was set to giggles and titters.

"Lady Daisy indeed," she laughed, getting back to her whittling. Just as he left, he heard her call out: "And my name's not Daisy!"

Milk, bread and linens. The linens cut to squares. And all for a single copper and a bit of barleycorn. He beamed proudly. He bound his satchel to Veg's saddle, taking careful steps to secure the milk pale, clasping its sturdy tin lid in place. He would not wish to spill a single drop, as his own cattle's milk was for their calves and tasted like sweet white water by comparison. Not like the creamy, rich milk of the great Brentiri cows.

Just a sip to ease my thirst, he thought, taking a long drink from the pail. The cream lingered on his top lip, and he gleefully licked it away—*all a man needs.*

"I look about our small village, and I see faces. Many faces. Faces who have not yet graced our Dragon's Temple."

The voice was familiar. The farmer looked about and found the source. Brother Kindur, standing on the cobbled auctioneer dais in the market square, arms outstretched, ready to speak. Farmer Bundon led Veg to the edge of the growing congregation and watched curiously. The Brothers of the Temple were known for their glamours and tricks, intertwining their weekly orations with clever sleights-of-hand and colourful enchantments. Bundon had little time to dawdle, he knew, but how often did simple farmers get to see such wonder? The promise of mystery and magic paused his stride.

"Come, listen, gentlefolk. To a tale as old as the mountains. A tale hidden and forgotten within the vaults of history. Of that time, long ago when dragons ruled the skies! Red dragons, gold dragons, bejewelled sea dragons of jade and silver. Fairy dragons that could sit a man's hand and fearsome fire drakes whose wings could block out the sun. But, stay here. Put a hand to your chest, just so. Feel it beating? Your heart. Safe within you. Dragons, though, aha, dragons keep their hearts in their hoard. A dragon is nothing without its chased goblets and cut gemstones, without its loyal subjects and leal servants. And above all else, a dragon values the undiminishing beauty, the yellow glow and clinking music of gold. For dragons have hearts of gold, you understand. The larger a dragon's hoard, the larger the dragon can grow. Power and beauty and cunning beyond imagining. But as the dragon grows, so do its failings. Greed. Contempt. Corruption. Pride. And evil. Unwavering, unyielding, untenable evil."

A crowd was growing quickly, with gasps echoing through the congregation as the Brother Kindur threw clouds of many-coloured smokes into the air with graceful flicks of his wrist, dazzling the onlookers as the clouds sparkled and took the shapes of writhing dragons, all clawing at one another, and breathing their foul fire. A hundred tiny dragons, perhaps as many as a thousand, all swarming through the coloured clouds of the Brother's divine illusions.

"And so, back then, when dragons ruled... wars were waged. Dragon against dragon. Each fighting to strengthen their hoards, strengthen their hearts with the hope that one day, they will be all that's left. For only then will they truly have won. What is the point of power and beauty and cunning if you are not the *most* powerful? The *most* beautiful? The *most* cunning? Dragons regarded themselves as second to none, so how could any but *one* exist? The wars waged, and many hundreds of dragons died, each one bequeathing their hoard to the victor. And the victors grew in power.

"Lesser dragons hid. Masked in glamours and guises with powerful spells. Walking the world in the shapes of men and women, coveting their remaining wealth. Resenting their fragile form. Ugly, in their eyes. Tempering their corruption with webs of endless lies and deceit. But for true dragons, the wars waged on. The fires that burnt turned the skies to ash. And the ash fell like snow, blotting out the sun with thick black clouds and allowing the icy hands of the north to sweep down from the Cold Beyond. The world froze over. Nothing grew. Nothing lived. The dragons had taken all. And the world would have stayed as such… if not for our Noble Dragon." The Brother stopped, picked up his blackwood staff and planted it on the ground with a solid thwack; a bright green cloud erupted from its tip, moving in the air to form the shape of a great green drake in flight. Bundon found himself awed by the spectacle, it had been many years since he had watched one of the Temple's sermons, and he did not remember them being so… magical.

"Behold, Kri!" The Brother roared as gasps washed across the crowd. "Behold our great green dragon. A hide of shining emeralds and wings of cloth-of-gold. And eyes that held great wisdom. For when he sat amidst the clouds of the Dalkamont and watched as an eternal winter buffeted the land… he did not skulk beneath the earth, as many of his kin had done. Nay. He called forth his brothers, lesser drakes with scales of obsidian and wings as bright as fresh shed blood." The Brother twisted his staff, and two clouds of black and red circled in the air, forming two more dragons that stood stalwart by their great green brother. The crowd gasped and cheered and clapped their wonder as the three illusions soared over Dalkaford, over the market stalls, coiling around the stone bell tower, and roaring their divine fire into the clear blue sky.

"The three of them soared over the icy wastes, grief marking their faces, golden tears cascading down to the earth below. And from their tears... the ice began to melt. They beheld this wonder and hatched a great plan. Kri bid his brothers burrow into the earth to rid themselves of their monstrous hoards, the hoards that had corrupted their kin so. To make the hills and the forests and rivers their hoard instead. To place their hearts in the natural riches of the world. To let the roots of a forest grow from their blackened scales. To let life thrive from the red fires in their black bellies. And so they did. And His brothers died to give that gift. But Kri knew it was not enough." The black dragon clouds faded from sight, dissolving into the bright autumn sun, and then the Brother grew sombre.

"So when the first buds of the new forest grew, when the rivers once more ran with crystal waters, and the hills rolled green, one over the other... our Dragon, our *Noble* Dragon began his prayer. A prayer we would not hear for ten thousand years or more. He said to us 'By my dragons-fire, so noble and strong. I give you my sacred flame'.

"The prayer was etched into every leaf on every tree. On each stone of the mountain. On every grain of sand and every drop of rain. So that we might hear it for all time. Hear it and be reminded of his final sacrifice. For when Kri gazed around the melting lands... he let out a slow and cumbersome breath. But this breath did not unleash the inferno that dragons were known for, no. It was a gentle warmth. The warmth of a summer breeze. The warmth of a lone candle in a dark room. It melted the ice back into the earth, and grass began to grow once more. The buds of the first forest rooted into trees, the lakes filled with pure water, and the ashen clouds subsided, allowing the sun to wash the world with golden rays. But the Green Dragon Kri had breathed away his dragon's hoard, the essence that made dragons immortal. He lay on the mountain as the first rains of the century beat down upon his back. He closed his eyes and melted into the earth. The green cloud faded now, carried off on the breeze. And Brother Kindur stood there, head hung in prayer.

"A sacrifice," he said. "For Tyr'Dalka. For us. For the possibility of us. For the kindnesses and falsehoods alike. All that we are. All that we can be. To realise, as he did, that the good in us will conquer the evil. By my dragons-fire, so noble and strong. I give you my sacred flame."

If the crowd had seemed excited before, they dwarfed that excitement now. Standing, and cheering, and making such a noise that Bundon had to cover his ears. Coins were thrown, coppers, mostly. But Bundon saw a glint of silver here and there. The colourful illusions had all faded now and left Farmer Bundon feeling something, something akin to sadness, but not so solemn as that.

By my fire. The farmer shivered, finding himself weeping from the tale. *That is what I try to live by, Brother; make no mistake. I always put a copper coin at the foot of the stone dragon come the new moon.*

'Paying Thanks' is how the devout phrased it. A small sacrifice to honour the grand one their noble dragon gave. Bundon walked to the Brother, busy as he was with collecting what coins strew on the cobbled steps.

"You have a commanding voice, Brother Kindur," Bundon commended. "I knew the story well enough but never heard it so, so… by my fire, I haven't the words for it. It was wonderful."

"Dragons sleep, and mermaids sing, and Brothers tell their tales," the Brother said, rather more coldly than Bundon had expected, not paying much heed to the farmer at all. Busy with the gathering and counting of his gifted coin.

"That word you said, though. Um, tay-dalka, or some such," the farmer began.

"*Tyr'Dalka,*" the Brother repeated, uninterested. "What of it?"

"What does it mean?" Bundon asked; the Brother turned his head and looked the farmer up and down with a scowl.

"It's elvish," he said, unmoved. "It's what the elves called the world. *Tyr'Dalka*. Land of Dragons. Now, are you making a donation or simply stinking the air with that horse?" Bundon was at a loss for words. Brother Kindur had been nothing but gracious in his visits to the farm, and his story just now had near enchanted him. How could he be so cold, so suddenly?

"No, Brother, no. I meant no harm. And Veg smells no worse than other horses,"

Bundon fumbled with his purse, spilling the contents again. He cursed under his breath and set about picking up the coins. He heard the Brother tut in annoyance. Once done, the farmer placed a copper piece in the Brother's hand and doffed his straw cap. The Brother regarded the coin coldly.

"All that fuss and bother for a single copper? I'd sooner pay you one to stop wasting my time." The Brother pushed past Bundon and continued on the road northward, back to the Dragon's Temple. He still took the copper, though, Bundon noted.

"Where was his sacred flame then?" Bundon asked his horse. "I'd have thought holy men to always be fair and kind, even when irked or angry." That was how the farmer tried to be, though he did curse more than he'd like. And unruly cows never cheered his mood. But his wife was always there for that.

By my fire, my wife!

He saw how low the sun was getting. He had lingered too long, distracted by the Brother's stories. He led the horse back to the edge of the village, back to the cobbled bridge he had crossed before. The sun was low, too low. It would be dark before he got back.

She will not be happy. Thank goodness the Sister is there with her.

The journey back always felt easier than the journey away. Perhaps the roads were more downhill, or perhaps the sun was more forgiving.

Or perhaps it is the thought of my beautiful wife waiting for me that speeds my horse's steps. Usually, she has dinner waiting with her.

Bundon noticed how hungry he was, and his belly moaned its discomfort. There would be no dinner waiting tonight, he knew. His wife, the beautiful Alaria, was in her birthing bed, waiting for their little fellow to usher himself into the world.

Ushered into Tyr'Dalka, as the elves would say. The Farmer chuckled and shook his head. *It's a complicated old world, and you don't know the half of it, Master Bundon.*

It got dark as he rode. The palfrey ambled down the ever-dimming road, quick and steady. But the light was failing them, and the moon was hostage to heavy clouds. The farmer had a long walking staff he kept tied to Veg's saddle; from a notched hook, he had hung a small lantern. He was loath to use the oil, but it was his own folly that bought him out this late.

Best be safe, master farmer. You've a wife at home, great with child. Like to burst any day - by my fire, she could be bursting now.

He spurred the palfrey forwards. He would like to be there for that. He had imagined holding his son warm from the womb. Pink and wriggling. He had grimaced at the thought, but it was not an unhappy grimace. He looked forward to it.

And I do not mean to miss it.

The farmer's resolve strengthened, pushing the palfrey into a gallop. Veg was a spirited beast, yearning always to show his true skill to a master who tethered him to a plodding amble. So the horse eagerly ripped through the air, his sandy mane whipping into the farmer's eyes. The wind buffeted Bundon's undyed woollen cloak and near ripped the straw cap off his head. It felt good to feel such speed. It felt almost as though he were flying. But then he heard something. A clatter. Metal on stone.

And a splash.

Not a splash, please, Noble Dragon, don't let it be a splash.

He slowed the palfrey to halt and turned, dreading but knowing too well what he'd see. The milk pail. Gone. And the milk along with it. That's just what he needed. And that was his finest milk pail. The big one with wooden handles and solid tin lid. He thought about leaving it.

What's wasted today is tomorrow's regret. You're right, mam.

He got down from his horse and straightened his back, a string of crunches running up his spine. He followed back up the curve of the dusty road and saw wet patches splashed across the dirt. He followed them and followed them.

Fire, take me! There will surely be none left at this rate!

The farmer worried. The milk trail ended, but Bundon saw no milk pail. Just darkness as the edge of the road gave way to a steep fall, a wide and craggy ravine, overgrown, it seemed, with briars and brambles.

And blackberries, too.

The farmer licked his lips. *I could fetch my pail and trade the wasted milk for blackberries.*

The crag was steep, but he was a surefooted rambler. He had walked the whole of the Dalka's banks one summer, King's Anchor to Buckbridge Glen and looping back around; three and twenty miles all told.

A rough road, too. Rougher than this in places.

He was on maybe his third or fourth step when his balance faltered, and he fell. He grabbed at something. Anything. But the briars were too fierce and the bramble too weak. Their thorns, fierce and weak alike, grabbed back, however. Pulling great rips in his cloak and tunic, raking stinging welts across his bare skin and stealing away his dutiful straw hat. He only saw darkness and only felt what came stinging at him in the dark and the scuffs and grazes of the crag's face on his back.

Noble dragon; preserve me. I have a wife at home great with child. Like to burst any day.

He prayed quickly amidst a storm of scratches and scrapes. But the storm passed. Quite suddenly. The pain lingered, but the rush had stopped, and there was solid ground beneath him. He knew as it had beaten the wind from his chest.

He couldn't see. He could feel, though, and already his body ached from his thousand little cuts. There was something beneath his feet. He felt along, squinting, forcing his eyes to adjust.

Loose rocks and pebbles. Logs, perhaps, dried branches. And a small boulder. Light. White. I can see the white of it. A skull. A great bird skull.

Bundon had never seen anything quite like it. Its skull was as large a bull's, larger even. With a vicious hooked beak and a crest of tough, spiny quills. Or feathers. Some cross between the two. He could see now. A bit. Better than before. The bones sprawled around him, dusted with a thousand quill-like feathers; long, white bones—light as paper. The wings intermingled with the ribs, a scattering of white knives on the ground; its long neck curved round, head nuzzled into its chest. Its tail, long and rigid, stretched from the nest, a fan of great, spiny tail feathers decorating the end of it. Its once-powerful talons crumpled beneath it, buried by the ghost of its belly.

It's no dragon. Too small. He studied the beast. *It's short a pair of legs for a griffon, and those aren't the quills of a manticore.*

His father used to talk of the great bird-bats of the coasts. He had told stories of seeing them on his visit to Kriscany, the capitol, on the mainland. Diving into the oceans and pulling great writhing eels from the waters. A vulture's head and a bat's wings, neither scaled nor feathered, but some odd union of the two. This was a fald—a dragon's smaller, uglier cousin.

By my fire, I'd have thought them all dead by now. He paused, and looked at the bones. *Of course, mayhap they are.*

The farmer dusted his hands and winced at the pain of it; he could see his hands were covered in blood. In fact, he was covered so head to toe in brambles, blood and blackberry juice that he looked half a blackberry himself.

Your father's father was prone to fits and fevers with a single prick from a bramble thorn, be glad you're not him, Master Bundon. He looked up and assessed the climb. It would be a hard one. He looked about the thicket; there were no clear pathways; it would be a long and painful road that way. No. There was only one thing for it; he would have to brave the climb.

But you are weary. And you're hungry. Your thighs are worn from riding, your eyes are near to closing, and your body is half a pincushion.

He tried to stand up. He tried. But he felt oddly comfortable leant against the crag's wall, a roof of thicket above him. The tangle of briars and brambles a stalwart shield from the cold winds beyond. This place felt half a home. And the night suddenly seemed so peaceful. What was wrong with him? His resolve was so strong before. Before it all went wrong. *Before that damn milk pail. Fire can take that blasted pail!* He had not even retrieved it, determined though he was. He had followed it halfway to the hells, it seemed to him, and even then, there was no sign of it.

Damn the thing. He cursed and thought on that a moment.

I would miss it, though. He relented; *it's a better size than the most, with nice wooden handles.*

Bundon never noticed his eyelids droop. He never even felt particularly tired. But sleep took him regardless. And he dreamt of milk pails.

BUNDON II

The Twenty-Fifth Day in the Month of Harvest

He did not stir until the first of dawn's birdsongs trilled from the bracken. He woke suddenly and winced a moment later as his mind recalled his sense of pain. He felt a walking scab. Covered in dry blood and aching all over, itchy from the brambles in his clothes and then sore from his own itching.

Dear Noble Dragon, when you breathed your life into the world... did you have to give us brambles? Why give the sweet, fat Lord Blackberry such vicious household guards?

In the light of day, the farmer was in no small part relieved when he found his milk pail, empty alas, but intact. And soon, it was filled with berries. He was about to embark on his climb back up to the road when he noticed something else. He hadn't seen it the night before, so black was its shell. But there it was amidst a sea of splintered, obsidian shards.

A stone. No. An egg. Large. Larger than any egg I've seen before. Its shell was shiny, black and jagged, as though it were made of cut glass. And what's more... it was *warm. Warm*, inside.

"A little one," the farmer said aloud. He felt nervous suddenly. As though this were a trick or a trap. People didn't just find fald eggs on the side of the road. Not once had that happened to anyone he knew. Ever. This was new. A new thing. Happening just for him. The farmer ill-liked that, he ill-trusted, he ill, ill... it was just ill. All of it.

I should leave it where it is. It'd be no mercy taking it home. It'd die without a mother.

But the farmer could not find the will to place the egg back down. It was warm. And alive.

You can't put a warm, alive thing back on the cold, dead ground, can you? Just to die? He hadn't the time to think. So he placed the egg in his satchel with great care, content to make the decision another time. But further back, deep into the recesses of the young farmer's mind, he had already made one.

The climb was hard, made all the harder by the pail of blackberries. But there at the summit, as the farmer had expected, was Veg. Dutiful as ever. He had waited all night, right where he was told to wait.

I care not one whit what the stable master says; you deserve all the apples under our Dragon's sun.

Bundon stood to one side of the palfrey, and leant his forehead against the horse's neck in silent thanks; before securing the milk pail to the saddle *extra* carefully and going on his way.

A fald's egg for his birthing gift. The farmer grinned. *That is better than a thousand wooden spoon horses.*

The sun was beautifully warm on his face, and the world somehow seemed more colourful today. His son would be born; he was sure of it. Upon his return, as though he were waiting for it. Alaria would need some days to recover, he knew, but he had made jam many times before. That's what the blackberries were for. And his stews could be as good as hers, different, he knew; humbler. But just as good.

She will scold you for your late arrival, he worried. *So you must be her stalwart companion, as you said in your vows. You must be her stalwart companion, her torch against the darkness of the world, and your sacred flames must burn as one. That is what you promised, farmer, be sure you don't forget it.*

They had their handfasting in the Month of Flowers, as Alaria had always wanted; 'ever since she was a girl' she had said. She was a finer match than he deserved, he knew. Good yeoman's blood in her veins. A trader's daughter from the continent. She had bought him a palfrey as her dowry. A kindness he had never asked for and one he'd never forget.

She didn't have to do that. He beamed at the thought. *She did that 'cause she cares. Truly. Cares. Only our Noble Dragon knows why. You're a scruffy old fool, Bundon. But she does. And she is like to burst any day now.*

His resolve strengthened as he pushed Veg into a gallop once more. Checking every few moments to make sure the milk pail was still safe.

He was nearing home. The bends of the road were fond ones to him, as they meant the farm was just a little further on. And soon, in the valley of two great, green hills, he saw it. The large barn, with its lopsided roof and big green doors. His herd, all three-and-twenty of them. His fields, waving their wheat and barleycorn in great seas of brown and sand coloured grass. He saw the old swaybacked Meat, grumpy as ever, slowly and gloomily grazing the emerald fields, all the world like the only grey cloud in a clear, blue sky.

My son will be born today. And I shall place the egg beside him in the crib. That'll win him luck, or strength, or favour with the Dragon in some small way, I am sure of it.

The farmer reached his gates, dismounted from Veg and took him to the stables to see him watered and scrubbed down. He deserved a good rest and some good food.

"And an apple, so long as you don't go tattling on me to Master Myko," he warned. Kissing the horse on his muzzle and leading him backwards into his paddock. After all was done, the farmer washed his hands and face in the basin by the stable's door and took a deep breath.

He might be here already.

He gathered his thoughts, and once he felt surefooted… walked to the farmhouse. *I shall weep; I know it.* The thought of his Alaria and his baby boy waiting for him, the fire roaring in the hearth, perhaps the good Sister had prepared a stew or some broth. There were vegetables in the larder, turnips, leeks and carrots. And there was bacon curing in the smoke shed.

And jam, of course, I'll make my wife some of my blackberry jam.

He was halfway up the path when the Sister opened the door. He lifted his hand in a jolly salute and smiled widely.

I have the bread; I have the linens, cut to squares. The jam will make up for the lost milk. What is that she holds? A bundle of blankets. A bundle?

The farmer hurried his pace, running to the Sister with a wide grin. The Sister did not greet him back, which he thought odd. In fact, as he drew closer, he could see she wore a dour look. And tears. Tears down her cheeks. And the bundle in her arms. A steady breath. A little arm. And a little kicking foot.

So small. He thought.

And covered in so much blood.

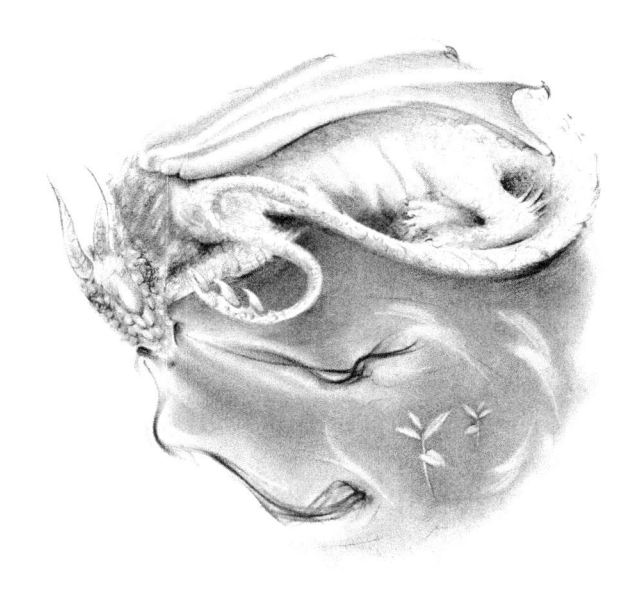

BUNDON III
The First Day in the Month of High Sun

What am I to do with her?

The farmer found himself thinking a few days later. It was the first time he had been alone with her. The good Sister had stayed awhile, caring for the babe while Bundon attended to other matters.

Alaria's pyre was a humble one. She had lost her father to a storm along the angry coasts of the continent, and she had no family but him. So the gathering was small. She was well-liked in the town-stead, and many friendly faces made quick, honest visits. But none stayed long. And when the last of the flames threw their sparks on the wind, Bundon found himself alone. Not alone, of course. But lonely.

It was a beautiful night; the sunset had painted the sky a thousand shades of pink and purple, and even the fireflies had come to pay their respects. A more perfect night, you could not have imagined.

This should be a cause for celebration. The farmer mused thoughtfully. *How different the night would be if you were sat here by my side.* He looked down at the sleeping baby in his arms—so pink and little.

I should leave it where it is. It'd be no mercy taking it home. It'd die without a mother; he remembered thinking when he had found the egg, what now seemed a lifetime ago. *I didn't mean it then, and I don't mean it now.*

He kissed the babe on her soft head and took comfort in the warmth of her.

"What am I to do with you?" He asked her.

Bundon's heart had grieved all it could and lay dully aching in his chest. But now, his head hurt from thoughts and fears of things to come.

"How am I to care for you? I am no fit man for the job. Your mother would have made your every day a joy; she would have, I know it. She would have braided your hair and told you grand old stories and seen you walk right in the world, as she saw me walk right in it.

"But how can I do that for you? I am just a farmer. I know of rearing calves and corn. Not girls. Not little girls. With little sparks in their hearts. Sparks that need to catch, and burn, and burn bright. Mine is but a dutiful flicker now Alaria's pyre is dwindling. How to stoke yours and tend to mine own? I am but a farmer. With a simpler mind than some. By my fire, your little spark, in the hands of such as me? Is that cruelty? That such a fragile little flame should be left with none but me? Your poor little fire. In there." He rubbed one coarse, calloused finger on her chest, and she wriggled and opened her lips a hair's breadth. Her tiny little hands cradled the finger and held it tight. The farmer was struck, and the oath came unbidden.

"I shall never let it go out, little one," he swore with a certainty the farmer ne'er knew he possessed. "And— and perhaps that is as simple as it need be. For if I am to be all you have, then

I best be all the best I can be." He wriggled his finger, and the babe's grip tightened. He raised the basket to his chest, slowly and carefully, as to not wake her.

"I will raise you *right*," he said, as promises gushed from him. "I shall teach you all the wisdoms I was taught and more. All of your mother's, and— and all of your grandmother's too, all of it. I shall see that all the great weights of the world do not smother your fire. And what's more, I shall see it fed with honesty, and goodness and all the good and honest things in the world. And— and of all the many kindnesses there are to give, you shall have them all. Freely. I— I promise. I shall endeavour, my little one, to give you all the best of what I am. And your mother. She will help. It will be her voice, always on my shoulder.

"She will steer me true."

The farmer looked up; he had not noticed how dark it was. The stars were out. The Bright Scythe curved across the sky with vivid static stars, while the twinkling far off beacons of The Maiden and The Fool courted each side of the moon. And Dalkarys the Dragon stood vigil in the centre of the sky, watching over the last embers of Alaria's pyre. Bundon placed the sleeping babe in her basket and let a hand linger on her soft curls. Joining the babe was an iron locket that belonged to her mother and the egg Bundon had found in the briars. Strange bedfellows, he knew. But all three were treasures.

"This one will watch you too," he dared a smile. "Of that, I have no doubt."

He sat in quiet thought for a time. Letting the stillness of the night wash over him.

"There will ne'er be need to tend *both* our fires, my girl, for they will burn as *one*. Bright. And warm. For I give you my sacred flame. Today, and all the days to come. All year. Every year. From Dance to Dirt. Everything I am is yours. My world; is yours. For that's what you are, m'girl. You're my world. My *whole* world.

"My little Tyr'Dalka."

TYR'DALKA I

The First Day in the Month of Harvest

Tyr'Dalka had always dreamed of fancy. Ever since she was small, she had wanted nothing more than to break the rigid confines of the farm and fly free. Fly free from the farmhouse. Fly free from the village. Fly free from her wicked stepmother and her two vile offspring, as the usual story goes.

She was at her happiest when trampling through the thickets of the surrounding wood or finding hidden caves in the dried out ravines of the old river. She had found things too, on these great adventures. She had found a bronze goblet, tarnished and green with age. Two axe-heads of old rusty iron, with the intricate Brentiri knots and wolf-head etchings still visible. And near a hundred old Sathillian coins - tiny paper-thin coppers or hollow bronze discs with crowned scorpions stamped on the back. Two were silver. Bright and shining, largely untouched by the earth and they sat as twin kings of her collection. She would sell them one day. She would find a trader out of King's Anchor who was bound for Autreville or Copperlee, someone rich and fancy with a heavy purse and a staunch fascination with all things old.

I will make our fortune then, she had promised herself, gazing into the pendant her mother had gifted her before she died. A simple iron locket, no larger than a hen's egg. Tyr had always wondered what her mother had looked like, but her father had only ever given the same answer.

"Go take a look at that locket of yer mam's," he'd chuckle. "For you two are like as one."

She'd taken great comfort in that, as a girl. And had grown a rather peculiar habit of seeking the counsel of her own reflection, thinking, or perhaps hoping, that some of her mother's wisdom might permeate through the veil. Reason aside, it always made her feel closer to her if nothing else.

I will pay all that father owes, mam. And see him gifted with a herd twice the size. I will see the barn door sat straight and see that poor Veg is retired before his back gives out. And help. I'll pay for help. Good help. Strong boys from the town, more than just me. And them.

And her.

And, as though the beast had heard her thoughts, the fald cawed into the sky and nuzzled her crooked, rough beak into Tyr's ribs. The beast was very strong now and pushed the farm girl near off her feet.

Tyr'Dalka snapped the locket closed and lay a casual arm around the fald's long, saggy neck, leaning into the crest of quills and feathers that decorated her head.

"Ugh, Alaria!" she cringed at the smell of her. "You have been helping yourself to the wood carrion! I can smell it!"

She pushed the stinking beast away playfully, who only nuzzled harder, pushing Tyr to the floor and attempting to groom her hair. Sharp but harmless jabs on the top of her head.

"This is not why we're here!" Tyr ordered in between laughter and jabs. She sat up, and in her best commanding voice, said, "Alaria! Enough!"

The fald straightened and sat with her wings folded by her sides; great leathery blankets of black and brown skin. The intricate pattern of hundreds of veins beneath were illuminated by the sun, like a confused and markerless map. Her tail was rigid and capped with long, trailing feathers. And her bronze-scaled feet were the size of a lion's paws, with talons three times the size. Vicious, cruel things they were. Tyr would have been frightened of them had they belonged to any other creature.

But Alaria was *hers*.

The curious beast cocked her head to one side with those tiny yellow eyes like distant star light. Sharp. Determined. And clever.

Her father must have told her the stories a hundred times by now. Perhaps as many as a thousand. Of how he had found her egg on his journey back from Dalkaford.

"I had gone to fetch milk, bread and linens for your mother, who was great with child and like to burst any day", was how he always began the tale. But his wife had died before his return, so he had nothing but a baby waiting for him. And a midwife, a Sister whose name had escaped him over the years. He told her of how he placed the egg in her basket the day they lit her mother's pyre.

And how, just shy of one year later, it had hatched.

"It hatched. And I tell no word of a lie; it hatched upon the utterance of your first word," her father had told her. "You never knew her. I spoke of her often, true, but never by that name. Not that name. It would be *your* name for her. But you never met her to name her so.

"Mamma, you said. Mamma. And the egg hatched before my very eyes. All pink and covered in bristles. An ugly little thing. But gentle. Gentle from the beginning. I don't know what our Dragon says of souls and spirits and all of that, but I remember thinking then as I still think now... there is a touch of fate to all of this. A touch of... dare I say, *destiny*.

"I had warned you away from her. 'Away from her, Tyr!' I'd say, 'away from her!' But you didn't listen, as you don't still. You just threw your arms around her, and they've scarce moved from there, I swear it."

He always laughed when he told that story. And wept. The two were inextricably linked to her father, she knew. He rarely did one without the other.

Alaria still peered at her through tiny, golden eyes. Tyr embraced the beast as hard as she could, filling her thoughts with thoughts of thanks and gratitude and hoping that at least some of their meaning might be felt through their embrace.

"I'd have no one else with me," she whispered. "Now come - that rise there- that's a good place to practise."

Holding the beast's reins, she began guiding her up the hill. She took the tambourine from her belt, a solid band of dark wood with intricate brass cymbals and a rawhide drum. It had been a gift from her father for the day she became a young woman. Alaria liked the noise of it. It intrigued her and scared the beast in equal measure.

They danced together on the hills around the farm.

Dancing is what Tyr called it. Her step-siblings called it 'prancing like an elf'. But if elves danced with their falds, Tyr could dance with hers. Her father was always understanding of it, allowing them the time to practise every morning or even in the evenings in the summer months. Tyr had caught him watching once. Smiling to himself, and weeping, of course.

"You dance so like your mother," he had said, or rather he had tried to say before he lost himself to sobbing and had flustered off red-faced and bashful. But Tyr's mother had never had a fald, as far as Tyr knew. So the dancing could not have been *that* similar. He had not watched her dance since then; Tyr presumed it made him too sad. So she never asked.

Alaria could be a stubborn thing, a stubbornness that reminded Tyr of her own, especially when faced with the prospect of tasks she disliked. The beast had no issue with pulling the plough. She gathered the herds well enough too. She raked the farmland with her talons, and when they journeyed to the Dalka's banks, she would fish them a supper worthy of kings. She enjoyed the work.

But she never flew. Ever.

There were times it looked like she might, and there were times she had even tried. None had been of any success, however. The more she tried and failed, the stronger her resolve to never try again. At least, that is how it seemed to Tyr, and Tyr always trusted her instincts when it came to her odd companion.

"The elves used to do battle atop the backs of your ancestors," Tyr said, shaking the blackwood tambourine that Alaria liked so well. The beast squawked and trilled along with the jingling cymbals, prancing about, head cocking and neck swaying, half dancing to the tambourine's gentle chimes.

"They would send showers of silver arrows down upon the armies below. You would be dressed in armour of silver and sea-green steel, and your riders in the same. Wielding curved spear-swords etched with magic runes, and old, lost spells ready on their lips."

Alaria screeched, and when she saw the rise of the hill, she began to resist. Tyr was now half pulling the beast. Her arms ached already, but she had to try.

"It would be all the easier if you flew us there," Tyr grunted. She heaved again, winning a foot of ground. But the rise was still a fair way up, so she sighed and began heaving again.

"If your ancestors carried elves on their backs; armoured and carrying swords and bows and arrows and who knows what else, then you can carry me one day. I am not so heavy as all that," Tyr told the fald, who upon hearing this news decided she had gone far enough. And so she sat. And would not move.

Tyr knew this mood well, and no amount of pulling, pushing or shaking the tambourine would compel her to move again.

"There is adventure, Ally," she called, jumping up with an eager smile, hoping to excite the beast. "At the top of this rise, come on! Imagine flying, Alaria! Imagine it! Imagine the fish you'd catch if you dared hunt above the open waters. Imagine the heights you'd reach,and the peace you'd find. *We'd* find. If you'd only use your wings!" But the words were not working. Tyr huffed her disapproval and sat heavily on the grass next to the fald; who delicately placed her head on the grumpy girl's lap.

"You little coward," she laughed, rubbing the curve of her sharp beak. "You big little coward. You're less fun than papa and more stubborn than me," she teased, trying to push the fald's head off her to little effect.

They sat for a time, just lazing in the soft grass and basking in the ceaseless rays of this summer's sun. It seemed a joy, now. But the summer had been long and hot thus far, and half their crop had failed; withering to paper husks from the heat. They had lost the five of their five-and-twenty herd as well, from the rivers running so dry.

Such thoughts made Tyr anxious. So as much as she could, she chose not to think about them. Out here, in the vastness of the world, she wasn't a farmer's daughter. She was an adventurer with a loyal steed—a loyal steed who never *ever* allowed her to ride on her back.

One day, though. Tyr always thought. *One day you will. And you'll fly. And then I'll be able to sell my collections. And then I'll save the farm. And then everything will be alright.*

Alaria suddenly sat up. Neck stretched and peering off into the distance, alert. Tyr knew what that meant, and she listened for it—getting louder and louder. Her name.

"Tyr!" she heard. "Tyr! Alaria!"

She made no answer. She didn't want it to end so soon. This was her time. Her only time. Had it been so long already?

But Alaria was nothing if not loyal, and she cawed her reply into the sky, a shrill and deafening screech. And before long, the weary-eyed farmer stood at the crest of the rise. His tattered straw hat perched on his head, fair-skinned and fair-haired, with a permanent patch of peeling sunburn on the bridge of his large nose. He had never mastered the art of growing a beard, but he held great pride for the coarse muttonchops that grew down both cheeks. He stood there, brow furrowed and arms folded.

"I wake to find breakfast half-eaten and chores half-done," he scolded. Alaria, ever-dutiful, raced toward him, the reins wrenching easily from Tyr's grasp as she charged up the rise and took Bundon off his feet. The fald nuzzled into the crumpled clump that was Tyr's father as he batted at the beast's head with a hundred little slaps to get her away.

"Get off, you horrible bird, get off!" He ordered her, holding her neck firmly, eyes scowling into hers, and batting her softly on the beak. "No! Hear me, beastly thing? No!"

"Aye, papa, she hears you," Tyr called to the clump. "But she does not listen."

"Now, who does that remind me of?" He mumbled from the ground. "Now, in all seriousness, child," he turned his scowl to Tyr. "Tis the first day in the Month of Harvest; dancing will have to wait."

"We weren't dancing," Tyr said defensively. "We were going to fly."

"As you were yesterday? And the day before?" Her papa asked in his fatherly tone. "You do not know for a certainty that falds can even fly, Tyr. Perhaps they are like those odd little cormorants on the coast? They have wings, but I've ne'er seen one so much as flutter."

"Alaria is *not* a cormorant," Tyr mocked. "Look at the size of those wings; they are *meant* to *soar*! And I recall no fairy stories of ancient elves riding *cormorants* into battle."

"Elves are rogues and scoundrels," Bundon tutted. "Perhaps their stories are just as false."

That didn't ring true to Tyr. But she decided not to push her certainty, lest it be mistaken for stubbornness, as it was ofttimes.

"Now, the dragon's long past had her breakfast, and the day's begun, so I'll need you working the fields today. Greta has —"

"Donned the plough? She's big enough for it."

"None of that," he warned, flatly. "Not this harvest. We can't afford it."

"Yes, papa," she hung her head, quietly proud of the remark.

"The Harvestman's Market is less than a moon's turn away, and we are behind in our reaping. I'll need you two to see to that this week, with Greta's help o' course. I'm taking three heads to slaughter today, early, I know, but we'll need the coin from the hides and meat if we're to survive till the end of harvest. We haven't the coins for help, and the Temple hasn't the hands to spare for boon work, so it will be a long month. But I'll see a good cut of beef is saved for our Harvestman's Feast. And all the offal for you, you greedy vulture."

He stroked Alaria's beak. She loved nothing more than a cow's liver but ate most of what came out of their bellies, lapping it up like honey.

"Will Hans—"

"No," her father looked almost ashamed. "Hans is sickening again."

He will be sickening throughout the Month of Harvest. And then he will be well again. And his slices of roast beef will be no smaller than ours. But there was no point in brooding on such things. Parts of life were unfair, Tyr's sixteen years (near seventeen) had taught her that if nothing else.

Her father, sensing her mood, lay a hand on her shoulder.

"It will be a trying harvest, Tyr," he warned softly. "But we'll see it through, as we always do."

But it's only getting harder, papa, she wanted to say. But instead gave her sweetest smile and said nothing.

❦ ❦ ❦

In the farmstead's prime, five strong lads would be sent from Dalkaford to help with the harvest. And with ten strong hands, as well as their own, they could reap twelve acres in seven days. But help dwindled over the years as more and more lads answered the summons to join King Doryn's Third Crusade.

Now, with her father's hands busy with the slaughter, it fell to her, her fald and her step-sister, Greta.

Greta was two years Tyr's senior and was a vile beast of a girl, in Tyr's eyes, if no one else's. She was closer to six feet than five. Taller than both her mother and stepfather. She was broad-chested and broad hipped and where most girls might curve between the two; Greta, so full of surprises, did not. She was a log. A log with a red, freckled face and two tiny blond plaits that sprung from either side of her big, square head. She wore an ill-fitting surcoat of light-pink linen; belted, (where Tyr presumed her waist to be) with a simple roughspun apron.

But while the two step-siblings had ne'er seen eye to eye, Tyr could not deny Greta's skill with a scythe. For every cart of wheat Tyr harvested, Greta did two. while Alaria and Veg were sent back and forth to store the stalks safely in the granary for later threshing and winnowing.

Of the farmstead's two-and-forty acres, only three fields worth were sown, as that was all the small farm could afford with what help they had. Wheat and barleycorn, with some beans, peas and pumpkins in the third field to see the soil nurtured.

"Some crops feed their soil; some crops drain it. So you spin your acres like a cartwheel," was how her father put it. They would see the winter crop first, the wheat, then the barleycorn in the Month of Honey, and finally the peas, beans and pumpkins in the Month of Brambles. All before the fields are left fallow, then rotated, then ploughed, then seeded.

And repeat and repeat and again and again… and again.

It was long and tiring work. The sun sizzled the back of Tyr's neck, and oozing blisters rose across both palms, but it was nothing she was not used to.

They worked in silence for the most part, as Greta spoke seldom and never to Tyr directly. The only noise Tyr heard her make throughout was when Alaria mistook Greta's straw hat for a rabbit, and a short-lived tussle arose. Greta, who feared nothing so far as Tyr could tell, was wrestling the ruined hat from the fald's vice-like beak when Tyr felt compelled to intervene, despite how humorous the sight had been.

"Alaria," Tyr snapped. "Drop it."

The fald did so.

"Control your gaffing monster," Greta grunted cruelly, placing the dilapidated hat back on her head and setting her hands back to the scythe. "It's a bloody terror."

So are you. Tyr thought, not brave enough to say it.

Greta's language was always foul out of earshot of the grownups and had been for as long as Tyr could remember. But Brynhilde never believed it. Hans and Greta could do no wrong in their mother's eyes, so if there was blame to be had, it was often reserved for Tyr. Or Alaria, most likely. Few things angered Brynhilde more than Tyr's cowardly fald.

And Greta will waste no time in telling her mother of this small misbehaviour, I'm sure.

※ ※ ※

When the first day was done. the farmhands had harvested just shy of an acreage of wheat and had stored it all within the granary, where Alaria kept her nest. A mess of ragged cowhides and straw, intermingled with many horrid pellets and the bones of rats, rabbits, fish and birds. The fald was partial to rats, and she did a fine job of keeping them away from their grain. The little of it there was. For the crop was small. Smaller than last year.

And next year, it will be smaller again.

Inside the farmhouse. she found her family huddled around the solid oaken table, with the hearth bright and warm to one side. A stew sat bubbling over the fire. Beef and onions. With yesterday's bread sitting on the embers, toasting to black on the outside but deliciously soft on the inside.

Hans sat in the only padded chair; it had become *his* chair in all but name, as none dared sit there while he was sickly, lest his mother clout you on the back of the head. His mother, Brynhilde, was a large woman who stood a few inches taller than Bundon, her husband. She wore a rough cotton surcoat, with an apron of un-dyed linen around her thick waist. Her broad head was covered in a white kerchief, with a few rogue curls of grey hair peeping through. She had thick wrists and thicker wits, but she had never been cruel. Stern, yes. Unfriendly, more so. But never cruel.

"That beast of yours nearly took off Greta's arm today," Brynhilde scolded, feeding hot stew to her poorly son. Hans was of an age with Tyr, and much too old for being fed like a babe.

He was small, a little stunted with a ratty face and mousey-brown hair, thin as his frame. He was buried under a thousand layers of fur and blankets, with his scrawny little feet poking free at the bottom. He sighed and groaned and tossed and turned upon the comfy chair like a feverish old man.

"Mother," he croaked, "So cold. So hungry."

Brynhilde stern stepmother suddenly transformed into Brynhilde kindly nursemaid, gently holding out the spoon for Hans to ineffectually lap up some morsels. But she quickly turned back a moment later.

"It should be chained up," she barked. "Dangerous for a beast like that to have free run the place."

"She hates chains," Tyr said simply.

"Not my concern; it's a beast."

"That '*beast*' has a name," Tyr shot back.

"As does the black rot plague, dear, but I'd sooner not have that in my home if it's all the same."

"If she unnerves you, don't go near her. It is as simple as that."

"Ungrateful child," Brynhilde tutted under her breath, holding out another spoon of broth for her son, who feebly took it in his mouth and moaned from the effort. "In my day, a girl would know three strikes of the switch for such a remark. Greta, small bites. That's a good girl."

Greta regarded her mother coldly as she insolently ate a whole stewed onion, letting the broth drip from her chin.

"You'd think I'd be worthy of the girl's respect," Brynhilde whined, "Me, who fed her at my own breast like she were my own. Me, who helped save this wretched farm. Me, who keeps a clean kitchen, a warm hearth and a hearty supper cooking for her whole family. Ungrateful child."

Brynhilde tutted again. She never looked at Tyr when she complained; she always talked to the room as though trying to urge the walls themselves to come to her defence.

"I see you've all been hard at work," Tyr's father said wearily as he entered through the crooked door. He placed his cloak on a hook and ran his hands through what remained of his fair hair, letting out a long, beleaguered sigh as the warmth of the farmhouse washed over him. He moved over to the hearth, where the old, weather-beaten cartwheel lay. It had been painted and treated to act as a rough calendar, with the months of the year painted around the rim, with the days; one to thirty, painted by the spokes. Her mother had even written the months in their old Sathillian names,in beautiful cursive letters —Amarys; the Month of Dance, all the way round to Terrasys; the Month of Soil.

One year. From Dance to Dirt, papa always says.

The farmer turned the days-wheel to one and the months-wheel to Messys; the Month of Harvest. And then he stood for a moment, staring at the calendar, before sighing wistfully, and mumbling, "It's been a long first day of harvest, but only nine-and twenty more to go.

"Cowhides are hanging by the smoke shed, Bryn; they'll need treatin' come morning. Give us a squeeze, Tyr; there's a good girl." The old farmer ruffled his daughter's hair before they both embraced, squeezing away the stress of the day.

"You two did very well today. Near an acre harvested, by my reckoning. I've seen three grown men struggle with such a task, but not my girls." He kissed the top of her head, then Greta's and finally his frosty wife, who coldly handed the farmer a bowl piled high with meat, onions and thick, brown gravy.

"I've been tending to my poor son all day," Brynhilde bristled. "I suppose that's not hard work in your eyes. And need I tell you again about that blasted bird? It nearly took off Greta's arm today. And Hans still bears the scars of her first attack."

"She barely touched him," Tyr mumbled. "She doesn't like her wings being touched, I tried to warn him."

"She didn't," Hans whispered to his mother.

"Liar!" Tyr snapped, to which Hans made a petulant face.

"Tyr," her father sighed. "I'll have none of that, thank you."

"She's wild," Brynhilde bristled. "As beastly as her fald."

"Not half so beastly as you," Tyr barked. "She is family."

"Ungrateful child," Brynhilde hissed. "In my day, a girl would know three strikes across the backside for such disrespect."

"She is family, Bryn," Bundon spoke softly. "She earns her keep and feeds herself, and us on occasion, when the Dalka's fish are plentiful."

"See!" Tyr grinned.

"Aye, I see," Brynhilde seethed. "I see that my loving husband won't see sense until one of mine is put in the ground by that vicious... *pet!*"

"Pet!?" Tyr stood, red-faced. "She helped harvest an acre of wheat today. Tomorrow she will do the same. Next month she will pull the plough, and the next month she will seed the fields, and she will work, and work, and work."

"A plough horse could do the same," Brynhilde chided.

"She is family!" Tyr said firmly. "Better family than some."

"Ungrateful child!" She roared, brandishing Hans's spoon with vigour. "In my day, a girl would know—"

"In my day! In my day!" Tyr mocked her loudly. "In your day, they did a splendid job of beating all the decency out of you, seems to me."

"Tyr," her father warned. "I'll have none of that over supper. Sit down." The farmer was still and calm as he settled at the table with a bowl of his own. He lit the three candles in the table's centre, the tall green one and the smaller blacks, and held out his hands to Greta and Tyr, who in turn held the hands of Brynhilde and Hans, who lifted his arms with no small amount of complaint.

"Noble Dragon, we hear your prayer and thank you for your sacrifice. We're grateful for the food before us and the bonds of family that keeps us together. By our Dragon's fire, so noble and strong, we give you our sacred flame."

The farmer opened his eyes and beamed his usual warm grin, and they ate in silence.

❋ ❋ ❋

Brynhilde and her brood had come to live on the farm when Tyr was a baby. Her father had sworn to raise his babe as best he could, but alas, as hard as he might try, he could not make milk. Brynhilde had just birthed Hans, so came to the farm as a wet nurse. And stayed as a wife.

"A partnership of labour, to see our children raised right."

That is how Tyr's father had phrased it. But in the many long years of partnership, Tyr had yet to see much dispersion of labour. Her father would breed the cattle, wash the cattle, feed them, brand them and take them to slaughter. He would make the hay and care for old Veg, all himself. He collected firewood and foraged for nuts and berries. He would gather hives of bees in the Month of Flowers and collect their riches by the Month of Honey. He mended the farmhouse, whene'er it needed it, thatching and whittling and fixing any holes with wattle and daub. He would plough the fields, sow the fields, weed them, reap them and scare away the foxes. He took their goods to market and bought what produce they needed. The old man was always on his feet and ne'er complained to be so. What little help she and

Greta gave seemed trite by comparison.

While Brynhilde was trusted with naught but the home, and the raising of the children, who had already grown well beyond the need of such coddling.

Brynhilde was not truly wicked. Tyr knew that, deep down. She kept a clean home. And cooked good food. And had shown generosity, at times. But she was not a mother to Tyr'Dalka. She had never shown her a mother's warmth. She had the capability, Tyr had seen it, and had often thought that were the affection shared three ways, instead of two, Greta and Hans might not be so greedy. Tyr opened up her iron locket and stared solemnly at her own reflection, snapping it closed a moment later with a resound scoff.

"They'd have me chain you up," Tyr snapped to a sleeping Alaria, well past midnight. She had snuck across to the granary, as she often did, to spend the night with her fald. She never liked being too far from her; their link felt taut and thin.

"They look at you, and all they see is a beast," she gushed. "If it were just you, father and me, everything would be better."

"Better for who?" She heard from behind her. It was her father, groggy and dishevelled, holding two steaming cups of warm milk.

"You weren't meant to hear that," Tyr said ashamedly. She accepted the hot milk and kissed her father on the cheek. The old farmer joined his daughter at Alaria's paddock, leaning over the edge and watching her sleep in her great nest of wings, feathers, straw and scraps of fur.

"You must not hate them," Bundon said flatly.

"I don't hate them," she said defensively, and it was largely true. They had never been unkind. That is what Tyr always told herself if she found herself thinking too long on their shortcomings.

They are never unkind.

But nor were they ever kind, especially Greta and Hans. They seldom spoke at all and never to her. They always watched her from a distance, shared looks of silent mocking and had deliberately left her out of games when they were younger. She had learnt to stay clear of them, and they of her.

Greta had once put a spider's egg sack in Tyr's boot, and she had screamed and screamed when all the baby spiders came crawling up her leg. That particular joke had halted any further attempts of friendship Tyr was like to make.

"But you don't love them, neither," her father said, sipping at the frothy milk. He grunted his approval at the taste of it and licked his lips. "All a man needs."

"They are your milk siblings, Tyr; there is a kinship there. An odd one, I grant you. But it's there all the same. They're family."

"They're not," Tyr snapped. "Alaria is family. You are family. Us three are the family. They're just imposters."

"My good wife fed you from her own breast; she didn't have to do that. You stand here now because of that woman."

"And you didn't have to take her in. But you did. You've paid her back for her damnable milk twenty times over or more." Tyr felt angry but felt guilty all the same for troubling her weary father with further worries. But there was injustice here, and he had always told her to stand up to injustice, whatever forms it took. "They are lackwits; all."

"Lackwits," the farmer repeated the word with a slow nod. "I was called a lackwit in my youth. No amount of cuffs and shoves hurt so much as that. Lackwit. I know, I am not so sharp as some, but I work hard. And I see you're fed. And safe."

"You do not lack for wits, papa," Tyr said sternly, if not a little apologetically. "You're a good man. Better than them."

"I had a good family. If I am a good man, the thanks are theirs, not mine." The farmer cleared his throat, looking deep into his daughter's eyes. "I had a good mam and a dutiful pa. I was surrounded by those who cared for me and wanted to see me safe. And when Brynhilde stood with her two little 'uns, with no one. No one at all. I thought. Well, no. I *hoped*. That I might be to them what my pa was to me. Perhaps my little lantern might help show the perils of the road. We'd all be the safer for company on this long march."

"I never doubted your intentions," Tyr allowed sullenly, growing glum as her father grew wise. "But they have not changed, papa. Not at all."

"Nor have you," he said.

"But I haven't done anything wrong!" Tyr snapped. "You never see my side in this!" Alaria woke. Tyr saw two bright yellow stars illuminating in the black mass before them. She made a throaty noise. The hour of their visit did not please her, Tyr knew, as the fald cawed her disapproval.

"Hush, damnable bird!" The farmer warned her. She did as she was bid, keeping wary golden eyes on the two of them. Tyr hung her head, ashamed of the outburst.

"I'm sorry, papa. That was ill-said."

"No. No, there is truth to that. I mustn't pretend they have no part in the divide. That jape with the baby spiders. That was ill done." They both shuddered at the memory of it and then caught each other's eyes and laughed. It was a long laugh, and her father wept partway through it, as was his way. Eventually, it ran to silence, and the old farmer was left thinking in the dim light. "Harvestman's Market at the end of the month should be quite the celebration, so long as the weather holds." Her father sighed. "And of course it will. This summer is looking like to cook us in our beds. Perhaps you—"

"Of course," Tyr sighed. This happened every year. She had wanted to go to the Harvestman's Festival every harvest since she could remember, but someone had to watch the farm, and Hans, he would undoubtedly be sickening with something.

"We'll need Bryn's hands here this year, cooking up our grand feast. And Hans would doubtless prefer his mother's nursing to yours. And the market falls on your birthday this year. The grand old age of ten-and-seven." The farmer beamed. "I'd have you accompany me if you'd like."

I would like. I would like very much.

She reached out and hugged her father tightly, knocking her milk into Alaria's pen, who wasted no time shuffling in her nest to lap it up.

"I could bring her," Tyr beamed.

"Now, Tyr," the farmer furrowed his brow and shook his head.

"Think on it," Tyr insisted. "I have practised some tricks with her, and she fetches well. She is trained, of a sort. And getting better. And she dances, papa. You should see us dance together."

"I've seen you practise," he said with a sad smile.

"Perhaps we'd raise some coin from the crowds. I bet they've never seen a fald before. Watch." Tyr cleared her throat.

"Now, Tyr, really—" her father began.

"Alaria. Cup. Here." Alaria cocked her head to one side and blinked cluelessly. "Alaria. Cup. Here. Now." Alaria shuffled again and straightened her neck, matching Tyr's height. She then trilled softly, a warm chirruping that would have sounded more fitting coming from a kitten than a fald.

"She is certainly trained. Of a sort." The farmer laughed, but Tyr would not have it.

"Hush up. She is better with the tambourine." Tyr scowled. "Alaria. Cup. Now." The fald chirruped and shuffled, agitated, knowing she was being asked something and frustrated she couldn't figure out what it was. But Tyr continued to give the order until the words had lost their meaning. Tyr could see the beast's poor mind struggle and decided it would be best to leave it for tonight.

"She'd best stay here, I think," the farmer whispered, not unkindly.

"She does fetch usually," Tyr said sadly.

"I am sure she does," he chuckled. "But for now, perhaps—oh. Oh, Tyr. Would you look at that?" Her father wore a face of both shock and glee. Tyr turned to see her loyal friend, trilling and chirruping still, holding a pewter cup gently in the tip of her beak.

"Told you," Tyr stood straight and scratched Alaria roughly around her chin, where she liked it most. "Can she come?" Her father thought long and hard, visibly chewing his thoughts over.

"A few extra coins couldn't hurt."

TYR'DALKA II

The Twenty-Fifth Day in the Month of Harvest

Tyr had never been one to fuss overly on her clothes.

But she had today.

Market day (coupled with her birthday) seemed a suitable occasion to fuss, so she had worn her finest surcoat, dark green wool with sandy coloured skirts, with her mother's fancy bodice atop that. It was thick black wool, embroidered with green dragons and flowers of a hundred coloured threads. Her boots were her usual riding boots, worn brown leather but not unclean. And over it all, she wore a simple cloak of un-dyed wool, clasped with an obsidian pin her father had carved for her birthday.

"Made from Alaria's shell," he had said, clasping it to her cloak with a humble smile.

She had even tamed her hair, wild bushel of curls as it was. It was a simple fishtailed plait, tied with a green ribbon. And, of course, her mother's locket hung around her neck. The cold iron pleasantly cool against her chest.

For the heat was stifling. She had removed her cloak when the sun had risen higher, and now even her fancy bodice was fast becoming a regretful choice. Her back was moist. Her mouth was dry. And the sun had brought washes of freckles out across both arms.

My face must be a red wash of them too. She worried, undoubtedly making herself redder still. They had attracted many eyes on the road, more than Tyr had thought. And now, her neck reddened from the attention. From the whispers, the gasps and the 'cor blimey's.

Alaria misliked it too and had tried to hide as best she could. She ducked her head low to the ground, following behind the carts, doing nothing to hide the six-foot tail and twenty-foot wingspan. But if the crowds ever gathered too densely, she would not hesitate to tell them so. She cawed and screeched and snorted, and the crowds gasped and chuckled and cheered. Some even threw coins.

That makes it worth the embarrassment. Tyr had thought but wasn't quite sure if she believed it. And Alaria certainly didn't.

Veg was plodding behind with Bundon pulling at his reins. The poor palfrey was near nine-and-ten, very old for a working horse, and too old to be pulling a cart loaded with wheat, barleycorn, tanned hides and salted meat.

When I sell my collections, I'll see my father gets a new palfrey, let Veg retire and roam around in the field where Meat is buried. It was one of the many things Tyr planned to do when she landed her first fortune.

I will buy some oxen too, a team of eight. We could plough all two-and-forty acres of land then, not just three fields worth. And a new packhorse. A big shaggy one, like old Meat was. Alaria was strong enough, Tyr knew, but she did not like being tethered. She just about tolerated the simple leash of plaited ribbons Tyr had made for her, but she'd suffer nothing more than that. She would kick up a royal fuss when presented with the plough, and harnessing it to her would take no small amount of effort and many dried fish for bribes.

You weren't made to pull a plough, Tyr thought, eyeing the beast fondly. *You were made for dancing.*

The town-stead was beautifully busy, with market stalls erected all around the square. Farmsteads from all across the island, as well as traders from King's Anchor and fisherfolk from Buckbridge Glen. There were striped canvas tents of red, yellow and green, with bunting stretched from stall to stall, criss-crossing to form a beautiful web of vibrant, fluttering colours. Most were selling their crops; wheat, barleycorn, maize and oats. But there was also pork, bacon joints and long links of sausages. Muttonchops, sheep's liver and sacks of wool. Leather, rawhide and great cuts of beef.

A leaner meat than ours. Tyr thought pridefully. *And our skins are much healthier.* These hides were patchy and pale, while theirs were bright and full, with a sheen across the dappled brown coat.

There were fire dancers, too, spitting their breath to the sky with great torrents of flame. And knights, real knights. Dressed in mail and light plate, heavy black cloaks around their shoulders and longswords at their hips. They had crossed bones painted across their kite shields, silver upon a sable field. They were from King's Anchor, knights in the service of Lord Tarbrand.

The Krillian was present also, in his green robes and golden mantel, with his two Brothers walking either side of him, dressed in black robes and red silken sashes.

Even the mysterious Lady DeGrissier was said to be making an appearance; that was the talk on the townsfolk's lips.

Until they saw Alaria, of course. And the talk quickly changed.

For the cowardly fald drew crowds everywhere they went. Everywhere.

It was busy in the town-stead *without* every villager, trader and guardsman stopping to gawp at them.

"Don't hide your head so," her father whispered to her. "They're curious. Show them how beautiful she is." Tyr wasn't sure she wanted to anymore. There were a lot more people than she had anticipated, and there was a sour feeling in the square. She couldn't explain it. When her father saw her discomfort, he gently took Alaria's reins from her.

"I need to see Veg stabled and watered," he said. "Go and see Daisy, and see this filled. She shan't take coin for it, but you have to offer." He handed her a large milk pail, the big dented one with the wooden handles.

Tyr had not been to market day since she was small; she had made visits to the town-stead before, but never for long, and never for fun. She knew the names and faces from the long stories her father would tell at day's end. She knew old man Myko and Daisy from the stables. She knew Owyn, the baker, who had grown very plump in his older years, so her father had told her, and even redder in the face. She knew of one-eyed Devyn from the smithy and Fat Hubb from the brewhouse, who was not fat but had been in his youth. She knew each of her father's fellow farmers and their crops. There was Farmer Mudge of beans, peas and mutton. Farmer Digby of olives, apples, pears and pork. Farmer Merren of eggs, feathers and game fowl, and the only other cattle farmer: Farmer Benniford, and he mistreated his cows fiercely, her father always said.

"He keeps a herd twice the size of ours and feeds them naught, but what they graze, he seeds no heather nor cowslip for them. Just dead dry grass. In this heat. Criminal. You can taste it in the meat, too, I bet."

But today, she was to see Daisy, who, as her father had always described, was sitting in her small shop completely surrounded by wooden spoons. She lifted her head when Tyr walked in.

"Who's this then?" She was old. Very old. Older than she ever imagined. "Is that a pail you're holding?"

"Morning, Daisy," Tyr beamed. "I'm Tyr'Dalka, Farmer Bundon's daughter. I've come for some milk, if I may."

"Are you like to pay?" She huffed. "As your pa never seems inclined." Tyr had not expected that. To hear her father speak of it; Daisy was always open-handed with her milk.

"No, no, I have coin," Tyr said.

"Hmf. Good." She snatched the pail from Tyr's hands and waddled from the room. She came back a moment later with a pail perhaps only half full. Daisy eyed Tyr as she inspected its contents, wary of complaint. Tyr gave none on account of feeling far too embarrassed. But she did hand over a copper piece.

"A man thinks he can throw a few stalks of barleycorn our way and drink as much of our milk as he pleases. Should 'ave gone to the guard years ago, but we do heed the Dragon's prayer; he should be grateful for that. You tell him from me." Tyr nodded uncertainly and turned to leave. "And if either you or him call me Daisy one more time, I'm like to spit!" She called after her.

That is not how papa described it. Tyr thought glumly. *Not at all.* But then, through the years, her father had said more and more how sour the village was growing. He blamed the heat. The Month of Harvest was always a trying time for farmers, and in recent years it had gotten harder and harder. A few years ago, there had been talk in the village of gathering coin to purchase Bundon an ox to better plough the fields, but they had spent the coin on a bronze statue of Good King Doryn instead.

"To help bring glory to his third crusade!" The townsfolk had declared. Her father had been hurt by that, she knew. But he never complained.

The baker had been no kinder. Nor the miller, the butcher, the brewer or the smith. The brewer had complained of how little barleycorn they'd harvested and had refused to pay the usual fee for such a light crop. Tyr had conceded, and measured out a fist full of coppers to make up the weight.

Her father had faired no better. Myko from the stables had charged him five coppers, for stabling Veg over market day, something he'd never done before. And had scoffed and huffed when he saw Veg's shoes were in poor knick; in fact, he had nary a nice thing to say about Veg, her father told her. His coat was too thin, his gut too heavy, his back too swayed, his saddle too tight.

"They say they'll buy me an ox and don't, and then complain that my poor horse is in ill-health. By my fire, what do they expect! There is a very sour mood in the village today." He had complained, but that would be all he'd say on the matter.

Perhaps they are just sour people now, papa. Tyr had wanted to say. *For they clearly favour Kings of bronze and stone over farmers of flesh and blood.* But she knew that would make her father dour and thoughtful, so she kept it to herself.

Tyr did not mislike the attention so much now; at least with Alaria, the crowds were curious and excited. A hundred faces, all wide-eyed and smiling.

Those smiles are like to be the only ones I see today.

When the miller had his wheat, the brewer his barley, the tanner his hides and the butcher his beef, Tyr and her father enjoyed a cup of pear cider from the grand and busy stall of Farmer Digby of olives, apples, pears and pork. His had been a healthier harvest than some, and his cider was dry and sweet. It was thick on the throat and a dragon's gift for coping with the heat. And when that was finished, there was no more hiding. If she were to do it, she would have to do it now.

Tyr took the tambourine from her pack, looped Alaria's leash around her wrist and escorted her to the raised stone dais, where an auctioneer had just finished selling off the chicks, lambs, piglets and calves of this years Month of Dance. A crowd had gathered before she'd even begun. Tyr's heart beat noisily in her chest, and Alaria could tell she was nervous. She poked at her shoulder with the point of her beak and tried to chirrup some comfort. But Tyr would not be dissuaded. She held up the tambourine and began to shake, letting the chime of its brass cymbals silence the onlookers.

"Good men and women of Dalkaford!" She called out, her nervousness already quite forgotten. "Back when these lands were ruled by elves, these beautiful creatures flew the skies!" There had been some hisses and boos at the mere mention of elvenkind, but the fald kept hold of their attention.

Tyr began a steady beat on the drum as Alaria and her began their dance. Moving around each other and over each other. Tyr weaved around tail, wing and neck as Alaria, with more grace than you'd expect, jumped from one talon to another, cocking her head inquisitively to the chimes and steady beat of the tambourine. There was laughter, and clapping and much gasping as Alaria rose taller, stretching her neck to its true length, her dancing strides becoming more spectacular as Tyr moved around her on the tips of her toes. Tethering her thoughts to her fald. She always felt their connection so vividly when they danced together.

Go here, and then here, and then jump over here. Don't stop. It's a dance. Spread your wings, curl your tail, duck your head low and then stretch it as high as it will go. Very good, Alaria. Perfect. And Alaria would listen. Tyr couldn't explain that, but she knew it. Alaria could always listen, even in silence.

The crowds had become a blur to Tyr; they were just faces, moving and changing and making noise. The dance was what mattered now. She heard the clinking and clattering of coins on stone, and that just made her dance all the more. Tyr quickened the rhythm. She was hot and tired and nearly spent, and Alaria was not far behind. But they had to finish with something grand. Something they would speak of when they returned home. No. Something they would still speak of a year from now. Or two.

I would craft memories to last a lifetime if I could. Tyr thought. *Dance, Alaria. Dance. Listen to the chimes. Move with me. Now stop. Stretch out that great neck and sing. Sing, Alaria.* The beast halted, reared up on her talons and flapped her great leathery wings. And she sang. A brief and tuneless song. But such a noise. A screech that every soul from Dalkaford to King's Anchor must have heard. The crowd paled, shrinking back. Before erupting into a final bout of applause, a noise so welcome that Tyr found her eyes glistening with tears. Joyful tears.

The stone dais was awash with coins. Most were humble, but there were some glinting silvers amidst the sea of dull coppers.

We should have done this years ago, Al. Tyr thought, struck dumb by the generosity. Her father came and helped her gather the coins as the onlookers dispersed. He clapped her on the shoulder and beamed at her proudly. Some lingered to watch the beast a little longer, but Alaria was done performing. She was wearing her weary, imperious look. A look that suggested that everything, literally everything, was beneath her notice. She had deserved that feeling, Tyr thought, and scratched the length of her neck, despite the fald's growing indifference.

Her father was hunched over, gathering coins, when the first onlooker approached. When the gentleman cleared his throat, the noise took Tyr quite by surprise. She jumped and then giggled to see a young man before her. She flicked her plait over one shoulder and played with it nervously.

"Beautiful," he said. "Very beautiful."

He was tall and well dressed. And handsome. Goodness, he was handsome. A mop of straw-coloured curls fell to his shoulders, framing a freshly shaven face without any trace of blemish or sunburn. His eyes were blue.

He has blue eyes. She was struck. *Bright blue eyes and curly hair.* And suddenly, she knew no words.

"Do you belong to a troupe?" he asked when he received no response. "I like to think I am well-travelled in the world, but I have never seen a beast like this."

"A fald." Is all she said.

He didn't ask, foolish girl. She felt herself redden.

"A fald, of course," he smiled, showing the dimples in his cheeks. Tyr was lost for words again.

Dimples. She thought simply. *I wonder if he dimples everywhere.*

He was a knight, she was sure. He led a horse, a beautiful

blood bay with a shiny coat and mane of braided black hair and red ribbon. The knight wore a mail hauberk with a surcoat over the top of heavy charcoal-coloured fustian. A sword hung on his belt, a true knight's longsword. Castle forged, with a red-leather grip and a rough-cut garnet set within its solid pommel. He a had true knight's shield on his horse, a kite of solid oak; a white seabird painted upon a field of red; a true knight's sigil. And, of course, he had a knight's lance. An eight-foot blackwood shaft capped with a simple steel spike.

Tyr had now been silent for longer than she knew was appropriate. The knight gave her a look.

"That was very kind of you to say, sir." The words felt clumsy. She meant them, she knew, but did they sound meant? She worried over that while the knight was talking, and by the time he had stopped, Tyr had quite missed what he'd said.

"You're very gallant," she said. He was struck by that and chuckled nervously, his neck reddening to match his horse. *You're embarrassing him, foolish girl; say something normal.* "My name is Tyr. Tyr'Dalka."

"A beautiful name for a beautiful dancer," he grinned, making Tyr match his shade. "I am Sir Willem. Sir Willem Gull. Knighted by Good King Doryn himself under the stricken banners of Brentir, where we held victory over the rebels of the north. And I am at your service."

"Not my service, sir," she giggled. "I have no need of a knight."

"None, hm?" He showed his dimples again. "Know of a noble soul who does? I am looking to join the service of a lord's household. My sword has sat in its sheath covered in nought but dust since peace was forged 'twixt north and south. Oh, here, allow me." He stooped to pick up some rogue coins, but when he neared Tyr, Alaria let out a warning. A low, scornful grunt from the back of her throat. He retreated a pace, and his horse whickered, pulling at its reins nervously.

"Al, be kind," Tyr batted the fald's beak. "She shan't hurt you. She's a big coward, really. Not like you, sir. I'm sure. You are a freelancer if I'm not mistaken."

"You have good eyes, both sharp and lovely," he gave a wry smile. "Perhaps I could assist you and your father? My lance is for hire—"

"The girl wants nothing from you, beggar knight," the voice came sudden and cold. "And if you'll insist on begging within the village, you might wish to rid yourself of that rusted sword in favour of a bowl for alms." The knight looked struck and paled.

"M'lady, I meant no—"

"No, no, I'm sure you didn't," she chuckled and looked him up and down. "But rest assured, the girl has no interest in the service of your lance." The knight, crestfallen, bowed his head, gave a sad smile to Tyr and left.

Tyr had thought the knight a fancy sort but stood next to this new arrival; he did look half a beggar. The lady's frock was one of heavy red velvet, with a bejewelled bodice of orange silks, red samite and cloth-of-gold. She looked fire in human form, bright and warm with a long, intricate plait of chestnut coloured hair. A diadem of red gold and yellow diamonds crowned her head and bought out the bright amber of her eyes. She linked arms with Tyr and let out an easy laughter that melted from her throat.

"And that, my dear, is how one handles an unwanted admirer."

Tyr was not so certain that he was unwanted. But she thought better than to argue. She glanced back to her father, who looked upon them with a brow knitted with worry. A look that urged caution.

"He was no bother," Tyr grinned. "He is looking to pledge his lance in service of a noble cause."

"He was looking to pledge his lance, have no doubt," she whispered wickedly. "But not the one tied to his saddle. And certainly, not for any noble cause, I promise you. Look at him." Tyr did as she was bid, watching as Sir Willem strode across the square. As she looked at him, she noticed how the sheen was fast disappearing.

"He's handsome, yes. But look at the patches of rust on his mail. And the mud and filth spattered all up his greaves and surcoat. That shield has blocked a hundred blows, splintered to ruin and good for nothing but showing off his ludicrous sigil. He might have thieved his arms and armour from a corpse and be no more than a robber. Such things happen." Tyr could see it now. His surcoat had once been black, washed to grey by the sun, not by choice. The garnet in his sword was just coloured glass; the scabbard's red leather was worn and ragged. And his horse was getting old, half lame with an awkward, lumbering gait. Even his pretty face suddenly looked a little gaunt, with shadows under his sky-blue eyes.

"He doesn't want a lord's service," the lady said in whispered glee. "He wants a lord's gold. Freelancers make mocking fools of true knights. He'd have wooed you, wed you and left you come morning." Tyr could feel how red her cheeks had grown and wondered if all of that was true. He had seemed gallant enough.

"What a charming gown," the lady said her expression at odds with her complimentary words. "Is this some grand occasion?"

"Only the market, m'lady," Tyr gave. "Oh, and my birthday — if such a thing interests you."

"Always," the lady gave eagerly, though clearly not listening. "Now, this beast."

The noble lady looked upon Alaria with a warm intrigue. "Tell me, how did a farmer's daughter find herself in possession of a tamed fald? One of the few I've ever seen?"

"How did you know I was—"

"That's your father, no? The Farmer Bundon of wheat, barley and beef." She grinned wickedly again. "Dalkaford is *my* fief, my dear; I make it my business to know its people. So tell me, truthfully, where did you acquire such a majestic creature?"

Her fief? Tyr realised and suddenly bowed as low as she could go. *This must be the Lady DeGrissier.*

"My pardons, m'lady. There was an egg. She hatched when I was small," Tyr noticed another noble, a moon-faced man in a fancy velvet doublet with tight orange curls on top of his head and a blond goatee that did nothing but accentuate his lack of chin. "Excuse me, m'lord, but she is tired from the show. Be careful."

When Tyr took a step toward the plump gentleman, another nobleman made his presence known—drawing his sword and standing steadfast between Tyr and the lordling. He stood tall and lean in a breastplate of shiny black steel and a visored helm of the same dark metal. He held Tyr's shoulder firmly with a gauntleted hand of lobstered steel. He gave a low, guttural warning in one of the continental languages and pushed her back a pace.

Tyr was suddenly afraid and didn't know what to do or say. The armoured man drew up his visor, and beneath was a sallow face with bushy black eyebrows that sat in permanent disapproval. His nose was hooked and long, his face was clean-shaven, and his lips were oddly red and wet. He spoke again, in that same unfamiliar dialect.

Angry. And happy to be so.

"Sir Richarde," Degrissier snapped, and in that same odd language, gave a firm warning. One that Sir Richarde wasted little time in heeding.

"Sir Richarde LaBotte," the red lady explained in a gleeful whisper. "Captain of my Riverguard. He came with us over the sea from Autreville, one of my late husband's retainers. His duty is his idol, and he worships it with grim satisfaction. But if one is to keep the banks of the Dalka safe, one needs a solid boot to kick away the thieves."

Our mighty Dalka can plenty protect herself. Tyr thought. It was something her father had always said.

"Apologies, Sir—" Tyr began before the lady interjected.

"Oh, don't waste your manners on him," the lady laughed. "He doesn't understand them, and courtesy is as strange to him as mercy."

"Mother, is this what we're looking for?" The plump lord asked, completely ignoring the confrontation with Sir Richarde. Too busy gawping at poor old Alaria.

"How did it come to be here?" His squinty eyes fell on Tyr. "Oh, you. I saw you dancing. It was very good. You're very comely, that is a fitting word, I think. Right mother?" he asked, and the lady nodded serenely. He never looked Tyr in the eye when he spoke, favouring instead everything or anything else. He fidgeted as though uncomfortable in his own skin. And his clothes, despite their great value, only seemed to exaggerate his odd proportions. His round belly and sloping shoulders, his quivering jowls and chins stacked three high. He wore a curved, gilded sword on his left and a bejewelled dagger on his right. And round his neck was an extravagant torque, smithed to the shape of writhing, golden flames. In its heart was a large gemstone, but none that Tyr had ever seen before. It had the look of red marble, with layers of yellow, amber, silver and pearl. But the layers seemed to move. They swirled and danced like molten metal within a thin glass casing.

It glows. It glows hot. Tyr realised. *I can all but feel the warmth from it.*

"That's kind of you to say, m'lord," Tyr bowed her head.

"The Lord Anguis DeGrissier," the lady explained. "My son. And Lord of Dalkaford. You've heard of him."

"Of course," she kept her head bowed.

"You poor pathetic creature," Tyr looked up and saw the lady talking to Alaria. DeGrissier suddenly looked to Tyr with accusatory eyes. "Her wings look a little withered. Does she not fly?"

"No, m'lady, no. She is a little cowardly if I'm honest. She mislikes heights."

"Mislikes heights," DeGrissier made the words sound a slur. "Does she not hold the blood of dragons?"

Blood of dragons?

"I can't speak to that, m'lady; she just finds them nerve-wracking, methinks." Tyr lay a soft hand on Alaria's neck; De-

Grissier's eyes shot to the hand and then to Tyr, her eyes pinched with indignation. But she hid it quickly, with a burst of laughter and a slow shake of her head.

"What's your name, girl?" She spoke with a golden voice, a voice that almost compelled you to answer simply from the asking.

"Tyr'Dalka," she bowed again. "Your ladyship."

"Indeed?" There was a foul edge in her voice, but she rounded her shoulders and let out a chuckle, soft and deep. "Elvish, I believe."

Tyr could see from the lady's expression that she knew full well that it was.

"Elvish, yes. For Land of Drag--"

"I know," the lady gave sharply. "Although, if we are being pedantic. *Tyr-na-Dalka* is the true elvish. *Tyr'Dalka* means simply: Land Dragon." The lady eyed Tyr up and down and smiled. "Which is perhaps a little more apt."

Is she... making fun of me? Tyr grew bashful, and examined the lady's pinched in waist, her ample bosom and long luscious hair. Her pale, unblemished face, her soft, thin hands and her large, round eyes. Perfect, as far as Tyr was concerned.

Do not risk the heartbreak of comparison, Tyr. You're a farm girl. She's a lady. That is just the way of it.

"A beautiful world is the land of dragons," The lady continued. "A proud name to live up to, my dear. A very proud name." She gave Tyr a long, inquisitive look before turning away and muttering a hasty 'good day', followed by the long powerful strides of Sir Richarde LaBotte and the waddling shuffle of her Lord son.

"Good day, m'lady, m'lord, Sir." Tyr mumbled after each had passed her by.

What was all that about then? Tyr worried. She only just noticed how sweaty her palms were, and how her heart fluttered noisily in her chest. Her father approached her after a brief spell of silence. Wearing a wide smile and childlike wonder.

"The lady bid me good day and gave me this," the farmer

opened up his hand, and a coin of yellow gold lay on his palm. The coins that noble folk called golden monarchs, for the likeness of Good King Doryn that was stamped on the back. It was gold. And heavy. And *gold.*

"She must have loved that show you put on," her father said excitedly. "We should retire this sad beast with this coin." He patted poor, old Veg on the side of his neck. "And see the barn door sat straight. By my fire, we'd have enough left over to start payments for an ox. Save Alaria's efforts for dancing! For dancing, it seems, will be the saviour of our humble farm."

TYR'DALKA III
The Ninth Day in the Month of High Sun

Tyr had not thought she'd ever see the Lady DeGrissier again. Returning to the farm, the family set to winnowing and storing what remained of their harvest. Putting that grand gold coin to good use, buying with it a young and eager plough horse, and naming it simply; Fruit.

The farmhouse had been in such fine spirits, Tyr had not thought much on the Lady DeGrissier, nor the strange fascination she had held with Alaria. But a half-turn of the moon later, a herald knocked on the old farmhouse door, declaring, "The company of Lord Anguis DeGrissier and his lady mother shall be here within short order."

And soon, the first sight of them sparkled on the horizon.

Banners. Glinting in the sun. A glitter of golds and crimsons. A rampant red dragon on a field of gold. They could see the dust clouds following behind the great retinue, thick russet clouds billowing into a blue sky.

The humble farm had never had many guests, save for travelling Brothers trading blessings and confessions for a warm meal and a roof for the night. It had certainly never had those of gentler birth grace its modest holdings, not for many long years. Tyr's father had oft told the tale of when Sir Geiger Greenwater, heir to Black Harbour, had taken refuge for a stormy night when Good King Doryn had sent him in search of brave men to fight under the Chainbreaker's banner. Tyr's grandfather had given them shelter and food, and the King's men had bought three heads of cattle to feed their new recruits. Two of whom were

Bundon's own brothers. The eldest, Will. was slain at the Battle of the Witchwood. And Colm fell to the flux on his journey home. Despite that, the noble visit had remained a point of pride for the small farmstead.

"Brave smiles stanch great sorrows," was what came to Tyr's mind. Master Dulcet had said it in her lessons once as a comment on her father. And Tyr had never forgotten it.

"They gave us ten silver marks and asked for no coins back," her father had always said. "A worthier guest we could not have asked for. The picture of gallantry and good graces, yer gran always said."

Brynhilde was wearing her finest. A surcoat of soft, blue wool. Stockings of cream coloured linen and a clean apron of brilliant white. She wore a blue ribbon in her grey, wiry hair, which she had plaited and curled on top of her head. Hans stood and gawped like a shocked rat, and Greta stood in pink and cream with the same level of enthusiasm she bore most everything.

Her father looked handsome, though, with neatly trimmed whiskers and sandy hair oiled back, in doublet and hose of russet and straw-coloured linen and wool. Tyr had worn the clothes she had worn to market. She owned nothing finer than that, and the lady had complimented the gown.

But all clothes were shamed when the Lady DeGrissier arrived in her usual flamboyant finery. Followed by the Autrevillian knight, Sir Richarde LaBotte, his jaw clenched tight, his eyes betraying his silent disgust. His hand ever-perched on the pommel of his longsword. Just waiting, it seemed, for an excuse to use it.

DeGrissier's servants helped her from the carriage as her guardsman took their horses to the stables for watering, led by a barrel of a man with a mean face and a knotted ear. A sergeant or captain, perhaps, but either way, he did not design to ask first; Tyr noted. In fact ,he, and his guardsmen, regarded the farm with little more than sneers and hushed laughter.

No one asked you here. Tyr thought bitterly. *If it's not to your liking, go back to your lady's lordly estate.*

"Where's the fald?" Anguis barked as soon as he was free of the carriage steps. He removed his fine, doe-skin gloves and held them out for a servant to take. One did, without delay.

"She is safe in the granary, m'lord," her father bowed low and smiled as widely as he could. "We do not have much, but what we have is at your disposal. We are graced by the visit; we did not believe our Tyr at first when she said—"

"The granary, he said," the fat lord barked to his mother, who had joined his side. "Where's that? This way? I want to see the beast again."

"My sweet son, where are your courtesies? We are guests here. Be polite." Her attention turned to the bowing farmer at her feet. "We were passing by, and we felt a sudden urge to visit with that extraordinary specimen in your care." She threw a knowing smile Tyr's way and linked arms with Anguis. There was no clear resemblance between mother and son that Tyr could see, save for their foul manners. He was fat; she was thin. His hair was the colour of bright rust, while hers was a deep, dark auburn. He had all the gallantry of a rotting beetroot, with a complexion to match. While she was fair and pale and wickedly charming.

"Hm. Apologies." The fat lord said to no one in particular. "Still. Is the beast this way?"

"Yes, m'lord. This way. Tyr, would you be so kind?"

"Oh yes, you." The young lord said, eyeing Tyr up and down. "I saw you dance. Very pretty. Mother says the same. Very pretty indeed."

"Sweet farmer, perhaps you could escort my son? I'd have a moment of your daughter's time, if I may?" The Lady DeGrissier did not wait for an answer before she gracefully stepped forward, swept an arm through Tyr's and began to walk.

"M'lady, I'm sorry to be a bother. But will you be supping with us tonight? I have food enough for you, but sadly not your men." Brynhilde's eyes never rose higher than her own bootlaces. The Lady shared a look with Tyr, smiled her sweet, poisonous smile and then turned back to the stepmother.

"You tempt me, good woman. Tell me, what grand feast can we expect to sup on tonight?" Brynhilde had just been about to answer when the lady spoke again. "The choicest cuts of that great, gowned sow you call a daughter, no doubt. She looks tough. I fear for my teeth." Brynhilde's face held a look of shackled indigence, chains taut, but she swallowed the bile at the back of her throat and put on her best cordial smile. Greta, however, could not have cared less.

"M'lady, no. I have some good cuts of beef though, roasted with rosemary and—"

"I must respectfully decline," DeGrissier gave. "Feed it to the men. Feed it to the horses. I care not. But I shan't risk the poisoning." And with that, the lady pulled at Tyr's arm, and they were gone. Off into the farmlands. Tyr had enjoyed that more than she knew she should. None had ever dared talk to Brynhilde in such a way while Tyr had known her. None. And to hear her shocked to silence was more beautiful than any song to Tyr's ears. DeGrissier rolled her eyes at Tyr and laughed behind her hand.

"She is an ugly mountain of a woman, isn't she?" She giggled, making Tyr giggle too. She felt cruel, of a sort. But she was forever the butt of secret jokes between the three of them; this laughter was well earned. Tyr dared not openly agree, however, so she simply stifled her laughter and nodded.

"Are they good to you?" DeGrissier asked as they began their ascent up one of the farmland's hills.

"Sorry, m'lady, I don't—"

"Kind, my love. Are they kind? One hears such dreadful stories sometimes, of wicked stepmothers and ugly, misshapen step-siblings."

"They are not unkind," Tyr said, truthfully.

"Who is they? The pig in the dress, or the weasel in the boots?"

"All. M'lady. All three. They are decent, but I shan't say they're any more than this, lest I be made a liar." Tyr explained, dabbing the perspiration from her forehead.

"You deserve better," the lady said sternly.

But what does she want with you? Is this about Alaria digging up the old riverbeds? Is she angry about the dancing? Or taxes? Or perhaps the crop is too small; she's had complaints.

"You're very pretty." Lady DeGrissier made the word sound anything but. "Not classically beautiful, no. But very pretty. The sort of young girl most honest men dream of, and most dishonest ones too. That knight, in the square, he *was* handsome; you're not a fool for thinking so. But my late husband was handsome too. The late Lord DeGrissier. He was an esteemed ambassador from the ducal courts of Autreville out west. He had made his meagre mark in the white city and was content with the small influence he had garnered for himself there." Kriscany, she meant. Kraigwyn's capitol. The King's seat on the southern island. "He lacked ambition, or rather, he lacked the will to seek ambition. Favouring instead, cask after cask of Farnesian red. We were wed at Kriscany's great Temple, and one moon's turn later, the drunken fool had fallen down the great palace steps. All three-hundred-twenty-six of them. There was not much left of him by the time he reached the bottom. And such an ugly stain on that lovely white stone."

"I'm sorry for that, m'lady," Tyr said sadly. The Lady wafted away the condolence like a bad smell.

"Do not worry yourself. The years storm on, from Dance to Dirt. As the smallfolk say. Yes. He *was* handsome, my husband. He *was* rich. He had it in him to be as fierce as the dragon on his banners. And the stupid sot fell down some stairs." She laughed then, quite unexpectedly. Lady DeGrissier noticed Tyr's reaction and took firm hold of her hand.

"Did I shock you? Should death never make one laugh? I apologise. But the point is the same. Handsome is fine. But the question is would you rather fair hands hold you for one night, or a fair heart keeps you safe for eternity?"

"A fair heart, m'lady," Tyr bowed her head. DeGrissier nodded wisely.

"Good girl," she squeezed Tyr's hand a little too tightly, then released it. Walking onwards.

"There is a spark in you," she said as they journeyed upwards to the highest rise of the farm's two hills, out into open country. Tyr saw two of the lady's guardsmen walking five paces behind them, spears in hand. Led by that towering brute Sir Richarde, his hand still resting on the pommel of his sword.

They look ready for a fight. Tyr thought that odd.

"Listen, girl." The lady snapped. Bringing Tyr's attention back. "It is rude to look elsewhere when a lady is speaking to you. Here. Right here. This is where you should be looking." The lady gestured to her own amber eyes, and she smiled imperiously.

"Yes. Better. I can see it now. A touch of destiny. Has anyone ever told you that before?" Tyr stayed quiet, but even so, the lady smiled as though Tyr had given some response.

"The show was a good one. That... *dance* in the square. Very good. Too good for the slack-jawed inhabitants of that sorry piss stream of a town," DeGrissier sneered. Tyr's laugh came unbidden, and she felt guilty all at once.

But why? What do I care for that sour old town-stead? They had been nothing but rude to her and her father. Well, save for the ones who threw coins for her. That had been a kindness. She felt guilty again remembering, that. Dalkaford had always served them well. *It is not a piss stream. The roads are cobbled, the buildings made of stone and good cut timber.* There were outlying villages that would fit her description. Sparse groups of hovels with simple dirt roads, none big enough to be worthy of a name. But not Dalkaford.

"I know, I am wicked, truly." The lady's laugh was a lyrical thing, deep and soft. "I own the village, girl. I know how petty and foolhardy the locals can be, generous with smiles while smiles are easy. But after some few hardships; some hot summers and cruel winters, there are no smiles left."

Tyr supposed that was true. That would explain the sourness in the streets. The thought made Tyr sad, somehow.

"Simple minds breed simple folk," the Lady stated boldly,

then turned inquisitively to Tyr. "But that's not you, is it?"

"I'm not sure I follow, m'lady," she swallowed nervously. DeGrissier's manner was as sharp as her cheekbones, and it left Tyr feeling rather beset. As though her words were all clever jokes that Tyr didn't get.

"Do you know your letters?" the lady asked, and Tyr gave a proud nod. "Quite uncommon. Who taught you? Not your father." She laughed, and Tyr's insides tightened.

She best not be mocking my pa. But she said nothing.

"Brother Dulcet, from the Temple," Tyr began.

"I know him not."

"No, no, m'lady. He sadly passed some years ago. He was a fine man, though. He taught many of us, young farmers, their letters and sums, taking no payment but a warm supper. Smartest man I've ever met."

"I wager I could count your acquaintances on one hand," the lady laughed. "I am sorry, I should not mock. Such souls as Brother Dulcet are rare indeed. Doubtless, some past sins had guilted him to such generosity."

"I can't speak to that, m'lady," Tyr mumbled, downcast. "He were always decent to me. More than decent, I'd say. He, he— I haven't a good enough word to describe him in earnest."

"Perhaps better tutelage could have taught you such a word," the lady quipped, continuing onwards. Leaving Tyr hurt in both head and heart.

I wish she would speak plainly. Her mockery seems like praise, while her praise feels like mockery. Tyr had never felt so simple-minded, and the more the lady spoke, the more Tyr wished for this chance visit to end.

"All these lands are yours, are they?" DeGrissier asked, stepping over a stile with more grace than Tyr expected; she even held out a hand for Tyr's descent.

"Two-and-forty acres," Tyr answered. "Gifted to my grandfather when the Good King sundered the chains of slavery." Tyr took the hand and expected some response. But DeGrissier gave a thin-lipped smile as though she weren't truly listening.

They strolled over a small stone bridge, where a placid stream lay below. They stopped a moment there, leaning over the side. Tyr gazed down at her reflection, expecting to meet the red lady's eyes. But she never looked down. Not once. The lady must have noticed this, for she gave Tyr a sideways glance and cleared her throat.

"Are you one of those girls that simper so over their own reflection?" She rolled her eyes and placed a firm hand on Tyr's shoulder. Tyr's eyes shot up.

"No, m'lady, no," she gushed.

"True beauty needs no looking-glass. Let the world look to you and behold it." She picked up a loose stone and threw it into the stream below, fracturing Tyr's reflection into a rippling web. "Mirrors are a foul distortion on reality, sowing naught but doubt and poison in the heart of the onlooker. I've seen some of the most beautiful women in the world lose themselves entirely to their own reflection. That's not you, I trust? Nothing is half so pitiful as the innately imperfect striving for perfection."

"Never, m'lady," Tyr hung her head. "I'm not so beautiful as you. I never even hoped to be *perfect*, as you say." Tyr thought of her mother's looking-glass, the locket tied about her neck, and chose to stay silent on the matter.

"There is wisdom in that," the lady concluded.

They set off again, nearing the highest rise. You could see the whole farm up there. A clear view almost all the way down to King's Anchor. Tyr had grown thoughtful and had said little since their walk across the bridge. She felt DeGrissier's eyes on her, though, waiting for her to speak.

"Sorry for the asking, m'lady," Tyr blurted. "But I do wonder. What calls for your interest in me?"

"To the point," her nose wrinkled delightedly. "The first step to getting what you want is having the gall to ask for it."

"Kind of you to say so, m'lady," was all Tyr could think to say in such heat. The day was beastly hot, and she already regretted her bodice.

Why do I always wear this thing on the hottest days the year has to offer us? Tyr complained in her head. But made no more fuss than that. She looked across at the lady, who did not seem troubled by the sun at all, not even as she walked the hill. Her fair features were in the full beam of the summer's rays, and yet she did not redden nor flush. Nor even sweat. Not one bead.

They walked through the rough hedgerow roads between each acreage, right to the summit of the farmland's highest hill. Once there, the lady sat herself down, straight onto the grass. Tyr worried for the gown, but the lady seemed unfazed and did nothing but gently pat the empty ground next to her. An invitation, Tyr thought. And sat quickly.

Tyr could not deny how beautiful the world looked from their highest hill. She had practised her dances up here many times, gently beating the tambourine while Alaria hopped along with the chimes. She had learnt so fast, Tyr remembered.

I thought, and she did; it was as simple as that. Tyr wanted nothing more than to be dancing with her fald right now. She longed for the familiar, and this lady and her mysterious walks were anything but. Tyr flushed suddenly, noticing the lady staring at her.

"You're very pretty." She said, sounding surprised almost. "I've said that, haven't I?"

"Yes. Very kind of you to say, m'lady," Tyr said again. *And you have said that already, foolish girl.*

"I never say anything to be *kind*, girl," she quipped and then smiled too sweetly. "No. I speak only the truest contents of my own mind. It's all one should ever speak, truthfully. Fewer misunderstandings that way. And the truth of the matter is this. I want the beast. The fald. I want it." Tyr was without words.

"M'lady—"

"And my son likes you, so there'd be no need to see you separated. You'll just stay with us." She had never asked the question, but Tyr felt as though she awaited an answer.

"M'lady is very kind—" Tyr caught the lady's glare. "Not *kind,* of course, but— but Alaria is family. And I'm needed on the farm."

"I'll see your quaint little farm never struggles, dear girl; it doesn't look like it should take much to see this place maintained," she laughed again, looking out over the barn, the crops and the cattle with a foul sneer.

"M'lady," Tyr began.

"Hush a moment. You see, my son is quite taken with you. It should not displease him to have you in our service, would such a match suit you? You did say you'd prefer a fair heart over fair hands if I recall. I know he is an odious specimen, but he is a good boy. Loyal, albeit dim. Like his father, and certainly *most* unlike me. But one cannot choose their children, however detrimental to one's standing they grow to be. They are still yours. A graceless, plump reminder that 'tis still the gods that rule over all; highborn and low. But a fair heart he has, even if it is the only trait of worth he possesses."

She seemed lost in her own words for a moment, gazing thoughtfully into the empty air before snapping back to winks and smiles.

"So. We have an accord?"

"M'lady," Tyr felt a flush creep up her neck. "I am no fit bride for your son." *And I am not certain he has as fair a heart as all that.*

"Oh, my darling," the lady wore a look of mocking sympathy. "No, you're quite right. No. That would be quite absurd a-notion. You're a farmer's daughter, bought to court only for the lucky happenstance that that *beast* finds itself in *your* possession. But you would not complain in becoming his mistress? Raise some strong bastard boys to join our growing militia as officers, and maybe knights? That is still a finer match than you'd ever hope to find else wise. And there are others. My son has a court full of beautiful, kindly maidens like yourself. Seven, I think at last count. And he showers all of them with gifts and gallantry. Think on it. You'd want for nothing. You and your pet."

Would she have me be her son's plaything? With seven others? Tyr felt a dull ache in her stomach. She didn't want to be here anymore. *By my fire, this is not gallantry; it is greed. And it makes me feel sick.*

"I'm sorry, m'lady, it's still a no; I'm sorry." Tyr tried to pull her arm free, but the Lady DeGrissier was holding it firm.

"I *said*; think on it." Her tone was darker, and her nails dug in at her wrist. "I needn't ask your permission, do remember that. The offering is a courtesy. Take it, or refuse it. At your own peril."

"You're hurting me," Tyr said flatly, not wanting to sound weak. Somewhere down below, Tyr heard Alaria screech. She turned to look, but DeGrissier yanked her chin back round to face her.

"Alaria," Tyr said in hushed desperation.

They're hurting her. Tyr thought. *They're hurting Alaria.*

"You don't understand yet, do you?" Her tone was wet with cloying sweetness. "You poor thing. If nothing else, understand this. Matters such as these always resolve in my favour. Fortunes breed fortunes, and I've been breeding mine for a long, long time." Tyr heard Alaria screech again and a man's shouting. Her father's.

They're hurting him. She worried. *They're hurting her.* She tried again to turn and look, but the Lady's sharp, red nails kept her in place.

"There is something to you," Lady DeGrissier looked her over, a look somewhere between a sneer and a smile. Like she had just solved a clever riddle. "A little spark of something. Perhaps that accounts for your impudence." Tyr tried to wrench free again and managed this time with ease. The Lady raised her eyebrows in faux surprise, her mouth agape in fake indignation with the hint of a mocking smile at the corners of her lips.

"She's not for sale, m'lady," Tyr said, trying to sound bold. "And nor am I, for that matter." And Tyr stormed off down the hill. To find her family. From behind, she heard the Lady DeGrissier laugh and call after her.

"Oh, such fire!" She roared, the words echoing through the small valley of hills. "Yes, Tyr'Dalka. There's a touch of destiny to you!"

Tyr found Alaria at the door of the granary, where the timid fald nested and protected their grain. With her, she found a panic-stricken farmer and a giant, wailing toad. Lord Anguis was crumpled on the floor, his crying, snotty face now as red as his doublet. The lady's guard had heard the commotion as the mean faced sergeant charged out of the stable with live steel in his hands. Tyr could see the others rearing their heads behind, grabbing spears, shields and crossbows.

"I tried to tell 'im," her father said, over and over and over. "I tried to tell 'im, I did! But m'lord insisted, truly insisted. He did."

"What happened?" Tyr asked, dismayed and already close to tears. She saw wet drops of blood seep through the closed grip of the crying lord. He held it tight to his chest, for all the world like his heart might fall out.

"It savaged me!" He wailed. "Mother! Where is mother!? It savaged me!"

"What have you done?" Brynhilde paled when she saw. "By my fire, we're ruined. We're ruined." She kept saying.

"He tried to get on her back, Tyr," her father whispered in her ear, the desperate cries of 'we're ruined' making it difficult to focus on anything. "She warned him; she really did. She backed away as far as she could go, she cawed, she cried, she flapped her wings. But still, he tried." The guards were nearing. Tyr couldn't think. There was nothing to be done. Nothing. She could do nothing.

"We're ruined! We're ruined! By my fire, we're ruined!" Brynhilde kept crying.

"Tyr, what can we do?" Her father panicked. "What should I have done? By my fire, what was she supposed to do? She was scared. Oh, Dragon, have mercy."

"Dragons have no mercy, Master Bundon." Lady DeGrissier's voice was cold and hard but full of so much unbidden glee. Standing next to her was Sir Richarde, who had never looked happier as his longsword slid enthusiastically from its sheath.

"Just gold… or fire," she concluded.

"Mother," the man-child wailed, lumbering to her side and burying himself in her straight and imperious embrace. DeGrissier stroked her son's hair like he were a loyal house cat, and wordlessly her personal guard drew their swords and lowered their spears. The guards approached slowly, cornering Bundon and Tyr at the door of the barn's granary. Tyr heard Alaria chirrup worriedly behind her, cocking her neck nervously and crumpling to the floor to hide behind her wings. *She is scared.* Tyr knew. *She is so scared.*

"The beast! The beast! It tried to eat me, mother! It ripped my doublet, look. It was going for my heart, I know it! I *know* it!" The red lord cried and sputtered, tears streaming down his pink cheeks and snot collecting in his thin goatee.

More likely, she was going for his liver, Tyr thought bitterly.

"As I told you, Tyr'Dalka," the Lady DeGrissier called to her. "Things always resolve in my favour. So which of the dragon's mercies will it be… Gold?

"Or fire?"

TYR'DALKA IV

The Tenth Day in the Month of High Sun

"This will ruin us," Brynhilde said, again, and again, and again. "Fire, have mercy; this will ruin us. Ruin us. For certainty, it will. It will."

Gold or fire, she had offered them. Fire was force, and the Lady had even threatened to take Alaria's life for attacking a man of noble birth. She had threatened to get the law involved, the Brothers too. So they had settled for gold.

"A fald's worth, to be precise," The Lady had quipped. But that, as it turned out, was a steep price and one they could never match with coin alone. So her father had sold the last thing he owned of any real value.

And it is all my doing.

They had loaded grain sacks with as much coin as they had, which was precious little. As well as the few bits of silverware they kept for feasts over midwinter. And the deed, of course. Though Brynhilde could read and write after a fashion, Tyr was the best with words, so she had written up the deed. Each stroke of the pen had felt like a stab through the heart. But the alternative was far fouler.

Foul of hand and foul of heart. Tyr thought angrily as she signed her father's name at the bottom of the paper.

"It has to be done," her father had said with an accepting sadness. "See she gets it. It shan't be too different; I don't think. We will simply work our Lady's farm for her until the debt is settled."

"As her slaves," Brynhilde spat the word, half in tears.

"As her serfs," the farmer corrected. The grief creased plainly across his weathered face. "Her ladyship told me that is how all farmsteads are run on the mainland. Good King Doryn saw an end to the slave trade, afterall."

More grief for the old man. Tyr brooded. *He has seen enough of that.*

"Aye, but he did not see an end to debt. And the two are like as one, if you ask me. My father worked off his debts in the copper mines, worked them off until he couldn't work anymore. And then his debts were ours. Bundon, you jolly fool, what have you done?" Brynhilde was all wrapped up in her finest cloak, a heavy stretch of pale pink wool, clasped with a copper pin.

"It is just until the debt is paid," the farmer said again.

"Aye, with a failing crop and barn like to collapse before next spring." Brynhilde was red with fury, spitting her venom at her husband, who was well beyond the hurt of her words. "She will seize any excuse she can to call you a thief or a layabout and claim that monster as recompense. You've gained nothing from this. Nothing. Why spare the beast? Why?"

"She is family," the farmer said quietly. "She is my daughter's guardian. She saved us. If I must sacrifice my farm to see her safe, then the Dragon will be all the happier to greet me when at last I join him."

"You holy fool," Brynhilde spat. "And you. Could you not

have taken her offer? You could have grown to love the boy. And you'd be with your blasted bird, is that not what you wanted? Had Greta been offered such a thing, she'd have the sense to take it." The look Greta gave was one of utter indifference, made ludicrous by the two tiny, blond plaits springing from either side of her head.

If you are so set on it, then perhaps both of you could go to him. Give him a total of nine mistresses. But Tyr said nothing and let her stepmother's words wash over her.

Hans had tried to weasel his way out of going, feigning his sicknesses with more vigour than ever. But the lady had said it plain; the *three* of them must go. And Brynhilde would not risk it.

And so, without farewell, Brynhilde set off. Hans and Greta were close behind, shooting Tyr and her father foul looks as they went.

For reasons unknown, the Lady DeGrissier's terms stated that Brynhilde, Greta and Hans must deliver the payment. They had caused the least offence during the Lord and Lady's visit, but that was never the stated reason. They never *gave* a stated reason.

They didn't have to.

They didn't want to. Tyr pondered anxiously.

"It falls to me to clear this mess," Brynhilde had said more than once. "I'll be the only one of us not to make a pig's ear of it, and our lady clearly sees such. But she expects a fald. And a farm girl besides. I doubt she'll look kindly upon this offer."

"But it's all we have to offer," Bundon had given wearily. "So it must serve."

If I had not taken Alaria. If I had stayed home and tended the farm, as I usually do. None of this would have happened. She wept if she thought on it too long. She could feel the tears now as Brynhilde and her milk siblings waddled down the road. Her father spoke no words of comfort either, too heartbroken himself to offer a firm shoulder to cry on. Alaria had been sullen too.

I'd have scratched the fop as well if he had tried to clamber atop me. Tyr thought miserably.

In the rucksack of coin and silver that Greta had hauled over her large shoulders, Tyr had placed the most valuable items of her collection. The two silver coins, and all of the coppers too. And the bronze goblet. That had made Tyr sad, but it was a small price to pay to keep Alaria safe and home. She'd kept hold of her mother's locket and the tambourine her father had gifted her. But all other treasures, big, small, old or new... all went in the sack. And all they could do was hope their meagre worth might satisfy the lady's grievance.

But Brynhilde is right. The lady wanted a fald. And she said, in no uncertain terms, that she always gets what she wants.

"These matters always resolve in my favour." She remembered the red lady saying. Tyr had nearly liked her too and had cursed herself many times for her girlish, eager trust.

❋ ❋ ❋

They had expected Brynhilde and her brood to return after two days. They had begun to worry after three, and after five, they were starting to despair. Her father had suspected they'd run-in with some foul company on the road, taking their meagre wealth and leaving the three of them for dead on the wayside. Such things were uncommon on the roads around Dalkaford, as they were watched closely by the Riverguard and Lord Tarbrand's patrols. But they were not unheard of. Especially as times grew harder and the sun shone hotter. And the whispered story on the roads was that an elven company had turned bandit, hanging any poor souls who stumble across their band.

I always rather liked the stories of elven wanderers singing songs for copper coins. But Tyr had thought the reality would be far more terrifying. She was fast learning that life rarely resembled her faerie tales.

It was the sixteenth day in the Month of High Sun when they found the note, seven days after Brynhilde had set off for the old Slaver Estates over the Dalkamont's ridge. It had been secured to the door with the point of a bejewelled dagger, gilded and inlaid with a hundred tiny rubies across the hilt. Tyr had found her father, shaking, half crying as he tried to decipher the words. He could not read, though, as hard as he might try. So Tyr sat beside her father at the table by the old hearth, took one of his shaking hands in hers and gently prised the note from his trembling grip.

"You took to yer letters well," her father said with an attempt at pride. "Brother Dulcet always said so in your lessons. Always said you were a sharp one. You can read them, yes? There's a seal at the bottom," her father said worriedly. "I need not tell you whose." Tyr looked over the letter. The parchment was sturdy vellum, written in a messy scrawl.

"They wanted the girl. They wanted the fald. You said we could pay their price in gold. They will not take it. They will not let us leave. The Lady is furious. She threatens to send her guard to settle the debt. Bring the fald, husband. Bring the girl. I fear they will kill us if you don't. Please. Hurry. Please. Please. Please." Tyr's father had his head in his hands, shaking from the words. Tyr concluded. "Signed. Your loving wife."

"This came with it," the farmer held a small plait of hair in his hands. Blond. "It is not their debt to pay, Tyr. Those three had no hand in this." Tyr was without words once more. They had given everything they had. Everything. And to them, it was nothing.

"Why would she write to you when she knows you can't read?" Tyr puzzled. "Papa, she was forced to write this. This is as much from the Lord and Lady as it is from Brynhilde."

"That is…" her father trailed off, lost in shock and grief. "They go too far."

What can we do? Tyr thought, still and sullen. *What can we do when the world is poised so readily in their favour? They'll take all, and think it their due.*

Tyr heard Alaria caw outside.

"We should tell the yeolderman, or the Krillian. Or Lord

Tarbrand at King's Anchor. By my fire, we should send word to the King!"

"How?" Her father asked, taking the vellum and looking cluelessly over the words. "How is this right? Why would our Dragon snub the fires of those like your mother while allowing the likes of *her* and her son to burn so hot and so cruelly?"

"I don't know, papa," Tyr said in a sad whisper. "I'm no Sister."

"The Krillian," her father said with a slow nod of the head. "Aye, he will see this put to rights. Our Noble Dragon would not permit this. Surely not. This has the smell of banditry about it, my wife and kin no better than hostages for ransom." Tyr had never seen her father angry. He cursed beneath his breath on occasion but would always apologise for it after. Even if the apology was to none but the empty air. He rose from his seat with two clenched hands and a quivering chin.

"Tyr, fetch me my cloak and my riding boots," he took the jewelled dagger and tucked it in his belt. "Your father will not stand for this."

TYR'DALKA V

The Sixteenth Day in the Month of High Sun

The Temple of the Green Dragon was boasted to be the grandest shrine to Kri on any of the King's isles. Tyr had never been before, not since her ashening as a babe, where her head was bathed in ashes, and her sacred fire was first kindled. But now, sixteen years later, she returned. The mountain of the Dalkamont shot from the horizon; its single peak shrouded in cloud. The mountain was covered in growing things; mosses in a hundred shades of green, yellow and all the colours in between, making the great peak shine bright and verdant in the rising sun. At the base of the mountain was the temple, its doors glinting with decorative flames of beaten copper and bronze. But apart from that, there was no vestige of civilisation to spoil the grand view. Untouched green hills rolled in every direction, with the crashing of the Dragon's Sea to the east, below the coastal cliffs.

"The Krillian is wise and generous," her father had said. He had been talking of all the kindnesses the Krillian had shown the good people of Dalkaford over the years. How he would give out alms every Midwinter Morn; a procession of black Brothers behind him with great platters of hot, nourishing food. Whole chickens roasted over a spit, with great haunches of lamb cooked with mint and mustard seed. Buttered carrots and mashed swede. Honeyed ham and crispy crackling. Mulled wines and spiced ciders too. Food and drink the likes of which Dalkaford would never taste, else wise.

The Krillian had seen the mill built and restored in recent years. On the temple's own coin. That was what tithes were for; they paid for the upkeep of the isle's homesteads, shops and roads.

"And... should they require it, its good people too," her father had said. "I pay my tithes as dutifully as any other man. The temple will see us safe." Tyr wished she could believe that. But the only experience of the temple Tyr had known was Brother Kindur, who called on them every Month of Seeds to accept their tithes. But he had always been glum and fiercely unlikeable in his duty, despite what her father had said.

"He was once a kind man. A heart full of stories and a mouth full of smiles. Fire knows what happened to *that* fellow," her father had always said after the Brother's yearly visit. Tyr had never liked him and did not wholly trust the temple as a result. No matter how much her father praised the Krillian's wisdom.

Tyr and her father found themselves at the crossroads. It felt strange not continuing on the road south to Dalkaford; she had never walked any other route before. But instead, they took the eastern road, the long and winding Pilgrim's Path. A young horse and a cowardly fald following behind them. Tyr beat the blackwood tambourine to keep Alaria's pace quick, as she was known to wander off or fall behind if left to her own devices.

And I cannot lose you now, brave beast. Tyr rattled the chimes, making Alaria cock her head, thoughtfully chirrup and then hurry to the girl's side. Tyr placed a soft hand on the fald's sharp, stony beak and longed for the simpler adventures they used to enjoy together.

They had not danced since the red lady's visit. They would practise whenever they could before, but now it did little but make Tyr sad.

She had tried to ride the fald again, just before they had left for the temple. Tyr had thought that if she could fly, she might be able to rescue Brynhilde and the others, and maybe then they could take a ship to the continent or beseech the king for a royal pardon. But Alaria had grown morose in the days since their dance; she sensed the unrest and thus would not even entertain the notion. She huffed, she puffed, she flapped her great wings, and impudently scraped at the ground with her talons… but she did not fly.

"What are you so scared of?" Tyr found herself asking, not unkindly. But she knew that were falds to speak, Alaria's answer would have been: Everything.

"You little coward," Tyr said softly to her friend. "You big little coward." Alaria trilled happily before spotting a rabbit and racing down the hill to secure it. She cawed her victory, threw the slain quarry into the air and swallowed it down whole. Working it down her throat with a wide variety of foul expressions and fouler noises. Tyr and her father shared a look of fondness as the fald did as falds do, but her father looked away suddenly. Crestfallen. Struck by a thought.

"Tyr," her father said wearily. "If they should not… if they should not help us—"

"I know, papa," Tyr answered simply. "I know."

※ ※ ※

"The Lady DeGrissier, you say," the Krillian pondered,

smoking on his long clay pipe, surrounded on all sides by bowls of sweet-smelling incense. He sat on the floor at the altar, where cushions of green velvet and blankets of soft black chiffon littered the sand-coloured flagstones. Two Brothers sat with him, Brother Kindur; the older, and Brother Whent; the younger. Though separated by two and twenty years, one seemed as young and clueless as the other. Whatever fumes the Krillian and his brothers were inhaling were having an adverse effect on their hospitality.

"The widow DeGrissier has shown us here at the temple nothing but grace and kindness," he said slowly, as though each word were struggling to break free of his throat. "Look at the protection she has gifted our mighty Dalka, all at her own cost," "We find these allegations very difficult to believe." He took a pinch of grass coloured sand from the altar and threw it down onto a brazier. The fire erupted, and the flames danced green thereafter. Tyr and her father were stunned to silence.

"Your G-grace," the farmer stammered, squeezing his straw hat to his chest. "The Lady's gentle son was harmed by… by one of the animals in our keeping. She will not deliver my wife and kin safely until I pay the debt in full."

"The boy has a foppish way about him," the Brother Kindur quipped and then giggled to himself stupidly. Tyr could not help but notice that as the years went by, the Brothers' robes had become increasingly vibrant. Kindur's had started as little more than a woollen shift to see him covered and warm. It had gained some silver threads first, decorating the hems and sleeves. And then it gained some rubies and garnets, encrusting its neckline. His red linen sash had become silken, and the simple blackwood staff had gained an ornamented dragon's head, cast in silver with eyes of red rubies.

"Foppish he well maybe, but he is of noble stock… and your beast *did* harm him." The Krillian said within his layers and layers of glittering, emerald robes; all silk, chiffon and samite. His mantel was of the richest cloth of gold, with a hundred emerald medallions hanging from it, softly chiming together as he moved.

Each one wears enough wealth to see our debt erased and yet they do nothing. Tyr fumed, but held her tongue.

The old Krillian paused a moment, cleared his throat and stroked his thin, withered fingers through the white silk of his beard. "I fail to see how this is a matter for the Dragon's Prayers."

"A good word from you, yer Grace, and she will see the debt wiped clean. I know she will." The farmer urged. There were groans from the smoking Brothers, who locked eyes on one another and fell to bouts of high-pitched and irritating laughter.

The air was thick with cloying smoke; a grey haze lingered at head height, like a roll of morning mist through and around the white-stone columns of the main chapel. Stone dragons watched the Krillian and his Brothers from their altars, breathing a steady stream of sweet-smelling smoke from their nostrils. The Temple's many initiates and Sisters walked about in a daze, it almost seemed. Tyr's father was at a loss for words.

"I know this one, Krillian," Brother Kindur whispered drowsily. "They might seem all smiles and flowers, but I have seen their manners wither to naught but mulch these last few years. If they find themselves indebted, it might be they deserve it."

"It is *your* manners that dwindle so, Brother!" Tyr snapped, her father grabbed her wrist as a warning. "My father always tries with you; he does. And he never thinks twice before offering you food and rest, even in the light of your sour mood." The Brother Kindur seemed sincerely surprised, looking almost wounded at the words.

"Brother Kindur's manners are not in question here," the Krillian placed a hand on the Brother's shoulder and squeezed some comfort. The Brother took it. "But the nature of your visit, however, is. What is it you think our Noble Dragon can help you with?"

"Coin, yer grace," the farmer said simply. "We need coin to see the debt paid."

My poor father. Tyr thought. *He is too honest.*

The Brother and the Krillian exchanged looks before they slowly started to wheeze and laugh once more.

"Yer Grace, my holy Brothers… this is no laughing matter. This is a crime, I'm sure. We cannot pay the ransom."

"Ransom?" The Krillian echoed the word like it were a curse, and the Brothers fell silent. "My dear Farmer Bundy—"

"Bundon, yer Grace."

"It might seem an injustice to you. But where would our grand temple be if we paid the debts of every unfortunate soul who finds themselves in their possession?" His Brothers nodded sagely, with mumbled noises of agreement.

"I place a copper coin at the foot of the dragon every new moon, yer Grace." The three priests turned their heads slowly to regard the farmer. "I have worked hard, without rest, for many long years now. I have asked for nothing from no one. But I find myself in troubling times. If our Noble Dragon cannot help me, we are lost."

"Our Noble Dragon always helps those in need, especially those with kind and forgiving hearts." The Krillian took a long puff on his pipe, and when he breathed out, a dragon of smoke soared from his lips and melted away before reaching the farmer. The Brothers all nodded sagely again. "If you are pure and good, our Dragon will see you through these troubling times."

"And if not?" Tyr asked, a little more sharply than she intended. "If we fall to ruin? Is that because our Dragon wills it? Does that mean we are attainted in some way?" The priests scowled softly. They looked on Tyr like three kindly yet disapproving grandfathers.

"That, child, is not for us to say."

"Then what use are you?" Tyr seethed. Her father squeezed her wrist, but she snatched it back. "If you will not help your people, what use are you? What do you do here? Smoke and ponder and practise your little magic tricks?"

"My dear girl," he said, unfazed by her words. "We pray."

"For what?" Tyr hissed. "More pipeweed and a bigger

golden hat?"

"Your words are sharp, and they are said to wound us," the Krillian held up his hand and blessed her, tracing old runes in the air with a long, wrinkly finger. "But our Noble Dragon has a forgiving nature. And I bequeath to you my sacred flame."

"But that doesn't mean anything," Tyr said, tearful. Defeated. "It only *means* something if you *do* something. Surely."

"It means as much or as little as the strength of your faith," the Krillian dismissed the both of them with a gesture. "The halls of our temple are yours, stay awhile and pray. Pay thanks to his sacrifice." Tyr's heart had sunk to her boots, and the Krillian must have made note of this, for the look he wore now was one of fatherly consolation. He held out a long, thin arm, and upon seeing this, his two Brothers rose, helping the old man to his feet.

"She is young," he spoke kindly, all but ignoring Tyr. Speaking, instead, to her father. "She has seen fifteen winters, perhaps sixteen?"

"Seventeen, y'Grace," the farmer agreed.

"Seventeen," he nodded knowingly, as though the number were the answer to all life's mysteries. He gently patted Tyr on the shoulder before moving to a stone font that stood to one side of the altar. "The fiery passions of youth. As yet untempered by the honest passage of time."

"Brother Dulcet always said she were a sharp one," the farmer interrupted. "She is wise, after a fashion. But, Krillian, our troubles burn hotter and fouler than my fair daughter's temper, I assure you—"

"Come, girl," the Krillian beckoned with a skeletal hand, ignoring the farmer's quiet protest. Tyr sullenly approached, casting wary eyes upon the font. It was a wide plate of black marble, subtly convex, so that it held a paper's width of placid, still water within. It acted as a perfect mirror. Tyr hesitated. When the Brothers saw this, they all grumbled and shook their heads.

"Do you fear your own reflection, girl?" The Krillian asked pointedly.

"It's not that I fear it—"

"For it is said that only demons and dragons fear the looking glass, my dear. Great power lies in the ability to simply accept the things that are. Dragons, though, lack such an ability. Seeing none of their beauty, none of their power... only the ugliness within. The flaws. The imperfections. Staining their precious pride forever. Driving them mad."

"But there need not be madness in the humble acceptance of what is, and what is not." Brother Kindur added over Tyr's shoulder, guiding her closer. "In fact, there is great wisdom in doing so."

"Tyr," her father whispered urgently. "Do as the Krillian bids; there's a good girl." And so, she looked. She stared down upon herself, with the Krillian and Brother Kindur peering over the black marble with her.

"What is it you see, girl?" The Krillian asked eagerly.

"I see my mother," Tyr said simply.

"She lost her mother, I should explain," her father added. "Died in the birthing bed."

"I see," the Krillian wore a look of forced pity, catching Tyr's eyes in their reflection. "And what is it you think your mother sees?" The dim light of the temple made it difficult to see much of anything, but the light kept catching on the Krillian's golden mantle and emerald charms on the Brothers' rubies and silver threads. Every time she tried to focus on her own reflection, the light would shift, and she'd be blinded by gold, silver, rubies and emeralds once more.

"Is it pride? Love? What do you think your mother sees when she looks upon you?" The Krillian pushed.

"She sees," Tyr began, her voice but a whisper, but her eyes were dazzled once more by the golden dragons adorning the holy man's shoulders.

That is what she sees. Tyr's brow furrowed, her heart filled with poison as she lifted her eyes from the font and fixed them firmly upon the Krillian's own.

"She sees straight through you," she said through

clenched teeth. Tyr retreated three steps, eyeing each holy man in turn. "You reek of her."

"Reek?" The Krillian's voice had a cruel edge to it suddenly; an air of poisonous, embittered tolerance ebbed through the temple. "Of what, pray tell?"

"Of her," Tyr backed away, a few steps more. "DeGrissier. Of ruin. Of deceit. Of fetid apathy and faithless prayer. Of fire. And *gold*."

"Dragons take you, girl," the Krillian snapped. "For you are truly lost. The both of you. Lost. Go. Out with you, I say, out!"

"Gladly," Tyr seethed and ran from the hall.

* * *

"That was poorly done, Tyr. Very poorly done," her father shook his head as her followed behind his daughter. Exiting the confining stone temple, and finding fresh air once more. "They are godly men. Who knows who you offend by offering them insult."

"I will not believe our Dragon sacrificed his sacred fire so that the greedy can smoke and giggle their way through prayers and call themselves priests," Tyr fumed. "They are no better than the old dragons. Hoarding their wealth. Besotted by their own sanctity and worthiness."

"I know," her father said sadly. "I know. They should place their hearts and riches in the natural beauty of the world. As our Noble Dragon once did. But there's no forcing the hearts of the unwilling, lest you lend your hands to conquest. And we're no conquerors, Tyr. Just a farmer and his daughter." Tyr moved to Alaria's side, who lifted her head as the two of them approached. She cocked it to one side inquisitively and let out a trill of tuneless song. Tyr held her fald's head to her chest, closed her eyes and tethered to her all her warmest thoughts and deepest sorrows. Alaria nuzzled into the embrace.

"Tyr," her father said over her shoulder.

"I know," she said. "I know. But perhaps you could ask if I might visit, on occasion." But her father gave no answer.

There was no long goodbye, for Tyr's heart could not bear it. She simply wrapped her arms around Alaria's neck and whispered a humble sorry in her ear. They separated at the crossroads, her father looping Alaria's reins around his hand and hiding both farmer and fald beyond the horizon. Tyr and Alaria had never been apart, not in seventeen years. And the grand creature cawed and fought against it with all the might she dare use, which for a timid creature such as her, was very little. Alaria's cries echoed over the fields and hills, long after Tyr had lost sight of them. It was a heartache so profound that all other pains seemed trite by comparison. There were no words for it. All Tyr could do was go home. Alone.

And weep.

BUNDON IV

The Sixteenth Day in the Month of High Sun

They hung there, blistering away in the last of the day's sun. Their cheeks had sunk back to their skulls, and crows had already seen to their eyes. Their hands were bound, each one, behind their backs. Bundon saw no wounds but the nooses tight around their crooked necks. Hanging from the man in the centre was a placard. It bore some old runes the farmer could not make out. But they looked different to common words and letters.

By my fire, this was the work of elves. Bundon knew elves to be rogues and scoundrels. Heathens who worship long-forgotten gods and drink human blood to spy out glimpses of the future.

Beastly folk, to truss up travellers such. The farmer shook his head. This seemed a tragic and brutal end for anyone, no matter what they did in life. There was no sign of struggle. Just three bound souls. Helpless.

Probably praying for home. Bundon thought sadly. *I pray you find it, my good sirs.*

Bundon heard a noise, a horrid wet noise. He turned and saw Alaria deftly picking strips off the hanged men with the tip of her beak. Not a care for the smell, nor the taste.

"Stop that, you horrible bird!" He called out to her, batting her beak softly. She lifted her neck, rigid and powerful and let out a shrill squawk. "Tyr might not mind you feasting on such, but you shan't do it in my company. Hear me?" If she did, however, she made no sign of it.

Aye, she hears me. But she does not listen. He remembered his daughter saying once. But then he grew sombre. Saddened to think of poor Tyr'Dalka walking, alone, back to the empty barn.

"She will weep," he told the fald, who seemed to know who he meant. Alaria softened. Her quills folded back and her neck drooped down until her head perched on the farmer's shoulder. He slung an arm around the beast's head. "I am very sorry for this, old friend. Very sorry."

At the crossroad, he had taken the western road, the least trod and travelled. Most of it was a simple dirt track, through woodland and marsh. Rougher roads than Bundon was used to and without a horse. He had let Tyr take Fruit; she was the lighter, after all. And the young plough horse would be needed on the farm.

Two days that is all. And then all of this can be forgotten. The farmer tried to think, but however much he wished, he could never believe it. Everything would be different. His daughter may never smile again. She would feel this heartache for the rest of her days.

And she will blame me, in part. He thought dismally. *And perhaps she is right too. What was I thinking letting a small girl take a fald as a pet?* He looked across at Alaria, who cocked her head and trilled a short song. She was no pet, he knew.

By my fire, you are family. And the only Alaria I have left. Bundon thought of his late wife a lot. Doing his best to voice her thoughts as though she were still there. But as time went on, he found it harder and harder to think on what she might say and do. He feared that might mean he was forgetting her, and that thought saddened him more than any other.

She wore a gown of cream and sage that day in the Month of Flowers when their hands had been bound together with a silken green ribbon. She had danced that night around the grand bonfire. At first, she stepped with her merchant father, all proud faced and stumbling. And then with Bundon. He had done his best, he remembered. But dancing had never come naturally to him. Alaria though. *His* Alaria. She could dance.

Aye, what an angel she looked, twirling round the grand fire. The farmer had never seen anything quite so beautiful. Not until he saw his baby girl and the bright soul she had grown into. A true beauty, with an honest heart, to match her mothers.

Her mother would say our girl had a brighter flame than hers. Bundon thought sadly. *But I'd say it were just as grand.*

Tyr looked so like her mother when she danced. It grieved the farmer every time he thought on it. For he wished, more than anything, that mother and daughter could have danced together. At least once. But he had wished for many things through the years, and so few of them had come true. What Bundon wished, for now, was his late wife's counsel.

She would know what to do. She would have advice to give. I know it. But Alaria's ghost was silent today, or perhaps her voice was too soft to hear over the thunderous worries that wracked the farmer's thoughts.

The farmer gave a final and heartfelt bow to the hanged men, wishing them well on whatever road they travelled now. Alaria gave a worried screech and pulled hard against the plaited ribbons of her leash.

She's scared. But then she scares so easily; perhaps it was just a fox.

Alaria misliked wolves and foxes. She ate weasels, rats, rabbits and small birds. But she turned coward when faced with anything larger—retreating into her wings and sounding her warnings from there.

Or perhaps she knows where she's going. He thought sadly.

"I do not do this for choice," he said to the beast. He avoided using her name when he could, it felt thick in his throat. "Do understand. I'd have you stay with us for all your days, but I have no choice. None." She resisted still, cawing and screeching her defiance.

"Behave, you horrible bird! Behave!" The farmer commanded, to little avail. "You'll make this journey take double the time, but you shan't change its destination. I am sorry. I truly am. Do understand that, please!"

"Begging of a beast," a voice came from behind as the farmer felt the cold touch of steel against his neck.

Bundon, you fool. He winced at his own folly. *She gave you fair warning, and you had not the wits to take it.*

"Turn around." The voice ordered. There was music to the voice, a colourful accent. One the farmer had never encountered before. Bundon took a deep breath and turned to face his attacker. And he was not alone.

There were five of them. Short men. The tallest coming up only to the farmer's chin. But as small as they were, he would not wish to anger a single one. They were lithe and athletic, with dark, hate-filled eyes. They were sour-faced, with skin of pale leather, in both colour and complexion. They had long silver hair, worn in an array of foreign fashions the farmer had ne'er seen before. Intricate plaits and braids, all secured with copper rings and humble ornamentation of onyx and malachite. Ornamentation that accentuated the impressive point of their ears.

Elves.

The farmer paled and thought himself as good as dead. The courtesy of elves was not held in high esteem. They waylaid honest travellers in the stories his mother had told him. And the farmer judged them to be such elves, by the odd recurved bows on their backs, the dirks on their belts and the long, serrated blade that was being held to his throat.

They wore armour of thick horsehide, with exquisite woollen cloaks of richly dyed crimsons, purples and greens. The likenesses of beasts and monsters embroidered onto every inch of them. Great, howling wolves, majestic silver moths, dragons of gold and too many horses to count. Horses that looked much like the three horses they led. Grey, dappled beasts, with long elegant faces and legs; lithe and powerful. Saddled, not with leather, but with the hides of wild cats and beautiful blankets of rich cottons and painted silks. A sixth soul sat a different horse —a beautiful chestnut mare. The man atop it was a stranger, though not a complete stranger. He recognised the face, grubby and gagged as it was. And it was not elven.

They all looked at him now, elf, horse and man alike.

"I mean no harm," the farmer said, holding up his hands but still holding tight to Alaria's reins. "I want no trouble with faerish folk. I have a daughter back home. If I do not return—"

"These three gave similar excuses," their leader said, looking over the hanged men. "But here they hang."

By my fire, they mean to hang me. Alaria screeched behind him, attracting the elves' attention. *Oh, be brave you, foolish bird. Be brave.*

"A fald," one said. "Must be worth a lot to someone."

"But not us, I fear," the leader said, his manner more sad than angry. "If we were to steal it, where would we sell it? We cannot even trade within their settlements. Not that we have anything of worth to them. No. No, I think just gold will suffice."

"Gold?" The farmer panicked. "Fire save me, I have no gold! I have naught but—"

"Naught but that dagger," another said, laying an arrow across the string of his bow. "Looks a mighty weapon to me."

"Take it!" The farmer urged, taking the dagger from his belt and throwing it to the feet of the elves. "It is not even mine, and I care not for the man it belongs to. He owes me much, this can make a start of it."

The elves exchanged a look of intrigue and shared a laugh. They spoke some words together, words the farmer could make no sense of. Their leader took the dagger from the ground and looked over it curiously. His eyes then fell back to Bundon, who gingerly put his hands back into the air.

"What's your name?" he asked simply.

"Bundon, if it pleases m'lord. Farmer Bundon."

"The picture of courtesy," the elf laughed. He stared at Bundon, long and hard, as though he were a riddle to be solved. After a time, the elf squinted, shook his head with a snort of laughter and handed the dagger back.

"My name is Evelys-o-Dah. And I cannot, in good faith, take this from you." One of his men shouted some words in their tongue, and Evelys shot back a short but stern reply.

"Sir," Bundon began.

"You said you have a daughter," he asked. "What's her name?"

"Tyr, sir," Bundon answered dutifully. "Tyr'Dalka, if it pleases—" But the elves were chuckling and sharing odd looks, which quite distracted the farmer from his words.

"Truly?" Evelys asked. "And why did you pick such a name?"

Bundon could not think. It was her name. That's all it had come to mean now.

Tyr for when she's good, Tyr'Dalka for when she's bad. He felt he should hurry and give some answer; he felt on borrowed time as it was.

"She's my world," he said. "My whole world. She is all I have."

"All you have. Could it be we've found an honest soul in a land of dragons?" The elf smiled warmly and sheathed his serrated blade. The jagged edges rattled against the metal of the scabbard. When their captain stowed his weapon, the others did the same, though not nearly so graciously.

"And what brings an honest farmer and his fald to the westward roads? Nothing lies this way but hovels, haystacks and hubris."

"It'd be the hubris, sirs; I am on my way to Lady DeGrissier's estate." Bundon felt a fool telling the truth so openly, he thought the whole affair reeked of secrecy and subterfuge, but he had made no oaths or promises. *And I shan't fall to thinking simple honesty a folly. Lies are like footsteps, everyone a little easier than the last. But the more you take, the harder to find your way back home.* That had been his pa's best advice, it did not have the same melody as his mam's. But it kept Bundon honest enough.

The elves exchanged wary looks.

"Lady DeGrissier," Evelys repeated and then spat at mention of her name. "She needs a dagger through the heart, that one. You have our leave to do so."

"I'm no murderer, master elf," Bundon assured him.

"No? More's the pity," the elf laughed softly to himself. "But you'd be disappointed. I doubt that she-dragon even *has* a heart."

"If she be a dragon," Bundon quipped. "Her heart is in her hoard." The elves shared a laugh over that.

"There is truth in that, Farmer Bundon," the elf captain chuckled and then eyed the fald over the farmer's shoulder. "To sell or return?"

"Exchange," the farmer answered sadly, laying a hand on the fald's rocky crest. "But not for choice."

"There is always a choice," Evelys whispered gleefully. "Come, share our fish and fire. The road is a dangerous one come nightfall." The elf spoke in such a way that Bundon felt he could not refuse. The elves readied their horses and set off. Bundon shared a worried glance with Alaria before bidding the hanged men farewell and following.

※ ※ ※

Later, around a campfire, a little ways off the track, the elves shared what food they had. Dried, salted fish and fresh berries from the woods. They ate very little, the farmer observed, and so the farmer ate no more than them for fear of seeming greedy.

The five elves seemed content with their own company, laughing and joking in their own foreign tongue. Shooting wary glances the farmer's way to make sure there was no trickery afoot.

The sixth man, the one bound and gagged, sat with them now. His hands were still bound tightly with hempen rope, but his gag now lay, sodden, around his neck. And he ate as much as he could. Using all the energy he had left to stuff his face with flaky, white fish. He was ragged and dirty. His linen shirt damp and filthy from the road. His lank blond curls were greasy, and his skin was taut across his skull, with gaunt cheeks and shadowy eyes.

"Sir," the farmer whispered as quietly as he could. "Are you their prisoner?" The gaunt man stopped eating for a moment, gave Bundon a sullen, defiant look and raised his bound hands in answer.

"Ah," the farmer nodded. "Forgive me, sir. But I know your face."

"And I know yours," he said back, giving Bundon a weary look. "I saw you at Dalkaford… at the Harvestman's Festival last month. You, that beast… and your daughter, I think. Lovely girl." The ragged man attempted a smile, but he lacked the energy to sustain it.

Lovely. The farmer thought with narrowed eyes. His daughter *was* lovely; he knew that well enough. But he had been youthful once and knew all too well what 'lovely' meant coming from a young man's lips. He had used it himself a hundred times to put a gentle veil over far less gentlemanly thoughts. But the farmer chose to ignore it.

"What did you do, sir? If you don't mind my asking?"

"Those three that were hanged, back at the roadside, they were Riverguard, the one's employed by the lady of the isle. Black chain and red cloaks," the young man explained. "They were midway through robbing me when the elves fell upon them. Only our Dragon knows why they spared me; perhaps they hope I am worthy of some ransom. But they shall be sorely disappointed. I am worth very little, I'm afraid." He grew thoughtful before going back to his food.

Even DeGrissier's Riverguard is poisoned. Is there nothing she touches that does not rot where it stands? He had been stopped a few times himself by the Redcloaks as he journeyed from bank to barn and back again. Taking only his share, mind. Less, in fact, when his rain stores had been plentiful. But they had been drunk dry some long, sweltering months back.

Cows are thirsty beasts. And it's thirsty work wrangling them. Bundon handed the young knight his waterskin, who eyed it warily but a moment before taking it eagerly and drinking his fill.

"It seems odd to save a man from robbery, only to murder him straight after," Bundon tried to sound reassuring, but he himself was unsure what the elves intended.

Elves are rogues and scoundrel;, trust them not. They had invited him to join their fire, and he had felt compelled to do so for fear of what they might do should he refuse. But they did not bind his hands nor gag him. They did not take Alaria's reins away either, and the great beast had even seemed comfortable in their company.

She is usually so wary of strangers. Bundon puzzled. But there she sat, curled up and content by the fire, snoring softly into her chest.

"Perhaps they mean us no harm," the farmer put forward. The boy scoffed.

"See their horses? Their bows? These are not just any elves, my friend. They're from the continent. They're goblins."

The chatter from around the fire suddenly silenced as the five elves turned their gaze to the ragged man, eyes filled with poison.

"What did you say?" Evelys demanded. "No. Do say it again, I insist."

"Am I wrong?" The man asked, with his best attempt at courage.

"Right and wrong in equal measure," the elf answered, getting to his feet and walking slowly to the weary man and staring down at him with studious eyes. "That is a name for us. A common one. But not a fair one. Nor one we are fond of."

"Sirs, he meant no offence," the farmer insisted. "We are scared and weary from the road." The elf thought that over for a time while the gaunt man puffed his chest and tried to look bold. The sight of him clearly irked the elf.

"Those men might have killed you, boy," Evelys gave with a sneer of contempt. "I saw none of this mummer's pride then."

"You need not have hanged them," the boy gave sullenly.

"You gave no protest at the time," Evelys smirked. "Or do you mean to say that it was moral conscience that stayed thy blade in place of fear?"

The boy said nothing to that, only averted his eyes and grew sheepish.

"Each of them, those *men* on the roadside, had looked mercy in the face and seen fit to ignore it. Taking water from those that need it. Taking coin from those that have it. Dealing justice while lacking a just heart. They'd have killed you, boy, if there was profit to be had from it." Evelys squatted, making the young knight meet his gaze. "Would you have done the same in their boots, I wonder?"

"I'm no murderer," the boy gave timidly. The elf captain nodded uncertainly.

"There is a grain of truth to that. Just a grain. A longing, perhaps. But it's enough, and that is why those ropes are tied about your wrists, not your neck. For now."

"For now?" Bundon asked,

"For now. Yes. Do you question, Master Bundon, why we keep this man alive at all?" The elf asked.

"I would wonder more why you'd harm him, sir; he seems a decent sort to me," Bundon answered; the young man looked across at the farmer with a look of humbled, if not a little bemused, gratitude.

"Does he?" The elf smirked. A wicked smirk that suggested some long-forgotten wisdom. Evelys turned to his companions and clapped his hands together grandly, making the farmer jump. The elves laughed and scooted closer to listen. "A test then. To see if you are right. A game of choice."

Evelys sat before them, hands on his knees, his back to the fire, casting his long shadow across the both of them.

"Sir knight, you first. You stand upon a hill, looking down upon two fields below. In one, there are one-hundred souls, men, women, children of all colours and creeds. Highborn and low. In the other is a single soul. A man, a woman, a child, rich or poor... it makes no matter. With you, on the hill, is a grand ruler, a captain. A king, perhaps. Even a god. He bids you cleanse one field. To kill either a hundred souls or just the one. Which do you choose?"

The young man looked nervously to Bundon, swallowed his worry and answered.

"The one, of course."

"Just the one?" The elf asked, surprised. "Very well. But as you go to do so, he falls to his knees. He begs for his life. He cries out. He beseeches his gods. He offers you all he has to offer so that you might spare his life. He swears he's done nothing wrong. He begs for the sake of his children, his wife. Do you still stand by your decision?"

"I do," the young sir nodded. When the elven captain asked the why of it, the knight shifted in his seat and gave a mumbled answer.

"It is still kinder to kill one soul than a hundred. I'd sooner have less blood on my hands." He thought a moment but nodded decisively. "It is the lesser evil."

"A good answer," the elf gave, making the young man breathe a sigh of relief. "And the one we expected. Farmer Bundon. Your turn. The question is the same. The captain, the king, the god... he bids you kill one, or one-hundred. What do you do?" Bundon had to think on that. He had to visualise it. Map it out in his mind. He imagined his high hill back home, with the one-hundred souls amidst the barleycorn and the single soul amidst the wheat. But then a thought struck him.

"I would ask my king what they had done to deserve such a fate," Bundon said, resolute.

"Nothing." The elf answered with a flicker of a smile. "They have done nothing. But he commands you all the same. Only angrier now, for the asking."

"Then I would choose neither, m'lord."

"Neither?" The elf gasped in mock surprise. "But your king will punish you. He might even make you join one of the fields below and name you as his enemy. Is that truly your decision?"

Fire save me. Am I being a fool? The farmer felt a knot in his guts. But his mind was made.

"Aye," the farmer nodded. "Aye, m'lord, I would choose neither. If that serves as an answer."

"It serves, Farmer Bundon. It serves very well." Evelys stood. "And that, sir knight, is why he is our guest… and you are not."

"That's not fair," the boy protested. "That's not fair! I was not given that option; I thought it had to be one of the two!"

"I gave you a choice, master knight; I said nothing of only two options. That was your king's command, not ours." The elves behind sniggered and started eating again, shaking their heads.

"I would kill no one, given a choice," the young man insisted.

"You always have the choice!" The elf roared, the fire seeming to roar with him, fuelled by a sudden breeze. "It is man's great illusion that life is but a coin toss of a greater or lesser evil. And honest souls can see through it." The elf captain's eyes fell on Bundon, with a nod of solidarity. The breeze calmed, the fire dimmed, and a long silence followed.

"What will become of him?" Bundon asked softly.

"He is not hanged. But he is not free. In earnest, master farmer, we have not decided," the elf drew his dirk, an ancient weapon of shining bronze.

"The world is forged by honest folk doing their duty," Bundon put forward. "A knight's duty is to his liege; he must do as he is bid. Or he won't be a knight for long."

"And would the world mourn the loss of such a man?" He seemed to be sincerely asking, his eyes two black wells, lost in thought, with no hint of white. He flicked the dirk deftly through his fingers, closer and closer to the young knight's face.

"It was dutiful men who torched our caravans, who enslaved our women and children, and cut our brothers down in their thousands with wicked iron blades." Evelys caught Bundon's confusion, and turned to him with a sage nod.

"Iron, yes. The beastly tool of man. It poisons our blood, festers our wounds, cleaves through our bronze and hide as though we wear no armour at all. And whatever magic we once possessed would break against that cruel, unyielding metal. Unfazed."

"I had no hand in the wars against your clans," the knight said, eyes set on the ground. "I had no hand in it, I swear."

"But were you ordered to," the elf seethed, holding the curved, bronze blade to the knight's throat. The young man winced, and his jaw clenched tight. "It would be your duty, no?"

"These grievances are from ages past," Bundon said quickly. "None live now who slew your people. Do you mean to charge all men for the actions of their ancestors? A thousand years dead as they are?"

"The well of elven memory runs deep and dark. We remember much that lesser races seem quick to forget. And we see much, much that man has blinded himself to through these long ages."

"Then it's true," Bundon spoke in a whisper. "Do your kind not age? How old are you?" The elves shared a look, and after a moment, they laughed. Loud. And heartily.

"Once that was the case, or so the singers say," Evelys gave. "But nay, it is just the memory that lives on now. Clear as morning sun. And dark as day's end."

"I wish I could trust my memory as you do," Bundon said back. "For I'd forget the day's numbers if not for my calendar. I'd forget what chores I'd done if not for seeing with my eyes. And I'd forget my favourite tunes if I did not whistle them every day."

"Meaning what?" He asked coldly.

"Meaning, that perhaps it is a false memory. Especially if it is bitterly held. They grow fouler in thought, not merrier."

"Oh, hear that?" Evelys called to his companions. "Bundon has cracked it. Our ancestors are just bitter and bring us bitter memories from the grave." They laughed, though there was no joy in the laughter. Hard and forced. Bundon felt mocked and so said nothing.

"I count three lives on this one's soul," Evelys continued, turning his eyes back to the bound knight. "And the guilt of a fourth."

"And how many souls do you count on yours?" Bundon gave quickly. "I saw three on the roadside. Already you've matched his sum, and I'd wager they're not the first. Nor last."

"Certainly not," Evelys did not look his way, instead holding the dirk ever closer to the knight's quivering face. "Perhaps just one more."

"Stop this. Stop!" Bundon called out. Making Alaria awaken and snort a wary warning at the elves.

Bundon worried for the boy. He had seen the elves' idea of justice upon the westward road, and he would have no part in it. "You are being hateful."

"Hateful?" The elf was taken aback. He withdrew the dirk and settled back down by the fire. He chuckled softly and lay a nurturing hand against the fald's neck, who chirruped her approval. "Do we not have reason to be hateful, Master Farmer?"

"I can't speak to that, master elf, but my mam used to say 'hate all those you've cause to hate, and hate is all you'll know.'"

"Spoken like a soul whose ne'er lost a thing," the elf said darkly.

"I've lost plenty, sir," Bundon said firmly. "Speak of your own pain, if you must. But leave mine be. That's between me and my Noble Dragon."

"Your Noble Dragon," the elf laughed bitterly. "He was our Dragon long before he was yours. But your kind saw fit to steal Him away too. Along with much else. No. No, I think we shall keep hold of this one. Trade his lame horse, rusted arms and patchwork armour for what little they'd sell for and string him up when he becomes a nuisance."

"And that's your decision?" Bundon put forward sternly. "You could let him go, sirs."

"We have not the luxury of such a choice," the elf dismissed.

"You always have a choice," Bundon raised his voice, which he did not like to do. "Don't you?"

"Careful now, farmer," Evelys held his dirk to Bundon now, leaning over the campfire, the flames reflecting perfectly in his black, whiteless eyes. "There is such a thing as *too* honest, be sure it's not mistaken for arrogance. You know nothing of the heart's of elves,nor the heavy grievances we carry."

"If you feel naught but grief in times as such, grief is all you'll know," Bundon gave slowly, as though only just truly understanding the words for the first time. The farmer immediately thought this a regretful thing to say, judging by the open mouths, wide eyes and expectant faces of the elf captain's companions.

Evelys's shadow grew long and dark and seemed to envelop Bundon's whole self. Inside and out. A bitter wind blew, and the fire felt a distant starlight, cold and far away. Alaria sat up for a moment and gave a defiant caw, bringing the elf captain back from his wrathful gaze. His shadow melted away, and he wore an almost apologetic look. A look of shock, cut with sadness.

The night grew quiet as the elves watched closely with eager eyes. Evelys lowered his blade after a time, sheathed it behind his back and smirked his particular smirk. The captain's shoulders rounded and relaxed as he picked up a bowl of flaked white fish and began to eat.

"Go when you wish, but the... *knight* is ours," he said, not taking his eyes from his supper. And said not another word all night.

Bundon had half expected to find that elves did not sleep at all. The five of them were up half the night, drinking their sour wines and laughing over stories in their melodious tongue. Bundon had lain his head down and closed his eyes, using the fald's flank as his pillow and her wings as his blanket. Bundon had often woken to find Tyr asleep in such a way, curled up with Alaria in the granary. It wasn't as comfortable as he had hoped, but that only worked in his favour, as he did not wish to sleep while the others slept.

The sky was a wash of browns and greys when the farmer began to rise, the first signs of dawn glittering to the east. The elf captain had lingered, awake, and thoughtful. Musing, clearly, on the words and conflict that had risen earlier in the night. As he lay, staring into the dwindling embers, he puffed thoughtfully on a long clay pipe, moulded into the shape of a russet dragon, breathing a steady tendril of smoke. He was singing, in the common trade speak too, not his lyrical native tongue. It seemed a merry song that sang of high hopes and fresh mornings. He seemed to be smiling sweetly to himself, and the farmer would have thought the elf in good spirits, save for the tears that caught in the faerishman's eyes.

"Why do you weep, master elf," Bundon spoke in a whisper. "It seemed a jolly tune to me."

"*Hiraethi*," the elf mused with drooping eyes. "The sorrow that follows after a taste of pure joy, or the joy that follows after a spell of deep sorrow. One cannot know one without the other." He lifted his eyes then, but for a moment, giving the farmer a knowing look. Those words struck Bundon; he had often wondered if there were a word for that feeling. For it seemed in recent years that sorrow and joy had become one thing to him. He seldom felt one without the other. The farmer thought in silence.

There is great wisdom in the elves. One I had not thought to find.

"You should get some sleep," the captain gave, closing his eyes while still puffing on his pipe.

"Dawn heralds fresh perspective."

❋ ❋ ❋

When the farmer felt sure that Master Evelys-o-Dah was asleep, he began his quick scape. Bundon removed his boots slowly, tying the laces together and hanging them over his shoulder. He lay a soft hand on the fald's dozing head, and her eyes shot open, two flecks of shining gold.

Stay silent, horrible bird, stay silent. He urged wordlessly.

The five elves slept noiselessly. Spread around the smouldering remnants of the evening's embers.

In the stories, elves never sleep. They gaze longingly toward the night sky and rest their weary souls amongst the stars. But that was clearly not the case. Bundon wondered what other elven magics were just tall-tales. They slept like men, rode like men, drank like men. They sang better than men, true enough. But they were the same bawdy songs, with the same ribald japes following after.

Could it be the world hates them for naught but the point of their ears? Bundon dismissed the thought with a shake of his head. It was too early for such complex thinking, and he had no sleep save for the moments he caught himself playing his part too convincingly.

Had I been any other soul, they might have hanged me the same as those robbers. The thought made his guts tighten and cramp, and then his eyes fell over the sleeping knight. His arms suspended above his head, tied to a low branch of a dead yew tree. The sight of it gave the farmer pause.

You have business to attend to, farmer. He tried to think. *If they should awaken and find him gone, they might well hunt you down. And then where would that leave your poor family?*

Alaria rose quietly. For such a large beast, she was remarkably moss footed. She prowled low to the ground, her great claws barely making any noise at all. She cocked her head from side to side, staring eagerly at the farmer. Bundon drew out the salted fish he'd saved from his supper and fed the hungry fald.

"Come on, you poor bird. This way." The fald, now with the promise of food, was even more eager. Prodding at the farmer's breast with her sharp beak. The farmer batted her away and took hold of her reins. But Bundon paused again. Turning to look at the young knight.

I'm worth very little, I'm afraid. He remembered the knight saying. He had seemed so gallant in the square, that long, long month gone. The farmer eyed the knight's horse, where all his arms and armour had been stowed.

Go. Go now. If they awaken, they might well change their minds and see you hanged. But the farmer did not move. Something was halting his progress. A dagger in his insides.

I am worth very little, I'm afraid. He heard the knight say again, and, without much thought, he untied the blood bay and led him to the knight's side.

What are you doing, foolish farmer? What are you doing?

Oh, hush. He told himself as he drew the bejewelled dagger from his belt and cut the knight's bonds. The young man was still half asleep when his eyes fluttered open, shielding his eyes from the fresh light of dawn and seeing his wrists free of restraint. The knight was suddenly awake, a mix of fear and joy and unbidden tears marking his face. The farmer put a finger to his own lips and told the knight to shush. The knight mimicked the action and nodded a silent understanding.

He clambered clumsily onto his saddle, throwing fearful looks toward the campfire every moment he could spare.

"Ride with all haste, sir knight. Their steeds look to be a spirited breed; I shouldn't chance a race against them." Bundon whispered. The knight looked struck but said no words. "Go. Go now. Before they awaken."

"I'll not forget this," the knight whispered back. "Fly, Duchess. Fly." He pushed the horse into a gallop and cut through the trees, back towards the road. The knight turned in his saddle and gave the farmer a final nod of thanks before disappearing into the woodland.

The farmer breathed a sigh of relief, scratched Alaria under her chin and turned his gaze westwards to join back onto the road.

"A brave soul, as well as honest," a lyrical voice spoke. "Good Farmer Bundon, I am lost for words. Are you so incorruptible as that?" Bundon turned suddenly and saw Evelys tending to his horse, not looking the farmer's way at all. *He must not have slept at all, merely closing his eyes to see me fooled.*

The elf lay a boar's bristle brush against the dappled grey coat and whispered some soft elven words in the beast's ear.

"Take the dagger," the farmer said, holding the jewelled hilt out for the elf to take. The captain stood straight and regarded the blade a moment. "I'll not be guilty of ridding you of the coin his arms and armour would have bought you. Take it."

"You might find better use holding it the other way," the elf grinned, returning his attention back to his horse. "It is far more effective, I find."

"I'm no murderer, master elf," Bundon said coldly. The faerishman laughed aloud, making his companions stir beneath their blankets.

"Killing elven bandits." He ran a careful hand down one of the steed's back legs, to his fetlock, where the horse obeyed and lifted his hoof. The bronze shoe was worn and caked in mud, but with a delicate copper hoof-pick, his master set about clearing it. "Most would not call that murder."

The elf captain shouted some words at the four stirring souls, who were beginning to notice their sudden lack of a prisoner.

"Most elven bandits would have hanged me when first they found me," the farmer gave back. "I'll not repay mercy with bloodshed." The elf captain laughed again and shook his head.

"Go, Master Bundon. Be on your way."

"You'll take the dagger," Bundon said.

"No."

"I'll not be called a thief, sir," Bundon warned. "This would fetch a fine price."

"I'll not take it. Just promise me this," the elf began. He lowered the horse's hoof and dusted his worn and calloused hands on his dirtied breeches. His black, whiteless eyes stared sternly into the farmers. "When the time comes, plant it in DeGrissier's glittering, gluttonous heart. Be it within a chest of gold and mahogany, or one of blood and bone."

"Sir, I am no murderer, as I said."

The elf captain laughed again, dismissing the farmer with another shake of his head. His hundred grey plaits and their bronze beads chimed against another. He lay his hands to another of the horse's hoofs.

"Be on your way, Master Bundon. Your journey does not end here."

"I thank you, sirs. Truly." Bundon placed his boots back on; now, the need for stealth was long past. He gathered his belongings and took firm hold of Alaria's reins.

"Do not thank us, farmer," the elf chuckled. "I feel a queer sense of fate surrounding you. Yes. Yes, for a certainty." He glanced up one last time and met the farmer's eyes.

"There is a touch of destiny to you."

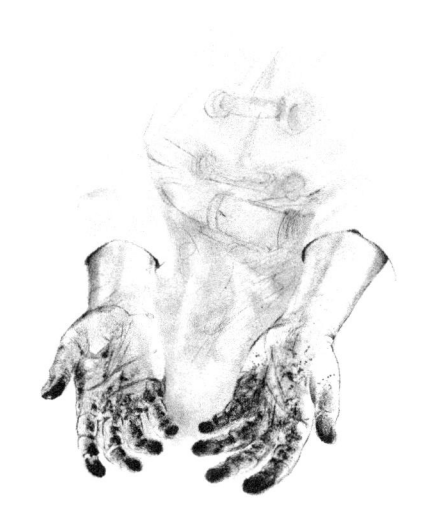

BUNDON V

The Seventeenth Day in the Month of High Sun

*E**lves are rogues and scoundrels.* His mam had told him, and his pa—many times. Every time, in fact, whene'er they were mentioned.

"Elves?" They'd always ask, shocked at their mere mention. "Elves are naught but rogues and scoundrels. Trust them not." Bundon had thought this good advice. Rogues and scoundrels were the last sorts of folk you should lay any trust upon; that was plain.

And yet. The farmer pondered. *Ragtag elves. Self-proclaimed bandits. They showed great decency even in the face of my deceit.*

And it was man, not elf, that ransomed his family now. His foulest treatments had all come from the hands of man.

And woman.

His timid companion let out a wheeze and the faintest suggestion of a screech and then clacked at the back of her throat horribly. The farmer lay a gentle hand to her neck.

I know, I know. I grow a thirst too. This heat could fell a phoenix, I'm sure.

The farmer had found a shallow brook and led the thirsty fald to its edge, where she started lapping up the mirky water greedily.

"Drink up, that's a good girl," he mumbled to her, patting her shoulder softly. He dared not drink the water himself; his bowels felt unhappy enough as they were. It was a silty stream, dusty, with a queer brown-grey foam that floated atop its surface.

"Drink your fill, girl. This sun is like to bake it to hard, cracked mud by day's end." He removed his straw hat and dabbed at his sweaty forehead with his sleeve. He took in the view around him. They were rising out of the Ploughman's Vale now; the roads were steeper and a harder trek than the lower lands.

"We should be there by day's end," the farmer said softly, to himself as much as Alaria. "There's the smell of nutmeg on the air, smell it? We're nearing the old slavery fields. It's but a few hours from there; perhaps we'll detour to Buckbridge on the way back, enjoy a night of rest at a proper inn. Haven't stayed there since my rambling days. They used to have this mead there, the honey wine the Brentirimen drink—" He looked sadly at the fald when he remembered.

Of course, she will not be with me for the journey home. Bundon felt the pain of that every time he thought on it. More for the pain his daughter would feel rather than his own. He heaved a sullen sigh, put the cap back on his head and guided Alaria back to the road.

But from the thicketed woodland beside the brook came a noise. A clanking. The heavy rattle of chain. And something else. A voice. A hushed voice muttering stifled curses.

Brigands. Rogues. Scoundrels. More elves, perhaps. These

might not be so kindly as the last. Bundon swallowed his fears and decided to flee before the hushed voice heard him. But his haste betrayed him when he stepped heavily on a dried branch.

Crack. It rang out, impossibly loud for something so small. Bundon held his breath and closed his eyes to listen harder. The rattle of chain had stopped. So had the voice. He stayed still, as though any movement might reveal him. After a moment, the rattling continued, and so did the curses.

Thank the fire. Bundon prayed silently before Alaria reared onto her talons and let out a deafening cry.

Screeeeeech. Screech. Screeeech. She cawed to the sky and flapped her grand wings, the force of which buffeted Bundon to the ground. The fald was beastly strong, though you'd never guess it from her timorous manner.

Bundon, in a hurried blur, scurried back to his feet and turned fretfully to the thicket, drawing his gilded dagger and praying he had courage enough to use it, should the need arise.

"Farmer? Is that you?" The voice asked, in a tone that would have sounded bold, save for the juvenile crack at the end of it. He knew the voice and breathed out a sigh of relief.

"Sir Knight," he answered. "Aye, it's me. Where are you at?"

"I am amongst the bracken, my good man. Hold there. I… I shan't be a moment." The farmer shared a look with Alaria, who seemed as confused as he was. He waited for a time. Listening to the desperate grunts and rustling chain emanating from the thicket.

"Sir, are you quite alright?" he asked, long after the farmer's generous measure of a moment had passed.

"Never better," he answered. "It is the buckles behind the, um, behind the shoulder, they—damn and blast— they are a little hard to reach."

"I have hands, Sir Knight if you're in need of some assistance," the farmer offered.

"No need; you have done quite enough. I just have to, almost— fire take you!" The knight continued. Bundon, after a time, approached the thicket and moved some dried branches from his path. Behind them was a half-dressed knight. His chainmail was donned, as was his sword belt, but he wore no breeches, nor boots, greaves or gauntlets. His bare, pale legs, looking impossibly thin, stretched from the rusty mail, ending in two filthy bare feet. His pauldrons clattered against the chain as he fumbled to buckle them behind his back.

"Sir," he said, hanging his head. "I am defeated." He reddened when he saw the farmer.

"You have need of a squire, sir," Bundon chuckled, tying Alaria's reins to a low branch and setting his hands to the buckles. "And before you ask, no, I am too old for such things now."

"Freelancer's squires are short-lived, sadly," the knight shifted where he sat, giving the farmer an easier reach. "I thought I'd best armour myself in case my captors came looking for me."

"They're not looking for you," the farmer assured. "They scarce seemed to mind, to tell the truth. Perhaps they ne'er meant you harm, only wishing to see you humbled, not hanged."

"Well, they succeeded on that front," the knight said miserably. Bundon was buckling the pauldrons under the arms and across the back when his finger fell across a gap in the knight's mail, delving into the thick doublet beneath. Dried blood still stained the wool. It was a large gash, of near six inches, right between the shoulder blades. His rough fingers traced the shape of it.

"The wound from such a blow must have near felled you, sir," he gave. "You must be tough as an ox."

"It's been said," the knight laughed. "Aye. Yes. That was a foul one. A Brentiri's axe blow. Did more harm to my mail than me, thankfully. But yes. What a scar. But every scar is a story, Farmer Bundon."

"My pa used to say the same," Bundon grinned and rolled up his sleeve to reveal the long, white streak up his forearm. The memory of the cut made him shudder. "When your father says not to enter the bull's pen, it's best to listen, I find."

"Aha, but the whole world is a bull's pen for a knight, my good man. Always great deeds to be done and grand stories to tell. Tell me truthfully, do you not take pride in the scar?"

"The pride of learning one's own folly, I suppose," the farmer nodded. "But I'd sooner have listened and saved myself the pain."

"I have scars like that one all over. From swords, axes, arrows. Scorned lovers." He gave a wry smile and chuckled to himself. "I took an arrow to the thigh once, wrenched the head free myself. Left an ugly scar. But then, ladies are said to like a man's scars." The knight laughed again. Bundon smiled to see some of the young man's gallantry returning, even if his humour was not to the farmer's taste.

"That they do, sir, that they do." It felt good to laugh, even in the blistering heat with all the worries of the world on his shoulders. He had forgotten how freeing it could feel, even in the face of such hardship.

The knight pulled on his breeches, patched as they were. And darned. But contriving, still, to be threadbare. His scuffed riding boots went on after that, with the toes peeling away from the leather foxing. And over those, he buckled his greaves; plates of dinted steel spotted with rust and spatters of mud. When all was done, the knight fastened a black cloak of old, moth-eaten fustian around his shoulders and turned to the farmer with an eager smile.

"You have saved me once again, master farmer," the knight laughed, sheathing his longsword and resting his hand on the pommel. "My name is Sir Willem. Sir Willem Gull. Knighted by Good King Doryn himself, beneath the stricken banners of Brentir."

"A King's man!" The farmer beamed. "The honour is mine, then, good sir. I had heard tell that King Doryn only knighted those who joined ranks for his third crusade? What grand quest brings you to Rhothodân?"

"Ah, yes. Yes. He does, for the most part. But there are those of us he sends forth to serve the realm. There is great honour in seeing the small folk safe. King Doryn himself told me that. Hold, Farmer. Wait a moment. You have saved me, not once, but twice. Where are you heading?"

"Sir, don't trouble yourself—"

"I insist."

The farmer felt he had no choice. "The old slaver estates, following westwards, then eastwards o'er the Dalkamont's rise." He pointed over yonder.

"I know the way," he beamed. "I shall be your guide. I owe you a great debt, after all."

A great debt? The farmer dared to hope. *A king's knight indebted to me.* He eyed his new protector curiously as he mounted his tired horse and started down the west road.

But what measure of a man is he?

"I bet you have a tale or two to tell, Sir Willem," the farmer called after the knight.

And the farmer was not wrong.

* * *

Impressions are like kisses. They can be good; they can be poor. But the first one is always the worst. Bundon remembered his mam's words as he walked with the knight, Sir Willem Gull.

When the farmer first saw the young man, trussed and gagged and greasy, he had never expected the sort of flamboyant soul he might be. But with a splash of water on his face, a set of chainmail about him and a horse beneath him… he was a different man. He bore great skill as a whistler, a skill he was not shy in demonstrating. Ofttimes Alaria joined her trilling to his, but those songs were thankfully brief. In between tunes, though, he would regale the farmer with stories from his many adventures. The farmer liked those best of all. The songs, after a time, got a little much.

"I was at the Battle of the Green Tongue when Doryn himself faced the northern usurpers. Clans of Blackwood, Grey-marsh, Whitehare and Honeyhill. But it was on that day that the black trees were felled. The green toads were skewered. The white rabbits; snared. And the brown bees now make their honey for better men." The gentle knight's tale was a lyrical thing, refined and perfected with each detailed and frequent retelling. "I saw old Jarl Ülver Blackwood, the one they called Bloodbark, breakthrough our ranks of billmen, making a final push for the king. To cut the head off the snake, as they say. But I could not allow that. No, sir. Not Good King Doryn.

"So I sallied forth and crossed blades with the Bloodbark himself. Near seventy as he was, he was still a vicious old mongrel of six-and-a-half feet. Arms like two, great hairy oaken branches. His great helm was filled with blood, and when he donned the steel, it showered down his shoulders like a crimson mantel, matting with his great beard and wild hair.

"It was a dance. A dance more beautiful than any I'd shared with a lady. He fought with twin axes, those Brentiri sorts with the great long-bearded blades. I had only my trusty sword and a shield that was more hole than wood. Three times the Jarl Blackwood struck me. Just three. Once across the left arm, splintering what little remained of my shield. The second; a graze across my elbow. The third, that havoc between my shoulders.

"He thought he'd struck a felling blow and assumed me killed. He left me, crumpled over as he cried out his victory. But, while bleeding at his feet, I raised my sword. And one strike was all I needed. Planting my steel up beneath his ribs and through the Bloodbark's heart. King Doryn had watched the dance and witnessed my valour. He saw that his own royal surgeons tend me. To clean my wounds and sew me back up. And when I was strong enough to kneel, the king bid me do so. And knighted me. Right there, on the battlefield. His murder cawed our victory, the princely ravens that follow our good king. And the field came alive with the chants of 'Gull! Gull! Gull!'.

"It was the finest day of my life," the knight concluded thoughtfully.

"And our Good King actually spoke to you?" Bundon

smiled widely. "Might I ask you, sir, what kind of man he is? Is he truly as good as they say?"

"No, Farmer Bundon," the knight sighed and smiled. "He is better."

Perhaps this knight is the answer to my prayers. Bundon thought more than once. He was well connected with friends and acquaintances in half the lordly courts of the mainland. Bundon had little to boast about, but he made mention of Sir Geiger Greenwater's visit to try and impress the gallant knight.

"Geiger Greenwater," Willem repeated the name, thinking it over. "Yes. Yes, I had the honour of feasting with Clan Greenwater at their new lordly seat of Black Harbour. There was a melee for the Jarl's ashening, his sixtieth or sixty-fifth. A grand age. I, while not boasting to have won, did break four of Sir Geiger's shields. And got closer than any other man to felling the Black Fox himself. He was so impressed that he invited me to dine with him and his at the high table. There were even talks of a match with his daughter, but alas—"

"The Lady Aethel," Bundon chimed but felt confused all at once. "He spoke of her. But she must be four-and-forty now. And married, besides."

"Aye. Yes. A widow, sadly, now. But still a handsome woman. And she certainly took a shine to me." The young knight raised his eyebrows and let out a dramatic sigh. "But alas, as I was saying, she was bound to another. Another of gentler birth than mine own. So our match was but a brief one. One night, in fact." The young knight flushed, chuckled softly and gave the farmer a knowing smile. Bundon shook his head but could not help but join the knight in his laughter.

Go on, farmer. Ask him. He owes you, he said as much. Go. Be brave. Ask. The farmer cleared his throat and stopped on the road.

"Sir," he said. "Might I have a moment?"

Sir Willem turned in his saddle and slowed his horse to a halt. Trotting back a few paces to join the farmer's side. "Of course, my friend. What troubles you?"

"You are a gallant knight, sir," Bundon put forward. "With ties and oaths and bonds of friendship that would put my meagre lot to shame. You serve our king. You see justice served in his name. And me and my family are in a beastly bind, sir. A beastly bind." The farmer went on and explained all to the young knight. Every detail. Tyr's dance. DeGrissier's visit. Gold and fire. The dagger in the door. Brynhilde's note. The Temple's dismissal. All of it. He retrieved the thick vellum scroll from his pack and held it out for the knight to read.

"I never took to reading and writing, but I am sure a knight such as you were taught young and under fine tutelage."

The knight said nothing, but gave a slow, thoughtful nod. His eyes darted left and right over the words, and after a moment, he handed the letter back and thoughtfully muttered, "I see."

"So, I've been doing some thinking, sir. And thought that perhaps, with such highly esteemed connections, you might see your way to having a talk with our local Krillian. He shares a kinship with the king. His cousin, I think. Great cousin, by blood too, not marriage. He will heed the words of a knight in his service, more so than a simple farmer and his plight." Bundon did not wish to stop talking as he saw the doubts and waverings creasing across the freelancer's forehead.

If I keep talking, perhaps some words will instil his valour.

"I know it is a kingly request, sir, I know. But I have no other paths to take. I'd sooner not part with my companion here. She is much loved by my daughter," the farmer lay a comforting hand on the fald's crest, and she nuzzled her great, rocky beak into the nook of his underarm, letting out a few quiet trills. The knight watched this his face still creased with doubt.

"The Krillian, you say," Sir Willem sniffed. "Yes. Yes, I know the man. And he is not fond of me; I am sorry to say." The farmer made no attempt to hide his disappointment.

"Why is that, sir?" He asked glumly.

"I once found myself taking holy vows and even got so far as midway through my trials." He said proudly. "So I'm not a priest, exactly, but rather I'm half a priest if you like. Half a year of prayer and silence and smoking those sickly smokes. The Krillian said I had promise, but I was bought into service by that ceaseless call to adventure instead. The Krillian was so wroth that he forbade it and challenged me. Aye. Indeed. That is how I broke his arm in a duel last spring. He was so irked by his defeat that he refused—"

"Last spring?" The farmer asked.

"Aye, sir. I think so. Or the spring before." The knight let out a snigger as he recalled. "Yes. I remember now, the temple's Brothers were all so surprised by my victory—"

"Surprised?" The farmer puzzled. "But the Krillian is an old man. Closer to ninety than eighty. And I never heard tell of him being much of a warrior."

"Aye, nor had I, to tell the truth," the knight gave a snort. "But the old goat was beastly strong for his age. Apologies, Master Bundon, but I fear the sight of me will do naught by anger him further." Bundon hung his head and continued down the road wordlessly.

"But perhaps," Sir Willem began, making the farmer turn his head and bare the beginnings of a hopeful smile. "Perhaps I would have more luck with this Lady DeGrissier. She is unknown to me, save in passing. I could have words with her and her son if that suits you? I owe you a great debt, after all."

"You would do that, sir?" Bundon beamed. "I would be forever in your debt, sir, forever. It would be a kindness the likes of which I have never known. Thank you. Thank you!" The farmer rushed the knight's side, cupping Sir Willem's hands in his own and holding them firm.

"I make no promises, Master Bundon," the knight looked troubled for a moment, but his usual, easy laughter came quickly. "But I will do all I can. Perhaps after that, I might have a proper audience with your daughter."

"Tyr?" The farmer asked. "Tyr is just a girl."

"But a beauty," the knight gave, making the farmer swell with pride.

"Aye, a beauty," he laughed. "She takes after her mother in that regard, thankfully. And her mother had good blood. Yeoman blood. But should a priest have such intentions?"

"Half a priest," the knight corrected.

"Then, sir, I'd say only half of you can marry her," the farmer laughed.

"Aye, but which half? I know my preference." The knight snorted his laughter, and the farmer sighed. He had heard tell of the clever tongues of nobility. A glibness, a wickedness and a charm, all rolled into one. He envied it in truth. Bundon's words always felt clumsy, no matter how much care he took to say them.

"You've a sharp tongue, master knight," the farmer allowed and gave the young sir a long, wary look. "It will take more than that to steal my Tyr away. But. Sir. You do have my leave to try."

"My good Farmer Bundon," the knight cocked his head to one side and gave a wry smile. "Are you giving me your blessings?"

The farmer could not help but snort himself now.

"My blessings are easily given; it is hers you'll have the trouble with. Just ask our gallant Lord Anguis." The memory of the pink toad made the farmer bristle. "I do urge caution with that one, sir, if you do happen to have words with him. And his mother more so. Their common decency is left… wanting, I'd say."

"Such a scolding critique," Sir Willem chuckled. "I was beginning to think you had not a bad word to say about anything."

"Bad words are bad words, no matter their reasoning. I'd sooner save my breath for the good ones." Bundon beamed. *Good ol' mam.*

The knight suddenly bore a sullen expression. A look that told tales of the dour, voiceless thoughts within.

"You're a good man, Master Bundon," Sir Willem gave with a stern nod. "I daresay that were you of gentler birth… you'd

133

have the makings of a fine Lord, sir. One that men would be proud to follow."

He means those words. The farmer could see and at once felt humbled.

"And were my cows to breath fire, they might be grand as dragons." The farmer gave a small shrug and a sad grin. "But they're not, sir. They're just cows."

❊ ❊ ❊

They were nearing the old spicer plantations now. The air smelled of nutmeg, grapevines and olive oil. It was the site of another of the Good King's many justices.

A better man than good. Bundon thought pridefully of his king. The farmer remembered his grandpapa's vibrant retelling of when Good King Doryn sundered the chains of all slaves within his kingdom. North Island and South, and all the smaller islands around the middle.

"Great ships of a hundred oars and more landed on our isle's shores!" He'd roar in his booming voice, the one he oft reserved for scaring off foxes. "Us simple farm folk had long been under the foul thumbs of slavers and greedy merchants. Our Good King changed that. Privateers in the service of the crown came and forced those crooked souls into exile and broke the chains and fetters of all those who called them masters. Captain Tarbrand, as he was then, led the assault. Clad in black plate. A morning star in his steel grip. His banners, and the banners of our King, held high throughout their procession. The crossed bones on black, and the black raven on blue.

"The old estates were plundered, and the loot was shared to each man across the isle, highborn or low. Captain Tarbrand was raised to lordship and gifted the port town of King's Anchor for his legal service, and to us honest folk who stayed to work the land, well, we now knew work as free men. With a wage and leave to raise a family. And then two and twenty years of prosperity followed, with temperate seasons and bountiful harvests. It was like the Dragon Himself was showing his thanks.

"And of them estates. Them evil estates, with their fields sown with blood. Well. They are naught but ghostly ruins, with nature vying to take them back." He would always spit at that point. "Nature can have 'em, I say. Let 'em moulder."

As they walked, Bundon saw what remained of the old estates. And nature's vying had been met with hard success, it seemed. The crumpled manses wore raiments of ivy, moss and mould. The woodwork infested with mites, woodworm and a hundred different varieties of mushrooms. Juvenile trees grew determinedly through thatch, beam and gable. While the fields that surrounded them were seas of tall, wild grass.

The wind made them whistle, a tune so high and shrill, the farmer found himself missing the fald's and the knight's discordant songs.

"Nearly there, Master Bundon," the knight called from ahead.

It seems we've been 'nearly there' for almost half the day. Bundon wiped his brow with his sleeve again. Both sleeves were so damp now, the act did very little but smear more sweat across his face. But the damp of the sleeve was pleasingly cool compared to the damp of his forehead, so he persisted with the habit.

With the good knight's words, perhaps she'll see fit to take the farm in the fald's place, as I originally hoped. The farmer busied his thoughts in an attempt to distract himself from the heat. *Or perhaps Sir Willem will speak so valiantly for our cause that she'll forgive the debt entirely.* He scoffed to himself. *Don't be a fool, Bundon. It was that lackwit thinking that got you into this mess.*

The world was full of crooks; the farmer was beginning to learn. He had hoped when all this madness had first started that Lady DeGrissier and her son had simply misunderstood the situation. That perhaps, once their wrath had subsided, they would see their side and take some small mercy upon them.

But in a world of liars, honest folk are nought but fools.

That was not one of his mam's lessons. Nor his pa's. Nor

Alaria's. That was one of his. A lesson all his own. And the learning of it still sat heavy in his gut. It did not fit within the world he thought he lived. The world he *wished* he lived. Where decency was assumed, and intentions never questioned. True, some did a better job of hiding their decency than others. But it was there, all the same. He felt a fool for believing such now.

There are truly wicked souls in the world. Souls who do harm, and wish harm and inspire harm in others. He felt guilty for thinking it. But could scarce deny it, either.

Sir Willem had grown quiet as they walked the ghostly road of those old crumbling estates. They had shared a solid half-a-day's ride together, and every moment had been filled with song, or story. Or both.

But now, the young knight was silent, chewing nervously at his nails and tugging constantly at the small hairs under his chin. He had slowed his pace down, and now lingered a few yards behind the farmer and his fald.

He fears the lady. He thought suddenly. *He said he'd speak to them, but now he fears it as the dawning of it draws closer. And I cannot blame him.*

"You speak well, sir," the farmer turned and called to the knight. "Don't fear them. You're of good birth and in the King's service. They'd be fools to refuse you."

"The world is full of fools." Sir Willem snapped a little more unkindly than the farmer expected. "And liars."

He wore such a sad look, Bundon could not help but feel sorry for the boy. But soon enough he laughed his laugh, arching his lips into a smile. A smile that did not reach his eyes. "Go, hurry. I'll not be far behind."

Bundon thought nothing of it as he turned his head back to the road and continued westwards, the knight still falling behind.

A moment later Bundon heard the ring of steel behind him but assumed it to be the knight's stirrups against his greaves or some such. And not even when he felt the cold point of a sword against his neck did he completely understand.

"I am sorry. Truly." He heard the knight say. And all at once, he understood.

In a world of liars, honest folk are nought but fools.
Fools like you, Bundon. Fools like you

※ ※ ※

"I am worth very little, I'm afraid." He remembered the knight saying.

Those were not the words of a King's knight. Those were not the words of an honoured guest at Jarl Greenwater's table. Nor the words of a temple's initiate, nor a lady's betrothed, nor the runner-up of a lord's tourney. He was false. A *false* knight. The elves had seen it back when Sir Willem was trussed up like a felled boar.

I should have left him there. The farmer cursed himself. *I should have let them hang him. I should have. I should.*

The elves had even said it. They had spied the sort of man he was and found it undesirable.

But you thought you knew better, didn't you, Bundon? And now look.

As the skies grew dark, the boy had guided both farmer and fald into the crumbling remnants of one of the forsaken slaver estates. A hearthstone and a chimney of baked red brick stood solid amidst the mould and crumbling mortar, and that is where they gathered now. Speaking in hushed whispers. Lest they disturb the sleeping.

Alaria was not happy. Bundon could tell. She whined and cawed desperately, encouraging Duchess to whicker and moan with her.

"They will bring the Redcloaks to us if you're not careful," Bundon warned coldly. "But o'course, you would nay mind. You'd call them allies, I s'pose."

"Never," Will spat as he tried his hand at starting a small fire in the hearth. But the wood was damp, and the air around the estate was damp as well. The whole place felt fetid and mouldy. A place where fire dare not tread. "They tried to kill me."

The false-knight had taken the bejewelled dagger from Bundon's belt, and the old farmer saw it glinting at the knight's waist.

I should grab it, he thought wickedly. *I should grab it and stab the traitor.* But he didn't. He didn't even linger long on the thought.

"This changes nothing, really," the knight had tried to say. But Bundon had closed his ears to the false knight's meagre reasons. "Think of it as doing me a favour. You were travelling to deliver the fald anyway if you allow me to deliver the fald *for* you… I might come into some money. I'll share it with you, once away from the walls. We could work this to our advantage; you might as well be paid for your woe."

"Work it how you wish, sir." Bundon felt nothing but a dull ache in his gut and a sharper one at his wrists, where the bonds cut. "But I'll have no hand in it."

Will's face creased with frustration, but whatever words he had wanted to say had stuck in his throat, favouring to stay silent instead.

He has the grace to feel ashamed, at least. The farmer thought, but it did little to prise the knight's dagger from his back. He watched on with petty satisfaction as the young boy struggled with the fire until he threw down his sticks and flint and cursed beneath his breath. The farmer let out a dark laugh, and the boy's eyes shot up; wounded.

"Untie my bonds, and I'll see to the fire if you wish it," Bundon gave, "I've no desire to freeze tonight for the sake of your pride."

"I can start my own fires," Will snapped as he grabbed his tinderbox and tried again with a fiercer determination. Alaria suddenly looked up, out into the darkness and cocked her head curiously from side to side. But there was nothing. Bundon felt his skin turn to goose flesh.

There are old spirits in these damnable ruins. He worried to himself. *I swear, I hear words on the wind.*

"You've paled," Will gave, making Bundon's heart skip a beat.

"There— There's an ill mood to this place," Bundon stuttered out. "Do you not feel it?"

"Always," the boy gave miserably. This irked Bundon. He shifted in his seat and made a grumbling complaint.

"You have a lot of cheek to be so sullen, boy, this is what you wanted, no?" Bundon barked. The boy looked up rather petulantly.

"No,"

"And I am to believe that?"

"It doesn't matter to me what you believe," the boy shot back, letting a lingering look of distaste settle on the farmer before returning to his fizzles and sparks.

"A freelancer who cannot even start his own fires," Bundon tutted. "Was any of what you told me true? Any word of it?" The farmer asked, making the knight bristle.

He has the gall to look almost offended.

"Aye," he answered simply but said no more than that. And silence followed, long and painful to behold. After a time, a spark flew and caught on a clump of dried grass, throwing a plume of grey smoke into the air. Excitedly the knight leant forward and blew on the embers as a little flame flashed into being.

"Ha!" The knight laughed with a beaming grin as he lay some meagre sticks atop his triumph. The fald cawed from outside, ridding the knight of his smile.

"Can you not quieten the beast?" the boy asked. "If the Redcloaks find us before we reach the Lady DeGrissier they will take all the credit themselves."

"I'd favour honest thugs over deceitful friends," Bundon mumbled miserably, and the boy looked struck once more.

"When we meet with the Lady DeGrissier, I shall see no harm comes to you," he gave with an attempt at sincerity, but if he expected the farmer to feel thankful, he was much mistaken. Bundon gave the false knight a hard, unforgiving glance.

"On my honour, sir," the knight's voice cracked, and he flushed red. Turning his attention back to the small fire that was spluttering and dying already.

The farmer had to laugh. "On your honour? Your honour as a false knight? Or a false friend?"

"As a soldier, if nothing else," he said thoughtfully, poking at the embers. "I know what you must think of me—"

"No, boy," the farmer snapped. "If you did, you'd cease these poor attempts at easing your foul conscience."

"Don't call me 'boy'," the knight gave, more glum than angry.

I'll not give you the satisfaction of my forgiveness, sir. Boy. I will not. The farmer looked up at his captor; the boy looked struck when their eyes met.

"You were my last hope," the farmer said gloomily, hoping those words would stay with the turncoat. Bundon turned his head away. Scoffing to say, "I doubt you were ever even a soldier."

"That's enough," the boy barked. "Just... rest, if you can."

Rest. The farmer seethed silently. *Rest, he says. A captive twice over, once to the Lady and her boy, and now to this one. How exactly am I to rest?*

The fire went out, and the boy did not curse. Nor did he try to rekindle it. He just sighed and stood, fetching something from his satchel; the farmer could not make out what. He then walked to his horse, lay a hand on her neck and kissed her softly on the muzzle.

"Good girl," the boy said in a whisper as he fed her the something from his pack. An apple, the farmer realised. And was reminded of his own animals, the late great Meat, grumpy old Veg and slow but sturdy Fruit. And all his cows as well.

My poor animals. Bundon thought. *Neglected beasts, I pray for the day that my greatest concerns are seeing them fed and safe once more.* A thought struck him. *That is dependent, of course, on if I can ever be free of these troubling times.*

They seemed insurmountable now.

I feel little more than an onlooker, just watching as my

world crumbles around me. Bundon looked up and met eyes with the knight, who bashfully looked away. The boy then looked through the hanging vines and half-rotten rafters, eyes upwards to the moon.

"I was a soldier," he said in a new voice, one free of pretence and pomposity. Rougher somehow, with the thick accent of Kraigwyn, the Kingdom's southern island.

"But no. No, I had no knighthood. No ravens cawed my name. No songs were written of my deeds. But I did kill, sir. I did. Not Jarl Bloodbark, no. But a boy, a little younger than me. And a wizened grandfather. And a grizzled old cripple too, with a pitchfork in his hands. Each swung at me first, but I was faster than most, so I stuck 'em. Quick. Before they stuck me. Doesn't make it easier, mind. You think it will when you're on that first long march from home. First battle, you can't spare the time to think on it. Not then and there. Not while the iron is clashing and the arrows are raining down around you... but after. Afterwards, all you have is time. To think. And remember.

"The sergeant who recruited me... I never saw him again after the first month. Lead by another by then. Split into ranks. If you'd a bow, you went with the archers. Had a spear, off to the frontlines with you. Axes, like mine, they were moved about all over. We were given no reasons, no whys, whos or whatfores. After the second month, all my brothers in arms were strangers to me. None of the friends I had listed with remained. They were scattered on the wind across the King's twelve armies. When a year goes by, you start forgetting yourself. You start taking what you need as your wages are late, then later, then late again, and possibly never coming. And you're in enemy lands; they *owe* you for this wretched war they started. But stealings stealing. You know that. You can tell by that ache in yer gut... the one that ain't hunger. After all, their sorry folk need it just as much as you do. But if you don't take it one of the other lads will. And at least if *you* do the stealing... you won't let the sin go further than that. I never thought myself to be a thief, but it were better than starving.

"By the end of the second year, you start seeing faces in your ranks. Faces of those you were fighting not six months earlier. Y'see allegiances are changing. Noble lords are shifting sides. No one tells you. You just notice. Your enemies are now your friends, and some of your friends now number amongst your enemies. And when you think on it, truly think on it. You have no clue why you're there—caked in mud. Cold to the bone. Blood always on you somewhere— you can never get all of it off. You've been marching around, island to island, siege to siege, banner to banner for four years. *Four.* You were a boy when you joined. And as you grow into a man, you never learn the why of it. Just one day, six-hundred miles from where you started, a steward in the service of some lord you've never heard of approaches your campfire and tells you peace is won, and you can all go home.

"But home is some far off, distant memory. And you've no compass pointing the way. The northern rebels knelt. And because of that, they kept their heads. They kept their lands and titles too. And then there *you* are. Left on your own. Abandoned, it feels like. Wondering what it was all for. Bundon. Look at me. What was it all for?" The knight had gone pale, and tears misted his eyes. His skin had turned to gooseflesh, and there was fear in him. A truer fear Bundon had ne'er seen in a man. "I killed men I didn't know, for a king I'd never met. And I shan't ever do it again. I will not join ranks, Master Bundon. Not for our King's third, fourth or twentieth crusade. I won't. Ever. So I will do what jobs I have to do to keep me from adding more nameless faces to my restless nights.

"And that is the *honour* of normal soldiers," he spat the words like an insult. "We bloody our hands and shatter our souls for the realm's nobility so that they might keep their own hands clean and their souls intact." Bundon had words on his lips, foul words, sneering words. Jabs and pokes and petty insults... but he kept them where they were. Tight behind his teeth. And he let the boy talk.

"You once asked me, sir, what kind of man King Doryn is? Here is the true answer. He is Lady DeGrissier. They are all Lady

DeGrissiers. And they don't give one wet *shit* for us."

And with that, the boy pulled up his hood and said nothing more all night.

BUNDON VI

The Eighteenth Day in the Month of High Sun

Bundon didn't sleep much that night. He lay awake, his eyes always drifting to the bejewelled dagger in the knight's belt. But every time the farmer moved, his cloak would brush the brickwork, and his captor's eyes would shoot open. His hand reaching for the hilt of his sword.

Would I be able to do it? The farmer mused through the night. *If I could grab the dagger?* He had thought he could. He had led countless cows to slaughter, after all, and he had cared for every one of them far more than he ever cared for this traitor.

But his thoughts never spurred him to action. And soon, birdsong and pale light heralded the morning.

"It would be faster if I took the beast," Bundon had given firmly. Seeing how the boy was struggling to wrangle the fald. But the boy had refused that and had snatched the reins away from the farmer, making him march ahead a few paces.

"It's not long now," the false-knight called. "Just beyond the next rise, I think."

Bundon must have seemed a dead man walking. With his head hung low and feet scraping the road, kicking up clouds of dust. Alaria was not much happier. No trills, nor chirrups. Just the soft *pad pad pad* of her footsteps and the hollow *clip-clop* as Duchess walked beside her.

As they exited the ramshackle manse, Bundon had thought DeGrissier to be half mad for choosing to make one of these tumbledown ruins her home. But the sight before him, when they walked over their final rise, was enough to chase his breath away.

A great manse of white stone, quarried from the cliffs of Kraigwyn. With blankets of dark ivy cascading down from every wall. She had transformed the tumbledown estate into a palace of sorts. The entry hall, whose roof once sported a gnarled old willow tree, had been gutted. The tree was one of the few things that remained. She had crafted a great courtyard, with the willow growing from its centre, surrounded with thick stone walls, made wide enough to stand spearmen and archers. He saw a dozen men walk the walls, each adorned in the crimson cloak of her infamous Riverguard.

Behind was the house itself. With a hundred paned windows, their thick glass catching the sun as they approached. The masonry had been repaired in twenty or so places with patches of white stone and clean mortar that sat like scars across the more dulled stone of the estate's original walls. And, ever the dragon queen, DeGrissier's banners fluttered over the gatehouse. A red dragon rampant upon a golden field.

After today, I hope to never see that blasted dragon again.

But by far, the most striking sight was what lay around the palace-cum-fortress. A moat. Of crystalline water, placid and glittering in the high sun.

"A moat," the farmer said, scowling. Stopping in his tracks

"Aye, and a deep one too," the false-knight agreed. "Look, there. They've diverted the water from one of the Dalka's hatchling streams. Oi, stay ahead. A good few strides, go." Bundon did not move, however. Too distracted by the moat. For it woke wrath in him. One rarely roused.

"I feed this island," Bundon gave bitterly. "I feed it with

beef. And warm it with leather. And the mills have fresh flour because of me. And yet I must have only three pails of water every week to see me through."

"Forward, Bundon," the knight warned.

"That is why the brooks and streams run dry. That is why the Dalka sits only halfway up its banks. It was not the heat. It was not the gods. It was not our people's greed. It was *her*." He found himself shaking and had to concentrate hard on steadying the angry wag of his chin.

"The water runs dry because of *her*. And she sends out her Riverguard and tax collectors, and without complaint, we pay her for the water she's stealing."

"You can voice all these complaints to her when we get there," the knight pushed the farmer on the back with the tip of his sword. But he didn't budge.

"Boy," Bundon's voice was thin and angry. "Is the realm seeded with naught but crooks?"

"Doubtless, she has some lord's permission," Will dismissed with an impatient sigh. "Castles need moats."

"Not so much as the good people of Dalkaford need it," the farmer mumbled back. "And castles need water like horses need clothes if you ask me." Bundon thought he was done with complaint, but more came forth.

"What defence does a castle need when none know it's even here? There has not been war on the isle for five-and-fifty years." The boy said nothing in return. Giving the farmer a small, sullen nod before continuing onwards.

"I suppose you see it as 'just the way of things'" Bundon called after him darkly. "If she offered you a place in her guard… could you do as the Riverguard do? Taking water from the thirsty? Taking silver from the poor? How long would it be before you're robbing lost hedge-knights on the road? Or stringing up elves like those that helped us?"

"Helped *you*," the knight snapped, turning in his saddle. "They took my purse, bound my wrists, and threatened me. They might hide it behind wise words and deceitful riddles, but they're robbers all the same."

"Deceitful riddles," the farmer shook his head. "They showed you, boy, that your choices are your own. Choices such as this one, which benefit none but you."

"All men make such choices," the boy dismissed. "You do what you can. You lie when you must. You fight when you have to. That is life, Master Bundon. That is how all men live. It's a foul game. And none play it fair."

"I did," Bundon said. The boy stopped on the road. "You can too, sir. Untie my bonds, give me the fald, set things right."

"Hush," the boy gave coldly. "There are horses approaching." Bundon saw the clouds of dust on the road ahead and knew he had little time.

"Sir," Bundon tried to reach the boy, gifting him back his title. "Sir. You can still choose to help us if you so desire it." Bundon looked at the boy's grubby face, all creased with doubts.

I am reaching him.

But after a moment, the boy only sniffed and gave the farmer a cold, lingering look.

"Get back," he ordered. "And be quiet." And the horses were with them.

"Halt," the man-at-arms warned. He was dressed in mail with a longsword on his hip and a thick, crimson cape fluttering behind him. His eyes fixed on the fald, who shrunk away timidly from the mounted sergeant. The rider gave a crooked smile. "You will come with me. Her Ladyship wants a word."

❊ ❊ ❊

The odd retinue was given a wide birth as they crossed through the gatehouse. The archers and spearmen were gazing down at them from the walls, faces hard and unmoving, glowering beneath conical helms.

Bundon heard murmurs and whispers as their eyes fell on the fald. Alaria misliked the attention as she screeched and fought against the false knight's grip.

You poor bird. You poor, poor bird. Bundon wished he could explain what was happening. Wanting to assure the beast that no harm would come to her.

But I do not know that. I do not know what these snakes intend.

In the walled courtyard with the willow tree in its centre, Bundon now saw just how grand this place truly was. Along the walls were topiary dragons of a hundred different bushes of gold and green and every shade between. Wildflowers grew cascading from their mouths and growing in patterned beds of swirling flames. Buttercups, cowslips, corn marigolds and evening primroses sparkled yellow and gold, while field poppies, campion flowers and pimpernels shone with warm ambers and scarlets. There was a smell of cinnamon everywhere. Along with honey and lemon. Sweet, rich smells that Farmer Bundon was not too familiar with.

The willow's golden, weeping branches hung down like a veil, and beneath it were awnings and soft seats. Servants were gathered in their crimson finery, holding plates and platters piled high with foreign fruits and honeyed nuts. Others held pitchers of what looked like hippocras, mixed with pulped wild berries. And sat, for all the world as though they were expected, were the Lord Anguis DeGrissier and his lady mother.

Alaria grunted in the back of her throat when she caught sight of the pink toad, the one who had tried to climb atop her at the granary. She halted, latching her claws into the ground and refusing to move any closer. Willem tugged and tugged at her reins, but she did nothing. Just scratching great gouges in the beautifully kept grass. Willem gave the farmer a pitiful look. And as much as the farmer wanted to leave the boy struggling, he could not sit idly and watch Alaria get herself into such a worrisome state.

He went to take the reins, but the false knight snatched them away. So the farmer lay a hand on the beast's neck, looked her in the eye and made a silent promise that all would be alright. Her talons eased from the raked ground, and Bundon felt the muscles relax beneath her scales. She still kept two wary eyes on the fat lord but obeyed and continued with the approach.

"They came, mother!" Lord Anguis jumped up from his seat; in his excitement, he knocked a flagon of wine from of a servants grasp, and it splashed all over the ground. He made no sign that he even noticed, deciding instead to grab his mother's hand and haul her to her feet. She gave a thin-lipped grin and rose gracefully.

The Lord and Lady favoured gold over crimson today, it seemed. Wearing bright, glittering raiment of golden samite and crushed yellow velvet, adorned with rubies and garnets about the neckline and sleeves. The lady's hair was worn up today, coiled into an extravagant knot atop her head, half concealed by her red-gold diadem. Her son still wore the bejewelled torque around his neck. The gemstone in its centre swirling and dancing within its golden confines.

The Lord Anguis rushed to the fald's side, who recoiled as the lord neared, lifting her wings to shelter her head beneath them. She let out a small, defiant screech but did no more than that.

"It's not so bold now, is it?" The Lord laughed and patted Alaria clumsily on the head. "Who's this?" His lips curled into a sneer when he saw the knight.

Willem, adorning his mantel of a well-spoken knight, fell to one knee, yanking Alaria's head downwards as he held onto the reins. She huffed and gave the knight a cold look.

"I am Sir Willem Gull, m'lord, at your service—"

"I don't want your service," he wrinkled up his face in disgust. "Mother! There's a man here." The false knight suddenly looked fearful.

"My darling boy, have you quite forgotten your courtesies? Come, gentlemen, sit." Lady DeGrissier gestured for them to do so. Warily, the two of them obeyed. Willem still clutching the reins of both horse and fald. The four of them sat together, an odd sight for a tea party the farmer was sure. A battered knight, two nobles, a farmer, a lame horse and a cowardly fald. In fact, it bore an odd resemblance to a joke he'd once heard. The punchline was long forgotten, but doubtless, it was vulgar.

"Care for a cup of hippocras? It's a godsend in this heat, I find." The lady did not wait for a response, calling over a servant to pour for them. Willem drank thirstily, all too eager to make himself at home. Bundon did not partake, as much as he may have wanted a cup of wine and a piece of fruit in this sun. But he saw the smiling contempt DeGrissier was throwing the knight, who greedily lapped up the wine and helped himself to a bowl of honeyed hazelnuts.

"Hungry work, was it?" the lady asked coldly, without inflection. Willem cleared his throat and set his cup down. Sitting up in his awned chair and giving his best gallant smile,while hastily swallowing down the last of his hazelnuts.

"Indeed, m'lady," he nodded.

"Indeed," her eyes stayed on him expectantly. "And who are you, exactly?"

"I caught this one, m'lady, trying to flee to King's Anchor." He dabbed at the corners of his mouth with his cloak. "I questioned, him and he informed me you were seeking this one, so I thought I'd lend my sword to your cause." DeGrissier regarded the knight coolly, raising a cup to him in silent cheers, giving him a thin-lipped smile. She then glanced to an elder servant, her steward, Bundon thought. The older man nodded and drew out a coin purse from the folds of his robes. The steward then withdrew a handful of coins from the pouch, pocketed them, and threw what remained to the knight, who caught it clumsily. He eyed the coins within.

"Ten silver," he said.

"And you may keep the purse too," the lady grinned. "You can put things in it if you like. More than generous, I think. For your assistance. So masterfully done, and all without being asked. How truly gallant." She turned then to the farmer, her eyes smouldering wickedly like two dimming embers. "And you. You are not the girl."

"I need some assurance that my family is safe. Bryn and the little 'uns." Bundon swallowed his fears. The lady tried to stifle her laugher but made a poor job of it.

"Little 'uns," she said, and laughed again, louder. "Truly? Very well. See the great sow and her brood are bought here." She mumbled to her steward, who nodded dutifully and disappeared. When he was gone, the lady turned back to the fald and smirked, rising from her seat and approaching the cowed creature.

"There she is," she admired, running a delicate hand over the quills and feathers of her crest. Alaria shrunk away from her touch, grumbling a low warning. "A vestige of a bygone age. Last of the dragonkin. Without a voice. Without a hoard." She lay a hand on the beast's beak and looked into her eyes. The beast stopped trembling and met the golden lady's gaze, cocking her head to one side inquisitively. "Poor thing. Poor voiceless thing."

"Begging your pardons, m'lady," Bundon felt obligated to say. "But the beast has a hoard. She's back home. Sobbing her eyes out."

"What do you know?" She hissed a glimpse of her true fury, behind all the mocking smiles and arched eyebrows. "A beautiful beast. Tethered so to the earth. Eating rats. Harvesting grain. Dragonkin are not plough horses." Her mask of cold courtesy came back with ease. "Ah, here are the little 'uns now."

"Husband," cracked the old familiar voice, so full of scorn already. The old steward led them from the manse, Brynhilde bustling in front with the two children at her heels. Rosy-cheeked. Well-fed. Dressed in gowns and doublets finer than any they'd owned before. Bundon rose slowly from his seat.

"Wife," the farmer's voice was paper-thin. "You are not bound? Nor gagged?"

"Gagged," Lady DeGrissier quipped. "Why that would have made her company far more tolerable."

"Brynhilde," Bundon felt a quiver in his gut. "What's the meaning of this?"

"Where's the girl, you faithful fool," Brynhilde barked.

"You were supposed to bring the girl!"

"No," Bundon shook his head. "No, no, no. You said. Your letter said. Tyr read it out to me."

"I said when I left that it would fall to me to clean this mess, and I have!" Brynhilde shot back. "Our lives back, Bundon, with Tyr and her beast safe here. I've seen to matters myself. It is done!"

"Aye, a cunning mind, that one. Resourceful. " DeGrissier praised mockingly, leaning to Bundon's ear with a whisper. "If I've not said so already, you are a truly lucky man."

"Not you too," Bundon hung his head. "Fire, have mercy. Why, Bryn? Why?"

"Why?" The Lady DeGrissier giggled behind her hand. "The answer is always the same, dear farmer. Ask your knight. Ask your wife. Ask the Krillian, who I know you spoke with." But Bundon was not listening. Something had broken. Something he had tried so hard to keep intact, year after year. He bowed his head and fell to his knees.

In a world of liars, honest folk are nought but fools. The farmer kept thinking, over and over. He just wanted to sleep. He didn't want to bother with any of it anymore. The lies, the false promises, the false friends, the false hopes, the betrayals, the heartache, the grief and the sorrow. Where had the good gone? Where had the decency?

Flew off, far away one day, and I scarce noticed.

"He didn't bring the girl," Lord Anguis worried at the lady's shoulder. "Why didn't he bring the girl, mother? That's still the deal, no? We haven't changed our mind?"

"Get up, Master Farmer, get up," he heard the false knight say. Nudging him with the broken toe of his boot. "Be strong."

Be strong. Be strong, he says. For what? For the next deceit? The next lie?

"Our farmer is in a bad way, it seems," the lady's voice oozed mock sympathy. "But it was my understanding that your lovely daughter would be joining us here. Look. Look, poor dispirited farmer. It's not so bad here. Flowers, guards, and gold.

She'll want for nothing. Can you promise her the same?"

"Don't be a fool, husband," Brynhilde chided in. "You'd be doing her a favour!"

"Get up, Bundon," the knight warned again; when the farmer made no movement, the boy spoke up. Getting to his feet clumsily. "Are you forgetting your courtesies again, m'lady?" He asked sternly. "I thought us to be your guests."

"Guests?" The lady looked shocked. "But Sir Willem, I thought you captured him on the road? Trying to flee to King's Anchor, I thought you said?"

"Aye, but… but he is a decent man, m'lady, just scared was all— is all. No, just scared." The false knight stammered out, turning back to Bundon. "Get up! Her guards are closing; you need to get up." Bundon glanced upwards and saw Sir Willem was right. The guards were encircling them, spears down and pointed toward him. And he saw the gangly rooster Sir Richarde strut into the courtyard, a sneer of contempt already plastered across his sallow face.

"The fald will stay here. And you, farmer, shall go and retrieve your daughter and bring her back. If you do *not*, then Sir Richarde and his men *will*. And they will not be so gentle as you; I'd wager." The lady took hold of Bundon's chin and lifted his gaze to face hers. "Do we have an accord?"

He gave no response.

"Well?" She pushed. He looked up at her passively and gave his answer.

"No."

"What?" The lady seemed surprised. "What did you just say? No?"

"Perhaps he did not understand the question, mother," her son put forward.

"I understood well enough, you great oaf," Bundon suddenly felt light as air. Fear had abated. Grief too. And sorrow. All gone. He batted the lady's hand away and gave her a look. A true look. Truer than any word or deed he'd done up till now. And in it, he made no attempt to hide the revulsion, the hatred, the scorn. All of it. He poured every ounce of his contempt into that look and spat at the lady's feet. Both lord and lady were wide-eyed, and Lord Anguis even looked a little fearful. "I said: No."

"He called me an oaf," Anguis stammered timidly.

"He's gone quite mad," DeGrissier's fair face contorted with a foul sneer, she tried to hide behind a chuckle, but her wrath was too great. "Sir Richarde," she called, and the swaggering knight stepped forward. Lean and powerful,

"Fetch the girl," DeGrissier ordered.

"Bundon, you great fool!" He heard Brynhilde shriek.

"You leave her be, sir, or you'll wish you had!" Bundon pushed himself to his feet, and turned to the towering knight. "You'll die if you touch her, sir; I promise you that!" Richarde LaBotte slowly approached, sharing a mocking look with his lady, and with the heel of his boot pushed Bundon back to the ground. The guards laughed.

"Leave him be!" Brynhilde called out to deaf ears. "Don't hurt him! Leave him!"

"And upon her arrival, I shall show her what we do to those who do not obey. Starting with her dear papa." DeGrissier lay a sickeningly slow footstep down upon the farmer's left hand, and he felt the knuckle-bones crunch beneath, with more than a little pain.

"And the others too. See them fettered and chained." The lady in gold suddenly turned to Sir Willem, who was looking, wide-eyed, as events unfolded. Bundon snatched his hand away with a helpless grunt, holding the bloodied fingers to his chest. He looked up and saw the false knight stand to attention, more from habit than anything else, the farmer thought.

"If you seek a lady's service, you'll have it," she beamed. "Take these commoners to the kennels." Bundon turned his contempt to the knight, but the boy looked utterly lost, and the contempt soon gave way to pity. Especially when the boy gave no answer.

Foolish boy, answer the woman. Answer, she will kill you! The farmer softened his face, nodding to the young sir, allowing him to say yes. Urging him even. He could not forgive himself if the boy should die for the guilt he already bore. And in seeing this, the knight slowly nodded back.

"Or you can rot with them, if you'd rather," the lady pushed. Her patience for the situation fast wearing thin. "That is a soldier's lot in life, after all. The choice of death or duty."

"A choice?" the boy's voice cracked again, and he winced to hear it. The guards laughed. The fat lord laughed. Even the Lady DeGrissier's anger softened into a mocking snigger. And the boy's face grew red as his blood bay.

"Yes. That's what I said," she teased. "Are you a little touched, boy?"

"I choose," he gave the farmer a final look, a small and sad smile creeping across his lips.

"You choose…?" The lady shared looks with Sir Richarde, her guards, and her staff. All of whom were tittering cruelly.

"I choose neither." The young knight drew the bejewelled dagger and cut it through the air, slicing through Alaria's reins at the neck. The startled beast panicked, rearing back and unfurling her grand wings, all twenty feet of them. They buffeted against the ground, making the guards shield their faces and brace against the storm. DeGrissier was thrown off her feet, her rich yellow gown smeared in green grass stains.

"Mother!" Anguis cried.

"Fly, Alaria!" The farmer screamed. "Fly! You have to fly!" He had never seen the beast so scared.

DeGrissier was shouting orders from the ground, though they were muffled behind the desperate screeches and squawks of a thrashing, thunderous fald. Guards stood too scared to approach as Alaria suddenly quieted, gazing longingly into the sky. She took a step. A sure, solid step. And then another. And another. And then she was running. Her wings slicing through the air and catching.

She will never clear the wall. The farmer fretted. *She will never take flight.*

Bundon was bellowing at her. "Fly!" He was shouting. *But*

that's not my voice, surely. I never scream or shout.

"Leap! Fly! Run! Back to Tyr! Go!" He continued. He never felt the cruel slap DeGrissier dealt him, and her incensed orders for silence went unnoticed. For Alaria was running. Leaping. And there she was. Weightless suddenly. Soaring and weaving through the air, circling around the estate, once, twice, thrice. The force of her wings throwing the willow's branches into a frenzy. And the entirety of the courtyard fell silent, all eyes on the fald as she flew. Further. And further. Now just a dot in the clear sky, getting smaller and smaller. Singing her victory to the whole island. And DeGrissier stood, her eyes fixed on the ever-shrinking dot in the sky, her face twisted with horror. Horror cut with sadness.

In the panic, Bundon had not noticed the guards seize him. They jabbed at his stomach with the hafts of their spears, and one lay a mailed fist to his chin. He felt the lip split, and the taste of blood filled his mouth. Brynhilde was still shrieking her desperate pleas for mercy. In a daze of pain, and tears and unfocused thoughts, the farmer saw him. The young knight. Leaping heroically onto his horse. He looked a proper knight all of a sudden. The sun made him seem a shadow, a halo of white lights surrounding him. A longsword glittering in his grip. The cries of a fald echoing into the distance.

He is the knight I prayed for. He is. He is!

"Find her, sir," the farmer called to him, finding his smile once more. As broken and bloody as it must have looked. "Find her, and keep her safe! I beg of you!" The knight gave a quick nod, and then he was away. Galloping out of the courtyard and ducking beneath the gatehouse. DeGrissier screamed, shrieking at her guards to raise the bridge, to lower the gate, to stop the boy, anything. But their eyes were on the fald, and they heard their lady not. Lord Anguis was wailing now, too. While Brynhilde and her children were huddled together, weeping.

Archers eventually loosed their arrows, and one struck true. A hard hit between the shoulders, but if the knight felt the blow, he made no sign of it. And then another loosed. He heard the horse whicker in pain, and he felt a pang of pity for the poor beast. And then another. And another. But before a fifth arrow could find its mark, the knight was gone.

And for good or ill… the boy was now, truly, his last hope.

WILL I

The Eighteenth Day in the Month of High Sun

W*ho are you?* His ghosts kept asking. *Who are you, Will?* But the boy had no time to answer. *Ride, Duchess. Ride. Faster. Faster. Don't look back. Can't look back. They're coming.*

Will had always dreamed of fancy. He had always dreamed of and yearned for adventure, and gallantry, and heraldry and the shining armour of knights. But his own adventures had rarely felt like the stories he had grown up on. If he wasn't marching to war, and bloodying his hands with rebel blood, he was collecting taxes for lesser vassals of the realm or defending small caravans along troubled roads. But most of the time, he just travelled.

Travelling was peaceful, and the sights he had seen had made up, in some small way, for the hardships he had faced since he first lifted his axe and decided the life of a warrior was for him. He had found himself on Rhothodân looking for a noble household to pledge his sword to for half a year or so. After that, the plan was to travel away from the Isles altogether, find work in one of the mercenary companies on the continent, across the sea.

None would question my shield there. A stranger in a foreign land is only the man he says he is. I could start anew. Do only honourable things, for honourable men, and scrub my past clean. That had been his thinking. But those thoughts seemed a lifetime ago now.

Why did you do it? He fretted. *Why, Will? She offered you a place in her household guard, and with a 'sir' before your name, you could have become a captain.* But he thought of the farmer, crumpled on the ground, guards kicking him and the lady sniggering behind her hand, and knew, with fresh resolve, that he had done good. Or had attempted to, at least.

Who are you?

"You were my last hope," he heard the farmer say from somewhere. Whispering amidst the rushes of wind that whipped at his hair and cloak. "You were my last hope," he heard again.

"Is this why you stole my arms and armour, boy?" The dead knight asked from Will's side. "So you could fool farmers and simple folk into thinking you're something you're not?"

"Shut up," Will mumbled back. "You're dead."

"Aye, dead. Dead and buried. And you remember the exact spot, don't you... *Sir* Willem?" The dead man-made the name sound an obscenity.

Under a yew tree. Against the banks of the Greentongue. With the magpies watching from the branches.

"Aye. That's right." The dead knight nodded sagely. Will could feel the man. The revenant. Standing to his side, racing down the road with him, though standing perfectly still. He looked no better than when he had left him. Blood soaked. Pale as death. Could have been thirty, could have been sixty. So ravaged was he. "All I asked of you was to help me with my hauberk and to clean the blood from my sword. I ne'er meant for you to keep it."

"But you weren't using it, sir," Will said aloud. "You weren't using it."

"You don't even remember my name," the dead knight said sadly, combing a skeletal hand through blood-streaked silver hair.

You never told me your name, sir. Will thought. *You just asked for my help, which I gave without question. It was not my fault you died, sir. It was the axe blow between your shoulders that did for you, not me. I tried to help.*

"Tried to help by stealing my horse, arms and armour," the dead knight chided. "And I wasn't even cold."

Duchess liked me. I was always good with animals. The rest, well, it seemed a waste was all. I never intended to be—

"Never intended to be what, boy?" The dead knight laughed. "To be a thief? To be a liar?'

"To be you, sir," the boy finished aloud.

Folk looked at me differently with your shield on my back. They looked at me with wide, awestruck eyes and met me with eager smiles. They looked at me, sir. And saw me in a way I had never been seen before. And I liked it.

A knight is only as valiant as the deeds he's done. Will had heard the adage a hundred times before. And, when the people took him for a knight, he thought that were he to do valiant deeds, he'd be as close to a knight as made no difference.

But none of his work as a freelancer had ever instilled much valiance in him.

"No, son? But what of saving that farmer?" His father asked from the knight's left, grizzled and grey, with his two hands black and skeletally thin. He rode with him too, standing still like the dead knight, but rushing with him through the wind and the hot sun. "Did that not instil any valiance, my boy?"

It instils fear in me. And I am not so sure I saved him yet. More likely, I helped lead him to slaughter and betrayal.

"If he is to help that farmer, as he helped me, he will wait until he's dead and take all he has." The dead knight quipped, and the two of them shared a haunting, ghostly laugh together. "You are no knight, sir. No true knight."

"A false knight and a falser friend," Bundon's voice whispered on the breeze.

"With a dying horse, my boy," his father said sadly.

"She is fine," Will hoped, squeezing a clump of the mare's black mane and praying he was right. But she had slowed, and cold sweat clung to every inch of her. Her breath was a rattle, and she was grunting and snorting her discomfort.

"You'll be alright, girl, you'll be alright," the boy insisted.

"Perhaps you'll find some help along the way," the dead knight said. "And should you fall, he will be within his right to take your arms and armour and bury you at a markerless grave. Not even an epitaph to tell your story."

I cannot read, sir, nor write. Will thought glumly. *I tried to speak some words. But I never knew you. So, what could I say?*

"You could speak the truth," his father added. "As I taught you. That is more than you ever did for that poor farmer. And he so reminded you of me. Is that how you'd treat your old man if he lived? Bundon. A man who ne'er did you any harm. Bundon. Who saved you. Twice. You'd be hanging from a tree branch if it weren't for him. Did you forget?"

"Never," Will pleaded.

"And you lied nevertheless," his pa shrugged. "I think that worsens the betrayal, my boy, rather than making it better. By my fire. Look at you. You'll never reach the farm at this speed."

"DeGrissier's guard is on your heels, boy," the dead knight gave. "Your old man has the right of it. You'll never get there."

But I have to try. Will thought desperately. *I have to try, and it may be that I succeed.*

"And what then?" His father asked. But Will had no answer. He would think on that later; for now, all he could do was ride. And ride hard.

His shoulder muscles ached, and his back felt sodden with sweat. So much sweat. He felt it pooling at the hem of his breeches and making his small clothes cling to his back. Hot, thick sweat that smelt of iron. And the pain between his shoulders; foul, and only getting fouler. He thought he must have wrenched the muscles in the panic or when he cut the fald's leash.

Will's head was pounding from the constant gaze of the sun, his thighs felt raw from the hard ride, and his waking dreams were dancing with reality, he knew.

Dead men can't speak. He tried to remind himself. But there were the dead men, and he could hear their words all too clearly.

Who are you? Who are you? Who are you, Will?

"Will. Will. Your pa's gone grey. One shade darker, and he's on his way." He heard the other children sing and laugh, as they usually did back home. "Will. Will. Your pa's gone black. Caught the rot from a barley sack. Will. Will. Your ma's gone white, saw your pa wear a noose one night."

Evil children. Will cursed them, wherever they were. *Sally the cooper's daughter, Gregor the miller's son, and the other Will, the one they called Well Will, the shepherd's boy. I was the unwell Will. Though I never had the rot. Never. They just said I did.*

"Your horse is dying, young sir," his father said again, sadder this time. "She's dying."

"No," Will shook his head. "No, she's fine."

"You are a liar to the whole world, Sir Willem," the dead knight grumbled miserably. "Don't start lying to yourself."

"She's fine," Will insisted, stroking a caring hand through the braided black mane. "She's fine. You're fine, Duchess. Nearly there, girl. Nearly there."

✽ ✽ ✽

Will had dug countless graves in his time. And he had

watched countless pyres burn. And he had not wept over a single one, but none had ever been this hard.

Duchess had carried Will on her back through countless journeys. She had never bitten nor kicked. Not even when she sprained her ankle last spring. The tumble that had given her that awkward gait. A lumbering quality that did little to diminish her spirit and one that Will had grown to find endearing. She had always been a kindhearted beast. Sensible. Dignified. Loyal. Brave. Always brave. And now she was gone.

Will had never seen the arrows in her haunch and the blood that had been marking their progress.

She must have been in agony. He thought, his tears misting and obscuring the shallow grave he was intent on finishing. *And she rode on regardless. Because I asked it of her.* He sniffed and wiped the fresh tears from his eyes.

I owe her this much. He pushed his helm into the hard, dusty ground and mined out another small chunk of earth.

"This is folly, my boy," his father's ghost said from above. "DeGrissier's guard will find you long before you finish digging."

"No, no, he will fall before that," the dead knight offered. "Look at him. He is ragged. He is killing himself; each helm of dirt might well be his last. You look tired, sir."

"I am tired," the boy barked, scooping out another helm of earth. "I can rest when I get there."

"If, sir," the dead knight corrected. "If you get there."

"It's a two-day journey." A new dead face gave. The cripple from the Greentongue. Brandishing his pitchfork. Will could see the wound he had left him, the axe wound where shoulder met neck.

"And now your horse is dead," said the young boy. The one who wore woven reeds as armour and fought with a butcher's cleaver.

What was he thinking, charging me with that? Will found himself thinking.

"A knight without a horse is no true knight," the grandfather said. The old man with the kindly face and the rusty mail.

Who stuck Will with his crooked spear and near killed him at the Battle of the Greentongue.

But I killed you first, old man. Will hung his head, ignoring the new faces, and set his mind to the grave.

"Why didn't you come home, Will?" His mother asked in tears, consoled by his pa, whose skeletal black hands squeezed his mother's shoulders in comfort. "Why didn't you just turn around and come back home?"

Our village had no name, ma, and I don't remember the way even so. I'm sorry, ma. He continued digging, but his strength was failing, and the ground was getting tougher and tougher.

I couldn't go back there. With the songs and the names and the constant cruel japes.

"Are you touched, boy?" One of them asked. "Has the sun addled your wits?" Will looked up and felt unsteady on his feet. He shielded his eyes. The man was squat and ugly, with wiry grey hair and a gristly knotted ear. He wore mail and a red cloak.

Clan Blackwood wears red. With a beastly black tree on their banners. They fought for the rebels. But I do not recognise his face.

"I never killed you, sir," he dismissed, returning to his digging. But the ground was wobbling now; he felt unsteady and increasingly seasick. He looked back up to his ghosts. The ugly man was still there.

"Begone with you," Will insisted. "Begone. You're not one of *my* ghosts. I have plenty, sir. Be off with you."

"That arrow wound looks painful," the ugly man teased. Will was confused but turned and saw the shaft sticking out from his back. Tipped in fletching of dyed red feathers.

So that is why it hurts so. He thought. He had never felt the arrow, in truth. And the sight of it now made him feel intrigued, more than shocked.

"Am I dead?" Will asked of the ugly man.

"Not yet," he answered. "But her ladyship has charged me with such, and I do not shirk my duty."

"Oh," Will sighed, felt faint, and collapsed into the hole he was digging.

"It appears you've dug your own grave, boy," the ugly man laughed. "I take it the fald's not with you. Here, allow me." The squat, ugly man approached, took hold of the arrow and yanked it out. The pain washed over the knight, but he hadn't the energy to scream.

"Got lucky," the ugly man said, inspecting the arrowhead. "Bodkin, for piercing armour. Might have gone a little deeper than a broadhead, but it's a damn sight easier to pull out. Looks like your muscle caught most of it. Shame, boy, you might've lived if you kept running. Why'd you stop?" The ugly man's eyes fell on Duchess, lifeless on the ground. "Oh."

"I won't be long," the boy said groggily. Trying his best to stay awake. But he felt ever so tired suddenly. "I have to finish."

"And you'll heave that thousand pounds of horse by your little lonesome, will you?" The ugly man cackled. "I haven't the time to waste, I'm afraid. So. Best get on your feet, boy."

"Sir, please," he urged. "I never killed you. You're not my ghost."

"Stop that nonsense, for a start. Pick up your sword," the man insisted, ignoring the young knight's words. "Be thankful I'm of Brentiri blood; it won't serve for a warrior to die without a blade in hand. Pick it up."

He does look familiar. The knight struggled to recall. *He means to kill me. He is my angel of death. Delivering justice in service of the fates.*

The world had never felt so small to Sir Willem; it felt as though the sun were fast disappearing. Though he could see it bright in the sky. But the light did not brighten the grass, nor the road, nor anything. It felt dark. And close. And constricting.

Ghosts are dancing. That's all it is. My ghosts are dancing. This isn't real. But the grip that closed around his neck felt real enough, as he was hauled from the shallow grave, a sword's hilt thrust into his hand. Willem steadied his thoughts and tried his best to ignore the raw heat and pain between his shoulders. His eyes focused. The ugly man, in his black chain and red cloak, had his sword drawn.

He means to kill me. Will thought again. *He means to kill me. Do something. Do something. Do anything!* Will thrust forward, aiming the point of his sword toward the sergeant's underarm. But the thrust was parried aside, and the sergeant was left laughing.

"A knight," he mocked. "Such a gallant knight." He began walking to Will's left, so Will lifted his blade to defend. But no strike came. The sergeant laughed again. "So nervous. Is this what knighthood has fallen to? I'll make it quick, boy, if you'll allow it."

"Stay back," he cut the sword through the air, but the cuts were clumsy and chaotic. The sergeant backed away, a horrid grin on his square, red face. He scratched his knotted ear, and cleared it with his little finger. Flicking the black wax onto the ground. He cricked his neck, sniffed and spat a globule of brown spit at the knight's feet.

"That was ill-done," the knight said, in a thin wisp of his normal voice.

"And what will you do about it, boy? You can barely stand." The sergeant grinned, showing a mouth full of brown, broken teeth.

"And yet I still stand," the boy gave.

"We'll see," the ugly man guffawed and followed with a thrust of his own. Willem avoided it clumsily, darting to one side, nearly losing his footing. The sergeant followed the thrust with two cuts, left and right, pushing Willem back into his shallow grave.

"There's just no keeping you from it, is there?" The sergeant bellowed. "Stay there if you want." He thrust forward again, and Willem moved to one side, grabbing the sergeant's grip and pulling him into the grave with him. They tumbled and fought. Pulling and prising at each other's grip. The sergeant smashed his forehead down onto Will's nose, and he felt the blood gush into his mouth.

I shan't let go. He held on tightly to the sergeant's grip. *I shan't let go. I shan't. You can't make me.* The sergeant pulled and pulled, but every last ounce of Will's strength was being used to keep hold, a tight hold. The sergeant grunted, cursed, and soon he abandoned the swords altogether. His mailed hands found purchase around the knight's throat, pushing his whole body's weight down onto his neck. Will's eyes went wide, struggling for air, struggling to find something. Anything to stab, to cut, to distract. But there was nothing. The swords were useless, trapped between them, with no strength to wrench one free.

The dagger. Will remembered. *The farmer's golden dagger.* He groped around, feeling for the blade on his belt. But the world was getting dark. And his arms felt weightless, his fingers numb.

The ghosts gathered around the shallow grave, gazing down at the two of them. Will saw the sergeant's face, contorted with murderous purpose. His ghosts' faces were almost a blessing; when they looked at him, they looked on with pity. The cripple, the boy and the grandfather. His dead knight. And his ma and pa. It was nice to see them together again.

Is my ma singing? He missed his mother's songs. They were much kinder than the songs his playmates would sing.

"My heart, my boy, a mother's heart is always with her son. Our hearts, my boy, you'll always find will beat and burn as one." He had quite forgotten that song. He hadn't heard it for years, years and years. A lifetime ago, it felt. A different life. A different boy. Not him. He cherished the song. The last thing he'd hear. He preferred it to the scornful eyes peering down on him and the mailed hands squeezing the life from his throat. No. The sergeant bore nothing but hate. And it was the last thing he'd see in a world fast fading.

I'm coming to join you. He told the ghosts, quite forgetting his search for the dagger. Every responsibility had melted away. *I'll be with you all soon. Very soon. I can feel it. My life. It's draining away. Shadows linger in the corner of my sight, growing larger.*

I'll join you soon.

"Not today, Will," his dead knight said with a sure nod. "Not today."

"You have things to do, Will" said his pa, an eager smile

on his lips. His mother nodding serenely in agreement. And suddenly, the sergeant's grip eased as his eyes shot wide, looking down on Will with a look of shock and betrayal. He coughed, and a dribble of blood spattered down his chin.

There's an arrow in your back. Will thought drowsily. *As there was in mine. Do all men sport such arrows? Oh. And another. And another.* And then the world grew dark around him.

"You will waken, sir knight," Will heard as sleep, or maybe death took him. As his waking dreams danced with reality once more, the faces of ghosts and goblins churned and spiralled into one. "You will awaken. You will see. I taste it in your blood, sir knight. You will not die today. You will awaken. You will. And you will find the answer you seek, should you start asking the right questions."

"What?" Will asked in a ghostly whisper. "What answers? What questions?"

"You'll find out." There was a blur of colour, a whicker of horses, the smell of sweat, and wine and beast. A song. *They're singing songs.* He saw a man hoisted up a tree. But Will's eyes could not make sense of it. "You'll discover who you are, sir knight. You will. You surely will."

"I'm Will," he nodded. "I am Will."

WILL II

The Eighteenth Day in the Month of High Sun - Part 2

Will found the sergeant when he woke. His face had grown even uglier since he last saw him. Bloated, purple and bleeding from his eyes and mouth. Hanged. Riddled with arrow wounds. And quite, quite dead.

Duchess had been covered in a cairn of stones, with a lock of her braided mane left atop. He lay a hand on the stacked stones, and his skin pimpled with gooseflesh.

Thank you. He thought and tried to think it loudly so that they might hear him somehow.

The sergeant's sword, armour and horse had been pilfered, along with Duchess's saddle and the knight's coin purse, lance and armour. And the ten silver he'd been given by the Lady De-

Grissier.

That's only fitting, I suppose.

He got to his feet, feeling a little vulnerable without his chainmail, greaves and pauldrons. His helm had gone too. But his sword remained. As did the bejewelled dagger. And, most welcome of all, a full waterskin. Will drank from it thirstily and thanked the fire when he discovered the waterskin was, in fact, a wineskin, filled with the sweetest, richest red he had ever tasted.

He had been propped up by a tree, wearing his padded gambeson, his threadbare breeches and his old riding boots. All were stained from dusty travel and perspiring use, and now blood as well, both dried and fresh.

Will's back still felt slick with blood, but the wound felt less now. Less hot. Less painful. Less likely to fell him.

Did they treat my wounds as well? These elves who might've hanged me? Why? Why? It was all he could think. *Why? Why? Why?*

But all at once, the memory and pressing nature of his task came flooding back. He bid a final farewell to the dutiful beast that had carried him where'er he went for the better part of two years and continued eastwards. All the while asking himself: Who are you? Who are you? Who are you?

Back past the brook where Bundon had found him, defeated by his armour. Back past the hanging tree, where he first met the elves. Back to the crossroads, he went. Back, back, back. Eventually, to Bundon's farm.

Wherever that might be. The sun was not much lower in the sky, Will noted. So he surmised that he had only lost a few hours of daylight. *Unless I slept for a whole day, and then some.* And going by the throbbing in his head and weakness of his grip, he thought it possible.

He had begun using his longsword as a staff, each step relying more and more on the crutch he had fashioned himself. The sun beat down mercilessly upon him, boiling the blood within, making his head throb endlessly, accentuated by each step. *Throb. Throb. Throb.*

Will drank the wine too greedily, and the wineskin was empty before long. And then his thirst was palpable. His mouth felt as though it were filled with sand, his lips dry and cracking like pigskin over a spit. But onwards he went. All the while, the ghosts around him asking, constantly.

"Who are you?" "Who are you?" "Who are you, Will?" *Not a knight; you've proven that already. Nor a hero. Heroes do not lie. They do not cheat. Or steal. Who are you, Will?*

"A thief," he answered, between rasping breaths. "A liar. A thief. A brigand." But the answer didn't satisfy. For the ghosts kept asking.

"Who are you?"

Onwards, and onwards he went. Until he found a crooked signpost with four directions. His eyes blurred when he tried to make out the words and images. A dragon to the east, flanked by straws of wheat, an anchor to the south, an olive sprig for the way he'd come. The knight's eyes drifted eastwards, where roads dipped and rose with natural valleys and tall, rolling hills. His breath was chased away at the sight of it. But he swallowed any doubts and did not give himself the chance to think on the strain.

"Just keep going, my boy," his father urged, clapping him on the back with a ghostly, black hand. "You'll get there eventually if you just keep going. Don't stop to think. Not yet. Not yet. You don't even know who you are yet."

"A soldier," Will put forward. But what a poor soldier he had turned out to be. Happy to linger behind, no interest in gaining ranks or killing folk.

"If you were a soldier, Will, you'd still be serving," the dead knight put forward. "You'd be off with King Doryn on his third crusade, in the sun and sands of Arencia, But you're not. You're here."

"I am a warrior, then, if nothing else," he told himself. But his ghosts only groaned and sighed. That answer didn't satisfy either.

"What kind of warrior are you?" the dead knight scoffed.

"Warriors fight for something; what do you fight for?" the cripple asked.

"The only men you've vanquished are vanquished at the behest of some lord you've never met," said the grandfather.

"And what glory is there in that?" said the boy in the reed woven armour.

"A mercenary then?" He had planned on such when he first found himself on the Isle of Rhothodân. "I'll join a company on the continent."

"You'll not serve a king, but you'll serve some other rich sot half a world away?" his mother asked him, not unkindly. "No, my boy, that's not you. You're not a killer. It's time you make peace with that."

"A beggar then?" That is what he feared more than anything. *But so long as I have a sword, I have no need to beg.* So he kept hold of it and a tight hold at that.

"But if you do not fight, my boy, what good is the sword?" his pa asked him. But Will misliked the question, so ignored it.

"It's not *his* sword anyway," the dead knight chuckled. "Best bury it; sir, you'll not find who you are while you wield it."

"But I need it," Will attested, squeezing the blade's hilt even tighter. "I need it. I'll die without it."

"No, Will, you'll die *by* the sword. Not without it. It's not yours. It's not you," his mother said softly, almost lyrically. Like it was a song. He missed his mother's songs.

My heart, my boy, a mother's heart is always with her son.

"But I don't know who I am without it," Will said, keeping back his tears. But feeling their presence tight in his throat and the sting behind his eyes.

Our hearts, my boy, you'll always find will beat and burn as one.

"No," the ghosts said, a voice all as one. "No, Will. You don't know who you are. And that sword fends off the answers."

"I'm no knight," he said. It felt good to say, oddly. Like a great burden had been lifted. The ghosts all beamed, smiling, laughing together. The dead knight stepped forward, and bowed low.

Is that pride he wears? But the knight was gone before he could make certain. Vanishing away on the breeze.

"I'm no soldier," Will said. And the cripple gave his thanks, bowed, and drifted away.

"Nor a mercenary, nor a warrior," and the grandfather and the boy said their goodbyes.

"Nor am I a beggar," he smiled to say that one, and his mother joined him before she turned and walked away. Will stopped at a curve in the road; a steep drop lay before him, down a rocky cliff face and right into a nest of brambles and briars. His father's ghost stood alone now.

"Not all heroes need swords, my boy," he told him. "Who are you? Truly?"

Will thought over what answer he could give as he looked over the longsword in his grasp. And, without prompting, he gave his answer.

"I don't know."

"At last... some truth", his father whispered. "So go. Find out." And without much thought, Will dropped his sword. It clattered noisily down the crag's face, disappearing into the brambles. He took off his scabbard too, and his sword belt... and down it went.

When the clattering ceased, he realised he was alone. No ghosts. No whispers. Just silence. True silence. He stood for a while, letting the breeze blow against him. And he bid a silent farewell to whatever it was he used to be.

✼ ✼ ✼

A farmhouse soon appeared. Nuzzled in the valley of two hills. He knew it was the right one. He knew. He could feel it. Will walked like a drunkard to the old farmhouse door, and knocked once. Twice. Four times. Eight. He would knock until there was an answer.

She's gone. She's not here. DeGrissier has her. With every knock, the thoughts became inescapable. But after sixteen, perhaps more... a lock's mechanism clicked. Hinges swung and squeaked. And there she was. Eyes, large and honest. With freckles across the bridge of her nose. Her hair a tangled braid over one shoulder. She had tears in her eyes, mud up her skirts, dirt beneath her nails, and she was the most beautiful sight Will had ever seen.

"Who are--" She began, concern and surprise creasing her forehead. But then a glimmer of recognition. "Sir? Sir Willem? Is that you?"

"No, no, that's not me," he corrected, taking a step and tumbling, weary, to the ground. Thankfully the girl was there to catch him as she propped his head on her lap.

"Fire save you," she lay a soft, cool hand against the boy's brow and then one against his cheek. The sun was eclipsed by her, glowing like a halo. "Then who are you, sir?"

"I'm Will," he said, the darkness fast encroaching. "I'm just Will."

When Will awoke, he bore no recollection of getting into bed. Nor had he any memory of removing his bloodstained clothes and dusty old boots. He awoke on his belly, half suffocated by spiky, reed-stuffed pillows. He panicked, thinking for a moment he was back in his shallow grave, with the ugly sergeant pushing his head into the ground. But furs and blankets covered his legs, and a pair of soft, caring hands were tending to the wound between his shoulders. Will eased when he realised, and in fact, could scarce remember a time he felt more safe.

"You're awake," a bright young voice told him. "I cleaned up your cuts and scrapes, but then I found this one on your back." She traced a gentle finger around the wound. "Was it an arrow, sir?"

"I'm no sir," Will corrected, muffled from the pillow. "But aye, it was."

"And why are you getting arrows loosed at you, sir?" She

asked. "If it's not impudent to ask, that is."

"I—" Will began, but the girl interrupted.

"And this," Tyr retrieved the golden dagger and presented it with quivering hands. "Where did you find this, sir? My father took this westwards with him."

"I told a lie to you," he began, and her face hardened. "That day in the square. When you danced. I deceived you, I... I'm no knight, truly. Just a boy, with armour and a sword."

"Did you encounter my father on the road? Is he safe, sir?"

"Your f-father," he stuttered. "Master Bundon—" That is when he heard a caw from outside, he reached out and grabbed the young girl's wrist.

"Is she back?" Will asked, sitting up with some difficulty and with a few mumbled protests from the girl. She sighed frustratedly.

"That? That is just a crow, sir, is who back?" She brandished the dagger again, and her tone grew sterner. "Where did you find this?"

"She. Her. What's her name? The fald." He hurried.

"Alaria?" Her eyes went wide, and all the colour drained from her. But she remained still and calm. "Were you with my father?" Will nodded and could not help but look a little guilty.

"And is he...?"

"He is alive," he assured quickly. "But. But there is much to tell you, I fear." He didn't know where to start, however. Or how much he should say.

If I tell the truth of it, she will think me craven, and a fool, and worse things besides. Will shrunk a little and bit his lip.

You owe her the truth, for her father's sake, if nothing else. Don't think, Will. Just say. As best you recall.

And he did. He told her all. Every story, every lie, every betrayal. He left nothing out. He spoke of the elves on the road and how her father saved him from hanging. He went on and explained their journey to the old slaver estates; he told her of his own betrayal, he told her of her mother's betrayal, and the betrayal of Lady DeGrissier herself.

Throughout it all, the girl remained stone-faced. Her breath quickening, her cheeks flushing, and her eyes misting with tears. But still, and quiet, and listening, without saying a word. Save for when he referred to Brynhilde as her mother, where the girl's scorn was visited on the boy.

"She's not my mother," she snapped and said nothing more. But in so doing, she resembled the large, brutish Brynhilde more than ever before. Will had thought the two were little alike, so it came as no shock that they were not related. It even relieved him a little, though he could not say why.

But when all was said, she wiped away a rogue tear, cleared the lump in her throat and attempted to look bold.

"She flew?" Is what she asked first. "My Alaria? Flew?" Will nodded, and the girl even dared a smile. It was a pretty smile that spoke well of her hope. Though the tears were running, and her nose was in dire need of a wipe. But the smile was gone quickly, and her brow furrowed with concern. Or was it anger? Will had never been adept at predicting the moods of women. Nor was he particularly adept at talking to them. But after she mulled over some thoughts and bit back some anger, she spoke.

"I should hate you, sir, for what you did," there was a tremble in her voice, as though she feared speaking the words. Although Will knew the truth of them. "But for whatever reason, sir, I don't."

You should, though. Will thought. *I deserve no less.*

She suddenly snatched her hand away and stood from the side of the bed.

"What's wrong?" Will asked as the girl pulled on her long leather riding boots.

"How can you ask that?" she snapped, busying her hands with the bootlaces, stopping every moment or so to dry her eyes. "She is out there, alone. Scared. I need to find her. I need to get my pa. I shall get him back, even if I have to kill Lady DeGrissier to do it."

"Kill?" The boy attempted to jump from the bed too, trying to match the girl's energy, but wincing when he rose and quickly seating himself back down with a long, tired groan. "I rather think not. Your father would think ill of me, first agreeing to keep his daughter safe and then allowing her to run into the hands of our foe?" The girl stopped, turned her head pointedly to the boy and scoffed, her face wrinkled up in derision

"Allow?" she snapped unkindly. "*Our* foe?" she asked as well, no kinder than before, with an affected voice, all prim and proper. "It seems to me, sir, that knightly pretence is returning." Her manner changed back, and her face dropped. "Do not start your lies again. Speak proper. As Will."

"I will," he agreed, a little shamefaced. "It's a hard habit to break."

"I understand. But it is not your place to allow anything of me, nor deny me that matter." She was angry, he could tell. And she was trying to not be. But the fury rose, and rose as she spoke. "And *our* foe is *my* foe, in truth. You have played your part already, *sir*, and done a fine job making things harder. For all of us. Rest here, and mend your body. But don't dare do anymore than that." Her words were fierce, but more fierce was the fire behind her eyes.

"I think your father's intention was that you run. Away. Far away. Take a ship from King's Anchor and find refuge on the mainland or further afield to the continent. I'll see us there safely." He tried to sound firm, to regain some of his dwindling authority, but when he tried to rise again, his energy failed him, and he let out another pained groan.

"Yes, sir," she attempted a laugh. "You shall see us there safely, half-dead as you are."

"I think your father—"

"I think, I think, I think," Tyr shot mockingly. "What I think, *sir* is that you best keep your treacherous mouth shut!" Will did not know what to say to that. So said nothing. She moved haphazardly to the hearth, where she wrenched a hatchet from a half split log. She held it firm in her grasp, studying it for a moment.

"I *will* kill her for this," she said through trembling lips.

"Will you?" he asked, quite sincerely. "For, as I see it, they are many, while you are only one. And a girl besides. Hatchet or no, you are no threat to them. You need to run, girl, you—"

"Tyr'Dalka," she said firmly through gritted teeth. "My name is Tyr'Dalka. Is that clear, *boy?*" She made the word sound half an insult, and Will took it that way too. And stayed silent as a result. "I will resolve this. One way or the other."

The other. Will thought sullenly. *It's always the other.*

The girl stormed about the farmhouse for a time, throwing bandoliers across her chest and hanging pouches, bottles and bags from her belt. She would then take the bandoliers off, and hastily reassess which pouches she needed. But to try and place any semblance of reason to her rampaging was a foolish endeavour, as Will came to learn.

She laced and re-laced her boots half a dozen times and adorned then unadorned a cloak of un-dyed wool. But most of the time. she simply paced. Up and down, room to room, round and round, all the while heaving angry, chaotic breaths. After a time, however, her pace slowed. And soon, she sat on the end of the bed and wept. Uncontrollably. Through a tight and rasping throat.

You've things to say, Will. Say them. While you can.

"I didn't learn near as much as you'd think on my four-year campaign," Will said, not looking the girl in the eye. "But it did teach me one thing."

"How to lie," Tyr sniped. Will ignored it.

"It taught me that the person you are before you hit someone with an axe and the person you are immediately afterwards are two very different people. Don't be so quick to change yourself, girl— Tyr, Tyr'Dalka." He met her eyes. "You are plenty good as you are." And he quickly looked away, a thoughtful silence lingering behind.

"But if I lose them," her voice was a whispered wheeze, almost inaudible. "My father, and my fald, I mean. If I lose them... I have no one else. No one. Nothing."

"I know," Will said thinly. "But don't go killing yourself

over it. Not in the name of grief, or grief will surely make martyrs of us all." Will mumbled bashfully, unable to look the girl in the eye. And quite by surprise, he heard the girl laugh. A single burst of it, breathy and through the nose, but a laugh all the same.

"If you feel nought but grief in times as such, grief is all you'll know," Tyr mumbled thoughtfully, somewhere between a smile and a sob. "You're right. You're quite right." Once more, Will was left speechless. The girl had grown dour and thoughtful, lost in her worrisome, labyrinthine mind.

"Turn around," she said after a spell of silence. "I'll dress your back and let you rest." Will did as he was asked and allowed the girl to treat his injury with strips of clean linen and what smelt like lavender oil. She worked in silence, and Will had decided he had spoken enough for today, fearful he might reawaken the girl's wrath.

"I know what you must think of me," she said after a time. "That I am foolhardy, rash, perhaps even selfish. For if I were to give myself, and Alaria, over to the Lady's mercy... all would be mended. What would you do, sir? In my position?"

"I'm no sir," he said softly, though his voice cracked again, and he flushed red.

When will your damnable throat realise you're not a pimple-faced stripling anymore? He cursed himself silently. "But I've seen many proud men lose all they have left in the fruitless pursuit of what was taken from them."

"So you would, what?" Tyr asked, not unkindly. "Leave it? Whatever shall be, shall be?"

"If you like," Will shrugged, and then winced from the effort.

"But it wasn't gold that was taken from me, sir. Nor land, nor honour, nor virtue. It was a person. The only person I have. To abandon him is to abandon the truest part of my soul, and, to be frank, sir... I *would* rather die." Her hands froze, and Will felt the warm trickle of tears on his back, the salt of them stinging his wound. He then felt her head rest against his shoulder, and he felt compelled to hold her there a while.

"I told the old man that I would keep you safe," Will reiterated. "If you should die without him, it seems I shall have to get him back or be called a liar." Will knew the irony of those words all too well but chose not to remark upon it. And, mercifully, neither did she.

"Dawn heralds fresh perspective," is all she said, lifting her head from his shoulder and wrapping a strip of bandage across his back and round his chest. She let a hand linger on his back. "We'll see if my Alaria returns. All other worries can wait on the morrow." She said, giving the boy a soft kiss on the cheek before getting up and leaving Will in his sickbed. "Rest up. Will." Upon saying his name she gave a nervous, tear-streaked smile before bowing her head and leaving the room.

When she was gone, Will felt sure that sleep would never take him. So active was his mind, with thunderous thoughts and wearisome worries all crashing and colliding with one another. But once his eyes were closed, they all quickly fled, allowing him some much-needed rest. Fast adjusting to this rare and very welcome feeling of safety.

A feeling of home.

WILL III

The Twenty-Second Day in the Month of High Sun

The days were bleary for Will. They came and went with every tired flutter of his heavy eyelids. And every dawn, every dusk and every midday, he heard his nursemaid's calls.

"Alaria!" She would call. "Alaria? Al? Al! Alaria!" Over and over, from the farm's highest hill. The small valley carried her voice on the wind; any passing would hear her summons, and perhaps, even further afield than that. Will half wondered if the Lady DeGrissier might hear them and send a score of spearmen to see them through once and for all. He thought of that often, and in his dreams, those nightmares had manifested more than once.

But in his dreams, DeGrissier had been a real dragon. With claws and wings and fire to match her temper. She chased them, though now she chased them across the banks of the Greentongue, back where Will had first tasted battle all those years ago in King Doryn's Second Crusade. Her fire burnt all. It cut through the woods like a roaring inferno, and the Greentongue's waters bubbled and boiled dry. Horses were helpless as her dragon's fire engulfed them. And the men. Good and bad. Highborn and low. All fell victim to her torrents of rich, red fire. Squires hugged their lordly masters. Rebel Lords and King's Men alike dropped their axes and swords and wept in each other's arms. Each whispering silent prayers to whichever gods might listen. Archers' arrows couldn't pierce her hide. Knights were cooked inside their armour. Swords and spears twisted and melted in their wielder's hands. And the screaming. So much screaming. The banks, north and south, were blackened fields, with thick ashen clouds blotting out the sun. The river rushed with hot, red blood. And Will and Tyr were left alone.

I can't save her. He remembered thinking. *I can't save her. I can't. I can't.* The ground was a maze of scorched tree stumps and writhing, twisting souls all afire. And she was coming. DeGrissier. Her eyes were on them. They ran as fast as they could. Never looking back. Never giving her a chance to breathe her wicked fire. Never. Never.

I cannot save her. He thought again. As the writhing, blistered souls all began to move. And move with purpose. They were blackened demons now, their skin cracked and molten, with the hints of hot red embers sizzling below the surface. Their eyes were cruel and hard but lost in the shifting shadows and glares of the fires within them. Wicked fires. All burning for her.

They scratched, and clawed, and grabbed. Their hard, black claws raking blistering scratches across their skin. They were surrounded. An army of demons. Soulless, empty, evil. They kept running. Running and running. The woods gave way to hills; the hills gave way to mountains. Up and up, they climbed. There would be safety at the summit. Will was sure.

But all that waited at the top was her. A red wyrm. Scales of hot, beaten copper, tarnished with red blood. The demons walked beside her, carrying tattered, half-burnt banners. The red dragon on gold. They loved her now. They worshipped her. This beast that had burnt their living souls, rebuilt them to serve her purpose. They loved her. They would die for her.

Four black walls rose around, enclosing the two of them in some twisted, obsidian courtyard. A sudden torrent of flame erupted in its centre. A fountain of fire and ash that sent demonic tendrils lashing at their faces. A thousand molten whips, the arms of some great, ancient evil. And peering through it was her. DeGrissier. Grinning. Laughing. Victorious.

I cannot save her. Will thought, looking across at Tyr. But the girl did not seem fearful. She did not seem fooled. She approached the she-dragon. The fires smouldering and turning to steam as she walked through them. Will tried to call to her. But he had lost his voice. He had lost everything, he realised. He couldn't move. He couldn't breathe. He could only watch as this girl, this young, bright, spirited girl, walked towards a fierce and fiery death.

"A dragon's heart is in his hoard," he heard Bundon say on the breeze. But the world was growing dark. There was no hope to be had. All he saw was Tyr, holding something up to the dragon's gaze... and then the world was cold. And wet. It was rain. Fresh rain.

Is that what awaits us when we die? Will wondered as the nightmare faded from his sights. *Rain? Wonderful, life-giving rain?*

But it was not raining when he woke. It had not rained in months now, Tyr had informed him. Will had just thought Rhothodân to be a beastly hot and unremittingly dry island, not knowing it was meant to rain six months of the year.

Thus why Bundon was so irked by the lady's moat, Will brooded in the dark of his sickroom. *But your concerns stretched only so far as the weight of your purse. A purse now empty. A purse now gone.*

It had been three days since he arrived at Bundon's farm. He had slept through most of it, though he had cherished his waking hours more than he had for some time. It had felt like being back at his nameless village, in his old home of wattle and daub, with his ma baking apples in the hearth fire. But best of all was the fact his bandages and dressings had been changed every day by a pair of skilled and caring hands.

Tyr'Dalka was a headstrong girl. A girl who detested the word 'no' and absolutely adored the question 'why?' Such a combination left Will's storytelling very little room for ambiguity or embellishment. She was not fooled by him; that was clear. And what's more, he felt no desire whatsoever to see her fooled. He liked the girl, in truth. Honest. Awkward. Tactless. Humble. And kindhearted. Certainly her father's daughter. But with something else. Something... wilder.

"Her mother's fire," he could almost hear the farmer say, with that swollen look of pride he would wear when talking of his late wife and daughter. And Will could well believe it.

She took my hand and kissed my cheek. Will had not been kissed by a girl since Sally, the cooper's daughter. And that had only been a mean-spirited jape, back when he was a boy of some twelve or thirteen years. His father had died of the rot, so most of the village had been wary of his mother and him. The kiss was a dare. And Sally had not been gracious in its execution.

I wonder where Sally is now? She had nice soft lips. Even if it was a joke, a kiss was still a kiss in Will's view. *Probably a wife now. Probably to old mean Gregor. Mayhap a few young 'uns of their own. Or mayhap they're both dead to the rot. Now wouldn't that be a cruel twist?* Besides, it was not Sally's kiss he dwelt on now. It was hers.

He had woken this morning to find a bowl of porridge at his bedside, with sharp stewed apple and a prince's portion of honey to sweeten it. The day before it had been toasted bread and bacon and the day before that it was pease pudding and stewed mint leaves. Will had never eaten half so often, nor half so well. And he cherished every bite.

It must have been dawn, as he heard the familiar cries of: "Alaria! Al! Alaria!" From outside. Tyr's daily searches had become the false knight's cockcrows. But today was the first day he felt he had the strength to join her.

"You are slimmer than papa but larger than Hans," the girl had said, handing over some roughspun breeches, an oversized surcoat of un-dyed linen and his own riding boots, with the toes now stitched back to the foxing. "You might look half-a-fool, but you'll be a warm fool at least. And still less a fool than if you wandered the farm in nought but skin." She had giggled and grown bashful when saying that.

He slipped the clothes on now, deciding against the tunic.

Fearing how it would graze against the raw, hot flesh of his arrow wound. So in nought but breeches, boots and bandages, he opened the farmhouse door.

The dawn's first light flooded in, and his eyes took a moment to adjust. In his sickbed, he had accustomed to a life of semi-permanent darkness. But now he shielded his eyes from the light and took in the world outside.

Bundon's farm was built in the valley of two hills, one of humble height and the other high, with a view that must have rivalled that of the royal palaces in Kriscany. The farmhouse was built beneath the humbler hill, with the barn, granary and smoke shed built beneath the higher. With the farm's fields stretching over hill and valley alike, following the gaze of the sun. Will saw a small herd of cattle grazing lazily on the hillside, most lying down in the shade of a looming oak tree. Will could not blame them. Even at dawn, the heat was relentless. But despite that, he saw her. High on the hill. Calling. Hollering for her fald.

She had finished by the time he joined her. She was sitting, knees hugged to her chest, looking out over the farmlands. A blackwood tambourine lay on her lap, accompanying the golden dagger that was tucked in her belt. She was gazing sadly into the iron locket she kept about her neck, barely acknowledging the boy as he approached.

"You should be resting," she said stoically, without looking up.

"I'll rest up here a while, if I may," Will attempted a smile. "That climb nearly killed me."

"Nearly killed seems to be your favoured condition, sir," she joked, without any outward sign that it *was* a joke. "I'm starting to think you have a death wish."

"Death would certainly make life easier," he laughed, but Tyr did not laugh back. She looked up to him with tear marked cheeks.

"For you, maybe. But not those around you, sir," she patted the patch of grass next to her, and Will did as he was bid. Letting out a pained groan as he sat himself down. Before he could chance a glance at the locket, however, Tyr had snapped it closed and tucked it beneath her bodice.

"A lover's cameo?" Will asked, giving his best attempt at charm. "Or perhaps a long lost twin holds a duplicate?"

"What?" Tyr asked confusedly.

"Perhaps it was a gift from your intended? Or does it hold a lock of your mother's hair?" Will pushed.

"I fear your fever's returned for all the sense you're making," Tyr teased.

"Your locket," Will referenced where she had hidden it, as she idly placed her hand where it lay. "There's a story there, I'm sure. I've caught you, a few times now, gazing upon it doe-eyed."

"My mother gave it to me," she said thoughtfully. Will cast his eyes down, ashamed to have made light of such a thing.

Tread carefully, Will. You know her pain well.

"You miss her," Will said.

"I never knew her," Tyr answered back. "But I've seen how much my pa misses her. I think overmuch on the nature of things and such. That's what papa says. But there was a time, a time I never saw, when that man— my pa; he would dance. And smile. And laugh; and only laugh, without it turning to tears, as it does so often now.

"There was a time he would hurry home to a loving wife. Not just three ungrateful mouths. Four, myself included. There was a time that he was loved and loved another back. A time when his daily struggle reaped blessed reward in his eyes. He works out of duty now, for me, for them. But ne'er for himself.

"And I catch him, on occasion, when deep in talks with me—or laughing with me. Or sharing some old story, he's told a thousand times before. I see it, in his eyes... the joy sours so quickly, for he thinks of her, and the joy they used to share. Of *that* time. That time seventeen years ago. And I can't help but wonder... mightn't he be happier had things stayed as they were." Tears came, but she did not sob. They simply fell.

"All that joy. All that love. All that promise. And all of that beautiful potential. Cut short. For the sake of me." She broke free from her musings with a loud sniff, whereafter she dried her eyes, apologised near a dozen times and set about taming her hair into a frizzy braid.

"And now," she sobbed as she plaited. "My father finds himself in yet another bind. And once again… it's all my doing. And, what's more, my ma has been very miserly with her advice on this matter." Tyr retrieved the locket from her bodice. "Haven't you, ma?" She asked of the open locket.

"Perhaps you're not asking the right questions," Will put forward. "May I?"

"It's not what you think," she gave him a sideways look.

"Then set my thinking to rights." Will held out his hand and waited. Tyr sniggered through her nose and held the open locket out for Will to see.

"By my fire," Will said upon seeing his own reflection. "Your mother certainly is handsome." Tyr snatched the locket back then, doing her best to hide her smile.

"I suppose it seems silly to you," she added, giving her own reflection a sombre glance before snapping the locket shut.

It is a sillier thing to speak to ghosts; I'd wager. Will mused.

"Not at all," Will assured her. "And, while my words mightn't mean much to you… I do not think your father would wish you away. Not the Bundon I met, no sir. Not for all the riches of the world. I think you may be the culmination of all that beautiful potential you spoke of. He thinks most highly of you. Most highly. And is not shy in saying so." She sniffed again, and despite herself, coyly asked what he'd said.

"That you were a beauty," Will began, and the girl reddened immediately. "And I see the truth of that claim. Another claim he made was that this said beauty came exclusively from your mother. Thankfully, he said. Thankfully." Will grinned at the recounting.

"Thankfully," Tyr laughed, and wept in equal measure. "None can best my father in the art of self-deprecation."

"Aye, I can well believe that," Will quipped. "I was always

rubbish at it, personally." Another smile came unbidden, and when it left, and the tears had stopped... she slowly, and gently, leant her head against his shoulder.

Will looked out once more over the expansive farmland beyond and sighed thoughtfully.

"How do you tend a farm with this beautiful view here?" Will asked, craning his head around to see the south road determinedly weaving over, through and under hill, brook and valley.

"Alone?" She asked. "I don't, sir. The barleycorn should be harvested ready for autumn and then sown with beans and oats, with the wheat field left fallow. Bek the Bull should be sowing his oats too, but my father always sees to the herd's breeding. Veg hasn't the strength to pull the plough, and Fruit needs breaking in before he's harnessed and put to work. The honey sits crystallising in the hives, and Bek is in no mood for dancing. And I haven't the mind to think on anything but, but— ugh!" She grunted her disapproval, letting it echo through the valley. "How can I tend the farm, find my fald and save my father... all without losing more, sir? How?"

"I'm no sir," Will said. She grunted again.

"Is that all you can say?"

"No," he added. "I'm no sir, as I said. But I am a farmer's son. I grew up in a farming village. My uncles tended my pa's pig farm when he died. And they grew peas, beans and barleycorn. They tended an orchard too. Pears. The big golden ones they grow on the mainland."

"Farmer Will," she grinned through her tears. "Of pork, pears, beans and barley."

"I can't boast much memory of it," he nervously pulled at the fine hairs under his chin. "But animals have always liked me. And I am sharper than some. I pick things up quickly."

"Very good. And how are you at putting them back down?" Tyr asked, a hint of a smile peaking behind her eyes.

"None better," Will smiled back.

"Perfect, you'll be a farmer in no time." Tyr clapped him on the knee. "You'll find picking things up and putting them down again will make up a good portion of your day-to-day."

"That's fair," he laughed. Placing his hand gingerly atop the one Tyr had let linger on his knee. "I owe you and your family a great debt. A debt I cannot hope to repay with coin. So, perhaps my hands might make a start?"

"Your hands?" She sniffed, watching as their fingers entwined, bashfully wiping her nose on her sleeve.

"Aye, my hands," he nodded. "Give me a pitchfork in place of a lance, and I'll make no worse a farmer than a knight."

"You'd be hard-pressed to," she teased and then grew thoughtful. "But your hands alone can't harvest all those beans and barleycorn. Nor will they strengthen Veg's poor legs. Nor can they help the cattle breed."

"That last one comes as a relief, I won't lie," he laughed, and despite herself, Tyr laughed too.

"But," she added, resolute, giving Will's fingers a squeeze. "These hands might just tip the scales ever so slightly in our favour."

"Only slightly," Will nodded. "You haven't seen me try yet. I might be more hindrance than help. I imagine the hours are long." Tyr guffawed at that, craning her head round to the east and pointing towards the sunrise, which was blossoming pink over the eastern hills.

"At dawn, every dawn, the sun rises in the east and perches, for a time, right in the crest of those two far off hills. Like a soft-boiled egg, look. My pa calls that the hour of the dragon's breakfast."

That sounds like Bundon. Will thought fondly, watching as the rising sun sat perfectly within its great, green eggcup.

"'Work starts when the dragon's had his breakfast', that's what he'd say," she laughed, doing a near faultless impression of old farmer Bundon before growing sad. "And work ends when you've done all that needs doing."

"We'll get him back," Will found himself saying.

"Oh? I rather thought I should be going elsewhere? Somewhere safer?" Tyr teased.

"We will," he added. "But after. After he's back. After we *get* him back."

"Oh, will we?" She dared a grin. "Have you much experience in storming strongholds, Sir?"

"I was at the siege of Caergully Castle during King Doryn's Second Crusade," Will began. "I was the first up the ladders, leading a small raiding party to conquer the walls and open up the portcullis. King Doryn saw my valour firsthand—" Will turned and saw Tyr's patient eyes staring into his. She knew.

That's not true, Will. He told himself. *That never happened.* He hung his head and did not bother finishing the tale, despite it being amongst his favourites. Their hands slowly broke their embrace. The morning breeze licked at them, buffeting at their hair. After too long a silence, Will spoke.

"During the siege at Caergully, I worked with the quartermaster, seeing the lads got food, water and wages. I never got close to the walls. King Doryn wasn't even there. He was at the capitol. We never even stormed their walls; they surrendered when they saw our host."

"So your experience in storming strongholds is...?"

"None," Will gave a thin-lipped smile. "Less, I'd wager, if such a thing is possible."

"A shame," she nudged him playfully with her elbow. "I was rather enjoying the tale. Perhaps I could hear the end of it one day."

"But it's a lie," Will said gloomily.

"A lie," Tyr nodded. "No value in a lie, true that. But a story. There is great value isnstories. The Grand Adventures of Sir Willem Gull." She teased, then cocked an eyebrow. "Why Gull, Will?"

"On the shield I... I *found*. It was a white bird on red. It looked to be a gull, I thought, so when some soul asked me my name, that's the one I gave. And Sir Willem Gull sounded far more knightly than just plain old Will."

"I like plain old Will," she whispered as though it were a secret.

"That first part was not a lie," Will gave. "We will find your pa."

"Not without her, though. This is the only home Alaria has ever known," Tyr explained despairingly. "Where would she go if not here?"

"And the tambourine? Do those calls go ignored as well?" Will asked, tinkling one of the brass chimes. Tyr grinned and held it tighter.

"We used to practise up here," she answered softly. "Dancing, I mean. And she always liked the noise of it. I thought the sound of it might bring her back. Foolish, I know."

Will looked across the countryside, all now awash with the morning light. All pinks, oranges and golden yellows. It looked still. A perfect picture. Save for a soft rumble and a cloud of dirt and dust marking a speedy procession: four horses and four men atop them.

"Tyr," Will said nervously, mouth suddenly dry. "Are you expecting company?" She looked downwards, and her eyes went wide when she saw.

"They're hers, aren't' they?" She asked with trembling lips. "They're here for me."

"They've seen us," Will said, grabbing Tyr's hand and pulling her to her feet. They stood together a while. Watching. Waiting. One, he saw, rode a mule. The others were on garrons, strong-looking beasts of black and brown, all three dressed in crimson barding. The four horses slowed as they approached the rise of the hill, where the men dismounted and began the climb toward them. Weaving through the hedgerows, crossing over the small stream and making quick progress toward them.

Two wore mail hauberks; greaves, gauntlets and pauldrons. Complete with the black mail and red cloaks of the Riverguard. Will recognised Degrissier's captain of the guard; the lithe Autrevillian knight in his shining black breastplate. Another, the man with the mule, wore a fine black robe. A red silken sash around his waist, its tails flapping in the wind. He leant on a solid blackwood staff capped with a dragon's head cast in silver.

"Brother Kindur," Tyr spoke breathlessly. "And that is

Richarde LaBotte, a knight, I think. I recognise the other men not."

"Redcloaks," Will gave. "DeGrissier's men."

And you threw away your sword, foolish boy.

"Your axe," Will said, holding out an open hand. "Quick." She handed it to him without question. It was a small hatchet, no axe, in truth. More fit for splitting kindling than splitting skulls. But it was something. And, despite Will's knightly endeavours, an axe always felt more natural in his grip than a sword.

"You!" the Brother called halfway up the hill. "You, up there! Drop your weapon. We're here from the Temple!"

"You're here from DeGrissier's estate!" Tyr called back down. The Brother and the Riverguard exchanged a wary look but continued with their approach.

"That man is wanted for the murder of a sergeant in DeGrissier's service," the Brother warned. "What madness drove you and your father to take justice into your own hands?"

"You know full well what!" Tyr barked down the hill. "Leave! Now! You're not welcome here!"

"Button yer lip, girl!" One guard called back. "You're to come with us. The boy will answer for his crimes back at the Temple."

"I murdered no one," the boy explained to Tyr. "It was the elves. The elves did it, not me."

"It was the elves that killed him, not us!" Tyr echoed his words down the hill with a childlike fervour.

"Guilty by your own mouth!" The Brother screeched breathlessly. "Cavorting with goblins and heathens! Elves are the ColdFire's children! You damn yourselves with your own words!" The Brother was fast running out of breath, red-faced and panting from the climb. The guardsmen by this time had drawn their weapons, two stout arming swords while Sir Richarde drew out his bastard sword. A mighty blade that stood near as tall as Tyr.

The Autrevillian knight began barking curses up the hill in his foreign tongue. The guardsmen followed suit, throwing foul words on the wind. Mean words. Ugly words.

"They've been taking water, Brother!" Will added his voice to the cacophony of shrieks and curses. "Taking water from the Dalka to fill a moat. A *moat*, brother! During a drought. What crime is that?"

"A lesser one than murder, sir," the Brother called back. "Put down the axe and come with us."

"Sarge was a good man!" One guard spat. "Deserved better than a hanging tree!"

"Your sergeant was a brigand, and he died a brigand!" Tyr added passionately. She was a hardy girl, foolhardy, maybe. But hardy all the same. Will wanted to urge caution, thinking Tyr's fiery words might incite further cruelty. But he found himself voiceless.

"They're not conceding," one guard scoffed, more pleased than anything else. "Stay back, Brother, wouldn't want blood spattered on your pretty gown."

"They're ceremonial robes, and it won't come to bloodshed!" The Brother turned back to Tyr and Will, calling up to them. "Will it?!"

"Not if you turn around," Tyr barked back. She was fierce. More fierce than Will. But Will knew well that it was his body being threatened. They wanted the girl alive. Not him. He was no one.

Fire save me. He worried. *This is it. This is how I die.* He held the axe firmly in his sword arm. Every muscle across his back was taut and pained. Red hot and raw. They were nearly upon them. And he did not like the eager steps of their captain. Head to toe in armour, the glint of his longsword's razor edge reflecting the morning sun.

He is a walking fortress. Will's sword arm shook from the pain. Or perhaps it was fear. *He has a good foot on me, both shoulder and spine.*

"Under the arm, sir," Tyr whispered to him. "And the neck. I see bare skin at his neck." Will was unconvinced he would even get a chance to land a blow. His grip felt weak. His legs felt unsteady. And the sharp, jabbing ache from his back could not be ignored. And through it all, the four visitors were fast reaching the hill's summit.

I have a chance now. Before they even near us. Do it. Strike hard. Strike true. Will threw the axe. It spun down the hill, haft overhead, landing with a soft thud into the ground by the brother's feet. The two of them paused their stride, shocked. The mule whickered behind them. But the blow had done little else. LaBotte's mean face twisted into a vile smile a moment later, and their approach continued. Will felt Tyr squeeze his arm tightly.

She thinks you a fool now. She will watch you die and think you a fool.

"That was a stupid thing to try, boy," one guard spat. "Brave, though. Were you a better aim."

"You attacked a Brother of the Dragon's Temple," the Brother trembled where he stood, incredulous.

"Stay back unless you want more of the same," Will warned in his gruffest voice, raising his fists.

"More of the same?" The guard glanced back at the hatchet embedded in the ground and laughed. "Are you speaking to us or the ground?"

"And either way," the Brother warned, lips tight. "You are now without a weapon."

"Did you hear that?" Tyr whispered in his ear, distracted by something.

"I didn't murder anyone," Will said again as the guard took another step closer. "I swear, I didn't. But he might well have murdered me."

"It's not murder if lawfully done," the Brother gave. The guardsmen gave the reins of their horses to the Brother and began circling the hill flanking Will both left and right, leaving them nowhere to run.

"Then the law is broken!" Tyr cried.

"Enough!" the Brother all but shrieked. "These are Lady DeGrissier's lands, granted to her by Lord Tarbrand of King's Anchor! You live and prosper here by her leave! That is the law! Now cease this folly and come with us!"

"There it was again," Tyr whispered. And Will heard it. A distant call. A caw. And then a shadow, flitting across the green of the hill.

"Fire take you!" the guard spat and lunged. Will dodged and punched at the guardsman, but his knuckles met iron chain, and the blow did nothing. The river guard then dealt a blow of his own. A mailed fist slammed into Will's stomach winding the boy and making him double over.

I'm gonna be sick Will fretted, as he glanced over his shoulder and saw the towering Sir Richarde approach Tyr'Dalka. She drew the bejewelled dagger, but the knight grabbed her wrist and squeezed until the girl relinquished the blade.

Will heard the noise again. A caw. A hiss. And a shadow. There was a flurry of noise,as a vicious shriek echoed across the farmstead. Shadows danced with quill and feathers. But before any could make sense of the noise and shadows, the air cleared, and Sir Richarde LaBotte was gone. His disembodied voice hollering on the wind from somewhere. Everywhere, it seemed.

Will glanced upwards, as did the guards and the Brother, even the horses. And they found him. And her.

A fald in flight. A writhing shadow in her vice-like grip. Where Sir Richarde seemed no more than an eel.

"Call her off!" The Brother shrieked. "Call that beast off at once!" Tyr's eyes were wide with astonishment. That and a touch of wonder. She heard the Brother's command, and she nodded her agreement.

"Alaria!" Tyr threw her voice on the wind. "Put him down! Now! You hear me? I said put him down!"

And, ever dutiful, the fald obeyed.

An ear-splitting scream echoed through the valley, growing louder and louder before stopping quite abruptly.

Sir Richarde LaBotte landed just short of Brother Kindur, who took one look upon the broken knight, paled... and promptly fainted. causing him to roll a good way back down the hill. The horses then reared up, giving fearful shrieks and fretful snorts before bolting in all directions. The Riverguard gawped, looking to the skies for where the beast might strike next. Will used this distraction and scrambled to his feet, finding his footing firmly at Tyr's side.

"Call it off!" One guard shrieked, his eyes searching the sky. The other guard did not wait, however, abandoning all courage and retreating down the hill.

"Alaria!" Tyr was calling, desperately shaking her tambourine, but the sound could not be heard above the fierce rush of wind as the fald beat her mighty wings. The remaining guard turned his malice toward Will suddenly, his face twisted with hate as he charged toward him, his arming sword held high above his head. But there was another blur. Another rush of wind, another dance of shadow, feather and quill. And the sword never swung.

The guard was fidgeting beneath Alaria's vicious grip as she pressed down harder, squeezing the breath from him, lowering her rocky beak down to his head and hissing deeply at the back of her throat. Her sharp, pink tongue dancing at his ear.

"Al!" Tyr called to her, shaking the tambourine. "Al! No! Off him, now!"

"Fire, save me!" The guard was praying from the ground. "Don't let it eat me! Don't! Please!" Alaria gave another sinister hiss, her talons pushing the guard's chain mail into the deep bloody wounds across his back. Tyr rushed and grabbed the sword, handing it to Will haphazardly. Will, who was still lost in the panic, took the hilt clumsily. Lowering the glinting point to the guard's neck.

"Alaria!" Tyr snapped, batting the great beast across the beak. "No. Off you get. Now!" The fald obliged, lowering her head like a scolded mongrel. Tyr then hugged both her arms around the fald's neck and held her in a long embrace. The fald's head cocked sharply from one side to another and then snapped a large dragonfly out of the air.

"You, up," Will told the guard.

"My back. Fire save me. It's killed me," he complained.

"You heard him; up!" Tyr echoed. The guard, through pained moans and grunts, got to his feet. Hunched over like an old man, quivering where he stood. The malice had melted away, and a fresh wash of fear had taken its place.

"You have my leave to go, sir," Tyr told him, looking down at him with cold courtesy. "Run back, find your horse if you can. But run back to her, and tell her what a vile woman she is. Go."

"Tyr," Will warned. "He will bring others back."

"They'll send others if he's dead, as they sent this lot to find the late sergeant," Tyr explained. "And are you a murderer, sir? If so, have at it. See him dead."

"It is my duty, I suppose," Will murmured.

"But first, sir... what's your name?" Tyr asked.

"Mine?" The guard asked, shocked. "Gregor." *Of course, it's Gregor. All the worst people in the world are called Gregor, it seems.*

"Aye, Gregor," she nodded. "And what's your favourite colour?"

"Do you jest?" He asked, but when no answer came, he flushed and said. "Red. No, green."

"And your mother's name?"

"Bessie," he gave. "Dragon keep her." With that Tyr turned back to Will.

"Bessie." She said simply. "And his favourite colour is green. But do, go on, do your duty."

"I fear I've killed finer men than him already," Will mumbled thoughtfully.

"Don't be so quick to change yourself, Will," Tyr gave warmly. "You're plenty good as you are."

"And what of me?" The guard asked.

"You." Will gave gruffly. "Go. As the lady said. Go back to your Lady DeGrissier—"

"That beast should be chained up!" the Brother called from halfway down the hill. "The Temple will not stand for this!"

"Take that one with you," Tyr told Gregor. And he did so. Without complaint. Running down the hill and grabbing the Brother by the elbow before scurrying back down the dirt track south. Tyr, Alaria and Will watched and waited until their unwelcome visitors were nought but ants on the horizon.

"Right, now will you agree with me?" Will asked fervently. "We're not safe here. We were lucky they sent but four. There were near a dozen swords in the lady's employ when I was there, and she has the coin to hire many more. She'll send an army next time. And I fear our font of luck is fast running dry."

"You're back," Tyr said, her ears deaf to Will's warnings. Too distracted by the fald sitting imperiously on the hill, head half-buried in her own quills and feathers, giving herself a good clean. "I never thought I'd see you again," Tyr whispered into the fald's long neck. Alaria chirruped happily in the girl's embrace, stopping only briefly to give Tyr's hair a fleeting groom.

"Tyr," Will said, exasperated. She looked up with tearful eyes, beaming a hopeful grin. "What now?"

"Now?" Tyr's grin hardened. "Is Sir Richarde—" Will felt unwilling to check, in earnest. But he found LaBotte's remains and quickly wished he had not, adorned as he was in much more red than before.

"You will die if you touch her, sir. I promise you that," he remembered the farmer saying. *Dear Bundon… you are certainly a man of your word.*

"Sir Richarde is…" Will began. "Scattered." Tyr looked troubled for a moment but swallowed her worries and decisively tucked the golden dagger back into her belt.

"Then there is little else for it," Tyr's face grew stern. "Now, we shall save my father."

Is she joking?

"Are you joking?" Will asked, approaching the both of them and laying a cautious hand on Alaria's neck. She sniffed and huffed at him but made no more complaint than that. "She has a coward's nature, Tyr; she jumps at crickets in the grass. One buck or kick, and you will fall. Even if you do stay aloft all the way to DeGrissier's estate, once there, you'll be met with nothing but a volley of arrows and crossbow bolts. The both of you."

"Then we best be careful," she chuckled, clambering atop the beast. But as she did so, the fald whined and angrily shook her head and neck. "Al, be still; you can do this." But the fald did not seem convinced. She gave a low, grumbled warning at the back of her throat. Tyr brandished the tambourine, latching it to her belt with a piece of leather cord. Alaria, distracted by the chimes, allowed the girl to climb her back. But still bore no obvious intention of moving from her spot on the hill.

"Alaria," Tyr whispered softly. "Fly." But she did not move. She said it again, but with a harder, more commanding voice. "Alaria. Fly." She said. But again, the beast did not move. Shuffling instead to the remain's of Sir Richarde, sniffing out a loose morsel.

"Don't you dare, you horrible bird!" Tyr barked, swatting Alaria cross the back of the head. "Alaria. Fly! Fly! Fly!... Fly!"

Tyr must have tried close to a dozen times before finally stopping. Lips trembling, she rested her forehead on the fald's quilled crest and huffed her defeat. Wild hair tangled with quill and feather alike, making an odd nest... where soft sobs could be heard from within. Will lay a hand on the girl's knee.

"None have ridden a fald since the elves held dominion," he tried to sound reassuring. But he was sure the words did little to comfort the girl. "Some are simply not fighters. You. Me. Alaria. What can we do against such... dragons?"

"Alaria has dragon's blood," Tyr whimpered stubbornly.

"But not a dragon's fire," Will added, making the fald bristle defiantly.

"And my papa?" Tyr sobbed from within her nest, lifting her head to reveal eyes red from tears and a nose wet from grief. She wiped her nose on her sleeve and sniffed. "You said we'd get him back."

"But the fald—"

"Alaria," Tyr corrected, punctuated by a tiny squawk from the beast herself.

"Alaria," Will repeated. "Same as your mother." She nodded solemnly, laying a comforting hand on the fald's feathered crest.

"Her name. Her spirit," she sniffed. "We're one, her and me. Our hearts. They beat and burn as one."

My heart, my boy, a mother's heart is always with her son.

"But she doesn't burn, Tyr, look at her. She is home. She is content. She's no fighter." Will tried to explain, but the fald took umbrage with his words. Rising clumsily to her feet and shaking the dust from her neck and feathers.

"Tyr, careful," Will urged, seeing the sudden concern in the girl's eyes as she rose from the ground, her feet dangling either side of the fald's great, long neck.

"No," she said, almost silently. "No. I don't need to be careful. Pass me the sword." He was about to do so when he glanced down the hill and raced to grab the hatchet.

"You'll swing this easier," Will said, placing the worn wooden haft in the girl's clammy grip. "Don't die, Tyr," was all he could think to say. She smiled, as sweet a smile as Will had ever seen.

"I won't," Tyr hugged her whole self to the beast. "She won't let me." After Alaria's first footfall, Will was sure Tyr would just topple off. But she stayed steady. The next step was easier. The one after that easier still. Weight transferred from talon to wing as she stretched their full twenty feet each side of the hill. Running down. Faster and faster. Will could feel the pounding of her talons as they trampled down the rise towards to farm.

But they never reached the bottom. They were up. Higher than the hill. Higher than the dragon's mountain. Circling around, singing. A dance almost. The tinkling of Tyr's tambourine announcing their flight.

Will could do nothing but watch. Skin pimpled like gooseflesh, a tear stinging one eye. The distant, tuneless song of a fald and her rider fading to echoes on the wind.

Will stood. Heart aflutter. Knowing now, what he was only guessing at before. Yes. Will, of some nameless village, with no lands, titles nor even a true family name... had fallen absolutely, and irrevocably in love.

TYR'DALKA VI

The Twenty-Second Day in the Month of High Sun

We're flying. We're actually flying. She had not dared to look more than a couple of times, but both occasions had made her stomach twist into painful knots, and a rush of nausea made her throat tighten, so much so she feared she might not be able to breathe.

But up high, swimming amongst the sea of clouds, was a world one had to fast adjust to... or fall and be damned. But Tyr had decided that would not happen to her. Not her. She was meant for greater things.

There is a touch of destiny to you. She heard the red lady's voice on the rushing wind.

I'm coming, papa. I'm coming to save you.

The hatchet's blade was digging painfully into her side, where it was tucked into her belt. But she dared not release a hand to move it. She had kept her eyes firmly closed throughout their ascent, opening them only briefly to make certain it wasn't just some fanciful dream. It wasn't. She had dreamt of flying countless times before, but it had never been like this.

The wind was the cruellest thing. Cold, even during the drought, even during the hottest days of the Month of High Sun. It whipped at her constantly. Strong, determined fingers, made of frozen wind. Pushing. Prising. Cruelly poking and jabbing at her. Wanting her to fumble. Willing her to fall.

But I won't. She hugged her arms around Alaria's thick, strong neck. Squeezing her legs around beast's breastbone, with her bottom firmly perched between her shoulder blades, where she could feel the muscles move beneath her with every great flap of her wings. Tyr would not move from there. She would not budge.

You have me. She spoke wordlessly to her fald. *You have me, and you won't let me fall.* Alaria heard her; Tyr was sure. As Alaria sang her song, and flew ever higher. Through the last of the clouds, where a moment of calm washed over the both of them. A moment where the cruel wind had abated. The cold still clung to her, but she could feel the warmth of the sun permeating through the chill now. It was quiet. Deathly still. And Tyr suddenly felt brave enough to open her eyes. And after taking in what she saw, she knew deep down; she would be unlikely to see anything half so beautiful again.

Alaria had climbed her way, high, higher than the highest peak of the Dalkamont. Where the Isle of Rhothodân sprawled below. Impossibly small. Ludicrously small. A speck amidst the vast blue and jade waters of the Dragon Sea that stretched as far as the eye could see.

But no. I can see further. A true tranquillity washed over her as her eyes beheld the far off wonders of the east, where the white cliffs of Kraigwyn rose from the blue and green curve of the world, with the long shadow of the Blackwoods falling beneath them, where the northern isle of Brentir lay. The twin islands of the Eastern Alliance. The beating heart of Good Doryn's Kingdom.

White gulls screeched and sang their songs, soaring through the air, Alaria singing with them. Dwarfing their meagre trills with songs of her own.

How many get to see the world with a bird's eyes? Waters rose and fell out west, an endless and angry sea. The frost-covered cliffs of The Cold Beyond stood stalwart far, far away up north. And south, beyond the Dragon's waters, she saw a scattering of islands, stepping stones they seemed, dotting a pathway of grey, green and brown isles all the way to the continent.

She could almost hear the endless storms as they crashed, forever, east and west. Snow guarding the north and great seas of sand guarding the south.

Snow to sand and storm to storm. Tyr thought calmly. *That is what the sailors call our world. Our whole world. So much bigger than Dalkaford. Or Rhothodân. Or the Eastern Kingdom. So much bigger than me.*

Tyr had quite forgotten how scared she was meant to be. For, somehow, all of her fears had vanished. In fact, the feeling of fear now felt rather queer to her. She could not recall it, even as she tried. A fresh resolve had taken root. A freshly seeded perspective, blossoming quickly.

But how to communicate such a thing to Alaria? Who was making a quick descent, with a will all her own.

"Alaria," Tyr said. "No. No. Up. We must keep flying. We must fly to—" But Alaria let out a stubborn and vicious squawk, which left Tyr rather speechless. She lowered to the ground, her wings kicking up a cloud of dust and debris that rose, twisting, forty— maybe even fifty feet into the air. Tyr shielded her eyes and closed her mouth and nose, but it did little to stop the sting of grit and gravel as it buffeted against her.

When the dust settled, Tyr sat up and batted Alaria softly on the crest.

"This is not DeGrissier's estate!" Tyr barked. "This. This is the Dragon's Shroud." She eyed her surroundings. Some rough-hewn steps and a simple moss-covered shrine were the only hints that any had ever been there before. An ancient, heavy slab of stone, decorated with the faint and weathered shapes of three dragons, coiling around each other. Two were black, and they flanked the large green drake in the centre.

"Kri," Tyr whispered. "This is where he gave his final sacrifice, Al. This is where our dragon died. Up here. At the top of the world." But if Alaria was at all interested, she was doing a fine job at pretending otherwise. She stalked, wearily, to a rough nest of matted furs and assorted skeletons. The hides and bleached bones of rabbits, weasels and fish of a dozen different sizes. "This is where you've been hiding," Tyr said quietly, clambering down and setting her feet firmly on the ground. The sensation felt odd, as though she might drift away at any moment, caught on the strong winds. Alaria let out a tired string of chirrups as she delved into her nest, nuzzling her head and neck beneath the tattered skins and huffing contentedly from within.

Tyr stood looking down upon the steep steps that curved their way determinedly down the mountain. Her breath was chased away at the sight of them. It would be a long, hard scramble down.

But one missed footing, and you'd reach the bottom far quicker. Tyr suddenly recalled the Lady DeGrissier's late husband. The handsome sot who fell down the palace steps.

She likely pushed him. Tyr seethed. *And if that's how she'd treat her husband, how is she treating my poor old pa?*

"We can't stay here," Tyr said sternly, turning back to her fald. But Alaria was beyond the reach of words as she lay there softly snoring. Head nuzzled into her breastbone. Tyr lay a hand on her shoulder, and the weary beast shuddered from her touch. "Rest then. And rest well. By nightfall, Al, we must be well on our way. Brothers from the temple are always walking these high roads, especially here. Al? Alaria?" No response. Not even a chirrup this time, just the slow and gentle rise and fall of her chest.

Tyr's eyes fell to the many pellets and bones that littered

the Dalkamont. Alaria had at least been eating well, which was more than Tyr could say for herself. She hadn't given food a thought since her father journeyed eastwards to DeGrissier's estate. And she had not eaten much since her knight had knocked on the farmhouse door. Her thoughts all too consumed with fears and frets. For her father. For her fald. For her farm.

Grrrrrrrrgh. Her belly moaned. She hadn't eaten today. Nor the day before. And all the days before that were half-forgotten medleys of worry, work and woe, in equal measure. But now, her stomach was beginning to grow unruly. Rumbling its discomfort and singing mournful, tuneless laments of breakfasts gone by and suppers long past. All Tyr could find atop the Dragon's Shroud were odd little berries growing amongst the brambles. They had the look of blackberries, only larger. Juicier. Green and black, and ripe to bursting.

Don't go eating anything the horses won't touch. Her father's wise words came to her. But there were no horses here. So Tyr was left uncertain. She picked up a handful of the berries and held them to Alaria's beak. She sniffed at them, and her barbed, pink tongue darted out and lapped up a couple. She swallowed them whole, working them down her throat with a series of foul clacking noises that none should hear in polite company.

"I suppose they will have to do," Tyr shrugged and ate. The first tasted horrifically bitter; the second berry was sour and made her face wrinkle up in protest. The third was sweet, though. And by the fourth, she couldn't believe they ever tasted anything but wonderful. And by the tenth, her belly started groaning and aching and twisting into tight, cramping knots. She cursed herself silently, holding onto her belly with both hands.

Tyr then slumped against Alaria's chest with a pained moan, with her wings acting as an odd blanket. And there, listening to the soothing tide-like rhythm of her sleeping fald, Tyr opened up her mother's locket, and prayed some guidance might find her.

But sleep found her first.

* * *

"The wisest souls that walk this world can't tell us why it is we dream or what significance those dreams might hold," her old tutor, Brother Dulcet, had told her once, before or after a lesson on letters. He had been a kindly old man, an old scribe from the temple, retired from brotherly duty and living out his last years teaching the sons and daughters of Dalkaford how to read and write, as well as basic arithmetic and the odd morsel of wisdom from his favourite philosophers.

"Elder Methwyn-o-Clydd, the wisest of the old elven thinkers, put forward that all souls live twin lives. The wakeful soul walks the world in daylight, and the weary soul walks the dreamworld come nightfall. Cursed, or perhaps blessed, to immediately forget the other when sleep takes you or the waking world beckons."

That thought had stayed with Tyr. It unsettled her. Oft times, she liked the thought when her dreams were bountiful with adventure and fortune. But she had been plagued with nightmares as a girl, and in recent years they had come back with a vengeance. She would dream of great waves of blood, crashing down over the farm's high hill, upon the barn and the farmhouse and all she knew. And as she lay down on the mountain, she woke to such a nightmare.

There was a storm brewing. Black clouds rolled in the sky, thundering a baby's cries. Shrill, hard shrieks, echoing across the isle, as crimson raindrops stained the ground red, sowing the fields with corrupted black seeds. The red waters kept rising, flooding the farm's valley with thick, dark blood.

She watched on as the familiar sinking feeling clawed its way, indelicately, into her mind. *My blood. My storm. My desperate cries. I broke the world.* She could not escape the sensation, as it tugged without mercy at the very heart of her. The bodies of villagers would start washing up then, on the banks of these vile, blood-filled lakes. The baker, the butcher, the miller, the smith. Myko and Daisy. The brothers from the temple, with the Krillian too. Will was there now, strewn across the hillside, the bloody waters lapping against his pale, lifeless body.

Not him too. She wept, but no tears came. Tears never came in her nightmares. For the horror for Tyr, the true horror, was always the grim sense of pride she beheld. The blood was hers. Or her doing, at least. And the thick red waters poisoned everything they swept over. Vile corrupted stalks of red wheat and black barley grew in the fields, sharp and cruel. While skeletal cows chewed on blood-soaked grass, their horns afire.

I did this. She'd always think, as she thought now. *I made this happen.*

Even when her father's body washed up on the high hill, she felt nothing. Nothing at all. Just a cold, bemused satisfaction.

"You have a great talent, my dear," the she-dragon whispered in her ear. "A great talent. None hold such skill with misery as you do, it seems." DeGrissier wore her usual crimson finery, but in place of gold, she now wore obsidian. Black glass, all jagged and cruel, formed scale-like armour across her chest, shoulders and hips. Swirling into the vicious shapes of a dragon's maw, horns and claws. She lay a delicate hand on Tyr's shoulder.

"You are a despicable creature deep down, like me. Like Will. Like your father. Like all those sour souls in the townstead," she explained in her lyrical voice, soft as velvet. "In a world of liars, honest folk are nought but fools. And the world is full of liars, my dear. Full of them. All scheming to get their petty wants, each thinking they deserve their foolish dreams of fancy. And you do dream of fancy, don't you, Tyr'Dalka?"

I do.

"And while the rest of the world lies and schemes to get what they want, here you are—flogging a long-dead horse. Each strike raking away a strip of rotten flesh, awakening the swarms of hungry black flies within. Do you not deserve your fancies,

Tyr?"

I do. She thought proudly. *I do deserve them. I have been nothing but good. Kind. Honest. And here I am, still in the same dishonest world.*

"Precisely. In fact. You deserve them more, don't you?" She asked head cocked and smiling sweetly. "More than anyone else. For you've suffered more."

She's lying. Tyr thought, or said. She could not tell within the dream. She heard the voice, but it was not her own. It was older, wiser. And kinder. *She's lying, Tyr.*

"Why won't you listen?" DeGrissier asked with tortured patience. "Why won't you do as I bid?" But a great red wave was washing over the hills now, the waters rising, almost lapping against Tyr's feet. The wave could vanish the whole world; it felt like—a big, abyssal mouth of blood and shadow, ready to swallow all in its path.

But Tyr did not fear it.

There was something protecting her, as there always was. A touch of destiny. A touch of fate. The grim pride turned to timid bravery. She did not want to swallow the world. In fact, the resolve against it was so strong... she felt as though she'd rather die.

And so she stood, defiant, on the hill, ready for the wave to sweep her away. It rose, relentless, a thousand feet in the air. A wall of red water. Ready to crash down upon her. But just before it struck... she felt spirited into the air, high in a clear blue sky, where the black clouds and thunderous cries melted away as she soared. She buffeted the storm from the sky, letting a great, golden sun illuminate the bloodied shadows below. On wings, great lofty wings. Not hers, but another's.

I have you, my girl. She heard whispered in the clearing sky. *I have you.*

TYR'DALKA VII

The Twenty-Third Day in the Month of High Sun

She awoke suddenly, her belly's aching cramps summoning her to the waking world. It felt empty. Once again, singing its familiar growling songs, with the aching cramps from those bitter berries fouler and more frequent than before.

The sun had not quite set, she saw, and the late hour had painted the sky a hundred shades of pink and purple. The first of the stars had come out too. The Bright Scythe curved its way across the sky while the Maiden and the Fool were courting each side of the pale silver sickle that was the moon. There was a smell of fire and smoke thick in the air. Fireflies danced atop the mountain, flitting in lazy circles around one another. Crickets sounded from the bushes. Tyr turned to console her fald, who she knew despised the songs of crickets. But she was not there.

Hunting, perhaps. Tyr thought. But never feared. Alaria would be back, she was sure. Her connection with the beast felt stronger than ever, as though she were right beside her still. So Tyr feared not. And rose groggily from her bundle of fur scraps and fish bones.

When she stood, her eye was caught by a glimmer of light. A flicker. She thought it to be a rogue firefly when she first saw it, but no. It was candlelight. Three candles, in truth. Two black, one green. And above them stood a cowled figure, lost in the purple shadows of dusk.

Tyr said nothing. Thinking, perhaps, that the figure had not seen her.

"You're awake," she said, turning her head to catch Tyr's eye. And it was a she. Tyr could see that now. A lady of similar age to herself. Whoever she was, she was a striking woman. Big brown eyes, freckles spattered across the bridge of her nose with a wild bushel of dark brown curls erupting from the shadows of her cowl. She was garbed in simple black robes, with a red sash tied about her waist. No silks, though. Nor rubies. And no silver dragon head decorated her staff.

"I didn't mean to trespass," Tyr gave timidly.

"Trespass?" The lady laughed and looked about the summit. "This is the Dragon's Shroud, my girl. It's as much yours as anyone. Kri's final prayer was meant for all."

"You're a Sister, then?" Tyr asked.

"Of a sort," she nodded and laughed a moment later. "In truth, I don't recall much of my life before our Noble Dragon took me in."

"And you won't tell your Brothers?" Tyr asked bashfully.

"My Brothers? My Brothers are far, far away. Consumed by larger concerns." Tyr stood to the Sister's side, facing the old, moss-covered shrine, where the three candles flickered away at its feet. The Sister met her gaze, where an odd mischief twinkled in the corner of one eye. "People tend to find themselves in this place at times of great change. You're changing." It was not asked as a question, but Tyr felt compelled to answer.

"I am." She gave a single, proud nod. And the Sister gave one of her own in return. Tyr's guts still twisted from the berries, and sleep and stress had turned the world to spinning. Or perhaps that was the berries too. She could not tell for certain.

But within the Sister's eyes, Tyr could feel a strange sort of kinship. As though she were some friendly acquaintance from long past.

"Do I know you, Sister? Forgive me, but you seem familiar."

"Perhaps a different life?" She put forward, wearing a girlish grin. Tyr tried to steady her thoughts, but the mountain felt as though it were floating on a choppy sea. Each rise of the tide making her feel like she might topple off the edge of the world.

"Perhaps," Tyr mumbled, half distracted by this new wave of sea-sickness.

Only you could get sea-sick atop a mountain, Tyr. She heard her father's friendly derision in her ear. *The furthest one can be from the sea and still be on Rhothodân.* A particularly painful cramp twisted in Tyr's belly, making her double over and groan.

"Are you sickening, my girl?" The Sister asked, a face full of warm concern. "I pray you did not eat the brawdberries."

Brawdberries. Tyr cursed her foolishness again, and the pain in her guts twisted once more. Tyr nodded bashfully. *Found a fald. Trained a fald. Rode a fald. And died eating poison berries, you foolish girl.*

"You shouldn't die, don't fear," the Sister's voice was a cool and calming sound. Her words felt almost a lullaby. "Unless you ate your weight in them, you'll be fine; I'd wager. The pain is just your body's way of telling you *not* to eat them again."

"They tasted sweet," Tyr whinged, still doubled over by the old shrine.

"Poisons often do," she nodded sagely, laying a caring hand on Tyr's back. Her touch felt healing, almost. Easing the pain a little. Tyr had heard of the healing hands of the Dragon's faithful but hadn't expected it to hold so much truth.

"Don't fret; you are not the first to eat them. And you certainly won't be the last. The Brothers at the temple dry them, you know. Dry them, powder them and inhale their sickly smokes."

"Why?" Tyr grunted, holding her belly with both arms and rocking back and forth on her heels. "Why would anyone do this to themselves?"

"They maintain it instils some connection to the Dragon's Prayer, some smoke the berries and see the prayer, as described, etched into every growing thing across the isles and beyond. Others boast of audiences with the great green drake himself. His grand counsel is said to strengthen hearts and bolster spirits and often reiterates much of what the Brothers already think and hold to. Which is certainly convenient, if nothing else." The Sister rubbed Tyr's back lightly, thankfully dissipating an oncoming wave of sickness.

"And then there are others who feel nothing but a sting in the gut, as you do now."

"And?" Tyr's nausea caused her mouth to fill with excess saliva. She grimaced and swallowed it down, wiping what remained away with the back of her sleeve. "What's the truth of it?" The Sister laughed at the question, and after a moment, she shrugged.

"Who can say? It's as real as it feels, I suppose. Come, sit. Here by the shrine. Our Dragon won't begrudge a sickening maid some small comfort." She chuckled again, and in her laughter, Tyr's feeling of recognition flooded back.

"I know you," she grumbled again as she sat herself down at the moss-covered alter and rested her back against the ancient stone slab. "I do. Did your sisterly duties ever bring you through the Ploughman's Vale?" The Sister thought a while.

"A Brother Kindur worked the vale, I seem to recall," she said softly. "Always gracious in his duty, if memory serves."

We have met two demonstrably different Brother Kindurs, it seems. Tyr brooded bitterly, thinking it best to keep these bitter thoughts unspoken. But then the Sister's brow furrowed as though remembering something more.

"But I do recall a farmhouse. Long ago. A lifetime, it seems. There was a babe, also. And a lot of blood." *It is her.*

"That babe was me, Sister," Tyr beamed. "My father, the Farmer Bundon of wheat, beef and barley, do you remember him?"

"Bundon, yes," she said, her eyes half-closed in concentration, visibly searching through her memories. "A sweet man. Kind. Honest. Yes, yes. I remember him quite well, actually. And the girl. The babe. How is she?"

"She's been better, in truth. These are trying times, Sister," Tyr tried to sound humble, but there were too many worries not to vent a few. "Much has changed since last you saw us."

"What troubles you?"

"Dragons," Tyr said frankly. "Heartless dragons. And they seek to tear my world apart."

"Dragons are only heartless through choice," the Sister gave, tracing a gentle hand across Tyr's now sweaty brow. "They cut out their hearts, unable to bear with the wickedness and ugliness they visit upon the world. Stowing them with their other treasures. Making them as heavy, cold and unyielding as the gold they sleep beside."

"A dragon's heart is in its hoard," Tyr gave, in between dry retches. It was something her father had often said when on the topic of dragons.

"While a mother's heart is always with her children," the Sister crouched down to Tyr's height and gave her a warm smile, and the warmth of it permeated the sickness within. Tyr was starting to feel the cramping pains subside. The Sister stood slowly as her eyes misted over, paled by whatever thoughts had come unbidden.

"I didn't want to leave you," she said sternly, reaching out to take Tyr's hand but withdrawing it a moment before they met. "Your father needed help. But our Dragon called to me, and when He calls, one must answer."

"My pa said you left us when I was but a babe in arms," Tyr puzzled. "How old are you? You seem no older than me. How is that? How do I know you so well?"

"Perhaps a different life," she laughed again, but through it, Tyr could see silvery tears budding from the corners of her eyes. "Or perhaps the same life. But through different eyes." Tyr didn't follow, and while the sea-sickness was abating, her bleary mind was as fuzzy as before. She could not decide if the Sister was behaving oddly or she herself was.

"Is that a locket you wear?" she asked, brushing its iron case with delicate fingers. Tyr clutched it tightly and nodded. "My mother gave me one similar. Keep it close, girl. Iron hides much from prying eyes."

"It does?" Tyr asked, not completely comprehending the Sister's words.

"It will be dark soon," the Sister said wistfully. "You should leave come nightfall. She's stirring. I can feel it."

"Who?"

"Who else?" She chuckled, and her eyes found Tyr's. She seemed to be gazing right through her. With big brown eyes, much like her own, though hers still harboured rogue tears. She smiled a moment later. "It's very good to see you, my girl. I never thought I'd have the chance."

"Who are you?" Tyr felt oddly nervous in the asking. But she had wanted to ask that question since she first woke to find the Sister. But she gave no answer, only wrinkled up her nose coyly, her voice a gleeful whisper.

"She's waking up," she said before removing a stray curl from Tyr's face and giving a final heartfelt grin. "My girl."

Alaria screeched then.

And Tyr awoke for a second time. Curled up against the warmth of her fald's chest, blanketed by her wings. The shrill cry had chased the gulls from the mountainside. Causing their startled shrieks to echo all across the isle. Tyr lay a gentle hand on the distressed beast. The fald's long neck stretched from her nest, alert, with her golden, needle-like eyes beaming through the growing darkness, staring, transfixed, at the altar. The old, moss-covered altar. Where three candles lay, snubbed out, their long tendrils of silver smoke, coiling and climbing together before melting seamlessly into the mountain air.

Tyr's mind was blank.

It was a dream, then. Or it was the berries. Or some odd mix of the two. But she could not make herself believe it. Nor had she the time to try. Through her abating sickness, Tyr rose; content was her mind to never question what it was that just happened.

Who can say? It's as real as it feels. The Sister's words reverberated through her mind. Though the details were fast disappearing from her memory. She could not recall the woman's voice nor smell. Save for the smell of smoke and fire. And her face had somehow warped into her own. And she could not, for the life of her, distinguish any difference between the two of them.

It was me. She looked like me. T'was a dream. An odd dream. Nothing more. The thought was a comfort, but the musings of a long-dead, elven philosopher came hurrying back to her. *Or perhaps that was your twin life. Cursed, or perhaps blessed, to forget it when the waking world beckoned.*

I shall take it as a good omen. Whatever the reason of it.

Alaria was up and about, chewing and crunching old bones that lay strewn around her nest. She spread her wings a few times, causing them to billow out from the great, strong winds atop the Dalkamont, but she was waiting for something.

Is it me? Tyr could often feel her connection with Alaria. If she closed her eyes, she could almost see it. The silver tether that entwined them together. *Does she wait for me?* Tyr withdrew the tambourine from her belt and beat it against her thigh once. The brass chimes twinkled, and the solid *thump* caught the fald's notice. Alaria lifted her neck and folded her wings, upright, as though standing to attention... and waited.

Tyr approached gingerly, twinkling the tambourine every so often to calm the beast.

It's me, Al. She'd think as she jingled the blackwood band with gentle flicks of her wrist. *You know me. You know me well. Let's fly, Alaria. Let's fly together. You and me.*

The fald chirruped, hopping inquisitively from one talon to another and cocking her head from side to side. They had done this dance a thousand times before, and it always ended in folly. But something had changed now. Tyr sensed a great fear in the beast but also a great sense of duty.

"That's called bravery, Al," Tyr whispered to her, stroking a loving hand down the quills and feathers that ran along her spine. "It's called bravery. And it's nothing to run from. I'll protect you. As you'll protect me."

The beast, now agitated, withdrew into her feathers, which she puffed out defiantly. Her scales' many plates separated, and her quills stood on end, making her look more sea urchin than fald, in truth.

"There'll be a time for hiding, Al," Tyr tried to explain. "There will. But I won't run now, not without papa. We need to get him back. And then we'll hide. I promise. The world will never find us again, even if DeGrissier searches for a thousand years!"

But through all her pleas, she got the distinct impression that Alaria did not want to go. Something was keeping her there.

Is it simply fear? Tyr wondered. *She has always been a timid thing.*

"I never wished any of this on you, Al," Tyr spoke softly. "Or perhaps I did." She grew solemn with that thought. For she had always longed for adventure. She had always dreamed of fancy.

What if these hardships are the price of such adventure? What if it was my hopes and prayers that summoned these troubling times? Tyr looked at the prickly ball before her, Alaria's two golden eyes peaking through the puffed up feathers of her mantle.

"You never dreamt of fancy, did you?" She asked of her gently. A humble squawk was her only response. "You were content to sow the fields, harvest the grain and dance upon our high hill." Her answer was another timid squawk.

"I'm so sorry, Al," Tyr whispered through trembling lips, placing a hand under Alaria's fearsome beak and resting her forehead against hers. "I'm sorry I brought this upon us. I'm so, so sorry." She closed her eyes, and the tether shone bright between them. The silver chain, strong, unbreakable. Stronger than ever before.

"But pa, Al," Tyr struggled to say, the words feeling tight in her throat. "We… no, *I*. I need him back. As I needed you back. My world is broken without him. And I can only fix it with you at my side." The fearful fald's neck rose from her chest, cocking her head to one side and letting out a playful trill.

"One thing more, Al," Tyr promised, and she meant the promise. More than any she'd given before. "This one thing more. And I shall never ask anything of you again. Ever. You will fly only when you wish to. Hunt only when you wish to. Dance, play and laze in the sun only when you wish to. But help me, first. Help me fix this small broken part of the world. By my dragon's fire, so noble and strong… I give you my sacred flame."

And the fald stretched out her neck, shaking the dust from her scales and feathers. She raked her talons across the dirt, kicking up thick earthen clouds. Her wings spread forth, all twenty feet of them. The silver light of the moon throwing her grand, imperious shadow across the summit of the Dragon's Shroud. Tyr beheld her. As she had never truly done before. And she was beautiful. Ancient. The blood of dragons. That is what the Lady DeGrissier had said of her. And for the first time, Tyr saw it.

"You're a force of nature, Al," She gasped at her fald. Swinging one leg over her back, nestling into the natural groove between her shoulder blades. "Your wings are a tempest. Your talons; a storm of swords. Your scales; a suit of armour. Your triumphant songs sow fear into the hearts of men." Tyr hugged herself tightly to Alaria's neck as she felt the mountain winds catch on the fald's wings.

"You, Alaria, are a dragon," Tyr beamed. Making sure every

word spoken was steeped in the delicious promise of adventure. "A greater dragon has ne'er flown the skies, not for ten thousand years or more. Show them. Give them something to speak of. Give them tales they will tell. Craft stories that will last a lifetime. Fly, Al. Fly."

Tyr tugged at the tether that bound them. Sending the words through the silver chain, willing her, pushing her. Through the darkness, Tyr could see little, but beneath her, she felt the world shifting. As talon raked against stone. She was running, flapping her great leathery wings... and then they were weightless once more. As though they had never left.

"Take me to him," Tyr whispered in the fald's ear. And she needed no sign that she understood. She knew. They both knew.

The Isle of Rhothodân was a different beast come nightfall; by the bright glow of the moon, it seemed almost ghostly. Surrounded, north, east, south and west by strong tides and crashing waves, all garbed in their silvery, moonlit raiment.

On the cold easterly winds, they flew downwards, following the Dalkamont's jagged peaks as they turned from cliff and stone to hill and valley. The winds grew warmer through their descent; even at night, the isle had grown stiflingly humid in recent years. Tyr could already feel her shift clinging uncomfortably to her back, and her palms were so slick with nervous sweat, she feared for her grip. But Alaria would never let her fall. Tyr knew that, somehow.

You're with me. We're one. We ride and fly as one. Tyr tethered to her fald. *To the kennels. Will said the kennels. Find them. Sniff them out.*

Tyr had long admired Alaria's skill with sniffing out prey. She always knew where to fish. Always knew where the rabbit holes were. And she could always find her if they ever got separated on their explorations.

So much has changed. The memory of digging for treasures in the old river beds felt like a different life to Tyr. *Or perhaps the same life, but through different eyes.*

They flew a while, travelling the length of the Sunset

Coast and back again. Tyr felt sure she'd recognise the she-dragon's estate when she saw it. Will, as colourful a storyteller as he could be, had remembered little and less of his time there. He recalled in great detail how the fald had flown, and how Brynhilde had wept and cursed, and how her father had hung his head in defeated acceptance. But short of walls, a moat and a willow tree... Tyr knew very little about the place.

"A dozen guards," she remembered Will saying. "With mail, shields and helms. Long spears and crossbows too. They'll pepper you with arrows and bolts the moment you get in range."

But not by nightfall, Will, my broken knight. Tyr thought wickedly, even daring a smile.

Tyr thought to see some lavish homestead made of fresh quarried stone. What she did not expect to see was the fortress that lay before her. A palace, almost. The bright chalkstone illuminated so completely by the light of the moon. So grand and pristine was the manor that it made the old slaver estates seem meagre hovels by comparison. With its tall walls of white stone and taller turrets at every corner. Its moat of silver, placid water. Its vibrant courtyard, boasting a grand golden willow as its centrepiece. And it's warm, amber glow within. The glow of half a hundred candles flickering behind thick paned windows.

Alaria let out a cry, a song of proud defiance.

Hush, Al. Hush. Tyr begged of the beast. *Not so loud. They mustn't know we're here.* Alaria gave an indignant huff but politely refrained from any more noise than that.

Tyr could see the patrols of DeGrissier's guard. Six tiny fires from six tiny torches. Fireflies, they seemed like, making slow progress atop the walls. But only atop the walls. She saw no torchlight atop the turrets, and the great round tower houses would comfortably fit a fald, and none would be able to see her while patrolling the walls or courtyard. None. At least, that was Tyr'Dalka's hope.

They circled the estate thrice over before Tyr had even begun to consider where to land and how. Upon the fourth inspection, Tyr had begun to see the pattern of the fireflies atop the walls. Two of the torches would vanish periodically as the guards holding them journeyed inside, only for them to journey back a minute or so later.

Upon their fifth inspection, though, Tyr felt brave enough to guide Alaria into a slow and quiet descent. Waiting for the four torches that remained to be as far from the turret as they would go. They flew effortlessly over the silvery moat, giving Tyr a feeling of bitter satisfaction.

Your stolen water might halt an attack by land. Tyr thought proudly, hoping the Lady DeGrissier felt this small spite. *But it's all but useless against an attack from the skies.*

As they swept closer and closer to the walls, Tyr found herself wishing she'd watched for a little longer, suddenly unsure of herself. Her stomach had turned to lead. Her throat was but a reed's width, with all the moisture of one too.

Quiet, Al. She pleaded with the beast. *Quiet. So quiet. Not one trill, not one squawk. Nothing. You're a shadow. A ghost. A breeze. Good girl.*

Two torches reappeared suddenly. Sooner than Tyr had expected, but the great fald's talons had already touched stone, and the world felt weighty and real once more.

Tyr slipped off the fald's back, sitting down on the white stone, resting her back against the crenellations and putting a firm hand to her chest in the hopes it might steady the quite unsteady beating of her heart.

She waited. And waited. Half expecting to hear the rattling arms and armour of mean-faced, mean-spirited men as they raced up the tower steps to snatch her. But she heard nothing. Just the breeze. Just the tide. Just her own shallow breaths.

They number many—you, just one. And a girl, besides. Perhaps Will had been right. Perhaps this was folly. Perhaps it was madness. None truly do such things, only in stories. Only in silly stories.

You live and die by fate's leave. By destiny's hand. You take the blows life dishes you and strive on regardless. None can change their fate. None can truly fix the world. On and on, the dismal thoughts came unbidden. Besieged, she felt, from both sides. Despair struck at her curtain wall while rebel tears fought from within. Capturing the winch tower and lowering the drawbridge, allowing them to storm down both cheeks.

"I can't do this, Al," Tyr stammered between breathless whimpers, barely containing the tremor of her hands. "This is not what girls do, not in reality. Only in stories. Silly stories—"

The fald gave a long exhale, resting her rocky beak on the girl's lap, as she often did. But to Tyr, it was all the reassurance she needed.

"But I'm here now," Tyr whispered, barricading the tears back behind her eyes. "And there's nowhere left to fly." She rested a hand on Alaria's beak, lay the briefest of kisses on her forehead and moved toward the hatchway.

The hinges were as new and shining as any other part of the holdfast. So they were, thankfully, all but silent. But as the heavy oaken hatch swung open, Tyr lost her grip on it, allowing it to crash down against the stone. Alaria shot up, alert and alarmed. The two of them locked eyes and stayed motionless, listening for... something. Anything. Voices. Alarms. The clatter of steel on stone. But after a moment of silence, Tyr felt safe in the knowledge that none had heard it, or at least, none had found the noise out of place. That is what she hoped, anyway.

Below the hatch seemed an abyss, a long dark tunnel with no end in sight. The steps down were solid stone but narrow and steep. The first three steps felt safe enough, illuminated by the moon as they were. But the rest felt a perilous trial. For within the tower was a world of absolute darkness, save for what light the narrow arrowslits allowed in, which was precious little. No, Tyr could see nothing. And could only hope, and pray, that each gut-wrenching footfall would find sanctuary atop the next step. The spiralling stairwell seemed impossibly long, for the steps kept circling round and round a central stone pillar. Twice, thrice, four times, five.

There must be an end to it. Tyr hoped in the dark. *There must be. There must be. There must.* She hurried her pace as her heart beat all the faster and found herself walking, face first, into a solid oaken door barred with iron.

She stifled her cry, wincing and rubbing her forehead ferociously to try and chase away the pain. She stopped and listened once more. Nothing.

Be brave, Tyr. Be brave. She told herself as her shaking, sweaty hand found the iron latch. She lifted it, and the door started leaning on its hinges and opening. Tyr held it firm, leaning it open but a crack to chance a look at the courtyard beyond.

The moon had chased away much of her cover as its white veil washed over all. She saw the topiary dragons and the grand, golden willow tree that Will had mentioned. And two guards. *Just two, the rest are on the walls.* One guard, the one resting a crossbow over his shoulder, walked the grounds. Slowly and without much care. His joy in the work clearly hindered by its slow monotony. The other sat, arms crossed and head hunched to his chest, beside a wooden outbuilding built within the furthest corner of the courtyard. An unsheathed sword lay across his lap, Tyr noted, but he did not seem particularly prepared to use it.

No guards at the main doors, but one spared to guard a shed. Tyr puzzled. *That seems queer to me. But I shall need a better vantage than this.*

The crossbowman walked a lazy circuit of the courtyard, stopping at every corner to heave a sigh and mutter a curse before continuing onwards. When he came to Tyr's respective tower, she half feared he might break his circuit and explore upwards. But one curse and one sigh later, he was off.

Tyr stole this chance, removing her boots and stowing them beside the door. The ground was rough-hewn stone within the tower, and she could not wait to feel the fresh green grass beneath her feet. She looked out once more, noting where the crossbowman was heading and giving a cursory look to the walls. If one were to chance a look at the wrong time, Tyr's plans would fall to tatters. If plans they were, for she certainly did not remember making any.

She chose a branch, a good, solid, low-hanging one. And she bolted. Leaping from foot to foot, fast as she could go. The willow's golden veil fell over her, shielding her from the moonlight. And with a leap and a hard scramble, she pulled herself into the tree, retreating to its innermost point and hugging herself to the trunk. Where she stopped. And she listened.

"Oi!" barked a gruff voice.

Tyr's heart faltered. She stayed deathly still and prayed.

"I'm marchin' about like a gaffin' toy soldier, and here you are blissful as ya please." Tyr peered through the golden branches on the willow, closing one eye to help her focus. She heard a scuffle of movement.

"Restin' my eyes, was all," a gruffer voice gave, sounding none too concerned by the comment. "Get to my age, and might be you can rest yours." The gruffer voice let out a yawn, and Tyr could see him fold his arms once more and close his eyes.

"Don't let her ladyship catch you," the younger warned. "You hear me? It'll be all our heads if them lot get loose." The crossbowman waited for a reply, but when nothing came but a thunderous snore, he drove a firm kick into the elder's boot.

"Lazy gaffer," the crossbowman spat and walked away, muttering foul curses under his breath. As he did so, Tyr saw a tricksterish grin spread across the dozing guard's face.

If them lot get loose. Tyr grinned to hear that. *They're in there. With only one of DeGrissier's guards keeping watch, and clearly not one of her best.*

Tyr crept along her low branch, intent on seeing what pathways were at her disposal. And saw a dismal sight.

She was not alone in the willow. A guardsman hung beneath her, swinging and creaking on a lower branch. His face was mottled and purple and white while his eyes bulged, near escaping their sockets. But despite that, Tyr felt a flicker of recognition.

He was at the farm. Tyr realised. *DeGrissier murdered her own man. Why?*

But as she peered closer, the hatchet on her belt snagged

and tumbled to the ground, haft over head, with a resounding *thud*. The dozing guard opened one eye and peered through the darkness. With a laboured grunt, he stood, took his arming sword in one hand, and began his slow investigation.

Tyr hugged herself to her branch, scrunching her face up and hoping, or praying, for some distraction. The weary guard moved ever closer, and his eye caught the glint of iron on the ground. He swept aside the golden willow branches and stooped low to inspect his find. When he realised what it was. he glanced about the courtyard, looking, perhaps, to see if one of his cohorts had misplaced it. Once satisfied that no one had, he picked it up, practised a couple of swings with it, and then tucked it into his own belt.

His eyes then drifted upwards, and Tyr dared not look. She could feel his prying eyes peering through the darkness.

I am not so well hidden as that. Tyr panicked. *If he keeps looking, he will find me. He will. A glint of skin, a hint of skirt, a single curl of hair... and I am discovered.*

"There you are," the old man said quietly, letting out a string of tuts. Tyr's heart froze. "You sorry gaffer. Why'd you run, eh? Never run."

He's speaking to the hanged man. Tyr could have wept with relief. *Breath, girl. Breath.*

"What are you playing at?" called the crossbowman from across the courtyard. The elder emerged from the willow's natural canopy and held the hatchet up for the younger to see.

"Found this," he said simply. "Heard something too."

"Hell's fire," the younger cursed. "That's all we gaffin' need, ya looked about, yeah? Perhaps it was just Sten's ghost. Is that his axe?"

"Might be," the elder answered, unconvinced.

The two of them convened together and spoke in whispers for a time. Tyr could not make out what it was they were saying, but they kept glancing about the place nervously, looking over their shoulders at the slightest breeze.

They concluded their secret discussion with a shared,

definite nod, and the two of them, weapons at the ready, stepped back beneath the willow's branches.

Noble Dragon, please. Please. Please. Please. If you do nothing else for me, do me this favour. Send them away. Make them disappear. Anything. Please. Please. Her hands gripped at the bark with such fearful vigour; she felt a hundred splinters break the skin. Her knees felt it also, but if she loosened her grip, her body would fall to relentless spasms and shakes. She ignored the pain and continued praying, for she knew not what else she could do.

"At what point should we tell her ladyship?" the elder asked in a hushed voice.

"When we find something, and not before," the younger gave, through gritted teeth. "She'd have us turn the whole estate upside down and say goodbye to any sleep we might chance. My watch is all but done; I'll not go tired tomorrow for the sake of a gaffin' hatchet."

"I've served under her ladyship longer than you," the elder gave, a touch of fear in his voice. "I'd risk a sleepless night and a fruitless search in favour of fallin' the wrong side of her. If she were to find out…" he shuddered at the thought and glanced back at where Sten swung and creaked.

"How would she find out? Are you like to tell her?" the younger seethed, making the question sound almost a threat. The elder wheezed a bitter laugh and patted the younger on his shoulder.

"You haven't a damn clue about her, have you?" He scoffed. "She'll know. She always gaffin' knows—"

"Dragon's fire," the younger cursed. "Quit your fretting and look. Somethin' ain't right about this." And the two of them continued their search in silence, and with only a meagre few places to search, Tyr felt good as found. She had even begun planning what it was she'd say or wondering if she might outrun them. They wore chain mail, and such a thing was weighty and cumbersome, but the younger held a crossbow. A bolt notched and ready. And while she might outrun the two guardsmen, she was not so certain she'd outrun the crossbow bolt.

If I submit, they'll take me to DeGrissier, and mayhap on the morrow, I might chance our escape. There is always tomorrow. Always. Dawn heralds fresh perspective. And the guards encroached ever closer, one disappearing and then reappearing a moment later with a flaming torch.

Well, Tyr resigned herself. *That is that. A poor and tragic ending to a poor and tragic tale.* The two guardsman were illuminating the golden willow branch by branch; the elder cast the light while the younger pointed the crossbow, with an eager finger fidgeting at the tickler.

Tyr closed her eyes and threw all her thoughts to Alaria. Alaria was here. Alaria could save her. The crossbow's mark shifted to her branch, with the torch soon to follow, but before it could... the quiet night sky erupted with the proud songs of a fald.

Screeeeeeeeech. Screech. Screeeeeech. She cawed, and the heavy beating of her wings soon joined the cacophony, as an angry, fierce fald swept down low, sending the willow branches flying in a hundred directions, whipping at the guardsmen at their centre and vanquishing the fire of the torch. Alaria drew back up in the air, and the two guardsmen rushed to the walls to chance a better view. Tyr could hear the calls and curses atop the walls, the clattering of chain mail, the ring of steel, the thrum of arrows and bolts. But round and round the fald flew, cawing triumphantly, and stealing away the focus of every soul around, and likely, within the vile estate.

Tyr threw her humble thanks to the wind and scurried down the willow tree, sprinting towards the outbuilding and ducking inside. She stayed a moment at one side of the door, and let out a long and trembling breath. A breath she had held since she first scaled the willow, it felt like.

The commotion was still roaring outside, and undoubtedly an alarm would be rung any moment. And as though the thought had summoned it, the resounding peal of a large bronze bell joined the fray.

Tyr knew her chance was a brief one; every ring of that foul bell might be the last. But as her eyes adjusted to the darkness within the outbuilding, she heard a brutish voice.

"Tyr?" It asked. "Tyr? Do my eyes deceive?" Tyr made no answer but gave a firm *shush* and rushed to meet the voice.

"Dragon's mercy. Dragon's sweet mercy. Bless you, girl. Bless you," the voice wept, quite ignoring Tyr's instruction. The building, judging by the smell of it, had been a kennel at one time or the other. Iron bars divided the room into six walled cages, with a central walkway between them. As her eyes adjusted, she found a haunting sight. Each cage was littered with broken eggshells, large black shards of obsidian, and intermingled within them were bones and grey withered flesh.

Falds. Tyr realised. *A hundred little falds, each barely strong enough to escape their eggs.*

There were some who had grown larger, but they too were stunted, runty looking creatures. Heads far too large for their bodies, with little withered wings. None had yet grown their true quills, still covered by small black bristles and soft fleshy beaks, not hardened and chiselled as Alaria's had grown.

She has tried before. A hundred times, it seems.

She lay a quivering hand through the cage and touched a few of the bones and mummified remains.

Their little silver tethers cut before they could leash. Tyr did not understand. *How could so many die? How could she try and fail so many times?*

"Tyr? Tyr, are you there?"

The voice came from the uppermost left, but Tyr could make out nothing more than writhing, shapeless cloaks on the other side of the bars.

"Brynhilde?" Tyr asked in a whisper. The weeping grew louder but now with a tinge of hope to it.

"Yes, girl," it wept. "It's me. Please. Please get us out. Please. We heard the beast, and I trusted to hope. I knew you would not leave us. I knew it." She was not being quiet, despite Tyr's insistent shushes.

Tyr looked at the cage floor and saw more little broken bones and many more broken eggshells.

"These are falds," Tyr said stoically.

"Aye," Brynhilde croaked out. "She's mad, she is. She's been lookin' for one still breathing. All her hatchlings died barely out of their eggs, as she tells it."

"Why?" Tyr asked, the red lady's motive truly lost on her.

"You were always second," Brynhilde added hurriedly. "Second to that beast— to *Alaria*, I mean. But she feared it'd die without you, as all her others had. She *needs* you, Tyr." The old woman cupped Tyr's hands in her own, and kissed her knuckles gently.

"Where's papa?" Tyr asked firmly, snatching her hands away. The weeping stopped for a moment.

"Inside," she said. "She called us dogs. Said we should live like them. But the farmer, the old farmer, I heard her say... he has value. He's the one she'll come for. That's what she said. But you came for us as well. I knew you would. I knew it."

Inside. He's inside. Tyr's heart fell to her bare feet, which were starting to feel cold against the loose, dry dirt of the ground.

I'm no thief, no spy, no assassin. I cannot hope to steal my father away from inside her walls.

"She called me 'friend', Tyr. We shared gossip and intrigue, and she watered us with Autrevillian vintages, gowned us in silks and damask," her hands were shaking. "I thought she'd take care of us. Of *you.* And that fald. I did. I truly did. I never—"

"Mother, does she have the keys?" She heard Hans whisper. "Ask her, does she have the keys?"

"Where would they be?" Tyr asked, and then again more insistently. "The keys, where would they be?"

"He has them," Brynhilde gave, pointing a shadowy finger toward the doorway. "The one that guards the door. Keeps them close, I reckon. I hear them rattle when he walks."

Tyr, loath to journey back outside, inspected the cage. A simple rusted chain and a thick, expensive-looking lock. Perfectly square and bronze. With a square, bronze keyhole.

Dwarven artificery. Tyr reckoned, judging by the runes. *None can pick a dwarven lock, but one can break a non-dwarven chain.* Tyr wished she'd kept a better grip on her hatchet but moved about the kennels in search of something. The ground was home to nought but dirt, but on a half-rotten wooden shelf, she found a pair of shears. Two dull blades attached with a curved band of iron. As a weapon is was near useless, the blades near rusted together.

But perhaps as a lever.

Tyr hooked the point of the shears into a firm link of the rusted chain and began to lever the link open. It was hard work, and Tyr feared the blades would break before the link gave way.

Tyr heard another distant caw from outside and the fuss of guards following her ascent atop the walls. Tyr thought it best to hurry.

"She thought you'd come back," Brynhilde gave timidly. "I feel I should say. I never... Tyr, do believe me, I never intended—"

"I don't care," Tyr shot in a seethed whisper. "Just stay quiet, and watch the door."

And they did so. Tyr could see them more clearly; now her eyes had time to adjust. They wore once-fine garments, tattered and grubby from their imprisonment. Brynhilde looked a gaunt and haunted thing, great bags under her eyes with ragged, limp hair and shaking hands. Hans was lost within a fur cloak, which he wrapped about him completely. While Greta stood watching Tyr's efforts closely. Without a word, the great beast of a girl in the pink dress grabbed the shears and lay her own strength to the task. There was a sickening creek as the iron link started to prise apart, but it was a slow process, slower than Tyr had hoped.

"Do you know where papa is?" Tyr asked the ragged Brynhilde. She thought a while, distracted by her constant glances at the doorway.

"We had apartments on the first floor, back when she named us as guests, not dogs," Bryn spat. "That'd be my guess."

"What else?" Tyr snapped. Brynhilde wracked her brain, her eyes forever wandering back to the door. "Locks on the doors? Guards inside? Windows? Tell me."

"Tyr," Bryn's eyes went wide, but she had no time to speak. Tyr felt a mailed hand grab at her hair, coiling the braid around his fist and pulling her to the ground. She felt as though her scalp had been near torn off, and her head was set to spinning.

"Get off her!" Brynhilde screeched, and Tyr could hear Alaria screeching too, flying over head with the comforting thrum of her wings. But now Tyr was on the ground, and the guard was pulling her, dragging her through the dirt by the braid of her hair. She swallowed clouds of dust and was set to coughing as the kennel's earthen floor raked grit, sand and stones across her back. Tearing at her bodice and skirts.

"Her ladyship wants a word," the guard spat through gritted teeth. He kept an axe on his belt. A small axe, a hatchet almost. Tyr fumbled to grab it, all the while Brynhilde and Hans spat threats and curses the guard's way. After a moment, he turned to the cage, waving the point of his sword through bars.

"Shut yer gaffin' mouths," he seethed, and the cage went silent. In this moment of calm, Tyr made another grab for the hatchet, stealing it from his belt and, without much pause for thought, slammed the blade into the back of the old guard's calf. Tyr felt the chain give way as the hatchet bit through iron, linen and flesh. Blood pooled around the wound quickly, and the guard let out a pained and angry grunt. He cursed loudly, with foul language Tyr had ne'er heard before. He snatched the hatchet from her grip and threw it to one side, yanking the girl up by her hair and dealing her a vicious backhand with his mailed fist. She felt her lip split and a deep cut open across her cheekbone as the blood seeped down into her mouth. She fought against him, but her petty blows hurt her hands more than they hurt her attacker.

He is strong. Stronger than me. So much stronger. Her hands pushed at him, scratching at him, trying to find soft skin to rake her fingernails across him.

Make him hurt. Make him scream. Make him stop. At last, she found purchase on his cheek and raked three deep gouges into the soft, leathery skin. He grunted and dropped the girl, and she fell back into the dirt. The guard lay a hand to his fresh wound and winced at the sting of it. Fouler language came pouring from him as he lay a great, iron-toed boot into Tyr's side, making her double over and heave all the breath she had left.

"My face!" The older guard roared, wincing harder. "My gaffin' face!" She tried to scramble away, clawing at the dusty ground. She felt a strong hand grab her shoulder, turning her onto her back as square, solid, mailed hands wrapped around her throat. From somewhere, she heard a sudden snap but knew not from where.

My neck. It must be. Such large hands. She thought. *I am small. Too small. Why did I think I could win?* Her neck felt impossibly thin within the guard's vice-like grip, as though it were just a meagre, pale twig he might snap with two fingers.

"Don't," she rasped out, but his eyes were full of cruel intent.

I hurt his pride. And now he'll kill me for it.

Tyr's eyes raced along the ground, hoping to find some tool, some weapon, something to cease the foul constriction of her throat. She spied the hatchet, bloodied and far away, too far. She reached nonetheless, but it only seemed to grow farther and farther away. It flew into the air, lifted by a shadow. A large shadow. A large pink shadow.

"Greta," Tyr begged, holding out her hand for the axe. But Greta stood, regarding the hatchet, regarding the girl, regarding the guard, all with the same, bemused resentment. With a fierce grunt, though, the hatchet's blade met its mark.

The guard's eyes went wide as his grip loosened, but Greta was not finished, it seemed. She heaved the axe from his back with an arched spray of thick, red blood and planted it back down again with a resounding *crunch.* The old man let out a slow, rasping wheeze as the air was hacked from him. As she struck again. And again. And again. Her tattered pink skirts covered so entirely with shiny droplets of blood; you'd be forgiven for thinking her gown were bejewelled with a thousand tiny rubies.

After the fifth swing, the guard had ceased his struggles and lay, lifeless, on the ground. Tyr scooted back against the farthest wall, kicking him off her and wiping away what blood had found her person. Tyr's eyes met Greta's, and all the monstrous girl gave in return was a single, slow nod. Brynhilde was, unsurprisingly, a little taken aback. Doubtless, she never, not in her wildest imaginings, thought she'd see her oddly large little girl hack an armoured sentry's spine through with naught but five blows. Well, five blows, thick wrists and a silent, brutal determination.

"G-Greta," Brynhilde stuttered. "Drop the axe now; there's a good girl." Greta gave her mother a look of sour dissatisfaction, favouring instead to tuck the bloodied blade through her belt. She then tore the conical helm from the guard's head and placed it, not unkindly, atop Tyr's.

"Protect that clever head," Greta said under her breath, knocking three times on her temple, wearing a glimpse of what could have been a smile. Perhaps. Tyr was not certain. But had it been, it would have been the first smile Tyr had ever seen her wear. Ever. In seventeen long, belittling years.

Perhaps that's why she is the way she is. She's a fighter. Not a farmer.

Tyr took Greta's hand as she hauled her up. Hans had already grabbed the guard's sword, and he was swinging it haphazardly around himself.

"Oi," Greta barked huskily. Hans needed no more instruction than that, lowering the sword and growing small and humbled. Greta moved over to her little brother and wordlessly exchanged her hatchet for his sword. He made no fuss, accustomed as he was with Greta always taking the prince's share. In food, drink... and even weaponry, it seemed.

Tyr then saw the iron chain lying in a heap, where the shears had prised open one single link.

One link. Only one. And the lock means nothing.

Brynhilde stepped through the shadows, inspecting the guard's body as though he might jump back up at any moment.

"Dragon's mercy," she gasped behind a shaking hand. "He's dead." She wasted no time in coddling her children, hugging Hans and Greta to her as though she had not seen them in an age. She wiped a few stray streaks of blood from Greta's chin and wrapped Hans in the guard's red cloak. Tyr was not saved, either. Brynhilde held Tyr's head in her hands, and lay a wet kiss on her cheek.

"You're a good girl," Brynhilde whispered to Tyr, tucking a stray curl behind her ear. Tyr withdrew the brutish woman's hands, in no mood to be fussed over. "Thank you, girl," she sobbed. "Thank you, thank you, thank you..." she whispered time and time again, but Tyr was quite distracted. A sharp, piercing pain washed over her, emanating from the muscle of her thigh. She heard her brave fald screech overhead, a shrill and desperate cry, as her heavy wings beat a hasty retreat.

Fire, no. Not Alaria.

"Is it—"

"Shush," Tyr snapped, opening her ears to the sounds of outside. But there was nothing. The commotion Alaria had stirred up had silenced. There was no swash or rattle of swords and chain mail. No tuneless songs of a fald in flight. No hushed voices, no footsteps, no crackle of torches. Nothing. Just the haunting whistle of the breeze blowing through the willow branches.

Something is amiss.

"Stay here," Tyr said, and the three freed captives, brows furrowed in uncertainty, nodded in slow agreement.

Tyr crept to the doorway before gingerly poking her head out to chance a better view, but before she did, a voice called forth, and a rough hand pushed her backwards a pace, nearly taking her off her feet.

"You certainly wasted no time," a gruff voice gave. "That skyward beast tried to have another go at me atop the walls." He took a step forward and pushed her again. He had a mean face, weathered and leathery and familiar.

"Best tell that sorry lot to drop their weapons, or I'm like to use this," he brandished an arming sword, and Tyr was curious as to why he'd not yet used it. Mean old Gregor eyed the felled guardsman on the floor and then turned his eyes back to Tyr.

"Did Old Oakley not get asked his favourite colour? Nor his mother's name? I dare say his answer would have been the same no matter the questions, and it wouldn't'a been suitable for a maid's ears."

"He was not so helpless as you," Tyr gave coldly. "He tried to kill me."

"Aye, Oakley had a mean streak, no denying that," Gregor laughed, an ugly hard thing. "But now you seem to find yourself in a helpless way."

"Tyr, get back," Brynhilde warned from behind.

"Listen to that one, all cuddles and kisses now, is she?" He laughed again. "She were the one who sold you out; I pray you know that."

"I know," Tyr gave.

Gregor chewed on that for a bit.

"No one's beneath your mercy, are they?" He asked uncomfortably. "No small wonder you and her ladyship are at odds. You saw poor Sten I trust. He ran, y'see. The lady suffers no cowards."

"You ran," Tyr gave.

"Nay, I was bested and returned with terms," Gregor gave a snort. "Her ladyship saw a difference."

"Her ladyship is a monster," Tyr gave with trembling lips.

"There's no denying that neither," he laughed. "But I've served worse."

"Will you help us?" Tyr timidly asked.

"Fire, no," he snorted and spat. "There's six crossbows outside, all trained on the door, all awaiting my wandering out with you in fetters." He held out a pair of iron manacles, linked by a thick chain. "Be glad I found you, not t'others."

"And Alaria?"

"That terror has a name, does it?" He sucked on his teeth.

"I saw that beast fly eastwards. One of the lads caught it in the flank. You're quite alone now, girl."

Alaria. Tyr worried. *My poor cowardly bird, that's what I felt.*

"If she is killed—"

"Killed?" He boomed out his ugly laugh. "Dragon's mercy, I hope not. Or her ladyship will have us all decorating the willow. You've seen the fruits of her labours thus far, I trust." He said, eyeing the little skeletons that dotted the kennel's cages.

"I spared you," Tyr said, downcast.

"Aye," he laughed. "Aye, you did. Now put these on, if you please." Greta stepped forward then, sword drawn and keen to use it. But Gregor only lifted his own to Tyr's belly.

"Drop those weapons, you sorry mongrels," he seethed. "Drop them, I said."

And they did so. Hans, without question. Greta took a little more time to think it over but ultimately heeded the guardsman's warning and yielded.

"I'll need that dagger too," he gave with an outstretched hand. And Tyr obeyed.

The fetters felt heavy on her wrists and likely to simply drop off her hands if she wished it. She had such skinny wrists. She eyed Gregor to see if he would notice, but he only gave a long, studious look followed by a slow, knowing nod.

* * *

The other guards were not so gentle in their duty; in fact, they twisted Brynhilde's arm so far behind her back she feared they'd broken her wrist. Hans came willingly soon after, but Greta needed three fully armoured guards to bring her to one knee. A petulant resignation clear on her face, an expression she usually reserved for being denied a second helping.

After some rough treatment and foul words were shared between the four of them, they were escorted to the estate's main entryway. A large set of solid oaken doors with twin golden dragons acting as elaborate knockers. They creaked open, and within was a large hall, with a twisting oaken staircase that split into two as it curled around to the first floor.

White stone columns were decorated with a thousand coiling, climbing dragons. Roaring twin fires flickered from left and right, burning within elaborate marble hearths. Floors were adorned with rich, crimson rugs. Walls were hung with oil paintings of long-dead kings, great elven scholars, and dark visages of horned demons, shadowy fiends and red wyrms spitting dark fire. Every display case, every mantelpiece, every bookshelf was wrought with the unmistakable, cold glow of gold. Every candlestick, every bookbinding, every cup, mug and pitcher. Every picture frame, every chandelier, even the fringing of every carpet. All of it. Gold. Bright, and yellow and glittering.

A stooped old man led them in, fear marking his weary eyes. He had dressed hastily, Tyr could see. The buttons did not align on his doublet, and a thin wash of grey stubble decorated his chin.

"The Lady Marguerite DeGrissier of the Dalkamont," the hunched steward bellowed, heralding the lady's slow walk down the curling stairs. "And the Lord Anguis DeGrissier, her son and heir."

The two of them walked arm in arm, dressed in their finest. The saunter in their step made Tyr feel sick, descending the steps as though they were joining some grand ball, garbed in their usual crimson velvet and cloth-of-gold. Tyr wanted to be angry; she wanted to fight and scream and *make* that evil woman *see* how much she hated her.

You feel it. Tyr seethed internally. *You know.*

DeGrissier's eyes fell on Tyr, and the red woman gave a slow nod, wrinkling up her nose in girlish delight.

The rest of the household was slowly waking up and joining the growing crowd in the entry hall. Tyr noticed a few young girls, like herself, peering over the balustrade from the first floor. They watched on, doe-eyed.

His seven mistresses. Tyr grimaced. *And I was to be the eighth. But I only count six.*

When the Lady and her son stood halfway down the stair, they stopped and rose their hands. The household, without a word, knelt down in a silent and reverent bow. All did, save for Tyr and Greta. Even Brynhilde and Hans fell to the social pressures and bowed, as low as they could, only rising again when the lady and her toad of a son lowered their hands.

"It seems a weed has taken root in my garden," DeGrissier announced, with a voice as sickly and sweet as honey. "Oh yes, a *nasty* little seed has sown herself, quite uninvited."

"They murdered Old Oakley," Gregor spat from behind. "Crushed his spine with this, if you please." He held up the bloodied hatchet, and the Lady rose a hand to her mouth in a mocking gasp.

"Old Oakley. Dear, dear dear," DeGrissier shook her head and tutted disapprovingly. "Exactly how many innocents do you intend to murder, Tyr'Dalka? Poor Old Oakley was just doing his duty."

"Aye, if his duty was to kill me," Tyr said, with an effort to sound bold. But she winced at hearing how small her voice sounded. "And Greta saw to her duty in defending me."

"Kill?" DeGrissier raised her eyebrows and turned her head to the mountain in a pink dress. "Why should he do that? He was given orders to see you safely to me."

"I scratched him. I- I hurt his pride, I think."

"Well, be that the case, good riddance." She dismissed her faux grief with a casual waft of her hand. "And this monster killed him, did she?" She seemed positively ecstatic at the thought. "Perhaps I should recruit it into my household guard? A couple of positions have recently opened up, after all."

"More than a couple," Lord Anguis shot. "Your faerish allies on the road made hedgehogs of three more of my guardsmen and even stole away one of my courtly maids! You shall bring her back to me, or I swear you shall rue the day!" Anguis screeched. "Rue it, I say!" If the Lord Anguis was attempting to sound threatening, he had sorely misjudged his tone.

Elves. Tyr thought curiously. *Are they the same elves that saved Will? That helped my father on the road?*

"How *did* you bewitch the elves so?" DeGrissier asked with a wicked curiosity. "They are beastly hard to charm in my experience, not so easily conquered as men. But then, thankfully, men slaughtered a great number of them. So, one should count their blessings, I suppose. But what is that now? Six? Seven dead?"

"Seven?" Tyr asked, shocked.

"All brave men," the lady hung her head. "Even my loyal knight. Sir Richarde. Who had stayed true to his oath since before my late-husband had his fall. Seven. Dead. Because of you."

"Because of you!" Tyr snapped.

"It baffles me; it truly does, that you can place seven men in the ground and still claim the— well, what to call it? Moral superiority?"

"I can't speak to that," Tyr said awkwardly, not knowing the words' meaning fully, but still feeling oddly cowed by the remark. "But I've only done what I've done to see my pa safe."

"Tis a common trait, I've found, amongst the wicked. To place the blame of one's wickedness upon the world—"

"Not the world," Tyr snapped. "Just you." DeGrissier bristled.

"Just me?" She whispered poisonously. "While your deeds stack seven bodies high? Eight. Including your mother's. Unless I'm guilty of that crime, also? Oh my, there it is. That look. That vile look. You really do *hate* me, don't you?"

Don't weep, Tyr. Don't. She said not a word, unable to rid herself of the lump in her throat.

"You came into this world covered in so much blood," DeGrissier said, her lip quivering with mock sympathy. "And by my fire, you seem quite intent on ending it thus. Is this truly what you wish? And I thought you to be so pure at heart. Tsk tsk."

"All I wish," Tyr struggled to say, "is to see things put to rights."

"To see things put to rights," the red lady repeated with

an edge of mocking laughter. "So, what would you have me do? Content myself with a farm girl's idea of justice? Should I learn some lesson in all of this? Allow you to slap my wrist and make me vow *never* to do it again?"

"No," Tyr said stubbornly.

"No?" DeGrissier seemed perplexed. "Then what, dear girl?"

"You can't stay here," Tyr warned. "Not after all you've done. You poisoned the village. You poisoned the temple. Poison seeps into everything you touch. So, first, you'll deliver my father to me safely, and then you must be on your way." There was a stunned silence within the entry hall as the guardsmen, mouths gawping, slowly turned their eyes to their ladyship and awaited her response.

"And where might I go?" She asked, with a foul edge in the asking.

Tyr had no answer to give, so rolled her shoulders and muttered, "Wherever dragons go."

A deathly silence lingered as the red lady eyed the farmer's daughter with a long look of bitter intrigue. She cleared her throat after a moment, affected a manner of dramatic nonchalance and laughed lightly behind her hand. She stepped forward, down the last few steps, coming near nose to nose with Tyr. Her breath was oddly warm and smelt of smoke and spices.

"You hurt Old Oakley's pride, you said. And for that, he meant to kill you," DeGrissier patiently explained with a whispered vitriol. "What do you imagine *I* will do to you for the sake of *my* injured pride? Hm?"

She did not wait for a reply before she signalled to a guardsman, who nodded and exited through an adjoining doorway.

"You've stated your terms, Tyr'Dalka. Now, allow me, if you will, to state mine."

"Just take her!" Anguis screeched, storming down the steps and puffing his chest. "I'm tired of all these words, mother! Take her! Take her beast, and hang the rest of them! Show her what we're capable of, mother!"

He was red in the face, his fists shaking from the childlike fury of his words. DeGrissier playfully tapped her son's plump cheeks three times, the third being a little firmer than the other two. Anguis put a hand defensively to his cheek as his eyes widened from hurt and brimmed with tears.

"Shush. My poor boy," she hugged him, leaving a hand resting on his rust-coloured curls. The boy said nothing and did little to accept the hug, just stood, shocked and hurt.

"You must forgive my son. He inherited very little of my patience and certainly none of my charm. Ah, here we are."

The guardsmen returned then, hauling a pathetic creature behind him. Bound and bare, save for his rough spun breeches, Tyr could hardly recognise her father, so battered and bloody was he.

Blood. So much blood.

His nose was broken, his lips had split in three places, and great purple bruises shadowed his eyes. Blood had matted his fair hair, making it red and slick across his forehead, while covering his bare torso were a hundred different marks. Brands. Cuts. Bruises. His wrists were bloodied where the bonds cut into his flesh, and his feet were filthy and scabbed. He stumbled in, and with desperate eyes, he looked to his daughter.

"Tyr?" He rasped and immediately hung his head. "No." He whimpered. "No. No. Why? Why are you here?" Tyr moved to him, but the haft of a spear barred her, and strong hands kept her in place.

"Pa," she said. "Pa, it's alright. I'm here."

"Oh yes, Master Bundon," DeGrissier chuckled. "It's alright. Your young daughter is here. Come to rescue you. And, as you can see, it's going just splendidly."

Tyr heard Brynhilde start weeping again and saw with a quick glance that she had huddled with her children. Greta stood defiant, gifting the Lady DeGrissier a merciless death stare.

They cannot help me.

She looked to the guards and chanced a look at Gregor,

but his face was hard and unmoving, not even glancing her way. And then she looked up at the growing audience above them. Shocked handmaidens and gawping, old ladies-in-waiting.

They will not help me. The guards, the staff, the wicked she-dragon and her son. None of them.

She thought of poor, lost Will. She thought of her humble, honest father. She thought of her brave, stubborn fald. She thought of every bond she'd ever made with any living thing... and all she felt was cold. And alone. More alone than she had ever felt before.

All for naught. All for nothing. Evil reigns. And dragons set the world afire.

"And so; my terms," DeGrissier whispered gleefully in Tyr's ear. She then stood back, lifting her skirts as she climbed up a single step of the stair. "Your father will go free, back to his quaint little farm with his quaint little cows. The great sow and her suckling piglets may go too. The farm, such as it is, shall be released of all its debts and shall be free to find prosperity or fall to poverty, whichever our brave farmer decides. It makes no difference to me.

"The knight— the *false* knight, Sir Willem Gull, must answer for his crimes. He will be hanged. Old Oakley has already demonstrated to you the ramifications of such disrespect. Sir Willem, you understand, hurt my pride. Refuse the gold, suffer the fire. One must stay true to their code, for we are nothing without them."

"Will, he never—" DeGrissier raised her hand, and Tyr felt compelled to stop talking.

"You will stay here. The beast as well. I'd see you hanged too, as a point of pride, but I rather fear the fald will take against such a thing, and I value her above all else. As for the elves—"

"That's a lie," Tyr said plainly.

"What?" DeGrissier raised an eyebrow. "A lie?"

"Alaria," Tyr said, bewilderment knitting her brow. "You don't fear she'd take against my death... you fear she'd die without me. As all your others have. I saw them."

"Hm," she regarded Tyr scornfully. "You should speak less on matters you know nothing about. That beast is only yours by chance, where I have sought a dragon's soul for near as long as I can remember. By what right do you feel entitled to something that others have spent long years searching for? You have not worked for it; you have not earned it, you have not suffered for it."

"I suffer," Tyr snapped. "I suffer daily for it because of you. If you feel you deserve Alaria, then kill me, and take her if you can."

The lady's cruel red lips curled into a grim smile.

"No," she said with relish. "The bond you share. She trusts no other. So no. Not for now."

"The fald trusts me also," her bloodied father spoke up, head still hung. "I shall stay; I shall tend the beast. Just let her go, m'lady, I beg of you."

"By my fire," the red lady cursed. "You are a simpering, self-righteous lot, aren't you? I don't want *you;* I want *her.* Their bond is... is, goodness how to phrase it for simple minds." DeGrissier puzzled for a moment before smiling widely and wickedly. "There are old and powerful forces in the world. They cannot be measured. They cannot be controlled. They surge as wildly and wondrously as a thunderstorm. It takes a trained and canny eye to see such, a skill I take great pride in. Your daughter and her fald share such a force, and from it, I feel some pull, some entanglement. A web of fear and fate. Of farmers and falds. Some grand and inescapable bond. I cannot say why I cannot even guess... but I know it. And I *will* understand it."

"A touch of destiny," Tyr raised her eyes and met the lady's gaze.

"Indeed," she gave slowly, studying Tyr's expression.

The bravest heroes make the largest sacrifices, Tyr. She closed her eyes, gave a silent prayer, and then opened them once more.

"I agree to your terms, m'lady," Tyr said in a reluctant whisper.

"Tyr, no," her father wept, making a pained attempt to

stand, only to be knocked back to the floor by his captor.

"Will must be spared. And the rest must be done, exactly as you—"

"Agreed," DeGrissier grinned, her eyes narrow with grim pride.

"Is it done, mother?" Anguis asked with quiet relish. "Is she mine?"

Mother, save me.

Tyr closed her eyes, and her hands, heavy from the loose manacles, lifted to her chest, where her fingers found the iron locket round her neck. She squeezed it, hoping to find some fresh resolve.

"What's that?" the fat lord spat. "Mother, she has something."

Tyr opened her eyes suddenly, and the Lady DeGrissier was looking at her with a poisonous intrigue. She sniffed the air once, as a bloodhound might to track its quarry.

"Iron," the lady remarked. "An iron locket." She held out her hand expectantly. Tyr squeezed it once more and shook her head defiantly. Anguis snatched it, and with a savage yank, snapped the leather thong that fastened it around Tyr's neck. There was a brief and pitiful struggle, but the sentries put a quick stop to it.

"Save yourself some teeth, girl," Gregor gave gruffly but not unkindly. "Do as she says."

"No," Tyr wept.

You've taken all from me. Do not take her as well.

"No?" DeGrissier asked, eyes wide. "If I were of a superstitious nature, I'd think you were trying to hide something from me. What is this? A gift? From your elven bandits? An old faerish charm?"

"Elves would ne'er use iron," Bundon gave. "It's poison to them."

"As poison is poison to man," DeGrissier dismissed the outcry. "Yet men use it all the same. And iron hides much from prying eyes. Be they elven eyes, or... others."

Anguis placed the locket in his mother's small, feminine hand and retreated a step behind her, peering over her shoulder with tentative curiosity. "What is this? Tell me. Now."

"It was my mother's," Tyr felt a pitiful thing, explaining herself to such an unfeeling and remorseless woman. But she had felt compelled to, speaking before her mind had time to refuse. "To remind me of her."

"A cameo, is it?" She laughed. "Most would favour silver or gold. Or at least bronze. But iron? Nothing reeks of secrecy half so much as iron. Tyr'Dalka. Hm. An elven name, for an elven spy."

"Spy? I don't understand—"

"Don't you?!" The Lady DeGrissier snapped, breaking the spell of her tortured patience. The fires roared from the twin hearths that flanked her, sending out sprays of vicious sparks. "A simple farm girl? With a tamed fald and an elvish name? You expect me to believe such? That you are just some witless onlooker? While the foul threads of destiny weave themselves about you like a winding sheet? What was it the elves divulged to you? A plot, perhaps? A virulent scheme?"

"The elves gave good counsel, but not to her," Bundon barked, a dribble of blood escaping his lips. "They proposed I stab you. Right through your cold heart!"

The sentry standing over him dealt a hard blow to the back of his head with the haft of his spear. Tyr could take no more. DeGrissier looked to him with hard eyes and crooked smile, a smile she was taking great effort to maintain.

"Aha," she let out a joyless titter. "Now we're getting to the truth of it. The Elves pride themselves on their insight, judging our souls even as their own hands are stained with blood!"

"It's just a locket!" Tyr cried desperately. "If you doubt it. Open it."

DeGrissier considered this, looking at Tyr as though the simple direction were almost a challenge. Her eyes then flitted about the entry hall, looking from guardsmen to staff, from captor to captor

And Tyr could swear... she saw a glimpse of uncertainty mark the red lady's face.

A look the Lady DeGrissier had never before shown in Tyr's company. She affected her untroubled manner once more, rounding her shoulders and baring her distinctive, thin-lipped grin.

"Fine," she said without her usual delicacy. Shifting her fingers gingerly to the clasp and clicking it open.

She looked, as her son looked on as well; and at first... Tyr was unsure if the Lady DeGrissier knew what it was she was looking at. Her expression varied from intrigue to bemusement, to a flicker of anger. The flicker shifted to fear, and as her breath hastened, she made her best effort to affect her usual manner once more. Though she did not wear it so well as before.

"What is that, Mother?" Anguis whispered into his mother's ear. A look of fearful repugnance painted across his pink, blotchy face. "Who is that? What is it?"

With trembling hands, DeGrissier looked up from the locket, but as she looked, her eyes kept darting back to her reflection. As though they were naturally drawn there, as one might watch a door awaiting an unwelcome visitor.

"Who—" she attempted a laugh, but it was a foul attempt. It sounded forced, half lodged in her throat. "Who told you?"

"You did," Tyr said uncertainly. "Do you not like what you see? Are you one of those maids who simper over their own reflection?"

The staff, the guards and all in the entry hall looked on, confusion creasing their brows, their eyes searching face by face for some answer.

"A damp cloak might be unpleasant to wear, but it's better than nothing if walking through a storm," she seethed, her eyes wide with grief, her pupils no more than pinpoints.

DeGrissier suddenly looked flushed as her cheeks turned red and sweat dotted her forehead. Her eyes fell upon her reflection once more as silent tears started falling down her cheeks.

"By my fire, look at it," she held the locket closer to her

eyes, inspecting every inch of it. Pressing her long delicate fingers into her skin, pushing, prising and adjusting it, trying, in vain, to change its shape. "Hideous. Pink and small and fragile. Soft and *weak*. How do you bear it? How do you live, every day, so devoid of beauty? So insignificant. So ugly. So... *human*." She spat the word as though it were the foulest word she knew.

"Mother—" Anguis began, but DeGrissier turned and struck the boy, hard, with a vicious backhand.

"Grotesquerie!" She spat. "Weak! Toad! Disgusting stain on my soul!"

Anguis retreated to the bottom step of the great curling staircase, where he sat, brought his knees up to his chest, cradled the golden torque about his neck and wept.

DeGrissier's eyes fell to the locket once more, and upon seeing it let out an ear-piercing noise. Somewhere between a shriek and a howl, and as though she had summoned it... her hoard began to glow. Yellow and hot. Every picture frame, every candlestick, every bookbinding. Every ounce of gold within the hall. All glowing. All emanating a hellish, otherworldly heat.

The guards lowered their weapons, taking shuffled, wary steps backwards towards the open doors, as shocked and terrified of the events unfolding as any of their captives. The staff edged away, as did Brynhilde, Hans and Greta. And one of the sentries suddenly broke, dropping his spear and fleeing to the courtyard. Another followed, edging backwards holding up his spear defensively.

"They run because they fear me," DeGrissier wept, near hysterical.

Brynhilde and Hans broke, too, moving toward the doors. But a wave swept through the hall, slamming the great oaken doors shut. Hans made an effort to heave them back open, but as he took hold of the golden handles, Tyr heard the sizzle of burning skin. Hans let out a pained shriek as he snatched his hand away, cradling the burns to his chest. All eyes turned back to the red lady, soaked in blood, rippling from the sheer heat of her.

"So. Do you fear me now, Tyr'Dalka?"

"Not half so much as you fear the looking-glass," Tyr stammered in a desperate bid to find her bravery.

DeGrissier did little but laugh, and weep, in equal measure.

A moment of calm washed across the hall as the lady in red stretched out her hand, holding the locket towards Tyr. And, with a petulant grin, dropped it to the floor. The glass shattered, the locket's iron casing broke in two, and Tyr's heart sunk to her bare and filthied feet.

"Oh," the lady cocked her head to one side with a flicker of delight. "Oh dear."

Tyr said nothing as she looked, broken-hearted, at the shattered remnants of her mother's locket. She felt a solid, mailed hand on her shoulder and a whisper in her ear.

"Time to repay that debt," Gregor gave. "Be ready."

"What—" she began.

"Your ladyship!" Gregor called, turning all attention to him.

Tyr turned, and she watched as mean-faced Gregor picked up a dropped spear. And, as though it were the most natural thing in the world, sent it soaring through the air. Tyr's eyes followed the arch of the spear's point as it landed, with a sickening, wet noise, into the very heart of the Lady DeGrissier.

"Fire save us, fire, fire fire," Anguis was chanting from the bottom step, fingernails clawing at the gem of his pendent. "She shan't be happy, no. No, no, no."

DeGrissier stumbled backwards, falling to one knee. She looked almost serene as she curled one hand around the spear's haft and, with a tranquil resolution, pulled it from her chest. Blood pooled, pouring down her fine golden silks and staining the velvet a darker shade of red. She rose, leaning her weight on the bloodied spear.

"The nerve of this one," she sighed, tucking a rogue strand of hair behind her ear. "Bravery and stupidity truly are two sides of the same coin. But, I am sorry to say, I cut out my heart many long ages past."

"Dragon's mercy…" Gregor cursed beneath his breath.

"Dragons have no mercy," she hissed. "Just gold, or fire."

And with a burst of preternatural strength, she returned the spear to Gregor; the iron tip erupted with dark fire as it cut through the air, planting with a sickening crunch through Gregor's chainmail, gambeson and finally his soft heart within. Striking him where he had struck her, so precise. And so *purposeful*. The mean-faced man took a step backwards and fell to one knee, dark blood cascading down his lips as he coughed and sputtered his last few breaths. His hand reached up and grabbed at Tyr's skirts pitifully, and all Tyr could do was kneel and take his hand in hers and squeeze it. His eyes were locked on Tyr as he died, wide with fear and confusion. And then still.

All who try and help me are damned.

Tyr's face twisted with hate as she slid the loose manacles off her wrists, allowing them to rattle to the floor. She stood defiant.

"You poison all the goodness in people," Tyr roared. "Any vestige of honesty, or kindness or understanding… you burn it away or chase it with gold. You corrupt everything you touch! And I know what you are." Tyr barked at her, and with that, DeGrissier's expression softened as the yellow glow of gold began to consume her.

"Indeed. Then it seems I can remove this damp, fetid cloak. But rest assured, the storm has just begun." She took one step downwards, and as her foot connected with the marble, scales of blood tarnished copper armoured her leg. A feminine hand took hold of the bannister as long, golden claws grew from her fingertips. And as she spoke, her voice warped and changed. Deepening, bellowing; from the earth, from the air around her. As though she were speaking with the voice of the ancients. And where once it came from her thin, red lips… now her words echoed from the hellish glow of her hoard.

"And behold, Tyr'Dalka. Power. And beauty. And cunning. Beyond imagining!"

She took another step, encasing her left leg in the same

burnished red and copper scales, her rich gown stripped away, billowing behind her, growing, fluttering and rising from the rippling heat below. As the cloth-of-gold and heavy red velvet shaped two monstrous wings.

"Tyr!" Her father grunted from the ground. "Run!"

Tyr did not hesitate to obey, taking a tentative step backwards before rushing to the closed, oaken doors. Ignoring the blistering heat, she coiled her hands around the golden handles and pulled as hard as she could. Greta rushed to her side, pushing Tyr out of the way and grunting as she lay her considerable strength to the task. Her jaw squared as the scorching metal seared into her flesh, but the pain seemed only to fuel her resolve, as her face twisted through excruciating exertion. The few remaining guards ran to the door, adding their strength to the effort. And, as fire and brimstone and primordial rage swirled behind them, the door fell open, knocking Greta off her feet with the effort. The guards rushed through without hesitation as the open door let a strong, cold breeze blow through the entryway.

"Where do you hope to go?" The hoard spoke again, a voice, deep within Tyr's own mind, issuing from all and everything. Brynhilde scurried past, pushing Hans through the open doors first before heaving Greta to her feet.

"Tyr," Brynhilde cried desperately. "Go."

But Tyr had to turn; she had to see. She had to *know*. And there was no mistaking it now. As wood splintered, mortar crumbled, and dark fires roared.

Dragons, Tyr knew, had not graced the world with their songs for ten thousand years, or more. Tyr *knew* that. All knew that. Even old Brother Dulcet had said so with his usual studious certainty, and he was the smartest man she'd ever known. But, as Tyr turned to look, all she certainly knew now was that nothing was known for certain.

For dragons live. And they are... beautiful.

Her great wings buffeted the flames, making them catch the estate alight. Her claws, like great vices, squeezed and crushed the marbled floor. Her long, slender neck coiled and twisted, bejewelled with a thousand shining scales, all rising to her large, horned skull, wrought in her natural crimson armour, as hard and unyielding as smithed steel. And burning and alive were her two molten eyes.

DeGrissier's eyes. Unmistakably.

She rose, perhaps fifty feet into the air, perched with picturesque grace on her four strong limbs; her wings folded behind her back. The beautiful beast gave a low growl as a heavy, taloned claw stepped forward, causing the estate's foundations to rumble. Making the white stone breath. As though it were alive.

Tyr could do nothing but stand and watch. So overcome, as all within the wyrm's company were, with an otherworldly sense of awe.

She is beautiful. Tyr felt a single tear stinging her eye. *She is magnificent. She is a hurricane. She is a tempest. She is fire and fortune. And what am I?*

"You." The golden voice echoed. "You are nothing."

She knows my thoughts, feels them as though I'm speaking them aloud.

"You are naught but *ash*." The bejewelled behemoth inhaled as the hoard's golden, rippling heat siphoned toward her. Tyr knew what was coming. She had read the stories; she knew she had to flee. But something was keeping her there. Be it through commonplace fear or some draconic... *magic;* she did not know. All she could do was stand, drained of all feeling, and gaze upon the searing breath of her destruction. If not for a small voice. Oddly calm and oddly pragmatic.

"Tyr," he said, standing hunched in the arch of a side door. "Tyr'Dalka." His eyes full of that humble wisdom she knew so well. "It's time to go."

And that was all she needed. Her heart regained its spark as she fled toward the door, as vicious gout of golden fire poured from the she-dragon's maws. She felt it, singeing her skirts and searing her hair. The golden willow stood before her as she flew past the hanging branches and threw herself behind the gnarled, twisted trunk. DeGrissier's volcanic breath streamed either side of the old tree, setting its golden tendrils alight. The force of the blast sent them into a frenzy, the tongues of a thousand demons licking at Tyr's skin, caught on a blistering breeze.

Tyr closed her eyes tightly, praying that this was all some foul nightmare. Praying that Will might crash through the gates with an army of angry elves at his command. Praying that the guardsmen might unite with her to fight this common enemy. But she did not awaken. And the gates remained shut. And the guards had all fled.

Fire save me. Noble Dragon, hear me, smite down your wicked sister. Please. Please!

"He can't hear you," the golden voice gave slowly, a touch of the lady's old manner returning. "And even if he could, he would not answer."

Noble dragon. I beg you. Some chance. Some miracle. Please. Please.

"You send your gold and your prayers to a green dragon. Paying thanks, you call it. A small sacrifice to honour the grander one *He* made," she affected a priest's manner, full of pride and pomposity. "And yet, you send no restitution *my* way. For all the good that *I* have done. Do you favour the colour green over red so much?" She laughed then, and the cloying sweet laugh of the *dragon* DeGrissier was a hundred times as chilling as that of the *lady*.

My dragon is good.

She heard the great wyrm's heavy footsteps. Each one sent a tremor through the earth as she charged through the oaken doors, twisting them off their hinges and sundering the doorframe, sending a vicious spray of mortar and debris into the courtyard. She was coming. She would find her soon enough. Tyr continued her prayer, only harder than before.

My dragon is kind. He is fair. He is—

"Dead," she gave hungrily. "Kri is dead, my dear. And the whole island and beyond still mourn him, and they think that the same as prayer."

"Then I shall honour the dead and live by his lesson!" Tyr screamed, eyes tightly closed, protecting them from the fiery whips of the flaming willow.

"You could live by *my* lesson, dear girl", the golden voice chuckled. "You always dreamed of fancy. You could have had it if you had only listened."

If all in the world were to live by your lessons, there would not be a world for long.

"You are sounding like those fools at the temple. Only, you actually seem to *believe* the things you say. Show me a thousand priests, and I'll show you a thousand men who favour preaching faith over keeping it."

Another tremor rumbled through the grounds. She was coming. Closer and closer.

Tyr glanced about the place, hoping to find some escape route, some pathway, some open door… but all was obscured by the bright, golden inferno of the willow's branches, the world beyond them an unbroken darkness. A flaming tendril suddenly lashed her cheek, and she winced in pain. And then another lash broke, and the tree itself began to creek, its solid roots starting to rip from the ground. Tyr stood and chanced the fire, jumping through the veil of flaming lashes just as DeGrissier's draconic strength tore the willow from the earth. A spray of hot soil and burning leaves showered Tyr as she lifted an arm to guard her eyes. When she lowered it, the willow was a giant smouldering ember, sundered and splintered. She had sent it crashing into the kennels, now a mass of twisted iron bars and broken, burning timber.

And there, towering above Tyr'Dalka, wings stretching a hundred feet across, if not more, was DeGrissier. That familiar look of tortured patience seemingly carved into the she-dragon's scales.

Tyr had never felt so insignificant, standing before a monolith of blood and gold and fire, no weapon, no words, no hope. Her lips quivered as she tried to find the will to accept what was surely inevitable.

All alone once more.

She went to hold her mother's locket but grabbed empty air in its place.

Not even my mother's memory to guard me.

"All souls abandon you. Or lie. Or cheat. Or steal," the dragon's golden voice gave. "The hearts of men are so easily felled. Better to do as I did, my dear. And cut. It. Out. Even your father has left you. Even your mothe—"

But the dragon's words were cut short, interrupted by the proud, defiant song of a fald in flight. DeGrissier's fiery eyes gazed upwards as Alaria, the fald with a cowardly nature, soared, talons bared, into the fray. She dove down as though she were fishing in the streams, clawing a scarlet streak across the red dragon's cheek. DeGrissier roared, and gout of golden fire poured from her throat, illuminating the night sky, making the white stone glow amber. The torrent flew high into the air as the fire dissolved to nothing, falling short of the moon. Alaria was quick, weaving around the font of fire, matching the dragon's shrieks with shrieks of her own.

Weave, Al, move. Like a dance. Just like a dance.

"You are my kin!" DeGrissier seethed hysterically. "We share common blood, you and I! Do not turn on me, do not turn on our kind, as all the others did! I command it!"

But whatever authority DeGrissier held over her servants and sentries... was not held over Alaria. She dove down again, raking her claws over the other cheek; the dragon ducked away clumsily, too big and too slow to outmanoeuvre the singing fald. Her dragon form seemed ill-fitting, as though it were a fresh pair of cobbled shoes she was breaking in for a better fit. Her movements were lumbered and slow, but the fury; that fit her well and came as naturally to her as breathing air comes to newborn babes.

DeGrissier shrieked once more, an earsplitting cry fuelled by some odd madness or grief. Some foul concoction of the two. Her blood flowed, hot and smoking, dotting the scorched grass and making the crimson fires hiss.

"You're breaking my heart, sister," the mad dragon wept. "We are the few who are left. We must command respect; we must *make* the world kneel to us, as is our *right!*" DeGrissier's long neck rose upwards, stretching out to her full height.

Standing as tall as the estate's highest tower, wings unfurled and catching on the scolding wind.

Alaria's mighty wings could take a grown man off his feet. But DeGrissier's... with one great beat, she sent the fires into a roaring fury, tearing the very turf from the ground and sending Tyr hurtling backwards, crashing into the burning remnants of the wooden drawbridge. Tyr quickly moved away, stamping out the flames that caught on her skirts and hair. She searched the skies for Alaria, hoping to see her safe. She spotted her, a blur of black and brown. She seemed so small; never before had she seemed small. Never. She was always big—her big little coward.

Like a dance, Alaria. Just like a dance.

Tyr watched as her oldest friend weaved around the stone towers, pursued by a dragon four times her size, perhaps even five. DeGrissier, too mad with fury, no longer caring for her golden home, tore through the white stone, sending the spires crumbling to the ground in white clouds of smoke and mortar. The beating of the she-dragon's wings churned the ruined courtyard into a hurricane as splinters of wood and fragments of stone swirled within fiery torrents. Tyr shielded her eyes, looking for some semblance of safety. Somewhere not burning. Somewhere not crumbling to ruin.

As her eyes made sense of the madness around her, she saw a shambling figure, struggling free of the ruins of the entry hall, as Tyr saw it.

Papa, Tyr thought desperately, sending a prayer of hope and bravery to her heroic fald, before rushing to aid her father. She ducked beneath the sundered doorframe, heaved a flaming timber out of her path and touched her father on the shoulder. He was crouched down, on the half-collapsed staircase, as though searching for something.

"Papa," Tyr said, warm tears marking streaks through her smoke-covered face.

"Where is he?" Her father asked desperately. "The boy. The Lord. The fat pink Lord, where is he?" He continued his search, kicking over debris and heaving great burning beams.

"We have to go," Tyr said, curling her fingers through his, trying to steal his attention.

"We have to find it," he squeezed back. Tyr looked on him and almost didn't recognise her father in the man. Covered in blood. Covered it smoke. A wildness in his eyes, not dissimilar to the madness in DeGrissier's. "We have to."

"Find what? Her son? We have to go, papa, we have to—" Her father stood suddenly and met her gaze, and in his eyes, she could see him trying to convey some meaning.

"Not her boy," he said in a harried whisper. "Her heart."

"It's here," came a solemn voice. "I'm here."

Through the smoke, the two of them peered, seeing a lone lump, crouched in the centre of the staircase, the estate crumbling around him. They approached tentatively, seeing the young Lord Anguis clutching at his precious torque, cradling it, as one would a swaddling babe.

"She—" he stopped and gazed down upon the farmer and his daughter, eyes drifting to their entwined hands, an odd sadness creasing his forehead. "She doesn't want me. I'm a stain. A weakness. She doesn't want me."

"Give me the gem," the farmer held out his bloodied hand.

"But she gave it to me," he squeezed it to his chest. "'Look after this, my precious boy', she said. 'Look after it.'"

He cocked his head to one side, confusion marking his brow. "But why would she trust it to someone so weak? So ugly? So insignificant as me?"

Tyr heard the thrum of giant wings above her, sending the fires roaring around her. The glow of gold permeated through fallen rubble around her, searing their skin. She could feel the she-dragon's fury. Feel it, like an angry sun.

Like these long, cruel summer's past.

"She's so angry," he whimpered. "We're the last of something, you know? Something ancient. You have to protect that. You have to. Even if it breaks the world."

Silent tears streamed down both cheeks, and, as Tyr looked on the pitiful boy, she saw he was falling apart. His hair was shedding in great, rust coloured clumps. His skin was sagging off his bones, his clothes were mouldering on his body, and all his gold accoutrements had tarnished to old green copper.

But the torque.

The torque was as alive as ever, swirling and dancing within its glowing confines. Beating. It was beating.

"You saw her, yes?" He tried to smile, but between his whimpers, it looked a horrid thing. "She's beautiful. Infallible. A titan of gold and fire," he squeezed the torque once more.

"A being such as that has no room for weakness. No room for ugliness. No room for anything but perfection. Best to be rid of them. Put them in a dusty box beneath the bed, and pretend they were never yours."

"The gem," her father said again, unmoved.

"Take it," he whispered flatly. "I'm too weak to stop you. Go on. Take it." And Bundon did, snatching the torque from around the boy's neck, the golden chain snapping as he did so. The gemstone was radiating a hellish heat, but it did not blister or burn her father. He wasted no time, throwing the gem against the ground as hard as he could. It ricocheted down the splintered stairs and landed with a loud clink on the shattered marble below. But it bore no mark. No scuff, no twist or bend. .

And from the stair, they heard an ugly laugh. A gurgling, wet noise.

"No," Anguis giggled. "T'was forged from dragon fire; no mere blow will sunder it. No mere weapon can unmake it. Evil, as you call it, can only destroy itself."

"Speak plain, or fire take you!" Her father barked at the broken lord.

"Fire take me then," he smiled. "If it be the choice of gold… or fire; let fire take me." And with that, he rose from his step and regarded the burning estate with a slow, tear-stained nod.

"I wonder what will become of me." He muttered listlessly to himself before ascending the stairs slowly and disappearing beyond a haze of black smoke.

Another thrum of wings issued overhead, sending a burning beam crashing down upon the staircase.

"Papa," Tyr pleaded desperately. "We cannot say here, come, please!"

"Her hoard," Bundon wheezed at Tyr. "Where's that dagger?"

Gregor. Tyr remembered, rushing to the felled guard's side and retrieving the bejewelled dagger from his belt. The rubies and emeralds dancing in the firelight.

Red and green.

"Thank you, sir," She whispered, clutching his hand one last time. "Thank you."

Tyr and her father then fled the fiery manse, making for the chaos of the courtyard outside. They heard the shrieks and screeches of dragon and fald alike as one pursued the other. Tyr had seen such a display before when Alaria would chase dragonflies as a fledgling, or seagulls when she was grown. But Alaria had always been the hunter. Not the hunted.

A little longer, my brave friend. Just a little longer.

But when she cleared the burning estate and entered the blustering, blistering courtyard, the she-dragon turned her eyes to Tyr, fixing them on the beating gem in her father's grasp. Her golden eyes burnt hotter with desperate and violent fear.

Wordlessly the red wyrm turned in the air, careening over herself in an elaborate weave and landing within the courtyard with ground-shattering force. An impact so fierce, the western rampart collapsed and crumbled into the moat.

"Why won't you listen to me!?" DeGrissier shrieked, her voice piercing through Tyr's mind, as she took slow and lumbering steps toward the girl and her father. "Why won't you do as I say!? Why!?"

"Because of her," Tyr said softly. As Alaria came soaring

down once more, raking her vicious talons across the dragon's left eye. DeGrissier shrieked, and as Alaria began her flight away, the she-dragon batted the brave beast aside, sending her with a hefty thud to the ground. The beast let out a desperate and pitiful trill from her pile of feathers and quills.

Tyr felt that strike; she felt it scarred across her heart. Tyr's eyes clouded with tears as her father presented the torque to her. The flames dancing within, red and hot and angry. Beating. Hard and fast.

"Strike, Tyr," her father spluttered, half suffocated on the smoke and smog. Tyr lifted the gilded dagger, the point resting on the torque. "Go, strike!"

"No!" DeGrissier roared, and Tyr could not help but stay her hand. "I am one of the few. I am one of the last. Do you truly have the heart, Tyr'Dalka, to rid the land of dragons? To rid the world of such... *beauty*?"

"Not beauty, no." Tyr gave the she-dragon a final, resolute glare. "Just you."

DeGrissier's eyes swelled with fear, but only for a moment. Her grand, golden voice gave a final burst of sweet, cloying laughter.

"A touch of destiny indeed..." she gave, as Tyr plunged the point of the gilded dagger down into the beating gem. The steel bit through the stone as though it were made of flesh, as hot, black blood oozed from the wound. Her father shrieked in pain as the searing blood fell across his knuckles, making him drop the jewel with a sickening, wet crunch. The glass shattered, the gold mouldered and twisted like a moth aflame.

Without a shriek, without noise, the she-dragon, the Lady DeGrissier, started withering to dust. Her scales fell away like autumn leaves, revealing a black obsidian skeleton beneath, which turned to ash on the breeze. Carried off on the hot winds DeGrissier herself had summoned. The ground became soft as her essence soaked into the earth. And grew bubbling, hot and poisonous. The vapours of brimstone and sulphur emanating from the fresh golden tar pits within the estate's courtyard. De-

Grissier had vanished. Her gravesite no more than golden oil, smouldering with fetid fume.

Tyr's hands were shaking, and as she removed the blade, the heart, the torque and the gilded dagger all turned to ash. Tyr felt a hand on her shoulder as her father helped her to her feet and held her, just for a moment, before Tyr felt the scars across her heart beat with a dull ache.

Rushing to Alaria's side, Tyr threw her arms around the fald's neck. And the beast merrily chirruped in her ear, nuzzling her great, crested head into the curve where Tyr's neck met her shoulder.

"You brave, brave bird," Tyr gushed into the fald's quills and scales. "You saved us, papa and me; you did." Alaria gave a proud screech before lowering her head back down.

"Come, let's get you home," Tyr wept, running a caring hand over Alaria's feathers, careful to go the right way. She hated being rubbed the wrong way; she would hiss and puff out her scales. But when Tyr brought up her hand to stroke her again, she noticed how wet it was. Red and wet.

And covered in so much blood.

"Al," Tyr said, almost silently. But the beast did not raise her head, not as she usually would. "Al, please."

The brave fald shifted where she lay, curling her long neck into the softer feathers and scales of her chest. She let out a long, tired wheeze as her sharp, golden eyes met Tyr's. Tyr lay the weary fald's head across her lap and placed a soft hand on her beak.

"You did it, Al," she whispered to her. "You saved us. The hard part is done. It's over. We won." The fald gave another tired wheeze and slowly blinked her eyes. Clouds rumbled up above as dawn shed its first light upon the smouldering estate.

Alaria blinked once more, and her eyes stayed closed for a little longer as Tyr's heart sank.

"Al," Tyr said, giving the fald a gentle shake. Her tiny eyes opened again, and Tyr attempted a smile. "There. I knew you wouldn't leave me. We have many more adventures ahead of us,

Al. Many more." The fald gave a defiant wheeze, slowly closing her eyes once more.

"No," Tyr said, shaking her a little harder, making the beast awaken wearily again. "No. You can't. I won't let you, hear me? Hear me, Al?" And she seemed to obey, as her eyes did not close. "You are a dragon, Al. Stronger, even. You— you're stronger than this. Al. Al? Alaria?" She did not stir, though her golden eyes stayed open. "Alaria. Don't you dare. Don't you—"

Tyr buried her head in the falds quills, and the tears flowed freely. "Don't leave me, mamma. Please. Please." The clouds rumbled above them once more as the farmer came and sat beside his daughter, laying his own caring hand to the fald's still beak.

And as they sat for a time, the fires smouldered and thunder clouds rolled up above, and fresh rain fell from the sky.

TYR'DALKA VIII

The Twenty-Fourth Day in the Month of High Sun

Alaria's pyre was a humble one. Tyr and her father stood vigil until the last of her embers smouldered to smoke and ash within the centre of the estate's courtyard. Where the roots of the willow tree lay, blackened and twisted.

Brynhilde and her children stood with them for a time, giving small words of comfort, but the few they gave were honest. They left the estate through the main gates, arms straining at the weight of what gold and fancy they could pilfer from the crumbling ruin. There was no long goodbye, and no conversations were needed. All knew that life could not return to the way it was.

"I've gone too far," Brynhilde muttered, teary-eyed. "I

know." It wasn't much, but it was all the apology the stubborn Brynhilde could muster. And Tyr felt oddly thankful for it.

DeGrissier's staff and sentries melted away like dew in the morning sun. Giving bemused, clueless looks to the farmer and his daughter, stalking free of the ruined estate with the nervous shame of an esteemed nobleman leaving a brothel.

And so Tyr'Dalka and her father were left alone amongst the blackened stones of the old estate, watching Alaria's pyre burn brightly, even as the rain fell around them, drenching the two of them and washing away all the blood and smoke that had stained them so. As the pyre turned to ash and ember, Tyr squeezed her father's hand and looked to him. His eyes wore heavy red and purple shadows, one swollen half-closed. And his nose. His poor nose, broken and bloody and twisted awkwardly to one side, with a swollen split across the bridge.

His perfect hopeful face. Tyr wept all the harder.

"My girl—" he began.

"Your nose," she said between sobs. "Your poor, poor nose."

"My nose?" He guffawed. "Right now, you think my mind is on my nose, of all things?" Tyr said nothing and looked away, but a strong, calloused finger held her chin and brought her eyes back to him.

"I've sanded my nostrils raw with soil and roasted its skin to blisters every summer," he spoke to her firmly but not unkindly. "And you think my pride lies with my damnable nose? I'd strike the thing off my face for my true pride, girl. For you. For that bright, beautiful spark in there." And he tapped her lightly on the breastbone, where her locket once lay.

"But it's my doing," she tried to hang her head, but his rough finger kept its place. "All of it."

"I'll have none of that," he snapped. "You did what you thought right. As I did. As that beast of yours— as *Alaria* did. She was brave for you. For us. Don't think her death was one of weary servitude... it was one of love. And bravery."

"A lonesome pyre seems a poor prize for bravery," she

blinked, the rain disguising her tears.

"She weren't brave for a prize, Tyr," her papa said softly, a lullaby almost. "It was a sacrifice. And we'll honour it as we honour our Noble Dragon's." Tyr closed her eyes and shook her head.

"But it was all for nothing."

"Well," her father cleared his throat. "That remains to be seen. We're still here, after all. With time aplenty to live, and live well. Because of her. If you focus on nought but the sad bits, then all stories become tragedies, Tyr. As your grandmam used to say. If you feel naught but grief in times as such-"

"Grief is all you'll know." Tyr finished sullenly.

"It's down to her, that horrible bird of yours, that we have an ending to make happy if we wish it."

"But my heart—"

"Will mend," he nodded sagely, scratching delicately as the tender bridge of his nose and letting out a humble chuckle. "As will my nose. Maybe not as before, and ne'er completely. But time heals much, and memory keeps those we've lost from drifting too far. And those old scars soon become part of who you are." Tyr slowly leant her head upon her father's shoulder as a strong, calloused hand cradled her head.

"I don't know if the world will ever know of what happened here today," he began. "And, might be better that it don't. But *we* know, my girl. We know. And I could not be prouder of you. And I know your mam would say the same."

It was weary grief, a pain that struck at the very heart of Tyr. And whatever words she might've said would not come, contenting herself to think them instead, knowing that wherever her cowardly fald might be, she felt the truth of them. As she always had before.

❊ ❊ ❊

They vowed to take from the estate only what they thought was owed them. Gold enough to put the barn door straight, to retire old Veg, and see to the down payments for an ox. That was all they needed. And they wanted nothing more. Not from that place. Not from her. But even that small prize was not to be, for when they looked within the rubble of the once-grand estate... the hoard had died with its hoarder. All tarnished green, as though it were made of old, weathered copper. The goblets, the book-bindings, the candlesticks, all. As though it had just been unearthed after long years of abandonment.

She poisons everything she touches. Tyr thought dismally. *Even gold. Brynhilde and the others are in for a dismal surprise when they unpack their scavenged wealth.* It did not even phase Tyr; she was surprised by little now. It all seemed sadly poetic and predictable. Things seemed to make more sense now, even if they, in fact, did not make sense at all.

All that I am certain I know; is that nothing is known for certain.

Mean old Gregor deserved a better end. And being of Brentiri blood, they buried him beneath a cairn of white stones, pilfered from the collapsed towers and walls. Then planting a sprig of the golden willow as a headstone. As was the Brentiri custom.

Brentirimen plant trees upon their graves. As the old Jaerls once did, in the rolling forested barrowlands in the Blackwoods of Brentir. She remembered from old Brother Dulcet's lessons.

"You needn't have died for us, Gregor," Tyr whispered, shuffling soil to keep the sprig in place. "You could have run and fled, as did the others of the Riverguard. I know little enough about you to give you a fair send-off. But I hope you find a fair green landing on your travels, with Bessie on the shore, awaiting your safe harbour."

And she could think of no more thoughts than that. Her heart already so weary with the grief of her next task.

They gathered Alaria's ashes into a humble wooden box, for Tyr wanted no vestige of gold to adorn it. Nothing tainted by the she-dragon. And, once gathered, they began a slow and silent march home. Hand in hand.

*　*　*

It was a welcome sight to see the natural valleys and rolling hills of Rhothodân adorned in sweeping grey clouds. Accompanied by rains so fierce, every step seemed a walk through a waterfall.

It feels as though the world is weeping. Tyr thought mournfully. *But it is only us who mourn her. No others knew her. They'll never know her sacrifice. Nor the dark fires she extinguished.* It was a dull, aching resentment. One, she knew, she should not dwell on. And as though her father could hear her worries, he squeezed her hand and bought her back from the shadows.

He is good at that. She admired quietly of her father. *And I shall endeavour to do the same for him.* And she squeezed back, silently.

As they crossed from open field to moorland, the two of them spied a small caravan on the road. Four horses, five men. They had the look of foresters, with quivers on their belts and bows on their backs. But they wore odd raiment. Bright coloured wools and waxed riding leathers made of patchwork pelts. There was a poetic melancholy to their slow, thoughtful gamble. And when they crossed on the road, the gentleman leading them drew down his hood and stopped to take in the view.

There is a sharp point to his ear, unless my eyes deceive me.

He sniffed the air and paused to shake the rainfall from his waxed leathers.

"A great storm has passed; it feels to me," the horseman said, with an odd, melodious accent.

"It feels to me as though ones' just brewing," the farmer nodded, with a brave attempt at camaraderie.

"Indeed," the elf laughed as he and his retinue continued on their way. "Safe travels."

"And to you, sir," the farmer gave soulfully. And soon, they were gone. And Tyr needed to ask no questions to know who they were.

It was a long journey home. Soaked to the bone, as they were, with a fresh, heavy grief slowing their pace further. But soon, they saw the familiar curve of the road north, and it was only then that they halted their progress. Tyr's father stopped, a thought worn clearly on his broken face. He gingerly peered over the edge of a steep fall, where brambles and briars tangled in a nest below them.

"It's a complicated old world," he said, in his usual medley of tears and laughter.

And you don't know the half of it, papa. She thought before giving his hand a comforting squeeze.

"I'm alright," he chuckled, wiping the rogue tears from his eyes. "Just, fresh scars, and all that. They itch the most, don't they? And hurt all the more when you— when you scratch 'em."

"I know, papa," she whispered to him. He squeezed her hand back and lifted it to his heart before placing a kiss on her fingers.

"We'll be alright," he kissed them again. "We will."

And there the farmhouse stood, in the valley of two hills. The barn's big green door leaning heavily on its iron hinges, the twenty heads of cattle grazing lazily beneath the shelter of an old oak tree, three fields of fertile farmland, one ready for seeding, and two in desperate need of threshing. And something else too. A farmer. Toiling in the barley field, in waxed linens and soaked to the bone. He stopped to wipe the rain from his hair, lifting his gaze to the hills yonder, and there he saw them.

Without hesitation, the boy threw down his scythe, climbing atop Fruit with very little grace, and galloping toward them, a boyish grin on his face. Before reaching them, he jumped from the young plough horse and began running, stopping only when he saw the grief that marked their faces. He approached slowly, his grin changing to a dour, inquisitive look... he searched the skies, and when he saw nothing, Tyr knew that he understood.

He said no words in his approach, casting his eyes downwards as he walked. Will looked baked from the sun, his hair sporting bright streaks of blond against his usual darker shade. He was soaked and grubby from soil, with dirt lodged beneath his nails, and he was the most handsome man she had ever seen.

"Sir," he mumbled to the farmer, his eyes not rising from his boots. "I've harvested a good portion of the barleycorn, ready for threshing. I fetched water; I mucked out the stable; there is even a humble broth bubbling in the house. There were leeks in the larder and bacon in the smoke shed. I hope they weren't being saved." His eyes found Tyr, and his cheeks flushed bright and red. "It's good to see you again. You both, I mean. Safe."

"I'm surprised to see you still here," the farmer regarded the boy coldly, folding his arms across his chest. "Thought I'd come back to find a farmhouse ransacked, with all of worth taken."

"Be glad then," Will gave with a nervous grin. "That you've nothing of worth to take." They stood in silence a moment as Will's eyes fell to the ground again. But to the boy's surprise, the old farmer gave a throaty chuckle.

"What made you stay then?" The farmer asked.

"Someone saved my life once, and he told me that there is always a choice to be made," he said, swallowing the clear lump in his throat. "And I made one. Sir. If you'll have me."

Will held out a shaking hand, and for a moment, Tyr feared her father would never take it. But after a brief silence, the old man gripped the boy's wrist before pulling him into a firm embrace. The boy stood nonplussed for a moment, eyes wide, before clapping the farmer on his back and whispering a croaking string of thanks and apologies in his ear. When they broke apart, Will turned his gaze to Tyr, who, unable to bear the bashful look in his eyes, wrapped her arms around his waist, and buried her head in his chest. One strong hand rested on her head while the other squeezed her shoulder.

She then, with a free hand, pulled her father to join them. And the three of them stood, for a time, lost in the stillness of the world. Safe in the knowledge that none of them, not one, would ever know loneliness again.

* * *

One more task lay before Tyr'Dalka. One she knew would not be easy, but one she felt most necessary. The climb to the top of the Dalkamont was a long and tiring thing, conquered only by the most devoted of pilgrims. But on a crisp autumn's day, the first day in the Month of Brambles, when the rain had washed away the cruelty of that ceaseless summer's heat; she found herself taking the last few steps to The Dragon's Shroud, where a familiar nest of bones and hides littered the mountain's peak.

She approached the stone altar, so overgrown with moss and vines, and with great care retrieved a simple wooden box from her satchel. She took a deep breath, nervous to say goodbye once more, before opening the box.

The ashes scattered on the strong mountain winds, swirling and dancing into the endless blue sky above. It was over so quickly; she thought she'd have longer. Longer to what, she couldn't say.

"Goodbye, my friend." She threw the farewell on the wind, hoping it might carry on the same breeze as Alaria's ashes. A solemn silence followed, and Tyr knew not what she was waiting for. A long and difficult journey back was all she had planned; whatever came next, that was yet to be seen. And Tyr was glad for it to remain that way, at least for a while. She had had enough of destiny and talks of fate.

"I'm ready for a few less surprises," she dared a smile and contented herself with that thought. She was ready to begin her clamber down, but something paused her stride. Her eyes fell to Alaria's old nest, strewn with bones and scraps of fur. The sight of it made her sad, to see a little remnant of her fald. A little something she'd left behind.

"I wish that you'd left more for me, Al," she told the empty nest. "You've left precious little to remember you by." She picked up one of the fish bones, but the sun had baked it brittle, and it crumbled to dust. The fur fared no better. But there was another thing, near-invisible within the mess of hides and pellets. A black stone. Shining and jagged like cut glass.

An egg. Tyr realised. She picked it up, feeling the gentle warmth within.

A fire all its own.

❋ ❋ ❋

Upon Tyr's return home, she was greeted with urgent news from the continent. Along with the whispers, rumours and torn garments of a fresh tragedy.

Good King Doryn had died on his third crusade. A lead bullet from the sling of some nameless Rynthian slave trader had caved in the back of his skull as the King and his retinue made a royal progress through one of their newly liberated settlements. This fresh sorrow seemed to cut through the growing sourness of the town-stead. And from that point, Dalkaford knew many years of mournful kindness and honest prosperity.

When it was discovered that the mysterious Lady DeGrissier had ransacked her own estate and fled to the mainland for some scandalous reason, the manner of her departure was much gossiped about in the town square. Some thought her to be escaping a scorned husband, others claimed her to be the daughter of an Autrevillian duke, who summoned her back to court on the mainland. Some even suggested that in the wake of Doryn's death, the lady had fallen to despair, and in her grief, thrown herself from the summit of the Dalkamont. The story the children of the island favoured was that she was a vicious, fire-breathing dragon. But none lay much credence upon that theory.

Lord Anguis, however, was never seen again. In the farmhouse, over the years, stories and tales were told of the plump little lord. A favourite amongst the dreamers and the young was that DeGrissier had kissed a pink toad and transmuted the poor thing into some rough semblance of a son. Another was that a dragon's spirit was too large a thing to squeeze into one human body, and all that remained after DeGrissier's transformation was channelled into some peculiar, blotchy byproduct. The ugliest leftovers of a dragon's soul. Another was that the Lord Anguis reformed himself, taking a new name and a mighty ship to the continent, there to battle the foul influence of dragons, wherever they might be found.

The truth of the matter was, of course, that none knew for certain. And none ever would save for Anguis himself.

The Temple, always keen to forget unpleasantries, said nothing more on the matter. Brother Kindur, when collecting tithes in the Month of Seeds, even told a joke. It wasn't particularly funny, and old resentments still permeated through. But it was a small effort. And one the farmhouse appreciated, and encouraged, as years went by.

But the mood in the town-stead favoured sweet over sour, for the most part. Disputes were made, as they are made anywhere. But the sourness was gone. And though mood and motive often deviated from good grace to villainy, it always managed to deviate back.

Of Tyr's wicked stepmother and her two wicked step-siblings... Tyr and her father would see the three of them again, in time, in the markets and busy streets of Dalkaford. Brynhilde would always be ready with some kind words and a treacle tart, while Hans worked as a dyer's apprentice, and Greta laid her strong and brutal hands to the anvil and was always openhanded in her trade, even wordlessly gifting Tyr with a small metalwork fald on one visit. Beaten copper, with little leather wings.

An unspoken bond of shared turmoil forged a strange kinship with the odd, broken trio. Hans, Greta and Brynhilde. A bond that would last for the rest of their days.

And of the farmhouse nuzzled in the valley of two hills, a contented and odd little family made their mark on the world there. Many smiles were shared, and many tears were shed, and often the two came as one. For hearts were mended, but not as before. And ne'er completely.

Will and Tyr had their hands bound in the Month of Flowers, as the false-knight cum storyteller regaled the guests with epic tales and grand old stories, captivating the young and old alike. While Tyr'Dalka and the Farmer Bundon shared a dance around the fire, where brown ale and a jolly tune were enjoyed, over a humble feast of bread and bacon.

And nine turns of the moon later, on the twenty-fifth day in the Month of Reeds, a new fire was kindled in the farm. A little baby girl with a little spark in her heart and a fald's egg in her crib. Which hatched upon the utterance of her first word.

Alaria.

ABOUT THE AUTHOR

J R Leach

JR Leach is a fantasy author, playwright, worldbuilder and graphic designer.

You can see more of his work on his website: jrleachauthor.com

Printed in Great Britain
by Amazon